LAST
TO
KNOW

MICALEA SMELTZER

- A WILLOW CREEK NOVEL -

Melissa,
Heagehog!

BOOKS BY MICALEA SMELTZER

TRACE + OLIVIA SERIES
FINDING OLIVIA
CHASING OLIVIA
TEMPTING ROWAN
SAVING TATUM

SECOND CHANCES SERIES
UNRAVELING
UNDENIABLE

STANDALONES
BEAUTY IN THE ASHES
RAE OF SUNSHINE

To my Favorite Cousin Jordan
—Because she said she'd hurt me if I
didn't dedicate a book to her.

Music gives a soul to the universe,
Wings to the mind,
Flight to the imagination,
And
Life to everything.
—Plato

CHAPTER ONE

THE GRASS CRUNCHED beneath my feet as I followed Sadie through the fair entrance. I hadn't even wanted to come. I would rather be home reading or playing the piano, but Sadie, who'd been my best friend since we were in diapers, was relentless.

It was the first official day of summer vacation and she didn't want me to lock myself in my house until school started in August and I was forced to emerge.

She called this fun.

I called it hell.

"Isn't this nice, Emma?" She chimed, clapping her hands together. Her brown eyes were bright and happy.

"Uh... *nice* isn't the word I'd choose." I wrinkled my nose at the trash littering the grass. Some guy bumped into me, knocking me to the side. I reached up to keep my hat from falling off. It was one of those large black round hats that helped to shade my face from the sun. Sadie said it looked ridiculous, but I liked it. I'd never been one to take another person's opinion to heart. My mom raised me to be a free spirit like her, so I always did my own thing.

"Emma!" Sadie groaned when she saw I'd been separated

from her. "Taking you places is like having a child. I take my eyes off of you for two seconds and you're gone." She grabbed my arm, dragging me through the crowd. "Willow Creek is playing and I won't miss this! I had to give Adam Carson a lap dance to get these tickets at the last minute."

"Ew! Sadie! You gave him a lap dance?!"

People turned to stare at us with my exclamation.

"A girl's gotta do what a girl's gotta do." She gave me a look like I'd know exactly what she meant.

"I don't even want to go!" I complained. "I don't know who they are, and I won't like their music anyway!"

"Well, we can't all be freaks that listen to classical music, like Beethoven," she argued.

"Why don't you go on without me," I pleaded, semi impressed that she knew who Beethoven was. "Look, food!" I pointed to a stand. "I'll get something to eat while you go listen to them play and we'll meet up afterwards."

"You *really* don't want to go, do you?" She frowned, her brows drawing together. Sadie wasn't used to me balking at her plans.

"Not really," I shrugged. "I'll probably just get a headache and want to go home afterwards."

She sighed. "Fine, you get something to eat, I'll go to the concert, and then we'll walk around for a while."

"Great," I said, prying my arm from her hold.

"I'll see you in a little bit!" She grinned, skipping off towards the bleachers in front of the stage. Her wavy brown hair swished around her shoulders.

I headed for the area with the food vendors, thankful that I'd gotten out of going to the concert. Willow Creek was the star act this year at the fair. Some local band that was making it big. I didn't know who they were or what they sang, and I didn't care to find out.

I grabbed a hotdog and fries before finding a vacant picnic table.

I heard the music start up a few minutes later with a clash of drums.

I sighed. Yep, so not my thing.

After I finished eating, I grabbed my purse—a large messenger bag with tie-dye strings of fabric hanging off of it—and pulled out the book I was reading. I never left home without something to read.

I got sucked into the fictional world of fairies and completely lost track of time.

I was shocked when I looked up and realized the sun was setting and people were clearing off the bleachers.

Where was Sadie?

I looked around, scanning the crowd of people for her.

I started to panic when I couldn't find her.

It wouldn't be the first time Sadie had ditched me, usually for a guy.

Some people might think she was a crappy friend, but Sadie was just... Sadie. And when I really needed her she was always there for me.

I tucked my book back into the bag, grabbed my trash, and dropped it in the nearest trashcan.

All the while I kept looking for Sadie.

I grabbed my phone sending her a text asking where she was.

Unfortunately, if she was with a guy I wouldn't get a reply—and cell service was spotty on the fairgrounds anyway. I was *so* giving her a piece of my mind for this. I hadn't even wanted to come! And *of course* I'd gotten a ride with her, so I was trapped at the frigging Clarke County fair twenty to thirty minutes from home. In other words, there was no way I could walk. And since my mom didn't even own a cellphone it wasn't like I could call her—and she'd be working in her studio at this time, which meant she wouldn't even hear the home phone ring.

"Are you lost?"

I squeaked at the sound of the voice and took a few steps back. I almost fell in a hole and the guy reached out to steady me.

"Whoa, are you okay?" He asked, flicking dark hair from his eyes. It was slightly damp with sweat, as was his whole body. I wondered what he'd been doing to get that sweaty, but then decided I'd rather not know. While I watched him he pulled a baseball cap out of his back pocket and fixed it onto his head, pulling the brim down low so that half his face was shadowed.

"I'm fine." I straightened my cardigan and squared my shoulders. "I'm... I'm waiting for someone." I didn't want to give this guy the impression he could take advantage of me.

He grinned crookedly, tilting his head. "Something tells me you're lying." He scratched his stubbled chin. He couldn't be more than two years older than me, maybe nineteen or twenty at the most, but something in his silvery gray eyes made him seem so much older. Like he'd had a rough life or something. It made me a little more trusting of him. I could relate to rough. My dad was an alcoholic and before he walked out on us things had been bad. "I promise I don't bite."

"I can't find my friend," I shrugged. "I'm sure she'll show up eventually." I looked around—for the thousandth time—hoping Sadie was about to jump out from behind one of the stands and scream, "Gotcha!" But she didn't, of course.

"Would you like me to wait with you?" He asked, tapping his fingers along his jean clad leg.

I looked around at all the people milling around and decided there wasn't much this guy could do to me in public.

"That would be great," I smiled. "Thank you for offering."

His lips twisted, almost as if he was trying not to laugh at me. "I'm going to grab a bottle of water and then we can find a table."

"Okay." I fell into step beside him. I checked my phone and wasn't surprised to find nothing from Sadie.

He bought a bottle of water from one of the vendors and cheese fries—the kind with the liquid cheese that grossed me out.

"Come on," he tilted his head towards a free picnic table. "Let's just sit down for a while and look for your friend. What exactly does she look like?"

"Tall, brown hair, pretty," I shrugged.

He laughed. "You just described half of the girls here. Although, none of them are as pretty as you," he winked.

My cheeks heated and I looked down. I wasn't used to being called pretty. Most of the people that I went to school with, guys and girls, thought I was weird. I was *different*, and people didn't seem to understand different. It was all too easy to pass me up as odd.

"Surely you know you're pretty," the guy added. "I think I might be developing a crush on your freckles."

When I was little I hated my freckles. None of the other kids had them and I'd been embarrassed, but as I got older I learned to love them because they were a part of me. My mom always told me there was no point in not loving yourself, because you can't change who you are and might as well embrace it.

"What's your name?" I asked him, wanting to steer the topic of conversation away from myself.

"Maddox." He answered, wiping his cheese covered fingers on a napkin. "Yours?"

"Emma."

"Emma," he repeated. "I like that."

"Um... thank you?" It came out as a question.

He chuckled, like my awkwardness was cute or something.

"Are you from around here, Emma?"

"About twenty or so minutes from here," I shrugged.

"Winchester?" He asked.

"Uh... yeah... how'd you know?"

"Don't worry," he laughed, "I'm not a creep, it's just where I'm from."

"Oh," I relaxed.

"We have a lot in common," he continued, eating another heart attack inducing cheese fry.

"We do?"

"Yeah," he nodded.

"I don't see how we have much in common except where we live..."

"Really?" He quirked a brow. "You look like you don't want to be here and I don't want to be here either. That's another thing we have in common."

"I don't like crowds," I mumbled.

"What a coincidence," he grinned widely. "I don't either!"

I narrowed my eyes at him.

"What?" He frowned. "You don't believe me?"

"I don't know you," I countered. "How could I tell if you were being serious or sarcastic?"

"Then why don't you get to know me," he suggested. "Go on a date with me."

I gaped at him, unable to form a coherent sentence. "You're very presumptuous."

"I'm not asking you to go to bed with me, *that* would be presumptuous. A date allows two people to get to know each other in a no stress environment."

"No stress?" I laughed. "I hardly consider a date as no stress."

He tapped his fingers against the top of the table. I was beginning to wonder if it was a nervous habit or something.

"So... are you saying no the date?"

"Yes. No. I don't know," I stammered. "You're making me nervous." My hands wrung together beneath the table where he couldn't see.

He chuckled, taking off the hat and running his fingers through his hair before replacing it. "I make lots of people nervous."

"I'm only seventeen," I warned, the words tumbling out of my mouth before I could stop them, "so if you're like twenty-five you might want to give up now."

"Do I looked twenty-five to you?" He laughed.

"No," I squirmed.

"I just turned nineteen," he supplied. "Is that too old for you?"

"I don't date," I mumbled, hoping he'd get tired of me and just leave.

"I find it hard to believe that a girl as beautiful as you doesn't date." He flicked the plastic top to the water bottle into the grass and I almost felt like scolding him for it, but I couldn't find the words. "And I hardly think one date is that dangerous."

"You're annoyingly persistent," I mumbled.

He grinned widely, his teeth perfectly straight and white. "I guess I just don't want to get old and look back on my life and wonder what would've happened if I asked the pretty girl with freckles that I met at the fair out on a date," he rambled.

This guy? Was he for real? And yet I found myself succumbing to his charms. "Fine, I'll go on a date with you," I mumbled, agreeing mostly to get him to shut up. As soon as I finished speaking I realized I'd just agreed to go on a date with a virtual stranger.

"Excellent," he grinned, and I couldn't stop my smile, "and wear that hat, I like it."

Wait until I told Sadie that one.

"Any word from your friend?" He asked, eyeing my phone that lay on the table.

I checked it even though I knew there was no message. "Nothing," I mumbled.

"You need to find a better friend," he joked.

"I think you might be right," I frowned.

He stood up and held his hand out for me. "Well, we're already here, we might as well have fun."

I eyed his hand like it was a live grenade that might detonate at any second. He wiggled his fingers, trying to coax me. Instead of accepting his hand I stood up to follow him. He let his hand drop to his side and smiled to show that he wasn't offended.

He started to walk away, assuming I would follow, and I called, "Maddox!"

"Yeah?" He turned around.

"Your trash... are you just going to leave it?" I frowned.

He narrowed his eyes at me. "Are you one of those girls that's always preaching about saving the environment and won't eat meat?"

"No," I scoffed. "I'll have you know that I can devour a cheeseburger in three seconds flat."

He laughed. "Good." He came back and picked up his trash, discarding it. "Coming?" He called over his shoulder.

I hurried after him.

"Nice boots." He pointed to my flowery Doc Martens styled shoes.

"Thanks," I smiled.

"What do you want to do? There's pretty much everything." He shoved his hands in his pockets. "There's the carnival setup over there," he nodded his head, "or the track... although it's probably too late for that. Or we could take a look at the different booths—we might find something interesting there."

I found Maddox's rambling endearing.

"I don't know, this isn't exactly my scene," I shrugged.

He chuckled, grinning crookedly. He peered down at me and I realized now how much taller he was than me. His white t-shirt stretched taut across his muscular chest, making his tanned skin seem even darker. My eyes ventured further down and I saw that he wore black jeans with a studded belt and boots.

"Are you checking me out, Emma?"

"What? No! Of course not!" I flailed.

He chuckled, rubbing his jaw to hide his widening smile. "You definitely were. It's okay. You can look, but no touching below the belt... yet."

I gaped at him. He did *not* just say that.

He laughed, continuing to play with me. "I like to know girls a little better before I unleash the beast. It might scare them."

I didn't know what to say and I kind of felt like running away.

He reached out, wrapping his arms around my shoulders, drawing me against his muscular body. "If you're going to go on a date with me, you better get used to my sense of humor."

"I'm not sure I want to," I mumbled.

"Oh come on, I'm delightful."

I wasn't sure delightful was the word I'd use to describe Maddox. Then again, I'd only met him thirty minutes ago.

"You say delightful, I say crude."

"Oh, you wound me." He grasped his heart with his free hand.

"I doubt your ego is bruised." I couldn't help smiling at him. There was something about him that was infectious and easy to like.

"Don't doubt my affection for you, Emma. I promise you it's more than bruised. It's downright shattered."

I couldn't contain my laughter.

"You know what, forget this madness," he waved his arm to encompass all the roaming people. His other was still slung around my shoulder, a heavy and warm reminder of his presence. "You wanna just talk for a while?"

"Talk?"

"Yeah, you know, where you move your mouth like this," he mimed with his hand, "and words come out."

"Uh... isn't that what we've been doing?" I asked, confused.

"Yes, but I think it's imperative that we get to know each other better before our date so that we can avoid the obligatory awkward first date and get to the fun stuff."

"The fun stuff?" I repeated. "This isn't the below the belt stuff is it?"

"Of course not, Emma. What kind of man do you take me for? I'm offended."

"Hey, you were the one that brought that up before," I defended.

He steered me away from the crowd and towards the now empty bleachers. A crew was packing up the stage equipment and loading it onto a truck with the Willow Creek logo—a willow tree with a tire swing.

"Anyway," he continued, leading me up to the very top of the bleachers and sitting down, "I figure if we know each other a little better tonight, then the hard part is out of the way for our date."

I was still shocked that I'd actually agreed to go on a date with him, but he had a point.

He stretched his legs out on the bleachers in front of him. "So, tell me a little bit about yourself."

"There's not much to tell," I shrugged, playing with a strand of my wavy blonde hair.

"You really suck at this whole getting to know each other

thing." He grinned.

"You're right," I frowned. I guessed I'd spent too much time avoiding people that now I didn't really know what to do. I took a deep breath and tried to think of something to tell him that wouldn't be too personal or exposing. "I play piano. Does that suffice?"

"It does," he grinned. "I happen to play the drums."

"Really?" I asked, surprised. "You're not just telling me that so that I'll think you're cool, are you?"

He laughed, ducking his head so that the brim of the baseball cap hid his face. "Not at all. Scoot over."

I slid away from him and he leaned over, plucking drumsticks from his back pocket and hit them against the bleachers—creating a beat. "Believe me now?" He quirked a brow.

"I believe you."

He continued to drum, spinning one of the sticks around his fingers in a fancy trick. "I can keep going if you don't believe me," he grinned boyishly.

"I said I believed you," I laughed.

He smiled, and the drumming ceased. "Ah, that's what I wanted."

"What?" I asked confused.

"To hear your laugh. It's beautiful, just like you."

"You're full of all kinds of cheesy lines," I laughed.

"Cheesy?" He faked that he was offended. Removing the baseball cap he said, "Most girls eat that stuff up."

"I'm not most girls," I stated. I wasn't like most people my age and I was fine with that. I was happy to be a free spirit like my mom.

"I'm beginning to see that." He smiled, closing the space between us so that our legs touched.

I hadn't even wanted to come to the stupid fair, and I'd been pissed at Sadie for abandoning me, but sitting here with Maddox made me glad I had come. Even if he was a bit cocky, I liked him for some reason.

Looking out at the dark sky, I frowned. "I better call for a taxi," I mumbled. Since apparently Sadie had left I had no choice. She was getting a mouthful later.

"Taxi?" Maddox's eyebrows furrowed together and he looked at me with a perplexed expression. "Why would you call for a taxi?"

"Uh..." Now it was my turn to look at him weird. "Because I need to go home. It's getting late."

"I can take you home," he offered.

"No, that's not necessary." I waved away his concern.

"Don't be silly," he stood up. "I'm heading that way anyway. We'll go together."

"I don't know," I frowned.

I might like Maddox, but I didn't *know* him. Getting in a car alone with him could be dangerous.

"Come on," he coaxed, "I'll find my brother and we'll head out. What do you think?"

Brother? So we wouldn't be alone. I guessed that made it better. "Yeah, sure."

"Great," he grinned. "Here, let me help you," he held a hand out to me.

"Uh..."

"It's just my hand and these steps can be shaky, plus it's getting dark. Just let me help you," he pleaded.

He was right and I was being stupid. He just... he made me nervous.

I placed my hand in his and he helped me off the bleachers. There'd still been enough light when we climbed up them that I hadn't had a problem, but now I was glad for the security his hand provided.

When we were on solid ground again he released my hand. For some reason I missed the feel of it.

He pulled his phone out of his pocket, texting his brother I assumed. A few seconds later his phone vibrated with a response.

"He says he's at the entrance."

"Cool," I said for lack of anything else to say.

"So, you said you were seventeen?" When I nodded, he added, "Does that mean this is your last summer before you're a senior?"

"It is," I nodded.

"Have you decided what you're going to do after school?"

"No," I admitted, wincing. "Are you in college or working?" I asked, tilting my head back to look up at him.

"...I guess you could say I'm working."

"You guess?" I questioned, confused.

"It's complicated," he shrugged.

I wondered exactly what he meant by complicated, but I didn't think he was likely to answer if I asked.

"I see him," Maddox pointed up ahead.

I squinted, not sure if I was seeing right.

"Uh..." I paused, looking from his brother to him. What the actual fuck? Were they clones or something? I guessed the more plausible explanation would be that they were twins, but a Maddox clone sounded a hell of a lot cooler.

We stopped in front of his brother and Maddox introduced us. "Emma, this is my twin brother Mathias."

"Hi, nice to meet you," I smiled.

"Whatever." Mathias rolled his eyes, and strolled off towards the parking lot.

"Sorry," Maddox frowned. "He doesn't like people... or animals... or living."

I laughed. "Is there anything he likes?"

"Sex."

"Of course," I sighed. I should've known that would be his reply.

"Just ignore him. It's what I do," he shrugged, and we followed after his brother.

Mathias stopped in front of a gray Nissan sports car I'd never seen before. "What kind of car is that?" I asked, pointing. It looked futuristic, like it could take flight to outer space or something.

"Nissan GT-R," Maddox answered, "isn't she gorgeous?"

What was it with guys and cars? Honestly.

"Looks nice to me," I shrugged. In my humble opinion a car was a car and nothing more.

Maddox looked at me like my simple statement was downright murderous. "Nice? *Nice?* This car," he reached out and lovingly stroked the hood of the car, "is what dreams are made of."

"If you say so."

"Can we get in the fucking car?" Mathias asked, sticking a cigarette between his lips and lighting the tip.

"No smoking in the car," Maddox warned with a raised finger.

"Fucking killjoy," Mathias rolled his eyes, tossed the cigarette on the ground, and opened the car door. I was surprised when he slid the seat forward and climbed in the back.

"Milady," Maddox extended his hand towards the car, "get in."

I gave him a smile and got in the car. Even though I wasn't that tall I had to practically sit on the ground to get in the low vehicle. Who the hell wanted a car like this? Well, obviously Maddox.

He started the car and caressed the steering wheel, making

a sound that could only be described as a moan. "Do you hear that purr?"

Was it too late to run away?

"You're scaring the poor girl," Mathias said from the backseat. "Shut up and drive or I will light a cigarette in here and good luck ever getting the scent out of the leather."

"Asshole," Maddox groaned, turning on the headlights and speeding out of the parking lot.

"Whoa," I grabbed onto the door.

"Sorry," Maddox gave me a sheepish smile. "I should've warned you about the power she has."

I'd never been in a car like this before. I drove an old 1972 Volkswagen Beetle that didn't start half the time, and it sounded like the engine was going to go up in flames anytime I actually drove it. This one sounded nothing like that. Maddox was right, it did purr.

Since Mathias was in the car we didn't really talk. Maddox turned on the radio and let that fill the silence.

When we got close to Winchester I started giving him directions, leading him to the simple brick one-story house that I called home.

To someone else it might've seemed like a dump, but I loved it.

My mom and I did our best to keep it up and decent looking. The front windows had white shutters and flower boxes overflowing with purple petunias. The grass was freshly mowed and green, instead of brown like the other houses on the street.

"Thanks for the ride," I reached for the door.

"Wait!" His warm hand wrapped around my arm and I turned back to look at him. "I don't have your phone number."

"Oh, right," I mumbled, rattling off the numbers so he could enter them into his phone. "I'll call you."

"Call?"

"Yeah, call. Is that a problem?" A single dark brow rose.

"No, not at all," I stammered nervously, "I just assumed you'd text."

He chuckled. "If I text you I wouldn't be able to hear your voice and that would be a damn shame. Texting is so impersonal."

"Oh," was all I said.

I'd never met a guy like Maddox before and I hadn't decided yet if that was a good or bad thing.

"I'll see you soon," I smiled at him. "Nice meeting you Mathias."

I heard a grunt in reply from the back of the car. Mathias was clearly a guy of few words. Besides their looks the twins were clearly polar opposites.

I was surprised when I closed the car door and heard another one close.

I looked over the top of the car and saw Maddox.

"What are you doing?" I asked, perplexed.

"Giving you a proper goodnight," he shrugged. "Did you really think I'd just drive off without knowing you got inside okay?"

"I-I don't know," I stuttered. Maddox had left me flustered.

We walked up the pathway together and stopped outside the front door while I fumbled for my house key. Once I got the door opened I expected him to leave, but he didn't.

Instead, he lowered his head and whispered, "Thank you for making tonight worth remembering. Goodnight, Emma." He pressed his lips to my cheek and walked away, leaving me standing there flabbergasted.

I forced myself to move and stepped into the house.

I leaned my back against the closed door, my mouth parted with surprise. I raised my shaking fingers to press them against my cheek and closed my eyes. A part of me was convinced that tonight had been a dream and I'd wake up in the morning and find that Maddox didn't exist. And that, surprisingly, left me feeling heartbroken.

CHAPTER TWO

I DIDN'T DREAM IT.

How'd I know?

Because at seven in the morning the next day the sound of my phone ringing woke me up.

"What the hell?" I groaned sleepily, slapping my hand against my nightstand for my phone.

I looked at the unknown number flashing across the screen. Who would call me at this time of the morning on summer-freakin'-vacation.

"Hello?" I asked, smacking a hand over my mouth to stifle a yawn.

"Emma!" A cheery voice chirped.

"Who is this?" I asked.

"Maddox," the person answered.

"Maddox?"

"Do you know more than one Maddox?" He chuckled.

"No, I'm just wondering why the Maddox I know is calling me so early?" I rolled onto my back and covered my eyes with the crook of my arm.

"Early? The sun is out, therefore it's not early."

"It's seven," I mumbled. "That's early."

He tsked. "Someone is clearly not a morning person."

"Nope, not at all," I agreed.

"Do you think you'll be feeling more chipper this evening?"

"Uh..."

"Great, I'll pick you up at six-thirty."

"Maddox, I didn't—"

He hung up.

I stared at my phone and the blinking screen that declared *call ended.*

I shook my head and set the phone back on the nightstand. Something told me I'd bitten off more than I could chew when it came to Maddox.

I rolled over and closed my eyes in the hopes of going back to sleep, but when I saw that it wasn't going to happen I pushed the covers back with a groan.

I padded down the hall and into the kitchen.

I wasn't surprised to find my mom sitting at the table reading the newspaper with a mug of hot tea.

She looked up when she heard me approach and smiled, her eyes crinkling at the corners. Her blonde hair, the same shade as mine, flared around her head in wild untamable curls.

"What are you doing up so early, Emmie? Are you sick?"

I waved away her concern with a flick of my hand. "No. I..." I couldn't exactly tell her that Maddox had called or she'd ask me a bunch of questions, particularly about who Maddox was, and I'd have enough explaining to do later before he showed up for our—gulp—date. "I had a bad dream," I lied.

"Let me fix you some tea then."

My mom thought tea could fix everything.

Your dog died? Drink some tea.

Your bike got stolen? Drink some tea.

The world is ending? Let's all drink some tea!

"No, thanks." I pulled a chair out and sat down, but she was already making the tea.

"How was the fair?" She asked. When I'd gotten home I'd showered and went straight to bed. I hadn't even bothered saying goodnight to my mom. She was working in her studio—the garage—and I knew she hated when I disturbed her cosmic energy or some shit like that.

"It was okay," I shrugged, taking a deep breath. I figured since she brought it up now would be as good a time as any to tell her about Maddox. "I met a guy while we were there." I purposely left out the part about Sadie ditching me.

"A guy?" She handed me the cup of tea, her eyes wide.

"Yeah," I nodded, blowing on the steaming liquid to cool it.

"Tell me about him," she smiled, sitting down once more. "He must be worth knowing if he's caught your interest."

"Uh... he's..." How did one possibly describe Maddox? "He's kind of a jokester," I supplied. "Very nice." I figured it was best to keep the details to a minimum.

"Is he cute? He must be cute."

"*Mom!*" I groaned, and felt my cheeks flush with color.

"Oh, he's definitely cute," she pointed at me, rolling her finger in a circle.

"Yeah, he's hot," I finally agreed.

"Oooh, do I get to meet him?" She asked excitedly. "Your first boyfriend! This is so exciting!"

"He's not my boyfriend," I snapped. "I just met him, so let's not go putting labels on it yet. And you'll get to meet him... soon."

"Soon?" She repeated.

"Yeah, like tonight... at six-thirty." I mumbled, staring into the cup of tea to avoid her eyes.

"Are you going on your first date, Emmie?" She started clapping her hands. It was safe to say that my mom was more excited about this than I was. Maybe she'd been worried that she'd be eighty and I'd still be living at home, unmarried, with a bunch of cats. But what was wrong with that? Sounded pretty peaceful to me.

"I guess I am," I sipped at the tea.

Despite his phone call this morning I still couldn't quite wrap my head around the fact that I was going on a date and that last night had been real. The whole thing seemed too good to be true. Guys like Maddox didn't have anything to do with girls like me. I was too quiet and different. I didn't go out and party, I stayed home and read a book. I didn't listen to popular music, read magazines, or even watch many movies. I was, as my mom liked to say, "an old soul", just like her. I couldn't figure out what Maddox saw in me that made him think I was worth his time.

"Emma," my mom said, jolting me out of my thoughts, "stop it."

"Sorry," I frowned. "I can't help it."

"You're a beautiful, sweet girl and this boy can obviously see that. Don't let your doubts hold you back."

I nodded, she was right. But it was more than my… quirkiness, that made me nervous. Ever since my dad walked out, I'd feared that if I met a guy he'd only do to me what my dad did to my mom, and I wasn't sure I could survive the pain of it happening again.

"Drink your tea and go back to bed," she picked up her newspaper once more, but her eyes remained on me. "We'll go out for lunch and do a little shopping. Get a new dress for your date. Does that sound good?" She smiled.

"It does. Thanks mom." I stood up and wrapped my arms around her shoulders. "I love you." My mom was all I had and the greatest person I knew. I didn't know what I'd do without her.

"I love you too, Emmie."

I picked up the cup of tea and went back to my room. Maybe it was the tea, or maybe I was just really tired, but this time I did manage to fall back to sleep—and I dreamt of a dark haired boy with a smile that stole my breath.

"WAKE UP!" SADIE bounced on my bed, jostling me from my dream.

"Sadie," I groaned, rolling over to see that the clock on my nightstand said it was after ten in the morning. "Get off my bed."

"Your mom let me in."

"I don't care who let you in," I mumbled.

She ignored my grumbling and settled onto the bed beside me. "What happened to you last night? You just disappeared."

I snorted. "*I* didn't disappear. You did. I couldn't find you and you didn't answer my texts."

"My phone died," she defended. "Josh and I spent at least an hour looking for you."

"Who's Josh?" I asked even though I didn't care.

"I met him at the concert. Anyway," she babbled, and I wondered if she ever stopped to breathe when she talked, "we ran into Kayla—you remember her from school right?"

"Uh... yeah." School had ended a few days ago for the summer and we attended school with the same kids we'd known since kindergarten, so did she really think I'd forget who Kayla was?

"Good, well Kayla said she saw you leave with some guy. She didn't get a look at his face but she said he had a great ass. I can't believe you didn't call and tell me. This is newsworthy information Emma, and as your best friend I should've known immediately. I've been waiting since eighth grade for you to get that cherry popped."

I gaped at her. "Well I'm sorry I can't be a slut like you."

She laughed, completely unaffected by my words, since we both knew it wasn't true. "So, tell me about him!"

"He's just a guy," I shrugged, rolling out of bed.

"Ugh, Emma!" She shrieked. "I need more than that!"

"He's hot! Does that suffice?" I growled, getting frustrated. "You *ditched* me, Sadie, so excuse me if I feel like I don't really owe you an explanation!" I snapped, anger lacing my tone. I didn't get mad at Sadie often, so my explosion was unusual.

Her face flashed with hurt and I instantly felt bad for my harsh words. "I'm sorry, I didn't mean that."

She stood up, straightening her clothes. "Yeah, you did. I'll see you later." She walked towards my bedroom door, her head bowed sadly.

When the door closed behind her I stood there staring at it. Maybe it was silly, but a part of me expected her to open the door and laugh it off. Sadie and I had never fought before—or when we did we made up before the other person left. This time felt different, and maybe it was because we were older, or maybe it was because I didn't really want to share Maddox with her. Right now I wanted to keep him to myself. Things were still so new and we hadn't even gone on a date yet—and what if after tonight he decided I wasn't worth his time? I didn't want to gush to Sadie only to have it blow up in my face. I wasn't like her, I didn't have a crush on a new guy every week. The fact that I actually liked Maddox was a big deal, and until I wrapped my head around my own feelings I didn't want to talk about it with her. I'd have to call her later to explain, but right now I knew I needed to give her a chance to cool down.

I knew my mom would want to leave soon, so I showered and dried my hair, letting it hang with its natural curl. I dressed in a plain white t-shirt, a pair of high-waisted jean shorts, and a pair of converse. I grabbed the black hat I'd worn yesterday and instantly thought of Maddox as I put it on.

I found my mom in the kitchen drinking a fresh cup of tea. "Is everything okay?" She asked. "Sadie looked upset when she left."

I shrugged. "I don't really know."

"Oh," she frowned. "Well, if you'd rather go to Sadie's house and talk to her we can do lunch another day."

"No, mom," I protested. "It'll be fine. I think we both just need to cool off."

She appraised me carefully and finally said, "Alright." She tossed me the keys to her car. "You drive."

While she finished her tea I headed outside and got into her teal colored Nissan Cube. It was a weird looking car, kind of reminded me of a bubble, but at least it was reliable unlike my old Volkswagen Beetle which had been a hand-me-down from my mom. Once I got my license she decided it was time that she upgraded her car—about thirty years too late, might I add. I wasn't sure how much longer the Beetle was going to last. Luckily it had never let me down when I needed it the most.

I had finished adjusting the mirrors when my mom walked out the door and slipped into the car. "Where do you want to eat?" She asked.

"Marigold's?" I suggested. Marigold's was a small restaurant on main street that offered the best sandwich's around, not to mention their sweets, which were all unique flavorings—my personal favorite being lavender cupcakes with lemon icing.

"That sounds perfect," she smiled, buckling her seatbelt, "we can check out the thrift store across the street after we're done."

Most girls probably would balk at the thought of spending the afternoon with their mom, but my mom was my rock. She'd always been there for me and I liked spending time with her.

We didn't fight like other kids did with their parents. Sadie's mom and dad were constantly mad at her for something, although she usually deserved it.

With traffic it took ten minutes to get to Marigold's. Luckily there was a free parking space right in front. My mom grabbed a quarter from her purse and put it in the parking meter.

I watched for traffic and once no one was coming I slipped out of the car and followed her into the restaurant.

Marigold's was a small café with only three tables. The walls were painted bright yellow and the tables were mismatched. The counter that housed the sweets and sandwiches was green.

Marigold's was in fact, not owned by someone named Marigold. Her name was actually Betty and I had no idea why she named the place Marigold's, but I guessed she liked the name, or maybe the flower.

A lone woman sat in the corner eating a cupcake and Betty wasn't at the counter. My mom reached out, dinging the bell. A moment later we heard a call of, "Just a minute!"

"Why don't you grab a table before someone else comes in?" My mom suggested.

"Sure."

I sat down at the table in the corner by the windows so we could look out. Little pots shaped like a watering can sat on the center of the tables with various flowers planted in them.

While I waited for my mom to order the food I checked my phone, thinking Sadie might have sent a text. Nothing. She really was mad at me. Maybe I was wrong to snap at her, but she was also wrong to leave me alone yesterday without a ride. If I hadn't met Maddox I would've been screwed.

"Are you sure everything is okay?"

I startled at the sound of my mom's voice as she sat our bag of food down and two cupcakes.

25

"Yeah, everything is fine," I assured her, putting my phone away.

"You look sad."

"I just hate having Sadie mad at me," I mumbled, reaching for the bag and pulling the sandwiches and chips out.

Betty approached our table then with two water bottles. "You left these on the counter," she smiled, setting them on the table. "Let me know if you need anything else."

"Why is Sadie mad at you?" My mom asked, unwrapping her sandwich.

"I wouldn't tell her about Maddox," I supplied.

"Oh," she said.

"Yeah, oh," I sighed. "Do you think it was wrong of me not to talk to her about it?" I wiggled nervously in my seat.

She shrugged. "I don't know. I thought you two told each other everything."

"I messed up, didn't I?" I asked, but didn't wait for her to give me a reply. "I was so mad at her for ditching me at the fair and I really don't even know what to think of this whole Maddox thing, so I didn't know what to say." I rambled, only realizing too late that I'd let it slip about the fair. My mom might've liked Sadie, but she wouldn't be pleased to know she'd abandoned me.

"She ditched you at the fair?" My mom's eyes widened.

Oops.

"Yeah…" I said slowly.

"I cannot believe she left you alone at the fair. Why didn't you call me, Emmie?" She frowned.

"You were working, I knew you wouldn't answer."

She shook her head and I wished I hadn't let that tidbit of information out. "Now I can see why you're fighting. I love Sadie, I do," she eyed me, "but sometimes she can be so irresponsible that I just want to shake her."

It wasn't funny, but I started laughing anyway. "I'm pretty sure Mr. and Mrs. Westbrook want to shake her too." And my poor mom didn't even know some of the more outlandish stunts Sadie had pulled—like skinny-dipping in the neighbor's pool with a random guy.

"Enough Sadie talk," she waved her hand in dismissal. "We're going to enjoy today."

I finished my sandwich and wadded up my trash, putting it in the bag. "I'm nervous," I admitted.

"Aw, honey, I'd be worried about you if you weren't nervous."

I reached for my lavender and lemon cupcake. "I... I'm scared that after tonight he might think I'm weird and never want to see me again."

"Emma," she scoffed, "you're a wonderful girl, who's smart, beautiful, kind... the whole package. Any boy would be lucky to have you in his life. Remember that."

Sometimes it was all too easy to compare myself to others and feel like I wasn't good enough. But the fact of the matter was, every person on the planet was different from everyone else and it was stupid for me, or anyone else, to try to compare to another person. We were all different for a reason and we needed to learn to embrace our uniqueness. Too many people acted like 'unique' was a disease, when it was the only thing that made you, *you.*

"Thanks mom. You're right." I needed to stop doubting myself and Maddox's motives.

We finished eating and headed across the street, exploring the thrift shop.

"What do you think of this?" My mom held up a simple red dress with small black buttons running down the front with a black belt.

"Um..." I was scared that it might be a bit too bold for me. "I don't really like that."

"Okay," she put it back, "what about this one?"

She held up a navy dress with short sleeves and different colored flowers all over it.

I reached over the clothing rack and rubbed my fingers against the material.

"This is perfect," I smiled, feeling my excitement build.

"I like this one the best too," she agreed.

I ended up getting a few more dresses and other clothing items before we headed home. It had been too long since I'd spent a day with my mom and I realized now how much I'd missed her company. No matter how old I got I always wanted my mom to be one of the first people I went to for everything. She'd always been there for me and I never wanted to be like those other kids that 'hated' their parents. I'd already lost my dad and the last thing I wanted was to lose her too.

I dumped the bags of new-to-me clothes on the bed and looked at the time.

Maddox would be showing up in a few hours and I felt completely unprepared. What did I do? What did I say?

I picked up the phone and called Sadie.

It rang and rang. Just when I thought she wasn't going to answer she did. "What?" She sounded sad.

"I need your help," was all I said.

"I'll be there in five minutes."

Sadie might've been a lot of things, but I always knew that when I needed her most she'd be there.

CHAPTER THREE

"WHAT DO YOU think?" Sadie turned me around to look in the mirror. She'd done my eyes in a smoky gray color and my lips were a bright red. The red was far more daring than I was used to, but with my blonde hair and the navy dress it worked.

"It's perfect, thank you," I hugged her.

I'd spent the last few hours picking her brain on all things boys and makeup. I think Sadie had been pleased. At one point she'd even said I was, 'a real girl now,' which had made me laugh.

"You look great and you'll be fine," she assured me. "I'm going to head out."

"You're not going to stay and meet him?" I asked.

"No," she smiled, "Josh and I are going to the movies. He's at my house waiting on me."

"Oh, right. Of course," I mumbled. "Thanks for coming over and I'm sorry about earlier."

"You don't need to apologize," she assured me, grabbing her purse. "You were right, I did ditch you, and I guess I got mad because you made me realize what a shitty friend I am. I mean, I did try to look for you, but not very well. I suck. Why do you even like me?"

"Because you're my best friend," I laughed, sitting on the end of my bed, lacing my converse.

"I think you have bad taste in friends," she started towards the door.

"You would know," I laughed. Once I had my shoes tied I walked her to the front door, thanking her again.

"Don't forget to call me to tell me all about your date," She waggled her eyebrows.

"Ew! Sadie! Nothing like *that* is going to happen!"

"Whatever," she laughed, "but seriously, you better call me." She narrowed her eyes.

"I will," I assured her. "Now hurry before you miss your movie!"

"Later, bitch!"

"Takes one to know one!" I shot back, laughing.

When I turned around from closing the door my mom stood behind me, suppressing a laugh. "I can see you two made up."

"We did," I smiled.

"I'm glad. I don't like to see you two fight, even if it's justified. So, what time is Maddox getting here?" She asked, perching on the arm of the couch.

"Six-thirty."

My heart started to race and not because it was almost time for him to arrive.

"Mom," my voice shook, "what if he doesn't show up?"

"Oh, Emma, don't be silly." She dismissed my concern.

"Sorry," I frowned, wringing my hands together. "I'm nervous."

"It'll be fine, Emmie. As long as he comes to the door and introduces himself to me," she warned. "If he stays in his car you're not going. Introducing himself is a sign of respect and if he can't do that then he's not good enough for you," she rambled.

"Okay, mom," I laughed.

I jumped when my phone chimed with a text message. My heart stopped when I saw Maddox's name flash on the screen. I was sure he was telling me he couldn't come now. I forced myself to read the text and breathed a sigh of relief when it simply said he was on his way.

I hadn't planned on meeting Maddox, or going on a date, but one night with him and I'd already turned into a giddy schoolgirl. Pretty soon I'd be sitting in my yard picking petals off of flowers chanting, "He loves me. He loves me not."

"He'll be here soon," I told my mom. I felt like this was my prom night and she was about to whip out her camera and start taking a million pictures.

"I can't wait to meet him. He must be a nice boy for you to like him."

I stood near the front door, watching for the car. When I saw it coming up the street I jumped in surprise.

He was here.

He was actually here.

Oh my God.

I'd been so focused on wondering if he'd actually show that I'd forgotten to think about being alone with him in the car and what on earth we'd talk about. All the information Sadie had given me went flying out of my panicking brain.

"I'll be right back," I squeaked, running to my room.

My mom gave me a peculiar look and started to say something, but then the doorbell rang and she let it go.

I closed my bedroom door behind me and paced the length of the small room.

I couldn't get enough air into my oxygen starved lungs. I was going to be alone with Maddox for hours and I had no idea what to do, or say, or even where we were going.

"What have I gotten myself into?" I mumbled to myself.

31

"Emma!" My mom called and I knew my time was up. "Maddox is here!"

"You can do this, Emma. Take a deep breath and calm down."

I grabbed my hat and a gray cardigan, and put them both on.

I walked as slow as humanly possible to the front room. Maddox sat on one couch and my mom sat across from him. I wasn't sure what they were talking about. My ears seemed to have stopped working and I felt dizzy. Was I going to pass out? Oh God, that would be beyond embarrassing.

"Emma," Maddox grinned, standing up. "I got these for you." He held out a bouquet of sunflowers. "I wasn't sure what you would like but these reminded me of you."

"Thanks," I took them from him. At least I could speak and didn't stutter. "I'll put them in a vase," I pointed over my shoulder towards the kitchen area.

"I'll come with you," Maddox stepped forward. He was dressed simply, much like he was yesterday only this time his shirt was black instead of white.

I opened the cabinet where we kept the vases and stood on my tiptoes trying to reach the nearest one.

"Here I've got it," Maddox stepped up behind me, his tall lean body pressing up against mine. While one of his hand reached for a vase the other was pressed against the counter near my waist. I held my breath, scared to move. My body was reacting in ways I didn't even know it could.

Maddox seemed to notice so once he had the vase in his hand he cleared his throat and took two steps back. I instantly missed the heat of his body against mine.

"Thank you," I whispered, filling the vase with water and emptying the packet of powered stuff into it.

"You're welcome," he grinned.

32

Once the flowers were fixed in the vase I pointed towards the back of the one-story house. "I'm going to go put these in my room. Wait here."

I hoped he didn't think I was rude by not inviting him to my room, but it would be my luck that I'd left a bra sitting on the floor and then I'd end up mortified. My cheeks were already coloring at the thought alone.

He chuckled. "Okay. I'll be here. Talking to your mom." I started to walk away and then he called, "I think she mentioned some naked baby pictures."

I dropped the vase and it shattered everywhere. At the feel of the cold water on my feet I screamed and jumped back.

Maddox started laughing uncontrollably. "Oh my God, I hate you!" I shrieked, chucking off my now drenched shoes. I slipped into a pair of flip-flops that sat in the hallway.

My mom poked her head around the corner. "What happened? Oh," she drew out the word when she saw what happened. "You two get out of here. I'll clean this up." She shooed us out the door.

"It was nice meeting you, Dawn," Maddox called over his shoulder. "I'll have her back by ten."

He placed is hand on my waist as we started towards the car. "You're on a first name basis with my mom?"

"Why does that surprise you? I'm quite charming and she clearly likes me. But what's not to like? I'm wonderful."

"You think very highly of yourself," I commented.

He chuckled, the sound warm and husky. "Should I not?"

I had no comment for that.

"Let me get that." He jumped in front of me and opened the car door.

"Thanks," I smiled, once again wondering why anyone liked having a car so low to the ground. I was surprised I didn't fall on my butt.

He got in the car, turning the music down so that we could speak. "Where are we going?" I asked. I hoped he planned for us to eat. I was starving. I probably should've asked him if this was a dinner date, because if he didn't plan to feed me I was going to turn into the kraken.

"The park. I thought we could feed the ducks, walk around, that sort of thing," he shrugged. "I want this to be casual and comfortable."

My stomach rumbled and he chuckled when he heard it.

"And I packed a picnic. I wouldn't let you starve," he glanced over at me, grinning.

"That actually sounds... really nice," I admitted.

His smile was so genuine when he asked, "Really?"

"Yeah. It's perfect."

He breathed a sigh of relief. "I was worried you might wonder why I wasn't taking you to a nice restaurant, but this felt like something you'd enjoy."

I was surprised that he admitted to putting so much thought into this date.

"How was your day?" He asked and I was surprised at the change of subject.

"It was nice," I told him, "I spent it with my mom. We got lunch and went to a couple of stores."

"You're close with your mom," he stated.

"I am," I confirmed, even though it was unnecessary. "After my dad left, she was all I had."

"It's nice that you have a mom like that," he whispered, and his eyes were sad when he looked at me.

"You don't?"

"Not biological."

"You're adopted?" I asked, shocked.

"No," he frowned, "my brother and I were foster kids. Luckily the family that took us in is great, and not like those horror stories you hear on the news. Why'd your dad leave?"

I wanted to question him further, but we were still in the getting to know each other phase and I didn't want to push him too far, too fast.

"My dad was an alcoholic," I spoke, "so I guess he chose the bottle over us. I think the worst part is, I was relieved when he left. He was always yelling at my mom and me. I felt like I had to tiptoe around the house and couldn't make a sound. I was afraid of him," I confessed.

"Living in fear is one of the worst things we can experience as a human being. It sucks the life out of you." His face darkened with shadows.

"You sound like you know."

"I do," he replied, but didn't elaborate.

"He wasn't always bad," I continued. Normally I wouldn't have said a word about this but I felt a sense of comfort with Maddox and it was nice to talk to someone about it. My mom never liked to talk about it and Sadie would rather talk about boys. "I remember times that were great, like when he taught me to ride my bike."

"It's nice that you have some memories like that," he commented.

"It is," I agreed. "And even though I'm relieved that he's gone there's a part of me that wonders if I'll ever see him again... there's so much I'd like to say to him."

"Maybe you should write him a letter," Maddox suggested, pulling into the parking lot.

"I don't know where he is." I looked at him like he was crazy.

Maddox chuckled. "You don't have to know. You just have to write what's in your heart." I jumped when he pressed his finger against my chest where my heart beat.

He startled, and jerked his hand away, as if he'd been

unaware as to what he'd done.

"Sorry," he mumbled, ducking his head in embarrassment. In the short time I'd known him I'd never seen him uncomfortable and I felt like it wasn't something he experienced often. Maddox oozed confidence and charm, even if I didn't want to admit it, so it was nice to see a more vulnerable side to him.

"It's okay," I replied, as he parked the car, but he wouldn't meet my eyes.

He reached into the back of the car and handed me a blanket. "Can you carry that? I'll get the rest."

"Sure." I cradled the blanket against my chest and got out of the car.

When Maddox emerged he gave me a stern look. "I would've gotten the door for you."

"Your hands are full," I reasoned.

He chuckled, smiling, back to his carefree ways. "Have you been here before?" He asked.

"Of course," I replied. "I think I was little though. I spend most of my time at home," I admitted.

"Really? Doing what?" He asked as we walked over to the picnic tables.

"Reading. Writing songs. That kind of thing."

"You write songs?" His eyes widened in surprise.

"Yeah," I said slowly. "Why?"

"I do too," he grinned. "I told you we had a lot in common, Emma."

I shivered at the sound of my name rolling off his lips. I'd never known that someone could make your name sound so... so... I didn't have words for it, I just knew it felt amazing.

"What kind of songs do you write?" I asked, sitting down at the table and placing the blanket beside me.

Maddox sat down across from me and placed the picnic

basket in front of us. Peering over the top of it, he answered, "Songs about life."

"Life... do you know a lot about life?"

His lips twisted in thought. "I might be young, but yeah, I'd say I know a lot about life. The rougher parts at least." Opening the picnic basket, he grinned. "And now I'd like to see you devour this in three seconds, I mean you did say you could," he winked.

I laughed when he pulled out a to-go bag from Five Guys.

"What?" He quirked a brow, that boyish smile still tugging his lips. "You didn't really think I'd slave over a home-cooked meal for you? I don't know you well enough for that."

I'd never met a guy like Maddox and I found that refreshing. "At least your honest," I reached for one of the foil wrapped burgers, "and for the record, I never said I'd eat anything you made."

He winced, his hand darting to his heart. "You wound me. Bullet straight to the heart." Dropping his hand, he leaned forward and waved me closer, like he was going to tell me a secret. "Just so you know, I make some wicked good mac n' cheese and maybe if you're nice to me one of these days I will bestow you with a delectable bowl of powdered cheese goodness."

"Powdered cheese? As opposed to real cheese?"

"Powered cheese as in the Kraft kind. You know, in the little blue box that contains everything childhood dreams are made of," he chuckled, grabbing a handful of fries.

"I can see why you write songs," I grinned. "You don't by any chance have any drinks in there do you?" I tried to peer into the basket.

"I hope you like water or Diet Pepsi. That's all I've got."

"I'll take the Diet Pepsi," I held my hand out for the bottle.

He handed it over, his eyes sparkling with laughter. "I think I love you."

"And I think it's a bit too soon for you to say that. I mean, you haven't even seen me in the mornings. My hair is a mess and my breath smells awful." I wasn't normally one to joke, but with Maddox it was effortless.

"Well, I guess you'll have to let me stay over so I can be the judge of that," he winked and I blushed. "But seriously, you play piano, write songs, you're not afraid to eat meat, *and* you like Diet Pepsi, you're my dream girl."

I snorted. "You don't have very high standards then."

"If my standards are here," he held his hand up as high as he could reach, "then you are here." He stood up, lifting his hand even higher. "Don't ever doubt yourself."

I bowed my head. "Thank you."

"Don't thank me for being honest." He shook his head. "But you can thank me for this food, this stuff wasn't cheap," he grinned, and I knew he was only trying to make me laugh.

"Thank you for the food, Maddox." I reached for a fry, dipping it into one of the containers of vinegar. "This was a great idea," I waved my hand to encompass the park. Pointing to the food I added, "And this is way better than mac n' cheese."

"I'm glad you approve," he chuckled. Sobering, he added, "I hope your burger is okay. I didn't know what to put on it since we haven't progressed to the state in our relationship where we share personal details such as which condiments we put on our food."

"I didn't know condiments were such an important thing to share." I twisted the cap off the Diet Pepsi and took a sip.

"It is. It's right up there with birthday's, blood type, and social security numbers."

Wiping my hands on a napkin, I joked, "It sounds like you're trying to steal my identity."

"That, my dear Emma, would require a sex change," he pointed a finger at me, "and I'm quite happy with my member. It's impressive, I assure you."

I snorted.

"Too far?" He sobered. "Sometimes my mouth has a mind of its own."

"I've noticed," I laughed. "I actually find it entertaining."

"Oh good," he breathed a sigh of relief. "I'll let the crazy run free then. But first, I'll ask you a normal question."

"What's your normal question?" I raised a brow.

"How's your summer so far?"

I thought about it for a moment before I replied. "Interesting."

"A good interesting?" He questioned.

"Yeah," I nodded, my lips quirking into a smile.

"Why is it interesting?" He rattled.

"You ask a lot of questions," I laughed. "But if you must know, it's interesting because..."

"Because?" He prompted when I trailed off.

I raised my eyes to meet his. "Because I met this really crazy guy at a fair last night and something tells me this summer isn't going to go at all how I had planned."

His grin was infectious. "And what was it you had planned, sweet Emma?"

"Nothing much," I shrugged. "Just sitting at home reading or whatever. I thought I might try to get a job."

"Well, you're right Emma, because this summer is not going to be at all like you thought if I have anything to say about it. In fact, I think it just might end up being the best summer of your life," he spread his arms wide.

"And why is that?" I questioned, wadding up the foil.

"Because I'm going to make sure it's one to remember."

He said the words with a laugh, but there was a seriousness

in his eyes, so I believed him. Something told me that while Maddox might be a jokester, he wasn't one to make idle declarations. I might've only met him last night, but I already knew there was something special about him. I'd never had this kind of connection with anyone. My mom would say we must be soul mates, but I wasn't sure if I could buy into that. I did believe that we met people for a reason and that each of them could impact our lives in some way if we let them. When I'd agreed to go on a date with Maddox my mind had already decided to go on a journey with him—whatever it may be. I knew that I couldn't pass off the opportunity to let him into my life, even if it was only for a short time. I wasn't even dreaming of a summer fling or anything like that. I just wanted to do something that pushed me out of my comfort zone, and being around Maddox certainly did that. He brought out a part of me in the extremely short time I'd known him that I hadn't even been aware existed. He showed me an Emma that was warm and fun, who laughed and joked, and wasn't afraid of getting hurt. When you met someone who did that for you, you didn't just walk away.

"I don't doubt you," I finally whispered, a shiver running down my spine.

"You shouldn't. Prepare for the most epic summer of your life," he rambled. "Nothing will ever top this."

"You're very confident in that fact," I laughed, finishing the last of the Diet Pepsi and dropping the empty bottle in the basket.

"I know how to have a good time," he grinned, tapping a finger against his lips.

And now my eyes were focused on his lips. My throat closed up and my heart raced as I thought about how his lips would feel pressed against mine. I wanted to smack myself for thinking about kissing him. I'd only known him *one day* and I was already turning into a swoony mess. By tomorrow I might name our children if I didn't snap out of it. I needed to think of Maddox as my friend and nothing more. I wasn't going to be one of those girls that had a summer fling that ended in heartbreak.

Maddox smacked the palms of his hands against the top of the table, effectively snapping me out of my thoughts.

"It's time to feed the ducks!" He chanted, throwing in a fist pump. "We'll just leave this here." He pointed to the basket and blanket I'd picked up to take with us.

"Oh, okay," I set the blanket back down. "You're very trusting of people, aren't you?"

"I've seen a lot of bad," he admitted, all joking gone, "but I still choose to see the good in the people around me. Once you lose trust in your surroundings, you've lost everything."

"Wise words," I whispered.

"I'm a wise guy," he quipped, pulling a bag of bread out of the picnic basket.

"Are you sure we're not going to get in trouble for feeding the ducks?" I asked, suddenly nervous.

"Don't you know, the first rule to having fun is *don't* follow the rules." He headed towards the water and I hurried to catch up with him.

"My mom will kill you if I end up in jail," I warned him.

"Your mom loves me, she'd never harm a hair on my perfect head. Besides, we're not going to get arrested. Now here, take a piece of bread and we'll play a game."

"What kind of game?" I asked suspiciously.

"One where we give each duck that comes up to us the weirdest name we can think of," he grinned.

"How do you win this game?" I started picking apart the bread he'd handed me, the ducks already waddling towards us.

"If you're having fun then you've already won," he

replied, tossing a piece of bread to one of the ducks. "That one's Casper."

"Casper?" I laughed, my hair blowing around me from the wind. "That's not a weird name."

"I think it is," he countered, his gray eyes lightening with laughter, "you've got a better one?"

"I've got lots of better ones," I grinned. I dropped a piece of bread to the ground for the duck by my feet. "That's Pipin."

"Myrtle," he tossed another piece.

"Trixie."

"Leviathan," Maddox chuckled as the ducks swarmed us.

"Uh..." I backed away from a duck that looked like it was ready to attack me. "Miggy." I threw the piece at the duck and it squawked, flapping its wings.

I let out a scream and Maddox hurried to my side.

"I think this was a bad idea," I hissed. "That duck looks like it wants to kill me."

It let out another loud bellow and more ducks started for us. "M-Maddox?" I stammered. "I think they're cornering us."

We became surrounded by ducks on all three sides as they herded us towards the small manmade pond.

"Throw all of the bread at them," he told me, tossing his own bread. I did as he said and felt his hand close around mine. "Emma, do you trust me?"

I glanced over at him, mulling over his words. Did I trust him? No, not the way I trusted my mom or Sadie—people I'd known my whole life. But I did trust him in a different way or I wouldn't be here right now.

"Yes," I answered, my voice nothing but a whisper.

"Then we're about to have some real fun," he grinned, pushing his hair out of his eyes.

"Huh?" Then I shrieked when he wrapped his arms around my waist and hauled me into the water. "Maddox!" I screamed.

"Put me down!"

"Okay."

I shouldn't have said that. The jerk let me go and I went straight into the water. It was chilly and murky—I couldn't see the bottom *at all*. I'd probably end up with some flesh eating disease from being in it.

I came up sputtering, wiping water from my eyes.

Maddox stood in the water, wet up to his knees, laughing hysterically at me.

My hat had come off my head and I grabbed it, tossing it onto the grass.

The water wasn't very deep, but it was deep enough to soak a person, and that's exactly what I intended to do with Maddox. He was too busy laughing to pay much attention to me.

I grabbed his arm and jerked. I was small compared to him, but it was enough to throw him off balance. He stumbled and tipped fully into the water. When he stood up his black t-shirt was drenched and clung to his chest.

"Oh, that wasn't nice, Em."

He surged forward, dragging me into the deeper part of the water. I wrapped my legs around his waist. If I was going down then so was he.

"I can't believe this is your idea of fun," I scolded.

He chuckled, kicking his legs to keep us both afloat in the deeper area. "But you're having fun, aren't you?"

"Yes," I admitted, wrapping my arms around his neck.

Water clung to his long lashes and his lips parted with a breath. I found myself imagining what it would be like to lean forward that last little bit and kiss him. I knew I would never actually do it, but a girl could dream.

"This isn't something I would normally do," I admitted, lowering my legs from his waist. I kicked against the water, but kept my arms around his neck.

"What? A date?"

I laughed, looking down bashfully. "Well, that part too. I just mean... this... makes me feel kind of fearless. Like I can do anything."

"You can do anything, Emma." His fingers tangled in my wet hair. "We're all capable of great things if we allow ourselves."

"I don't know what my great thing is," I confessed.

His voice lowered and he pressed his forehead against mine. His damp hair brushed my skin and I shivered. "Then we're just going to have to find that great thing."

"Hey!" An unfamiliar voice called. "What do you two think you're doing?"

Maddox and I turned to look for the sound of the voice.

"You can't swim in there!"

"Oh, shit," Maddox mumbled. "Come on, swim. Faster, faster," he coaxed me, as we swam to the other side away from the police officer.

Once were in the grass he grabbed my hand.

With a smirk, he cried, "Run!"

And so I ran.

CHAPTER FOUR

ONLY I WOULD get arrested on my first date. And not even for something cool like smoking pot or indecent exposure. Nope, we got arrested for fleeing the scene—which somehow turned into resisting arrest—and were being charged a fine for trespassing.

"This is unbelievable." I grasped the metal bars of the holding cell in my hands. "You told me we wouldn't get arrested for feeding the ducks," I hissed.

"Hey, at least it will be a nice story to tell your grandchildren one day," Maddox reasoned. "And we *didn't* get arrested for feeding the ducks." I guess he was right about that—but feeding the ducks, did lead to the reason for our arrest, so it still counted in my mind.

I turned around to glare at him where he sat on the thin metal bench. "You think this is real funny, don't you?" I shivered, because my clothes were still wet.

"I think it's hysterical," he grinned. "I mean, who knew swimming in a pond could get you arrested?"

"Apparently when there are signs telling you not to swim," I glared at him. He wasn't taking this seriously at all.

"Admit you were having fun," he challenged. "Sometimes a

little fun is worth the consequences."

"And sometimes a little fun leads to getting arrested!" I shrieked. "And other times it leads to babies!"

He laughed, leaning his head against the cinderblock wall. "Boy, that escalated quickly. From arrests to babies—does this mean the next time we want to have some fun we try for the baby part?" He grinned crookedly, waggling his brows.

My mouth fell open. "You are unbelievable!"

"And you're adorable when you're angry," he smirked.

"Oh, if you think this is angry then you haven't seen anything yet." I put my hands on my hips and leaned forward, leveling him with a glare.

"I see your boobs, does that count?"

With a squeak I threw my arms over my chest and turned around. Maddox's chuckle echoed around the small space. He might've been driving me nuts, but I was secretly glad they hadn't separated us.

An officer passed by and I implored, "When's my mom coming?"

He stopped, looking at the two of us, and shrugged. "If they'll do the right thing then they'll leave you in jail tonight to teach you a lesson."

He walked off, leaving me standing there in shock.

I turned to Maddox. "All night?! I won't last a night in jail! I want to go home! I want my bed!"

"Yeah, well I want my bed too, Em. And Sonic."

Why the fuck was he talking about Sonic right now? Food was the last thing on my mind.

"You are so infuriating."

"And yet you like me," he countered, leaning his head back and closing his eyes. "Just sit down and relax. I'm sure your mom will be here soon. There's no way she'd leave you here."

I sat down beside him, but not because he told me to. It

came from the fact that my body was no longer strong enough to hold me up. I sniffled, wiping the tears off my face.

I felt his body turn towards me. "Are you crying?"

"Y-yes," I stuttered, wiping away more tears.

"Please don't cry, Emma, it'll be okay." He wrapped an arm around my shoulders and pulled me close. I let him, simply because I needed the comfort. "I know I didn't say it, but I'm so sorry. I didn't mean for this to happen."

"I k-know."

"Oh, Em." He swiped his thumb under my eyes. "I didn't mean to make you cry. I just wanted us to have a good time."

"I d-don't even k-know w-why I'm c-crying," I stammered, clinging to his shirt for support—and I might've purposely wiped some snot on it because he deserved it.

He smoothed my hair away from my face. "We're going to get out of here any minute, you'll see."

"MY MOM'S NEVER coming to get me! She's going to let me rot here in jail for the rest of m-my l-life!" Sobs overtook my body. I sat on the floor with my back against the wall. We'd been at the police station for over an hour and Maddox's foster mom had just shown up to release him. My mom was MIA. Actually, she was probably at home in her studio slaving away over her latest piece and wouldn't know I was in jail until tomorrow.

Yep, I was going to end up spending the night in jail.

Maddox stood outside the jail cell with his mom by his side. "Don't worry, Em. We'll get you out of here."

"B-b-but y-you're n-not m-m-my m-mom."

I was having a full on breakdown like a five year old, but I didn't care. I'd been *arrested*—there had seriously been handcuffs involved—and I was in *jail*. I was pretty sure that was worth a breakdown.

"I'm very aware that I'm not your mom," he chuckled, staring at me through the bars. "But I promise I'm going to get you out."

"H-how?" I questioned, raising tear-rimmed eyes to meet his.

"I have my ways," he winked. To his foster mom he said, "Stay with her, please." I watched him leave and I started to cry harder.

"Hey, sweetie," his mom said through the bars. "I know this isn't exactly the best way for us to meet, but I'm Karen."

I took several deep breaths, trying to stifle my sobs. "I-I'm Emma."

"Emma," she repeated. "That's a lovely name. I always wanted a daughter named Emma, but I ended up with three sons."

"T-three?" I asked, trying to distract myself from the fact that she would no doubt abandon me within minutes, because there was no way Maddox could sweet talk me out of here.

"Yes," she smiled, squatting down so we were eyelevel. "Ezra, Maddox, and Mathias."

"I t-thought M-Maddox and Mathias were f-foster kids?"

"He told you?" Her voice squeaked with surprise and then she smiled. "You must be special. To answer your question, yes, they're my foster sons—but they've felt like real sons from the moment I met them as little boys."

"I d-don't like Maddox v-very much r-right now." I hiccupped, drying the last of my tears. Crying was going to solve nothing and I had to toughen up if I was going to spend the night in jail.

Karen laughed and it was a light twinkling sound. "No, I don't imagine you do." She looked down the hallway and stood up. "Here he comes."

I gathered myself to my feet, prepared for him to tell me that I was staying here.

His head was bowed and his shoulders were slumped.

My stomach rolled and I thought I might throw up. I knew there was no way he could pull it off.

I almost started crying again when the fucker held up a set of keys and jangled them.

"They gave you the keys?!" I shrieked, jumping around excitedly. "I'm free! I'm free! I'm free!"

He chuckled, unlocking the door to the holding cell. "Yes, they were really quite accommodating once I explained things." Once I was out he closed the door and removed the keys.

"For the record," I stared him down, "I hate you." I slapped his cheek—not hard, but enough to leave a sting. "And that's for getting me arrested." Kissing the spot I'd just slapped I whispered in his ear, "*That* is for getting me out."

I walked off and behind me I heard Karen say to Maddox, "I like her."

"Yeah, me too," he agreed.

KAREN WAS KIND enough to drive us back to the park for Maddox's car. I thanked her profusely and might've promised her my firstborn child for coming to get Maddox since he was able to bust me out.

Maddox and I walked back to his car in silence. He unlocked it and opened the door for me. He handed me the keys. "Start the car, I'll be right back."

I gave him a peculiar look, but did as he asked—mostly because I was still cold and wanted to turn the heater on despite the fact that it was summer.

I pulled my phone out of the pocket of my cardigan and cringed. The cop that arrested us had confiscated it, but I'd gotten it back once we were discharged—although that was kind of pointless since the thing was now ruined.

The night had started out great and then turned into one big ball of disaster. I didn't regret going out with Maddox, but I wasn't jumping up and down to go on a second date with him either. Maybe that was unfair of me, after all it's not like he planned for us to be arrested, but I was still mad.

The car door opened and he slipped inside. He tossed the picnic basket into the back and held out my hat. "Here you go," he grinned.

"I forgot about this," I mumbled, taking it from his hand.

"Well, I didn't," he boasted.

I rolled my eyes. I didn't know how he could be so happy considering all the crap we'd been through tonight. I wanted to mouth off at him, but it wasn't in my nature. Besides, without him I would still be sitting in a holding cell crying my eyes out. So, I guess he was good for some things... like getting you arrested and then breaking you out of jail.

I set the hat on top of my head and went back to fiddling with my phone—basically willing it to live. I didn't have the money to buy a new one.

Maddox looked over and saw what I was messing with. "Is your phone okay?"

"No," I sighed, pinching the bridge of my nose. I was tempted to throw the thing out the window, but I thought maybe I could still salvage it.

"Aw, Emma, I'm so sorry. I'll get you a new one," he promised, his voice ringing with sincerity.

I winced. "I'm not a charity case. You don't owe me a phone."

He snorted, driving through town towards my home. "I never said you were a charity case, but it's my fault your phone's ruined, so the least I could do is get you a new one."

"You got me out of jail, so I think you've repented enough," I mumbled, propping my elbow on the edge of the window and my head in my hand.

"I also got you into jail." His fingers danced along the steering wheel.

"Don't remind me," I grumbled.

"Does this mean you don't want to go on another date?" He rambled. "Because that whole getting arrested thing was a total fluke, I swear. I mean, it's not like I make a habit of getting arrested," he shrugged his strong shoulders, "that was actually a first for me. I'd like to promise that it'll never happen again, but hey, you never know."

"Do you ever stop talking?" I interrupted him. My words might've been harsh, but I didn't mean them that way. "You're like a toddler that's just learned to talk and won't shut up for five seconds."

Ignoring me, he added, "Basically, I think I deserve a second chance."

"Oh, you think so," I snorted. "And why is that?"

"I'm hot, you're hot, together we can make magic happen."

I pressed my lips together, trying to contain my laughter but it eventually burst forth. "I think it's safe to say I've never met anyone quite like you."

"I strive to be like no one else," he winked. "It keeps things interesting."

"Mhmm," I hummed, looking out the window.

"So..." He started. "You never gave me an answer about a second date..."

"I need to think about it and unfortunately," I held up my

phone and gave it a shake, "I won't be able to let you know what I decide."

"Bummer," he winced. "But I stand by what I said about getting you a new phone, so there's hope for me yet!" He cried like a man about to go to battle. I was learning quickly that Maddox was the dramatic type. I wondered if he'd ever tried acting.

My house came into view and I breathed a sigh of relief. I was exhausted, my eyes hurt from crying, and all I wanted to do was shower off the nasty pond water from my body and climb into my bed.

Maddox parked in the driveway and I reached for the door handle. "Thank you for a... uh... interesting evening. I can assure you it's one I'll never forget... like ever."

Maddox chuckled and leaned towards me. I scooted away from him so that my back was pressed firmly against the car door.

He ducked his head and lifted his eyes to peer at me through the veil of his dark hair. "Oh, Emma, you're like a little bird the way you quiver around me. I might have sharp teeth," his eyes lowered to my throat, where my heart fluttered erratically, "but it doesn't mean I *bite*." His voice dropped to a low, throaty octave.

My body heated all over. I'd never felt the sensation before—but I'd heard about it plenty from Sadie.

If I didn't get away—and stay away—from Maddox, I was going to end up in big trouble.

"I-I-I have to go," I stammered, clawing at the door handle. I tumbled from the car, falling onto the gravel driveway. "Shit," I cursed, when the sharp rocks dug into my knees.

"Emma!"

A moment later Maddox was out of the car and in front of me. He grasped my elbows and lifted me from the ground.

"Are you okay?" He looked me up and down. "You're bleeding." His eyes zeroed in on my knees and he frowned.

"It's just a scrape," I mumbled, backing out of his hold. I went to walk around him, but squeaked when my legs went out from under me.

He cradled me against his chest and strode up to the front door.

"What do you think you're doing?" I shrieked.

"I'm carrying you inside, cleaning your wounds, and slapping a Band-Aid on these suckers," he explained. "Now give me your keys before I'm forced to breakdown the door and don't doubt my ability, because I'll do it."

"Oh. My. God." I rolled my eyes.

"Emma," he groaned. "Key."

"There's one under the mat, I didn't bring mine with me. It looks like you'll have to put me down," I smiled triumphantly.

Maddox noticed my smile and returned it with one of his own. I let out another shriek when he tossed me onto his shoulder so he could grab the key.

He carried me inside and straight back to the bathroom. He flipped the light switch on and set me on the counter.

"This is… cute." He commented, looking around at the outdated décor.

"We haven't had the money to update," I mumbled, ducking my head in embarrassment.

I'd never been ashamed of being poor, but it didn't mean I wanted to show it off to the masses… or Maddox.

"I like it," he smiled. "It's old-fashioned."

I snorted. "Yeah, I don't think it's been updated since the seventies." I nodded towards the pea green bathtub. "But this place… it's home," I shrugged.

I startled when his warm hand cupped my cheek. "Shh," he hushed, rubbing his thumb against my bottom lip. "You don't need to explain anything to me." He tilted my head back and pressed his forehead against mine. His voice lowered to a whisper. "I know I literally just met you yesterday, but it feels like I've known you forever. I've only ever had this feeling of... of *belonging* with my foster family, and I know this sounds crazy, but I feel like we're supposed to get to know each other."

"Maddox—" I started.

"Let me finish," he hushed. He shook his head so his dark brown hair brushed against my forehead. "I'm not asking for anything romantic—although I'll admit to really wanting to kiss you," he grinned. "But it's summer vacation for both of us and I think we should make this the best summer of our lives."

"H-how?" My voice shook with nerves. Maddox affected me in a way that one minute I was mouthing off to him and the next I was a nervous and shaking mess.

His smile widened. "I guess we'll have to find out together."

Without another word he opened the medicine cabinet and set about cleaning my scraped knees, slathering them with Neosporin, and sticking Band-Aids—Hello Kitty ones—on top.

He lifted me off the counter and kissed my forehead.

"Get some rest. The most epic summer of your life begins tomorrow."

I opened my mouth to reply, but he already had his back turned and walked out the bathroom door. A moment later I heard the front door close.

What the hell had I gotten myself into?

CHAPTER FIVE

AFTER DELETING THE messages from the police station off the voicemail I'd gotten into bed and fallen right to sleep. I'd been exhausted, but this morning I felt refreshed and ready to conquer the day.

"Mom," I called, stifling a yawn as I headed into the kitchen.

I stopped when I found a note sitting on the kitchen table explaining that she was gone for the day, restocking her supplies.

I grabbed an apple and sat down to eat.

Since I was currently phoneless and had no plans it looked like I'd spend the day doing what I typically did—playing piano and reading. I wasn't complaining, though. I enjoyed spending time by myself.

I finished the apple and tossed the core in the trashcan.

I got dressed for the day and sat down at the piano. I picked a random song, placed the sheets of music in front of me, and let my mind empty.

I'd started playing piano at an early age. My talent had been a source of conflict for my parents. Many said I was a prodigy and early on my dad had wanted to push me to make a name for myself. I'd been so young, though, and my mom had been firmly against it. She felt that talent was meant to be enjoyed, not forced, and she didn't want to see me learn to hate something I loved so much. I was thankful that I had a mom like her. While my dad had ended up a drunk asshole that abandoned us, at least I had one parent that was amazing when a lot of people had none.

I was so lost in the music and the way the keys felt against my fingertips that when the doorbell rang I squeaked and fell off the bench.

Gathering myself I straightened my clothes and pushed my hair out of my eyes.

I was sure it was Maddox at the door, but I was surprised to find that no one was there. Instead a plain brown box sat on the Welcome mat. I picked it up and gave it a little shake. The rustle of sound didn't give any indication of what might be inside.

I kicked the front door closed and headed to the kitchen for a knife.

I cut the tape around the corners and burst into laughter when I found what was inside.

"Really, Maddox?" I laughed out loud. Inside was a white box containing a shiny new iPhone. What made me laugh though, was the cartoonish drawing of, what I assumed was Maddox himself, asking for forgiveness. I peeled the drawing off, careful not to tear it. I carried it and the small box back to my room. I don't know what possessed me, but I stuck the drawing to the mirror above my dresser. I didn't want to get rid of it.

Once the piece of paper was stuck to my mirror I sat down on my bed and removed the lid off the small box.

Inside the phone lay nestled. I'd never owned anything so... so *shiny*. Or new.

I picked the phone up out of the box and pressed the round

button to light up the screen. Since Sadie owned one I already knew how to work it.

I snorted when I saw the wallpaper. It was a photo of Maddox pouting with a little comic bubble added, asking, "Am I forgiven *yet?*"

I jumped when the phone started ringing in my hand. Maddox's face popped up again, but this time it was a different photo—a normal one where he wore an easy smile and seemed to be laughing at something in the distance.

"Hello?" I answered.

"How about now?"

I laughed, ducking my head. "You are relentless."

"So...?"

"You're forgiven," I sighed. I decided then that it was impossible to stay mad at Maddox.

"Excellent," he said, and I knew he was grinning. "Don't forget, adventure number one starts today."

"When?" I asked.

"Right about... now."

He hung up and a moment later a text popped up on the screen.

Go out your front door. Walk down to the stop sign and take a right. I'll be waiting.

I shook my head and muttered, "Maddox."

I hoped my shorts and t-shirt were appropriate since I didn't seem to have time to change.

Stuffing the phone in my back pocket I followed his directions.

When I rounded the street corner and saw him I laughed.

"You were mighty confident I'd show up, weren't you?" I pointed to where he stood leaning against a shiny red motorcycle. It shimmered like a candied apple in the sunlight.

He shrugged sheepishly. "I hoped."

"So," I waved a hand at the motorcycle, "is this our first adventure?"

"It is," he grinned. "Have you ever been on one?"

"No," I admitted.

His smile widened. "Does it scare you? You can hold on tight, my abs won't mind." He rubbed a hand over his smooth stomach concealed behind a tight gray t-shirt.

I rolled my eyes. "I'm not scared."

"Maybe you should be, because when Mathias finds this thing gone he's going to try to kill us," he frowned, rubbing his chin.

"Or we might end up arrested again, this time for stealing a motorcycle," I pointed out.

"Well, at least we'll be mixing things up," he shrugged.

"Why would you take Mathias' motorcycle?" I asked.

He held out a leather jacket for me. It was the perfect size and I noticed a price tag still dangled from the sleeve so I ripped it off. Maddox seemed to have a lot of money and I wondered momentarily where it came from.

As I shrugged into the jacket he began to explain. "Well, I had one..."

"You had one?" I repeated. "What happened to it?"

"Uh..." He ducked his head, scrubbing his hand against the back of it. "It's kind of a long story."

I crossed my arms over my chest. "I have time."

He peered at me with hesitant gray eyes. "It's really not worth telling."

"Mhmm," I harrumphed. "I'm waiting."

He let out a sigh and looked up towards the sky like he was trying to gather his strength. "I... uh... I... crashed it."

"You crashed your motorcycle and now you want me to get

on your brother's with you? That sounds like a sure way to land myself in the ER."

"I only broke my arm!" He defended. "Besides, I'd protect you!"

"You'd protect me while crashing the motorcycle? That makes a whole lot of sense," I snorted.

He mumbled unintelligibly. "You know what I meant."

"So, despite the fact that you crashed your own motorcycle, and we might get arrested for stealing your brother's, you still think this is a great idea?" I raised a brow, waiting for his reply.

His face crinkled. "It's an excellent idea," he corrected.

Of course he thought it was.

I was a smart girl. I never did anything I wasn't supposed to do.

I was normal, and some may say boring.

I was plain.

Ordinary.

Nothing special.

Unmemorable.

And that's why, even though I knew going home and pretending this encounter never happened would be the best thing to do, I said, "Okay, let's do this."

Maddox's grin split his whole face.

"I thought you were going to tell me to take a hike there for a second," he chuckled.

"I considered it," I admitted. "But only for like a second," I confessed, when his head fell. He grinned at that. "You're right Maddox. This is a summer for adventures."

His smile was blinding. "I'm glad you agree." He reached behind him and held out a helmet. I tried to take it from him, but he refused. He set it on top of my head and secured it. "Look at you," he chuckled, rapping his knuckles against the hard surface. It felt heavy and uncomfortable on my head—like my small frame might topple over from the weight. "You make for a very sexy biker babe."

"Thanks... I guess," I laughed.

He put his own helmet on and straddled the motorcycle.

"Come on, Em." He reached out a hand, waving me over.

My whole body shook. I couldn't believe I was actually doing this. Despite my previous confidence I was terrified. Motorcycles had two wheels and an engine that was fast—that was enough to send me running the other way.

But I refused to be the girl that shied away from everything—so I squared my shoulders, pretending my fear didn't exist.

I grasped Maddox's shoulder and swung my leg over the side. I wiggled my body against his until I was seated and didn't feel like I was going to fall off.

"Comfortable?" He chuckled warmly, reaching back so his hand grasped my thigh.

I bucked against him and made a choking sound.

"You okay?"

"Mhmm, yeah. I'm good." I tried to gather my breath. He hadn't meant anything by touching me and I was making a big deal out of nothing. "Where exactly are we going?"

"I have no idea," he answered truthfully, "and that's where the fun lies."

Before I could respond we were speeding down the road. I let out a small scream and wrapped my arms tightly around his chest. I felt him chuckle rather than heard it. I squished my eyes closed and laid my head against his back. He was going so fast that I was scared to look around.

When we were stopped by a red-light he said, "Emma, you're holding me so tight that I'm going to have bruises from your fingers."

"Then don't go so fast!" I defended.

"Fine," he chuckled. "I'll slow it down… a little bit."

I gulped.

The light turned green and he kicked off again.

"Maddox!" I shrieked. If this was his idea of fun, then I wanted off of this ride.

"Open your eyes, Emma!" How the hell did he know I'd closed my eyes? "The world is passing you by!"

I wrapped my arms tighter around his body and slowly peeled my eyes open.

Everything was a blur around us—like we were going so fast that time had come to a halt.

It wasn't as scary as I thought it might be.

Our small town soon disappeared as he headed towards the city.

An hour later he pulled into the parking lot of a restaurant. My arms shook and I couldn't move if I wanted to.

He reached up and removed his helmet, musing his hair with his fingers. "Em? Emma?" He probed, when I didn't move.

I was frozen.

"I can't move." I mumbled against his back.

He chuckled huskily. "Of course you can."

I tried to wiggle my fingers. "Nope."

"Aw, I didn't scare you *that* bad, did I?" He asked, grasping my arms and removing them from the stranglehold around his torso.

"I'll be okay," I assured him. "Just give me a minute… or five."

He kept still, waiting for me to muster the energy to get off the motorcycle. When I finally got brave enough I nearly fell thanks to how bad my legs were shaking.

"Whoa." Maddox's hand shot out to grab me before I could fall.

"Thanks," I replied, steadying myself. When he was sure

that I was okay he let me go and climbed off as well.

He reached up and removed the helmet from my head and stowed it away.

I smoothed my fingers through my hair, hoping he couldn't see how bad my hands were shaking. The ride hadn't been terrible after he slowed down, but I'd still been scared that if I didn't hold on tight enough I might fall off.

"M-maybe it won't be so bad on the way back?" I reasoned.

Maddox laughed, slinging his arm around my shoulders as he towed me towards the restaurant. "Maybe."

"You sound like you don't think so?"

He pulled me closer. "Well, you seemed pretty scared. I have the scratches on my stomach to prove it. Would you like to see?" He winked, reaching for his shirt with his free hand.

"Nope. No. I'm good," I stuttered.

He chuckled, shaking his head.

"What?" I prompted.

He shrugged as we started up the steps to the restaurant. "I think it's cute how embarrassed you get about certain things I say."

"That's because you have no filter," I countered.

"True," he agreed with a laugh. Opening the door to the restaurant, he added, "I hope you like pizza."

"Pizza is my life," I stated. "It's more important than showering and breathing."

He laughed, his lips twisting into a smile. "You really love pizza, then."

The inside of the restaurant was fancy for a pizza place. I looked around at the shiny wood floors and rich wood accents. I could see the kitchen where a wood fire burned.

"That's how they cook the pizza. Wood-fired. They're delicious." Maddox commented when he saw me staring at the fireplace.

"Two?" A hostess spoke up.

The pizza place had a freaking hostess?

"Yes," Maddox answered, "and could we be seated outside?"

"Certainly," she smiled, grabbing the menus. "Follow me."

Once we were seated and she had disappeared I hissed at Maddox, "I thought you said this was a pizza place?"

He arched a brow as he looked at me over the top of the menu. "It is."

"I was picturing like... Pizza Hut with red and white checkered tablecloths and paper plates," I mumbled. "This place is too fancy."

Maddox chuckled and set aside his menu. "Well, the way I see it, I kind of owe you after last night. So I thought a nice lunch would suffice."

"After you nearly killed me on the motorcycle?"

He rolled his eyes. "I did not nearly kill you. Don't be dramatic."

"I'm pretty sure I was holding on for dear life."

A playful smirk lifted his lips. "Maybe on the way back I can do some tricks."

"Don't even think about it," I narrowed my eyes.

He chuckled and picked up the menu once more. "I'd never really do that to you."

"I would hope not," I mumbled just as the waiter appeared at our table.

"I'm Tyler, I'll be your waiter. Can I start you off with something to drink?"

"Water, please," I smiled at the waiter.

"Diet Pepsi."

The waiter winced. "I'm sorry, we only have Coke products from the vending machine right now. Our machine is down."

"Fucking Coke," Maddox grumbled, "it's a conspiracy, I tell you."

I snorted and then tried to cover it with a cough.

"Water for me too, then," Maddox mumbled.

"I'll be right back." The waiter turned and disappeared inside the building.

I looked at the menu once more.

"Order whatever you want," Maddox stood up. "And if he comes back before I do, order me a large pepperoni pizza... and no, I'm not sharing. I'm eating that sucker all by myself."

"Where are you going?" I asked, puzzled.

"To get a Diet Pepsi, of course." He looked at me like I was the crazy one.

"Well, okay then," I laughed.

I watched him walk away and shook my head

"Are you ready to order?" The waiter asked, sitting the glasses down.

"Oh, uh... yeah. A large pepperoni pizza for him and cheese for me. Ooh, and some of these pepperoni rolls." I pointed at the picture on the menu. "Those sound good."

"Sure thing." He took the menus. "I'll put that right in."

While I waited for Maddox to return I studied the nearby buildings. Most seemed to be occupied by lawyers and other professionals, but I did see a pet store and ice cream shop.

"Found one!" Maddox chimed, breaking me out of my thoughts. He flopped into the seat and held the bottle of Diet Pepsi up proudly.

"I take it you really like Diet Pepsi," I laughed, sipping my water.

"I love Diet Pepsi the way you love pizza, with all my heart." He slapped a hand dramatically against his chest before unscrewing the lid.

"That's a lot then," I commented.

Maddox opened his mouth to say something, but the waiter appeared at the table with the pepperoni rolls. "Here's your starter," he smiled at me. His gaze flicked towards Maddox and he startled. I thought maybe he was about to scold Maddox for the Diet Pepsi, but that didn't happen. Instead, the guy stared at Maddox with a puzzled expression. Finally, he said, "You look really familiar."

Maddox squirmed uncomfortably in his seat. He covered his mouth with his hand and mumbled, "Nope, don't think so. You must be confusing me with someone else."

The waiter lingered for a moment longer, before shaking his head. "Yeah, I guess so, my bad." He smiled awkwardly at me and backed away from our table.

"That was weird," I wrinkled my nose, and looked across the table at Maddox.

He stared off into the distance. "Mhmm, weird... I'll be right back."

He stood up once more to leave and was gone before I could say anything else.

What the hell?

I watched him leave with a mystified look on my face.

He wasn't gone long, but returned with a black baseball cap perched on top of his head. He kept the brim low so that his eyes were bathed in shadows.

When he sat down I glared at him. "You're really bad at this whole date thing."

He grinned. "What? Are you kidding? I excel at everything." He reached once more for a Diet Pepsi.

"What's up with the hat?" I asked, reaching for one of the pepperoni rolls and dipping it in marinara sauce.

He reached up and touched the brim. "The sun was in my eyes."

I stared at him for a moment. "Maddox?"

"Emma?" He grinned.

"If the sun was in your eyes why didn't you put on your

sunglasses?" I pointed the fancy pair dangling from the collar of his shirt.

He looked down and smiled sheepishly. "I forgot about them."

For some reason I didn't believe him. I had a gut feeling that his sudden desire to wear a hat came from what the waiter said.

"Do you really know that guy and not want him to remember you?" I asked.

"What? No. I don't know him." He scoffed. "Like I told you, the hat was for the sun."

I sighed heavily and decided to let it drop. "These are really good," I said instead, pointing to the appetizer.

Maddox reached for one. "Yeah, I love this place. Good food and good atmosphere."

"But no Diet Pepsi," I jested.

He chuckled and I noticed that some marinara sauce sat adorably in the corner of his mouth. "And that's a shame."

Maddox polished off the rest of the pepperoni rolls just as the waiter brought out our pizzas. My stomach rumbled as I eyed the delicious cheesy goodness. I hadn't been lying when I told Maddox I loved pizza.

After the exhausting drive here I was starving.

I grabbed a piece and took a bite. "Oh my God." I had to suppress a moan. "This is the best pizza I've ever had."

Maddox stared at me for a moment and cleared his throat.

"What?" I asked.

"You... uh... might not want to make noises like that in public." He nodded his head in the direction of a table occupied by three men old enough to be my grandpa. They all stared at me with an open mouthed expression.

"Oh." I blushed, and set my pizza down, suddenly embarrassed.

"Now behind closed doors with me on top... yeah, I could go for that," he winked.

"Maddox," I hissed, my cheeks flaming red.

"Sorry, I couldn't resist." He chuckled.

I'd like to say that I lost my appetite, but that would be a lie. This was pizza and nothing, not even my embarrassment, would stop me from enjoying it.

We finished eating and Maddox paid for our meal. Normally I would've protested, but after getting arrested last night and the scary motorcycle ride this morning I figured he owed me.

As we walked through the parking lot my stomach twisted.

I had to get back on the motorcycle.

Oh, God.

I stood frozen and Maddox turned back to look at me when he noticed I was no longer beside him. "Emma?" He prompted. "Are you okay?"

"Uh..."

"Aw, Em," he strode up to me and reached for my hand. "It'll be okay. I won't go fast this time, I swear."

I closed my eyes and took a deep breath. It was only a motorcycle. I could do this. This was all about having an adventure and pushing myself outside my comfort zone.

"Slow?" I asked.

"So slow a baby turtle could pass us," he chuckled. Sobering, he added, "I'm sorry I scared you earlier."

"You're forgiven," I mumbled. "But seriously, if you scare the crap out of me again on this thing you better sleep with one eye open."

His lips quirked into a smile. "I'm intrigued by the idea of you sneaking into my room at night. This has possibilities."

I rolled my eyes. "You are..." There were no words for what Maddox was.

"Amazing?" He supplied with a grin.

"More like unbelievable," I countered. "But you can go with amazing if that makes you feel better."

He chuckled, rubbing his fingers through his hair. We reached the motorcycle and he grabbed the helmet I'd worn on the way here. Before placing it on my head he said, "I think I've met my match with you."

He cut off my retort by shoving the helmet onto my head. I wobbled with the extra weight and he grasped my hips in his hands, drawing me against his body. Our bodies lined up perfectly. In fact, mine curled against him—like my brain had completely shut down and my body had taken over. I swallowed thickly and was silently glad for the protection the helmet provided.

"I'm not quite ready for our first adventure to end." His hands flexed against my hips.

"You're not?" If this adventure continued on the motorcycle I'd have to put a stop to it. I might have a heart attack if I was stuck on the thing a second longer than necessary.

"No." He shook his head and his unique gray eyes darkened to the color of rain clouds before a storm.

"Oh... what do you have planned? Because this motorcycle and I aren't very good friends."

He chuckled and his hands skimmed higher up my back. I shivered from his touch, despite the fact that it was well over eighty degrees outside.

"I thought you could come to my house." As if he sensed my distress he hastened to add, "My mom will be there, so you have nothing to worry about. I just... you said you liked music and there's something I want to show you."

Behind the safety of the helmet I took a deep breath to steady myself. I knew I would agree, because there was something about Maddox that was impossible to resist, but a part of me was screaming that I was insane. After all, I'd only met him a few days ago. But I didn't want to be that same girl I'd been my whole life—spending the summer locked in my house playing piano and reading all the time... and occasionally getting dragged to the mall by Sadie. I wanted to *live* and with Maddox I... well... I felt *alive*.

"That sounds okay," I squeaked.

His hands disappeared from my waist. "Excellent." He rapped his knuckles against the helmet. "Let's get out of here."

My body broke out in a sweat at the thought of the ride back.

He climbed on the motorcycle and put his helmet on. "It'll be okay, Emma." He reached out a hand to me.

I nodded and forced myself to get on behind him. Since I had no experience with guys whatsoever it was a bit awkward being pressed so close to him, but I had little choice.

"Hold on tight—" He warned, revving the bike. I wrapped my arms around his torso and felt him chuckle. He reached back and put his hand on my upper thigh. My gasp was so loud I swore he had to have heard it over the roar of the engine. "— And don't let go."

CHAPTER SIX

THE RIDE TO Maddox's home wasn't nearly as bad as the first time. In fact, I kind of enjoyed it.

Despite that by the time we arrived at his house I was ready to get off the thing.

Removing the helmet I gaped at the massive house. "Holy crap, you live here?"

He chuckled. "Yes. Mathias and I actually live in the guesthouse out back, but we have rooms in the house as well. We just prefer our privacy."

"Guesthouse? You have a freaking guesthouse?" I gasped. Due to the large size of the home I should have suspected as much, but still...

Maddox chuckled and removed the leather jacket he wore. Heading towards the back of the house he nodded for me to follow him. "The guesthouse is actually where we're headed." He pushed open a wrought iron gate and we stepped into a nice backyard. It was flat with bright green grass and a shimmery blue pool. I'd only ever seen homes like this in a magazine. It definitely didn't compare to the shabby ranch-style home I lived in.

"I'd say for foster kids you and Mathias really lucked out

with Karen," I commented, still looking around at the palatial house. It really was gorgeous. While it was large it wasn't overly intimidating. In fact, there was something rather homey to it, and I thought that was thanks to the cape cod style. It looked like a home you'd see by a lake somewhere. "This place is beautiful."

"Yeah, we did get lucky." Maddox's smile was small and his eyes darkened. "But after all the shit we went through as kids with our parents, I think we deserve every little bit of happiness that's thrown our way."

I nodded. I knew Maddox didn't know me well enough to spill the secrets of what life was like with his biological parents, and the details behind his foster parents, but I was curious. Normally I didn't care to get to know anyone. I was happy to bury my nose in a book and forget the real world existed, but I felt connected to Maddox. I *wanted* to get to know him. I *wanted* to spend time with him. I was drawn to him in a way that even at seventeen years old I knew it was different. *He* was different.

"Emma?"

I stumbled and realized I'd been completely lost in my thoughts. Maddox stood by the door of the two-story guesthouse. It looked like a small version of the main house.

"Are you coming?" He prompted.

"Oh, uh, yeah." I scurried over to his side.

He smiled down at me before swinging the door open. "Home sweet home."

Inside the downstairs area was decorated sparsely, a small kitchenette lay to my right, and a rug was scattered over the wood floors. The back and sidewalls were painted white and brick. I didn't think I'd ever seen brick used inside a room before.

"This is what I wanted you to see." Maddox swept his arm to

the side and his smile was almost shy.

In the living room, the only pieces of furniture were a futon laid flat like a bed covered in random pillows and blankets and a desk covered in scattered papers.

I knew the futon wasn't what he was talking about though.

"Wow," I gasped at the full instrument set up. There was a mic, drum kit, guitar, bass, and a piano.

Maddox ducked his head. "You said you liked music and could play the piano... so I was hoping you might want to do a song with me."

I stood in shock. I couldn't get over how unsure Maddox seemed all of a sudden, since he was always so cocky. This was a side to him that was very much boyish.

I opened my mouth to tell him that I would love to when I heard a scuffling sound behind me. I let out a shrill scream and grabbed his arm. "What the hell was that?" I gasped.

He pressed his lips together, trying to hold in his laughter. He grabbed me by the shoulders and turned me around. Against the wall sat a small cage and I could see some sort of creature scurrying around. I stepped forward, peering inside. I expected to see a hamster, but it wasn't. It lifted its head slightly to look at me and wiggled its little black nose.

"Is that—?"

"A hedgehog," Maddox supplied with a grin. He opened the cage and reached inside to grab the little guy. "Emma, meet Sonic."

"Sonic?" I questioned, remembering last night at the police station. I'd thought he'd been talking about the fast food restaurant. "Why would you name him Sonic?"

Maddox gasped, clutching the hedgehog against his neck. "You don't know who Sonic the Hedgehog is?"

"Uh..." I looked at him like he'd lost his mind. "Isn't he right there?" I pointed to his pet.

He shook his head rapidly back and forth. "Sonic the Hedgehog... the videogame? Ringing any bells?"

I thought. "No. Sorry."

He gasped. "This. Is. A. Tragedy." He pulled his phone out of his back pocket and typed something in. He proceeded to shove it in my face. "*This* is Sonic the Hedgehog."

I stared at the cartoon drawing of a blue hedgehog. "That doesn't really look like a hedgehog, but if you say so."

Maddox sighed and put his phone away. "Well, when you get a hedgehog it's only appropriate to name it Sonic. Although, I did have a weak moment where I considered Aquilla the Hun."

I snorted. "Like a pun on Attila the Hun?"

Maddox gaped at me. "The fact that you know who Attila the Hun is, but not Sonic the Hedgehog, is appalling, Emma. It's downright blasphemy."

"You feel very passionately about this hedgehog," I laughed.

"I'm going to get a Sonic the Hedgehog videogame and make you play it. Just you wait and see," he mumbled. "Here, do you want to hold him?"

The spiky creature was shoved unceremoniously into my face. "Uh..." I eyed the hedgehog. "How do I hold him?"

"Just like I am," he chuckled, "but be mindful of the quills."

I held my hands out and he placed the hedgehog in them. Sonic sniffed at my hands, and I guess he decided he liked me, because he promptly fell asleep in my hands. I giggled. "I think he likes me."

I looked up in time to see something flash in Maddox's eyes. "What's not to like?" He murmured.

I startled at his words and warmth flooded my body.

Clearing his throat, he crossed his arms over his chest. The gesture pulled his shirt taut over the muscles in his chest and stomach. I swallowed thickly at the sight. "Maybe I should get you a hedgehog," he chuckled, "since Sonic likes you so much."

"Sonic and Aquilla the Hun?" I joked with a raised brow.

He laughed and took the hedgehog from my hands, putting him back in the cage. I watched the little guy burrow his way beneath the bedding.

Maddox put a guiding hand on my waist and led me over to the piano. I sat on the bench and he took the spot beside me. Since the bench was so small our bodies were squished together.

"What should I play?" I asked, my voice shaking with nerves. Normally I only played when I was alone. The most audience I had anymore was my mom. I was terrified that I might mess up with Maddox watching me.

"Whatever you want." His voice was soft and close to my ear. I jumped when his fingers touched my neck, pushing my hair over my shoulder. "I wanted to see your face." He whispered the words, looking at me with an intensity that left me breathless.

I gave him a shy look in return, my heart thumping madly behind my ribcage. I was mystified by this boy.

This crazy, cocky, insanely good-looking boy, that I had only just met, but managed to jumble my insides.

Even though I was nervous, I had truly never been so immediately comfortable with someone like I was with Maddox. There was something so infectious about him and impossible not to like.

"Okay," I finally replied.

I closed my eyes and my tongue flicked out to wet my lips.

I didn't think about any particular song. I just let my fingers guide me.

Typically I played with sheet music, even though I didn't have to. I'd always had an ear for music and could pick up on almost any song after hearing it once. It would take me a few tries to get it right, but I'd always been able to master even the most complicated of pieces.

This piano was much nicer than my one at home.

The keys were smooth and soft—almost as if it was brand new and had never been used.

When the song finished I opened my eyes to find a mystified Maddox staring at me.

"You're amazing," he whispered.

I ducked my head. "Hardly."

Shaking his head, he smiled. "Do you think we could do one together?"

"Sure," I agreed.

His smile was blindingly bright, causing my stomach to flip and flop.

"What instruments do you play... besides the drums, of course?" I asked.

"A little of everything. Drums is my favorite. I love the feel of the beat thrumming though my body and vibrating in my bones." He spoke with passion. "I can play the guitar decently, a little piano—nothing like you can, I assure you," he chuckled. "I sing... but not in front of people, only when I'm alone writing songs."

"You're such an overachiever." I joked with a smile, lightly bumping his shoulder with mine.

He smiled down at me. "It's only because I love music so much. It's my life."

I could see the love he spoke of shining in his eyes. I envied him for that. I was going to be a senior in high school and I was clueless about what I wanted to do. That scared me.

"What do you want to do for the rest of your life?" I asked Maddox, the words tumbling out of my mouth.

He grew quiet and his eyes were serious. "Music, of course."

I bowed my head.

"What do you want to do?"

I took a deep breath and forced myself to look at him once more. "That's the thing. I don't know and it scares me. I have to get it figured out, but I don't know if I'm as passionate about anything the way you are with music." I frowned. "I want... I want to have that sparkle in my eye that you have."

He reached up and smoothed the hair away from my forehead. "You do have a sparkle in your eye, Em. One for *life*."

"Somehow, I'm not feeling better."

He chuckled and bowed his head. His dark hair tumbled forward into his eyes. I itched to push it away from his eyes like he had done with me, but I wasn't nearly as bold as Maddox.

Finally he rested his fingers on the keys of the piano and began to play. "Do you know this one?" He asked when I didn't immediately join him.

"I don't... keep playing."

He did, and I closed my eyes, listening to the sound.

"It's Counting Stars by One Republic," he said.

"Never heard of them," I replied, still listening.

The music cut off and I opened my eyes.

"You don't know who One Republic is?" He gaped at me "That's like... impossible."

"Uh... sorry?" I laughed. "I don't really listen to anything but classical."

He looked like I'd just broken his heart. "Emma, I must introduce you to the amazing awesomeness that is One Republic... and The Fray, because they're fucking amazing too." He slid off the bench and said, "I'll be right back."

I watched as he headed to the upstairs part of the guesthouse.

He wasn't gone long and he returned with a black iPod. "Here," he held it out to me. "You can keep it."

"I don't want to keep it. I'll just borrow it for a little while," I slid it into my pocket.

"No, no. Just keep it. I don't even use it anymore. I've got everything right here." He pulled his phone from his pocket and waved it around. "Which reminds me, you can put music on the phone I got you. We'll do that another time though. Mathias is still sleeping and if I take you upstairs and we wake him up he'll be even more pissed than he would've been if he saw his motorcycle gone."

"Still sleeping? It's like two in the afternoon?"

"He was out all night," he shrugged, sitting down beside me once more. He started to play the song again and glanced at me. "If I play it once, then do you think we can play it together?"

I nodded. "Yeah."

He smiled and I closed my eyes again so that I could focus on the music. It didn't take me long to pick up on the song and by the time it finished I was ready to play.

A shy smile graced my lips as we started to play together.

I gasped in surprise when Maddox started to sing along. His voice was soft and husky. He became completely lost in the song and it was a sight to see. I wondered if I looked the same way when I was absorbed in a song. Or even a book. There was a look of such pure satisfaction on his face. If he looked this way singing and playing piano I longed to see him on the drums.

The last note lingered in the air and I dropped my hands into my lap.

Maddox glanced at me. His eyes were a light and happy gray. "Thank you."

I ducked my head, a few strands of hair falling forward to hide my face. Maddox made me feel things I hadn't believed possible.

When I lifted my gaze he still stared at me intensely, with

those unique silvery gray eyes.

"Do you want to do something crazy?" He asked, his voice no more than a whisper—like he was afraid if he said the words in a normal voice I might go running.

"What?" I asked, my brows furrowing together.

"Anything we want." His eyes darted to my lips. My heart jolted in my chest at the look of longing in his eyes. "I want more adventures with you like we had today. I don't want it to stop here."

I stared at him, puzzled. I didn't understand his sudden train of thought, but I rolled with it.

"Yes," I grinned. "Let's do it." I heard what he said last night echoing through my head, *Prepare for the most epic summer of your life. Nothing will ever top this.*

I *wanted* that epic summer he spoke of. I wanted to do the craziest things I could think of and finally allow myself the chance to live and stop fearing getting hurt by opening myself up.

His smile was blindingly bright and I squealed in surprise when he wrapped his strong arms around me in a hug. Mine hung limply at my side for a moment before I lifted them slowly to wrap around his torso. I could feel his muscles flex at my touch and the warmth of his body heat wrapped around me.

He let me go and I let my arms drop—hoping it hadn't seemed like I was feeling him up.

I swept my hair out of my eyes, hoping he didn't notice the way my hand shook.

"So," he started, and his lips turned up crookedly, "what's the second adventure you'd like to do this summer? —Because the motorcycle was number one. In case you didn't know." He winked, his smile playful.

"Knitting." The word fell out of my mouth before I could stop it. I slapped a hand over my mouth, like I thought the gesture alone could put the word back in there. Yes, I wanted to learn to knit—I was a dork like that—but I felt silly to have admitted that to Maddox.

"Knitting?" A brow quirked. "You want to sit around and knit sweaters and baby blankets like old ladies do?"

"Yes," I winced. "We don't have to do that, though. I don't know why I said it."

"No, no," he rushed to assure me, "it's okay. Knitting could be fun. Maybe I can make a Christmas present for Mathias," he grinned impishly. "I think he needs some new socks. What else?" He asked. "The craziest thing you can think of."

"I've always wanted to jump into a massive pool of those plastic ball things," I admitted with a shrug. "I never got to do that as a kid."

"Done. What do you think about skydiving?"

"Like jumping out of a plane?" I asked and he nodded. "I would do it.'"

"I think I love you, Emma," he chuckled.

I hated the way my body warmed at his words. I should *not* be thinking about the words *love* and *Maddox* in the same sentence. I'd just met him—and I'd vowed to never fall in love, anyway. Love made people weak. It made you do stupid things because you cared too much.

"Ooh!" He clapped his hands together. "Let's go to the aquarium in Baltimore."

I shook my head free of its previous thoughts, dismissing them from my mind.

"I've never been to the aquarium so that sounds fun to me," I grinned.

He gaped at me, his eyes bugging out. "You've never been to the aquarium? Even as a child?" I shook my head at his question. "That's just wrong, Em." He tapped a finger against his full bottom lip as he thought. "How about hiking?" He asked. "There's supposed to be an amazing view from the mountain not too far from here."

"I'm in," I agreed. Hiking really wasn't my thing, but this summer was meant for going outside my comfort zone. "I'll do it, but I won't be happy about it." I stuck my tongue out at him. "So when I get blisters on my feet I expect you to carry me the rest of the way up the mountain," I jested.

He chuckled. "I can do that." He proceeded to flex his arm muscles. Sobering, he said, "This sounds like one epic summer to me, Em."

I stared into his silvery eyes, getting lost for a moment. "Yeah, epic." I agreed, and I wasn't being the least bit sarcastic.

CHAPTER SEVEN

"RISE AND SHINE! We're going to the mall!"

I peeked my eyes open and hastily slapped a hand over them, wincing at the sunlight streaming through my now open windows.

"Sadie," I groaned. "I was sleeping."

"And now you're awake." I felt her hand slap against my feet. "Get out of bed, get dressed, and drink some of this lovely tea your mother made. I actually like this one, it doesn't taste like mud like the last one she gave me."

"I don't want to go anywhere," I pleaded. "Let me sleep."

"No can do. It's summer and we're going to have *fuuuuun*," she sing-songed.

"I was having fun... sleeping."

"Emma Rayne Burke, I will drag you from this bed if I have to. I need best friend time."

"Fine," I groaned.

"I'm glad you could see things my way," she clapped her hands together.

A moment later I heard my bedroom door close.

I forced my tired body from my bed and pulled on a pair of shorts, a white tank top, and the black hat Maddox loved so much—simply because there was no time to tame the beast. The beast being my hair, of course.

I found my mom and Sadie in the kitchen.

"Here you go, Emmie." My mom handed me a plate with an egg sandwich. "I'm glad you girls are spending some time together." With that she headed into her studio and I knew I'd be lucky if I saw her the rest of the day.

I sat down at the table beside Sadie and took a bite of my sandwich.

"Do we really have to go to the mall?" I whined. Our mall was the bane of my existence. It was a crappy mall—but even if it had been a nice mall I still would've hated it—with stores that charged too much and burnt food smelling up the place.

"Yes, we really do," she laughed, finishing her sandwich. "I need a dress for my parent's barbeque this weekend. You better come." She eyed me, daring me to say no.

"Of course," I agreed. "I'm there every year."

Sadie's family held a barbeque the week after school ended every year to celebrate the start of summer. It had been a tradition in my life as long as I'd been friends with Sadie— which was my whole life.

"I know," she frowned. "But you've been weird since the fair."

I knew this was the perfect opportunity to tell her more about Maddox, but I couldn't seem to open my mouth and get it to work. I thought a part of me was afraid that if I didn't keep Maddox a secret, he'd suddenly disappear—or become a figment of my imagination.

"Yeah, I know," I sighed.

"You were really mad at me, weren't you?" She frowned.

I shrugged. "You've done it before. I should be used to it."

"God," she smacked her hand against the top of the table,

"I'm such a shitty friend. You should really fire me and find a replacement."

I cracked a smile at that. "You know there's no one else quite like you."

She laughed, the tension bleeding out of her body. "You've got that right. I'm one of a kind."

I finished my sandwich and washed our plates. "Okay," I sighed heavily. "I'm ready to be tortured."

She rolled her eyes and grabbed her purse. "You are so fucking dramatic, Emma. You should really consider joining the drama club." She started towards the front door, leaving me in the kitchen.

"Yes, because I like people so much." I dead-panned.

She stopped in her tracks, laughing. "Oh yes, I forget, I'm your only human friend. The rest are fictional."

"At least they don't piss me off like you do," I jested.

"Whatever, Emma." Her tone was light. "Get your ass out here before I leave you!" She called, going out the door.

"Yes, because I would be heart broken if you left without me!"

The glass storm door swung closed but she turned around, giving me the finger.

A lot of people probably didn't understand our friendship, but when you'd known each other for forever you stopped caring what you said to one another.

I grabbed my purse and followed her outside. I slid into the passenger seat of her old Hyundai Elantra. "I better get some pretzels out of this with that yummy mustard sauce, it's the only good thing that ever comes out of the mall."

She laughed, backing out of the driveway. "Don't worry. I'll make sure you get your pretzels. Maybe, if you're a good girl and don't complain too much I'll even get you Cinnabon." She patted me on top of my head.

I clapped my hand over my heart. "I think you love me."

"Only a little." She held her thumb and index finger apart slightly.

In many ways Sadie was like the annoying sister I'd always wanted but never had. Sadie had her own little sister, Abby, and an older brother named Sam. When I was younger I used to be jealous of the fact that she had a brother and sister—even when they argued I wanted that. Now that I was older, and had grown up with my dad being such an asshole, I was glad that I didn't have any siblings.

As my thoughts turned to my dad I frowned.

There was a part of me that missed him. He was my dad after all.

And I knew I was still angry at him for abandoning us the way he had. My mom didn't deserve to be walked out on with a house and bills to pay for—not to mention a kid.

My dad was probably—okay, *definitely*—the reason I preferred the company of books and stayed away from guys.

Except for Maddox.

He was different.

But I didn't quite understand *how* he was different.

I didn't trust him, though. I couldn't. And he'd never get my heart. I wouldn't give it to him. But we could be friends.

Friends—wasn't that a joke with the way I was attracted to him.

I would be better off staying away, but I *couldn't*.

He was the sun and I couldn't help but be drawn to his warmth.

"Emma? Emmmmma?"

"What?" I shook my head free of my thoughts.

"We're here." Sadie pointed to the mall.

"Oh." I looked up at its brick exterior. When did we get here? I couldn't remember.

She shut the car off and climbed out, slinging her purse over her shoulder and fluffing her hair.

Sadie always looked like she was ready to pose for a picture—and not of the selfie variety.

Sadie was always put together—hair done, makeup impeccable, and her clothes stylish.

I followed her into the mall, praying that we didn't run into too many people we went to school with.

Small talk was the bane of my existence.

Sadie seemed to be on a mission, though. She power walked through the crowds and I hurried to catch up.

"They better still have this dress," she muttered. "It's on sale and it's perfect."

I had no idea what dress she was talking about, but if I knew Sadie it was probably short and would have her boobs practically spilling out of the top.

When she looked back and saw me dragging behind her she grabbed my arm and pulled me along. "Come on," she groaned.

She didn't let go of me as she practically ran into the store.

She scanned the racks and squealed. "Cross your fingers that they have my size!" She finally let go of me and went through the dresses. "Yes!" She exclaimed, holding up a strapless dress. The top was a corset design with flowers while the skirt was aqua colored. "It was meant to be." She clutched it to her chest.

I thought she was seconds away from kissing it and offering to have its children.

"Now we have to find a dress for you!" She jumped up and down.

"Uh, no." Clothes like this weren't my thing. They were too fancy and far too pricey for what I could afford. Sadie was always trying to buy me clothes and other things—even her parents tried to spoil me, since they all knew things were hard on my mom since my dad left.

She rolled her eyes and clutched the top of the metal rack. "Yes, you're getting a dress. I owe you for the fair and all the other shit I put you through. Pretzels and Cinnabon is not enough to make up for it. Please don't fight me on this." Her bottom lip curled down.

I was powerless to the pout and she knew it. It was how she'd gotten me to do many things over the years—usually to go to parties.

"Fine," I agreed. "But nothing over fifty dollars. I mean it." I pointed a finger at her warningly.

She didn't say anything in response. Instead she started darting around to the different racks like a demented fairy on crack.

"And nothing too revealing!" I yelled after her, causing several people to look my way.

I hurried after Sadie, lest she get too carried away.

She pulled a dress off a rack and held it out to me as I approached. "This one is perfect!"

I had to admit, she actually chose well for me. The dress was cream colored with pink, red, orange, and blue flowers embroidered on it. It had thicker straps and didn't dip down low in the front.

"You like it," she stated, smiling like the Cheshire cat. "Say it, Emma."

"You did good," I groaned. "I really like it." In fact, I might've even loved it.

I reached out, rubbing the fabric between my fingers.

"See, you should trust me more often." She beamed, her light brown hair swishing around her shoulders. She carried the items towards the checkout area, stopping at one of the spinning displays of jewelry. She grabbed a set of simple silver bangles and then placed her items on the counter by the register.

I nibbled my bottom lip nervously. "Sadie, you really don't have to get me that dress."

"Shut up. You deserve it and I'm getting it for you. End of discussion." She nodded her head firmly.

"Thank you," I said, knowing I'd end up thanking her a hundred more times before the day was over.

Once she'd paid she grabbed the bag and we headed towards the food court.

As promised she got me those pretzels I loved so much and Cinnabon. We sat in the food court eating and laughing. I was glad that I wasn't fighting with her anymore. I hated being mad at Sadie.

After hitting a few more stores we left and she dropped me off at home.

"Thank you again for the dress," I told her, clutching the bag in my hand. I was thinking about asking Maddox if he'd want to go to the barbeque with me. I was still scared to introduce him to Sadie—that was my insecurity showing—but I wanted him to come. I was already imagining his reaction to seeing me in the dress.

She rolled her eyes. "And for the thousandth time, Emma, you're welcome."

We both laughed and I got out of the car. I waved briefly before heading inside.

"Emmie, is that you?" My mom called from the kitchen when I closed the front door.

"Yes," I answered, wondering whom else it would be.

I found her sitting at the kitchen table with a cup of tea. Clay was caked underneath her fingernails and her light hair was pulled back messily and secured with a clip.

She looked up from the notepad where she was making a grocery list and smiled. "There's some more tea if you want some."

I poured a cup and sat down beside her. "I'm going back into my studio tonight. While I've got this..." She paused, searching for the right words, "...creative mojo going on I want to keep going. I thought maybe you could order Chinese or something."

"Sounds good," I agreed.

My mom rarely ever cooked dinner. It wasn't for a lack of care, she was just scatterbrained and often lost track of time. I didn't mind fending for myself, though. Especially since on the rare occasions when she did cook she liked to experiment—and all of her experiments ended badly.

She set the pen down and stared at me.

I gave her a peculiar look and asked, "Why are you looking at me like that?"

She shook her head and a sad smile turned her lips. "I was just thinking about what a beautiful young woman you've turned into. You're going to be a senior in high school, and then off too college. I know whatever you want to do with your life you'll excel at it. You've always been a brilliant girl. How'd I get so lucky?"

I didn't get emotional over much, but I felt tears well in my eyes.

My mom always went out of her way to tell me how smart and pretty I was. She was constantly telling me she was proud of me, and praising my accomplishments.

But sometimes I felt... almost worthless.

I wasn't an idiot, I knew where those feelings came from.

Having my dad treat me like crap and then abandon us had left a sour taste in my mouth.

If I wasn't good enough for him, then how would I ever be good enough for something or someone else?

I forced a smile. "Thanks, mom." I took a sip of my tea to

mask the quake in my voice. I set the mug down and traced my finger over the design of the skeletal T-Rex, smiling at the words painted on the mug: Tea Rex. It always made me smile.

She gave my hand a pat and stood up from the table, finishing the last of her tea. She set the empty cup in the sink. "I'll see you later, Emmie." She bent down and kissed the top of my head as she passed.

I picked up my cup of tea and headed back to my room.

Since the last few days had been... weird—that was the only word I could think to describe it—I hadn't been reading. But I was going to change that tonight.

I scanned my bookshelves for something new to read.

I read all genres, and even the occasional non-fiction book. I got bored easily if I read the same thing all the time.

When I couldn't decide I finally closed my eyes and picked a random book off the shelf.

I sat on my bed and turned the TV on for background noise while I flipped through the pages of the book.

I got lost in the imaginary world—picturing myself as the heroine. After all, wasn't that why people read? So they could live someone else's life for a little while?

Several hours passed and I was finally pulled from my fictional world by the rumbling of my stomach.

Clearly, it was time to order takeout.

And since I was starving I ordered enough food to feed five people.

My mom was going to kill me—but at least I remembered to order her chicken fried rice for later, so hopefully that counted as bonus points.

I settled on the couch in the living room, with my book in my lap, and listened to Maddox's iPod. I twirled one of the wire headphones around my finger, bobbing my head along to the song playing. It actually wasn't bad, and I found myself putting it on repeat. Maybe I was missing out on something by only listening to classical.

When the doorbell rang I set my book aside, but kept the iPod clasped in my hand. I grabbed the cash off the kitchen table and opened the door.

I stared at the guy standing there.

"You're not the Chinese guy." I eyed his empty hands.

"No," he chuckled.

"Who are you?" I asked, starting to ease the door closed. I'd seen *48 Hours*, so I knew a strange guy showing up on your doorstep was never a good thing.

"Ezra," he replied, sweeping curly black hair from his dark almond shaped eyes. "I'm Maddox's friend."

"Best friend and foster brother!" Another voice called from near the driveway.

I stepped outside and eyed Maddox, who strode towards me with confidence clear in the way he held himself. "Why are you here?" I asked.

"Are you not happy to see me?" He feigned a gasp.

"I'm confused," I countered.

"We were nearby," he shrugged, "and I needed to ask you a favor. Can we come inside?" He pointed towards the house.

"Sure," I shook my head, moving out of the way. Once they were inside I closed the door and pulled the iPod out of my pocket, sitting it on a side table. "So, if you had a favor to ask why didn't you text me? Or call?"

"And miss the chance to see your pretty face? I don't think so," he jested, sitting down on the couch. "Now, for the introductions, Emma, this is Ezra. He's Karen's real son."

Ezra rolled his eyes. "Please, I might be the biological son but you know she loves you more."

Maddox chuckled. "True, I mean, what's not to love?" He motioned to himself.

"Can we get to the point as to why you're here?" I interrupted. I wasn't normally so snappy, but I was hungry, and when I was hungry... watch out.

"Someone's grouchy," Maddox muttered under his breath to Ezra.

"I'm hungry," I defended, crossing my arms over my chest.

"Anyway," Maddox continued, rubbing his hands together, "We, and by *we* I mean my whole family, have to go out of town through the weekend. We leave tomorrow morning and I need someone to watch Sonic."

"Are you seriously asking me to babysit your hedgehog?" I resisted the urge to laugh. "I don't know the first thing about taking care of one."

"It's easy. You feed it, give it water, and shower it with love and affection. What's so difficult about that?" He countered.

"My mom's never let me have a pet. She's not going to let me," I warned him. The truth was my mom wouldn't care—it had always been my dad that was the real animal hater—but Maddox didn't need to know that.

"It's not like you're keeping Sonic. The moment we get back I'll pick the little guy up. It's only a few days."

"What if he dies?" I hissed. "I will not be responsible for the death of your hedgehog." I'd once killed a fish just by staring at it. True story.

Maddox looked at Ezra and back at me. "You're not going to kill him, Em. You're going to take care of him."

"What if by taking care of him I send him to an early grave!" I shrieked.

"You'll do fine," he continued. "I have the utmost faith in your hedgehog babysitting abilities."

I knew then that I wasn't getting out of this.

"Please, Em?" He begged, his gray eyes were wide and pleading. "You're the only one I trust with him."

I sighed in defeat. "Fine, I'll watch the hedgehog."

"Thank you!" He jumped up from the couch and wrapped his arms around me, planting a wet kiss on my cheek.

"Um... you're welcome," I mumbled.

The doorbell rang and before I could move Maddox was striding across the room to the door. He opened it wide, screamed, "Ooh! Food!" and pulled his wallet out his back pocket. He handed the guy a wad of cash and closed the door with his booted foot.

I stood there, shell-shocked at Maddox's take-charge attitude.

"I had money for that, you know."

"And I beat you to it," he winked, sitting the bags down on the coffee table. "It's like you knew we were coming. You ordered enough food for all of us, which is great since I'm *starving*."

He proceeded to sit on the floor and start pulling out the white boxes.

"Just help yourself," I muttered with a shake of my head.

I headed into the kitchen to grab plates and forks—I'd never been able to master the art of using chopsticks.

I set the stuff on the kitchen table and called, "Why don't you bring it in here?"

After a moment of shuffling the guys appeared in the kitchen doorway. Half of an egg roll stuck out of Maddox's mouth.

"I hope it's good," I stuck a hand on my hip, "because that was mine."

He chewed and swallowed. "There are like six in here."

"And I was going to eat all of them," I joked.

"Well you can have the other five then," he chuckled.

The three of us emptied out portions of everything onto our plates. "Seriously, why'd you get so much food?" Ezra asked, looking around like he expected a group of people to pop out from behind a hidden doorway.

"I was hungry, and I like this stuff left over," I shrugged. "And since you two showed up and want to steal all my food, I guess it's a good thing I ordered so much."

Ezra had the good graces to look ashamed, but it was clear Maddox didn't care. He was the kind of guy that was used to doing what he wanted, when he wanted. I wasn't annoyed, though. I liked that about him—that he wasn't afraid to be himself.

"Maddox said you guys met at the fair?" Ezra questioned.

I nodded, but before I could say anything Maddox spoke up. "She was overcome by how hot I am and fainted right at my feet. But just like Sleeping Beauty, my kiss awakened her. It's a very romantic story, one I'm sure we'll tell our grandchildren."

I looked at Ezra and we both started to laugh.

"You're so full of shit." Ezra pushed Maddox's shoulder.

"Excuse me if the truth was boring and I saw fit to stretch it," Maddox harrumphed. Maddox looked around and asked me, "Where's your mom?"

"In her studio, oblivious to the rest of the world." I wasn't angry about that fact. After all, I was very much like my mom. I got lost in my own little world all too easy where the passage of time ceased to matter.

"Well, then I think we should eat until we burst and then go for some ice cream," Maddox suggested.

"Yes, because gorging myself until I want to throw up and then eating ice cream sounds like such a good idea," I laughed.

"Fine," he chuckled, ducking his head, "maybe we should watch a movie?"

Ezra cleared his throat. "I feel like you've completely forgotten I'm here."

"Aw, sorry, sweet pea," Maddox feigned a high voice, "please forgive me?" He leaned towards Ezra, making kissy lips.

Ezra pushed him away. "We can't stay late," Ezra warned. "We still have to pack."

"I'll throw some clothes in a bag in the morning," countered Maddox.

Ezra rolled his eyes. "Yes, but our flight is at nine in the morning and we have to drop Sonic off here. Plus, you know what a delight Mathias is in the mornings."

Maddox frowned. "I wish we could just leave him."

"Yeah, well, we can't," Ezra muttered.

"Just one movie?" Maddox pleaded, looking between Ezra and me.

"Uh..." I started.

"As long as it's not a three hour movie I'm okay with it."

"It's settled then," Maddox grinned at me. "Movie time!"

The guys helped me clean up our mess and put away the leftovers before we settled in the living room. Ezra removed some cushions from the one couch and put them on the floor. That left the loveseat for Maddox and I.

I couldn't help wondering if Ezra had done that on purpose.

Maddox scanned the DVDs we owned. "You don't have anything recent," he muttered. "What's with that?"

"We don't really watch movies," I shrugged, "so we stopped buying them."

"Looks like we're going with *Air Bud*."

A moment later the movie started to play and Maddox sat down beside me.

I didn't know why, but I desperately wanted to close the space between us and curl my body around his.

It was silly.

Stupid even.

He wasn't my boyfriend, and I wasn't even sure we were *friends*.

My mind and body were fighting a battle of reason and attraction.

I didn't want a boyfriend—after all, I couldn't trust that a guy wouldn't abandon me just like my dad.

But my body... oh, my body wanted Maddox.

I'd never experienced this kind of attraction.

Sure, I'd had crushes here and there, but nothing compared to this.

It was like the moment I decided to close my heart off forever Maddox came along.

I kept telling myself that I'd only just met him and my feelings would fade, but somehow I didn't believe it.

I startled when I felt Maddox's arm fall around my shoulders. "Come here," he coaxed, pulling me against his side. He reached behind us on the back of the couch and grabbed the blanket, draping it over my body.

He made me feel protected and cared for.

I was totally screwed.

But I guessed there were worse things than crushing on the hot guy you met at the fair, right?

At least I hoped so.

CHAPTER EIGHT

I WOKE UP sometime after midnight and blinked my eyes open.

"What?" I asked blearily.

"Shh," Maddox crooned. "We fell asleep."

I startled.

Oh my God.

He was carrying me to bed.

He laid me down gently on my bed and pulled away. "I'll see you in the morning." His voice was soft. "Goodnight."

His lips pressed tenderly against my forehead and my eyes closed at the touch.

"Goodnight, Maddox," I whispered as he walked out of the room.

Once I knew he was gone I changed out of my clothes and into pajamas.

I snuggled beneath the covers, and soon dreams floated behind my closed lids—all of them starring a gray-eyed boy.

I SAT UP and threw the covers off my body.

Why was the doorbell ringing at—I searched for my alarm clock—six in the morning?

"Oh crap," I muttered, suddenly remembering my hedgehog babysitting duties.

I ran out of my room and down the hall, throwing open the front door.

My poor mom didn't even know I'd agreed to take care of the little creature. I knew she wouldn't care, but I still felt bad for not letting her know.

"Morning," Maddox grinned, standing with a grumpy looking Mathias who held Sonic's cage. Sonic, himself, was clasped in Maddox's hands.

I stepped aside and waved the twins into my house, while stifling a yawn.

"You can put him in my room."

Mathias grumbled something unintelligible, and I figured it translated to how much he hated the world and life itself. He just seemed like the type of guy to bitch about everything.

"This way." I guided the grumpy twin to my room.

He set the cage on top of my dresser, muttered, "Bye," and left the room.

"He hates mornings," Maddox shrugged.

"Your brother and I have that in common." I pushed my messy hair out of my eyes.

He chuckled. "Here, I made you a list." He pulled a piece of paper out of his pocket and shoved it in my hands.

I opened it up, squinting to make out what he'd scrawled.

He began to recite everything he'd written. Telling me how much food to give Sonic, bath time instructions, and even how often a day Sonic liked to play.

"I thought Hedgehogs were nocturnal," I muttered.

"They mostly are, but Sonic is special." Maddox grinned proudly at the hedgehog. Maddox reminded me of some of the crazy people I saw with dogs. You know the ones that talk to them all the time and kiss them? Yeah, that was Maddox, but with a hedgehog.

"Of course he is," I sighed.

Maddox frowned at the spiky creature. "I don't want to leave him."

"When will you be back?" I asked.

"Sunday night." He shoved his fingers through his messy hair.

I frowned. I remembered him saying yesterday they'd be gone through the weekend—so that meant he couldn't come to the barbeque.

A car horn honked and Maddox cursed. "I really have to go." He handed the hedgehog over to me and said, "Thanks, Em." He started to pass by me and stopped, lowering his head to kiss my cheek. "I'll miss you," he whispered. "But when I get back it's time for another adventure."

"Sounds good," I smiled. Clutching Sonic to my chest I followed Maddox to the door. I didn't understand why my chest ached at watching him leave. We hadn't even known each other a week yet. It made no sense, but in the back of my mind I remembered my mom telling me once that the greatest things in our lives have no explanation, they just are.

"Bye," I called, when he started to get in the car.

He smiled and my stomach stirred with butterflies.

As the SUV—one of those big black Suburban's—backed out of the driveway I lifted my hand to wave. Then, feeling silly, I even lifted Sonic's little hand—or whatever it was called—so he could wave too.

Once the SUV was out of sight I looked down at the hedgehog.

"Well, it's just you and me now, buddy."

He sniffed my hand and then proceeded to pee.

"Oh, gross," I gagged. I ran back to my room and put him in his cage, before washing my hands five times.

When I returned to my room Sonic was snoozing peacefully in his cage. I climbed in bed once more and promptly fell asleep.

THIS TIME I woke up to the smell of tea and my mother standing over me.

"Emma," she eyed me with a stern expression, "what on Earth is this?" She moved out of the way to nod her head at the cage where Sonic was currently drinking some water.

"That's Sonic," I sat up, rubbing my eyes, "Maddox's hedgehog."

"Well, if this thing belongs to him why is it in our house?" She raised a brow, giving me her stern 'mom' look.

"Uh... I said I would watch him. Maddox and his family are out of town until Sunday and he needed someone to take care of him," I explained.

She sighed. "Well, he is kind of cute."

"The hedgehog or Maddox?" I laughed.

She rolled her eyes. "I was talking about the hedgehog, but Maddox is cute too." She sat down on the end of my bed and her eyes grew serious. "He's a nice boy too. Sweet... I like him."

"Do you want to date him?" I giggled.

She swatted lightly at my leg. "Emmie, I'm being serious. He seems like a good guy. I know you've never dated before and I'm not stupid, I know it's because of your dad, and I guess I don't want to see you push him away because of that."

"We're not dating, mom," I groaned. "We just met."

She smiled. "I see the way he looks at you. I might be old,

but I still know what that look means."

"You're not old," I told her, "and he doesn't look at me in any certain way."

"I know what I saw last night." Her smile widened.

"Last night?" My brows furrowed together.

She nodded. "Mhmm," she took a sip of her tea. "I came in last night for some water and found the three of you in the living room. You'd already fallen asleep and the way he looked at you..." She smiled wistfully. "It reminded me of a boy I loved one summer, just like this, before my sixteenth birthday. He used to look at me like that and I've never forgotten it. It was so... pure."

I'd never heard my mom talk about any man besides my dad. "What happened to that guy?" I asked.

She frowned. "I don't know," she shrugged. "He was only visiting family for the summer, and I never saw him again. Then I met your father."

"And we know how that ended," I grumbled, rolling my eyes.

"Emmie," she clutched my hand, "you have to stop hating him. I know things were bad there for a while before he left, but it wasn't always that way."

"Why don't you hate him?" I asked, my lower lip trembling with the threat of tears.

"Because, he gave me you. How can I hate the man that gave me such a precious gift?"

I wished I could be more like my mom—so kind and forgiving.

I held my arms out and she enveloped me in a hug.

I didn't care how old you were, you were *never* too old to hug your mom.

She smoothed her fingers through my hair. "I love you so much, Emma."

"I love you too, mom." I wiped my tears away with a swipe of my hands. "What was that guy's name?" I asked.

"Matthew," she replied.

Were Maddox and I doomed to be like Matthew and my mother? Nothing more than a carefree summer fling?

I shook my head forcefully.

What was I thinking? This wasn't a fling.

This was nothing.

Okay, that was wrong.

It was an adventure.

And an adventure had nothing to do with love.

But if I never saw Maddox again after this summer would I be okay with that?

I knew, without a doubt, that the answer was no.

I wouldn't be okay.

Not at all.

CHAPTER NINE

THE WEEK PASSED by at an obnoxiously slow rate and was rather boring without Maddox around.

I'd planned to read books and basically do nothing all summer—but now that held no appeal to me.

Staying in the house day in and day out was getting annoying.

At least it was Sunday, which meant I had Sadie's barbeque to attend this afternoon and Maddox would be home tonight.

I'd heard from him several times every day—and he got antsy if I didn't give him regular updates on Sonic.

It was cute how much he worried about the hedgehog.

As if he was triggered by my thoughts alone, my phone flashed with a text.

MADDOX: SEE YOU TONIGHT. GIVE SONIC A KISS FOR ME.

I laughed.

EMMA: WHAT TIME ARE YOU GETTING IN? AND, NO, I'M NOT KISSING HIM.

MADDOX: Pls? 4 me? And we should be in by 10pm but u know how flights can be.

EMMA: Actually, I don't.

MADDOX: Don't what?

EMMA: Know how flights are. I've never been on a plane.

MADDOX: I guess it's a good thing we're jumping from one. ;)

EMMA: I forgot about that.

MADDOX: Don't chicken out on me.

EMMA: I won't.

MADDOX: Hey, sorry, I have to go.

EMMA: K. See you later.

I set my phone aside and looked at Sonic. "He'll be back soon."

His little head perked up, like he knew what I said.

I opened the cage and reached in to take him out. After giving him a brief cuddle—which was hard with the quills—I proceeded to coo and tell him how cute he was per Maddox's instructions. Seriously, he put it in writing.

I set Sonic on my bed while I got ready. I changed into the pretty dress Sadie got me, fixed my hair in a messy bun, and applied some makeup. I didn't normally wear much—only mascara and lip-gloss—but I decided to do a little more today. I rubbed the foundation on my face watching my freckles nearly disappear.

When I finished with my hair and makeup I went in search of my mom. "Are you ready?" I knocked on her door.

"Almost!" She called.

I went back into my room to put my shoes on and gasped. "Sonic?" I looked all over my bed. "Sonic?" I moved some pillows around, thinking he was hiding behind them. "Sonic!"

Oh no! I'd lost Maddox's hedgehog!

I dropped to my knees on the floor, looking under the bed. "Sonic?" I couldn't see him, but then again it was so dark under there that I couldn't see anything... and I was pretty sure I'd hidden some Cheez-It crackers down there. Maybe Sonic found them and was having a little hedgehog feast. Did hedgehogs even like cheese crackers? What if cheese was bad for them?

Oh my God, I was going to end up inadvertently killing Maddox's hedgehog with Cheez-Its!

I grabbed my fancy new phone and turned on the flashlight—and seriously, how cool was it that this thing had a flashlight?

I shined it under the bed, but Sonic wasn't there.

The Cheez-Its were though.

"Mom!" I called. "Mom! Come here!"

I was really starting to panic now.

"What?" She stumbled into my room, her hair half done.

"I can't find Sonic."

"What do you mean you can't find Sonic?" She practically screeched. "Isn't he in his cage?"

"I took him out and put him on my bed while I got ready. I felt bad for him cooped up in that cage and I didn't think he'd wander." I clutched at my chest, gasping for air. "Maddox is going to kill me."

"Don't panic," my mom warned, "he couldn't have gone far."

She moved the pillows around, just like I had, but Sonic definitely wasn't there.

"Oh God," I muttered. "This is bad. So bad."

"Calm down, Emma," she grumbled. "Wait... what's that?" She pointed to the pillow I slept on which contained a mysterious lump.

"Sonic!" I cried. I lifted the pillowcase and reached inside to grab him. "You scared me!" And then I proceeded to kiss the hedgehog, just like Maddox had wanted me to. I guessed he always got his way in the end. I put Sonic back in his cage and made sure everything was secure. "You're not going anywhere now."

"I'm going to finish getting ready," my mom said as she backed out of the room. "Try not to lose the hedgehog again."

"Don't tell Maddox!" I called after her.

Her only response was to laugh at me, and even I had to admit that it was pretty funny.

"EMMA!" SADIE SHRIEKED, running towards me. I only had a moment to brace myself when her thin arms wound around my shoulders as she crashed into me. "I'm so glad you're here. I can't handle all these old people," she muttered, looking around at her various family members that were gathered in the backyard. "Grandpa keeps asking for potato salad, and every time we give it to him he bangs his fists against the table and says, 'I did not ask for this! Bring me potato salad!' And then he doesn't believe us that it is, indeed, potato salad."

"Wow."

"Yeah, I know."

I looked around. "I thought you invited some people from school."

She shrugged. "I did, but it seems like everyone is having a more fun summer vacation than we are." She threw an arm around my shoulders, guiding me to one of the tables covered in food. My mom had brought a cake and tea... iced tea this time, and not her traditional hot tea. "Whatever happened to that guy you went on a date with?"

I'd always shared everything with Sadie, but suddenly I just... didn't want to. Maddox seemed like a fairytale to me and I was afraid if I started telling her about him it would break the spell.

I was kind of shocked that she was just now asking me about him, since I'd promised—and failed—to call her the night of our first date.

"Uh, we've just hung out a few times," I shrugged casually. "No big deal."

She gave me a doubtful look. "Sure. Let me know when the wedding is."

I laughed. "You're crazy."

"And *you've* never even batted your eyes at a guy before. This is a big deal."

I picked up one of the paper plates and started piling food on it. "Hardly."

Sadie settled into line behind me. "We should see a movie tomorrow," she suggested.

I frowned. "I don't think I can."

She snorted. "What could you possibly be doing? Reading? Come on, Emma. Wait..." She paused. "Are you going to be with *him?* Mystery boy?"

I blushed.

"You are!"

"I don't know that," I mumbled. "And he's not a mystery."

"But you hope," she countered, "and he is to me. I know nothing about him."

"He's amazing," I finally muttered. "I really like him, okay? We're just friends, though."

"You went on a date," she reasoned as we headed to one of the tables to sit down, "so that means you're more than friends."

"It does not," I grumbled. I searched for any topic that didn't have anything to do with my own life. "So, who do you have your eyes set on this summer?"

Sadie never stayed with one guy very long, but she usually picked one guy for the summer and then when it was time for school to start she cut ties. "Meh," she shrugged. "Everyone hot is gone for the summer. Figures." Smiling, she added, "I'm trying to get my dad to let me spend the summer at my aunt and uncle's beach house." She licked her lips like she was already imagining the guys she'd find there.

"I'm sure your dad is being really agreeable about that," I laughed.

Mr. Westbrook was one of the strictest parents I knew, but it was only because he cared so much about his kids. He wasn't an asshole like my dad. In fact, growing up, I'd often wished I could have Sadie's dad. The kind of dad that would've thrown me up on his shoulders, taken me to the zoo, and just spent time with me.

She huffed. "He's being an ass about it. But I'm going to be eighteen in a few months, so I don't see what the big deal is. I'm an adult."

Calling Sadie an adult was laughable.

"At least your dad is looking out for you," I commented. "He cares."

She flipped her brown hair over one shoulder and peered at me with searching honey colored eyes. "Your dad cares about you, Emma. You're his daughter after all."

I eyed her. "He has a funny way of showing it."

"It's been two years," she said softly.

"I know," I sighed. "I'm over it, I am. But sometimes it's all too easy to get mad."

She smiled sadly. "Maybe when you get mad you should think about how much better off you are with him gone."

Sadie could be crazy. She could be loud. She could even be annoying.

But at the end of the day, we were best friends for a reason and sometimes she was wiser than me.

"You're right."

"You say that like you're surprised," she laughed. She stood and came around the table to hug me. "I love you, Emma, like a sister and I hate it when you get sad."

"I know... where do you think he is?" I whispered.

She pulled away and gave a small shrug. "I don't know anymore than you do, but wherever he is, I hope he's getting the help he needs."

"Yeah," I agreed.

My emotions were always a rollercoaster when it came to my dad.

I was so angry at him for leaving us—for not being the dad I needed—that if he showed up at our home today I'd probably slap him.

But another part of me was sad and missed him. He might not have been a great dad, but he was my dad.

And then, like Sadie said, I also hoped he'd decided to get help.

I might've hated his guts most days, but I still didn't want him to suffer.

Sadie sat down once more and changed the conversation to lighter things.

Soon thoughts of my dad disappeared, along with the light from the sky.

Once it started to get dark was when the true party started.

Mr. and Mrs. Westbrook had twinkling lights strung up around the yard, and music pumped from a set of Bose speakers.

"Come on," Sadie grabbed my hands, "let's dance."

I let her drag me into the middle of the yard, where her older brother, Sam, danced with one of her baby cousins.

Sadie started to dance crazily and I mimed her movements. We looked like goofballs, but I didn't care. I was having fun.

My mom laughed at us from the table where she sat with Sadie's parents. I waved her over to join us.

"No!" She laughed. "Y'all keep going."

I smiled and reached up to pull the elastic from my hair. I let the blonde strands flow around my shoulders as I danced and sang.

I felt like a butterfly breaking free of its cocoon.

And even though Maddox wasn't here, I couldn't help thinking that he was responsible for my metamorphosis.

CHAPTER TEN

MADDOX CALLED ME last night and told me that their flight had been delayed and he'd be home too late to pick up Sonic. I assured him that it was fine, and that I'd even grown fond of the hedgehog. I left out the part about losing him.

Since I knew Maddox would probably arrive early to pick up his beloved pet I made myself get up and ready. Last night when we spoke on the phone he told me to be ready to cross off another adventure today. I was excited and scared, all at the same time, to see what he had planned. I mean, I might've known what the possibilities were, but I had no idea which one he'd picked.

I stared at my reflection in the mirror.

The girl I saw there almost looked like a stranger.

Yeah, it was definitely me—the same wild and untamable hair, full lips, and freckles—but what I saw reflected in my eyes was where the difference lay. My eyes sparkled with happiness. Even my skin glowed and my cheeks had a natural and pretty flush.

Maddox was bringing back the carefree Emma that had rolled down hills and sang songs without abandon—the girl who'd been unaware of the world's cruel punishments.

It was strange to see her reflected back at me again.

She'd been gone so long I thought she was lost forever.

In fact, I'd stopped looking for her.

I had accepted that this melancholy way was how my life was meant to be—but I'd been wrong.

I smiled and smoothed my hands down my cardigan.

This excitement I felt at seeing him was foreign, but exhilarating.

I wasn't supposed to like him—or any guy—to avoid getting hurt, but I knew without a doubt that Maddox was impossible to ignore.

The doorbell rang through the house and I stepped out of the bathroom. My cheeks lifted in a permanent smile as I headed towards the door. I tried to tone it down, but I couldn't. I was just that happy to see him.

It hadn't even been a week since the last time I saw him, but the moment I opened the door and saw him standing there it felt like forever.

I couldn't control my reaction to seeing him, even if I had wanted to.

I jumped into his arms, wrapping mine around his neck. "I missed you," I admitted against his shoulder.

His chuckle was warm and pleased sounding. His hands rubbed against my back and he didn't seem to want to let go either.

I forced my arms to fall and took a step back. Now, the embarrassment came. "Sorry about that," I mumbled, toeing the ground with my shoe.

He chuckled and I felt his fingers connect with my chin. He slowly lifted my chin until he could look fully at my face. "Don't apologize. I enjoyed it." His eyes were serious for once, with no laughter sparkling in the gray depths.

I didn't know what to say, and since I was quite possibly one of the most awkward people on the planet I stuttered, "Uh... you should... uh... get Sonic."

His lips twisted into a smile. "Really?" His brows rose. "Because I think there's something else I should do first."

"Really? Wha—"

My reply was cut off by his soft lips connecting with mine. I was shocked and didn't know what to do at first.

My brain was all like, *"Oh my God! He's kissing you!"*

And then a moment later it yelled at me, *"Do something! Don't just stand there and make him do all the work!"*

With my heart skipping a beat in my chest, I wrapped my hands around his neck. My fingers played with the silky strands of his hair. His hair was so soft and the feel of his stubble brushing against my face was actually quite pleasant. His fingers dug into my hips and I gasped at the pressure.

Suddenly I found my back against the wall—the breeze from the open doorway tickled my face.

He slanted his lips over mine.

Claiming me.

Devouring me.

Owning me.

And I let him.

His lips fell away from mine and his breath fanned across my face. Both of us were breathing heavily. His hands flexed against my hips and I'd yet to drop my hands from his hair.

"I wasn't expecting that," I panted.

He chuckled, brushing his lips lightly over mine. My eyes closed at the feel of the feather light touch.

"That's exactly why I did it." He nuzzled my neck. "I've been wanting to kiss you since the moment I saw you, but I wanted to wait until I knew."

"Knew what?" I croaked, my voice suddenly hoarse.

"I wanted to know that you felt it too," he whispered in my

ear and I shivered, "this crazy connection we have."

"C-connection?" I stuttered, my fingers now digging into the tops of his shoulders for support.

"Mhmm," he hummed. "I don't normally pick up girls at fairs," he laughed, "and then plan a whole summer of adventures with them." His voice lowered, "But I knew you were different, and I selfishly wanted to keep you around."

My whole body shook.

"What are we doing, Maddox?"

"What do you mean?" He asked.

"Are we a couple?" I said before I could decide against it.

"If you're asking me if I want you to be my girlfriend, the answer to that question is very much... *yes*." He murmured the last word lowly in my ear.

I shivered, grasping his arms so that I didn't fall.

"I-I don't know if I can do this," I admitted.

His eyes filled with sadness and his lips thinned. "I was afraid you might say that."

"It's t-too soon," I stuttered, my throat closing up. Did I really believe that? I felt like I knew Maddox better in a week than I knew most of the people I'd went to school with since Kindergarten. But I didn't feel like I was ready to take that leap yet.

His forehead touched mine and his eyes closed as if he was in pain. "It's okay." His tongue swept out to moisten his lips and his hands came up to form a cage beside my head. His eyes darkened with a promise. "Just so you know, I don't regret kissing you, and one day you're going to ask me to, and I'm going to kiss you until you forget who you are."

My breath shook. I believed him.

He stepped back and with a wink he headed down the hall to my room.

I still stood stunned. I couldn't move if I wanted to.

I tentatively reached up and touched shaking fingers to my lips.

The last—and only—time I had kissed a guy had been before my dad walked out, and that kiss was in no way comparable to this one. If a kiss could set off fireworks it would be Maddox's.

"Wow," I whispered, lowering my hand.

I did my best to compose myself before Maddox returned with the cage clutched in his hands and Sonic sitting on his shoulder.

"Aren't you afraid he'll fall?" I asked.

"No," he tilted his head to peer at the hedgehog, "Sonic knows to hang on. He's used to it. Would you mind holding the door?" He asked.

"Oh, yeah, sure." I bumbled over my words and hastily opened the door so he could head to the car.

I hurried after him and helped him get the cage in the backseat—which wasn't an easy feat since the car was a coupe.

"Are you ready to go?" He smiled down at me and my stomach flip-flopped. I hated the way my body reacted to him—how he was impossible to resist.

"Let me say goodbye to my mom."

My mom already knew I was spending the day with Maddox, so there was really no need for me to go back inside, but I had to get away from him and his hypnotizing gaze before I did something stupid. Like, ask him to kiss me again and prove him right.

I left Maddox standing by his car and walked swiftly into the house and straight to my mom's studio.

She looked up when I entered and stopped what she was doing. "Are you okay?"

"Yeah, I just wanted to say bye... so, bye." I stood awkwardly in the doorway.

She laughed, her smile bright and happy. "Bye, Emma. Have fun with Maddox, but don't get pregnant."

"Mom!" I groaned, my cheeks flaming.

She laughed. "Sorry, I felt like it was the responsible parent thing to say. Although, I know I don't have to worry with you."

"Thanks, mom." I whispered, suddenly overcome by an emotion I couldn't begin to describe.

She tilted her head, still smiling. "Why are you thanking me?"

"For being there for me... for always being the best mom you could be."

"Oh, Emma," her hands fell to her sides and some of the clay got on her jeans, "you never need to thank me for that—though it is nice to hear. It's my job as your mother to always be what you need. Whether it's a shoulder to cry on, or a disciplinary figure."

"I just want you to know that I think you're a pretty amazing mom," I shrugged. "You deserve to know."

"Well, thank you. I love you, Emmie."

"Love you too, mom." I took a step back and started to close the door. "I better go before Maddox comes to find me."

She chuckled. "Yes. Go on, and have fun."

I smiled one last time before closing the door.

I slipped into the sleek sports car and laughed when I saw that Maddox had Sonic balanced on the wheel.

"Is everything okay?" He asked, worry wrinkling his brow.

"Yeah, everything is great," I assured him.

"Okay," he said, "here, hold Sonic while I drive."

I took the hedgehog and placed him on my lap while I buckled my seatbelt.

"Ready?" He asked.

I wasn't sure if he was asking if I was ready to leave,

or ready for another adventure. I guessed it didn't matter since the answer was the same.

"Yes."

"OH MY GOD." I gaped at the swimming pool that had once been filled with glimmering blue colored water. Now, all the water was gone and replaced by plastic balls. "You know, when I suggested this, I didn't quite expect... *this*."

Maddox smiled proudly with his hands on his hips. "Isn't it wonderful?"

"Aren't your mom and dad mad?" I countered.

He waved a hand dismissively. "They don't care as long as I fill it up with water again."

"Uh-huh," I nodded.

"What are you waiting for?" He asked.

I shrugged. "You go first."

He chuckled, his eyes squinting from the sun. "I can do that right after I put Sonic away."

"Oh, right." I'd been so overcome by the site of the ball pit— or I guess *pool* was the better term—that I'd forgotten about Sonic.

"Wait here," he said, like he was afraid I might run away.

I wasn't scared though—just stunned. I hadn't expected this at all.

A slow smile began to spread across my face.

This was going to be fun.

Maddox returned and took in my expression. "I take it you're not stunned anymore?"

"No," I shook my head. "But I am wondering how you got all of these."

"I know people," he shrugged. "You still want me to go first?"

I nodded.

He grasped the bottom of his white t-shirt and started to pull it over his head.

"Whoa, whoa, whoa! What are you doing?" I cried.

He threw the shirt over his shoulder into the grass. "Taking my shirt off, isn't that obvious?"

"Why do you need to take your shirt off to jump in there?" I hissed.

"It's a pool, Emma."

"Yes," I agreed, "but that's not water!"

He smiled impishly and reached up to ruffle his brown hair. The movement caused my eyes to zero in on the way the muscles in his arms flexed, which then led my eyes to wander down over his sculpted chest and stomach. His body was filled out and not at all scrawny. I'd never blatantly checked out a guy before, but I couldn't tear my eyes away from Maddox.

"Like what you see?"

I squeaked and covered my face, embarrassed at being caught.

Maddox's laugh echoed around me and I startled when I felt his hand close around my arm. He pried my hands away from my face. "Don't get shy on me now, Em. We're about to jump into a pool of balls."

I snorted and he grinned.

"How about we go together?" He suggested, peering into my eyes.

I nodded. "Yeah, that would be good."

His smile was blinding. Reaching into his back pocket he plucked out a pair of drumsticks that I hadn't noticed earlier and set them down. He then reached for my hand—his larger one nearly swallowing mine whole.

Excitement pulsed through my body. I felt giddy like a little kid, where you were too young for the bad things to touch you and things like ball pits seemed like the coolest thing ever.

"Ready?" Maddox asked, and when I nodded he counted, "One, two, three!"

We ran forward together and jumped into the pool of plastic balls. I giggled as my body began to sink into the multi-colored balls.

"This is kind of amazing," I grinned.

Maddox smiled at me. "It is."

I moved through the ball pool laughing and smiling.

I was pretty certain that no one could be mad when doing something like this.

I didn't know how much time passed, but suddenly I heard an exclamation of, "What the fuck is going on?"

I turned to find Ezra and Mathias standing by the edge of the pool. Ezra was grinning and Mathias wore a scowl on his face.

"Having fun," Maddox responded to his grumpy brother.

"This is so cool," Ezra clapped his hands together. "Cannonball!" He yelled, jumping in with us.

Mathias rolled his eyes. "Y'all have lost your fucking minds."

"Come on, Mathias! Have some fun!"

Mathias wrinkled his nose at us like we were all disgusting. "No."

"Mathias." Maddox growled.

"Oh, fine." Mathias huffed. He turned around and fell back into the pool like a crowd surfer at a concert.

"Way to go Mattie boy!" Ezra cheered.

"Oh, shut up," Mathias mumbled. His voice lightening he said, "This is actually kind of cool, but may I ask why you filled our swimming pool with balls?"

"It was Emma's idea," Maddox responded.

Mathias turned to look at me. "Why?"

"I thought it would be fun. I certainly didn't expect Maddox to go to this extreme to make it happen, though." I smiled, lifting a blue ball and throwing it towards Maddox. He wasn't paying attention and it bounced off his head, making all of us laugh.

After a while Mathias and Ezra left and it was just the two of us once more.

The excitement was wearing off so we climbed out and headed to the guesthouse.

Maddox called someone to come remove the balls and fill up the pool once more. I sat perched on the couch, not sure what I should do. I felt a bit out of place. I still wasn't familiar enough with Maddox to make myself at home.

You sure were familiar enough to let him kiss you, my conscience spoke up.

My cheeks started to heat at just the thought of the way his lips moved so effortlessly against mine.

After hanging up the phone Maddox strode past me and sat behind his drum kit. He'd put his shirt back on so I could no longer embarrass myself by staring at his bare chest.

"Do you mind if I play?" He asked, grabbing his drumsticks from his back pocket and raising a brow at me.

"No, not at all. I'd love to hear you play." I sat forward, intent not to miss a moment of this.

He lowered his eyes, trying to fight a smile.

Flicking his wrists he began to beat out a rhythm. At first it was slow, like he was almost hesitant to play in front of me, but soon his passion overrode his fear. His eyes closed and his head fell back as the speed picked up. The symbols clashed and the beat of the drum flowed through my body.

I had figured he'd be good, but I hadn't expected him to be *this* good.

I sat in awe as he played.

I was quite certain that Maddox might've been the most amazing person I'd ever met—and I didn't even know his last name.

Ten minutes passed before he stopped. He reached out, silencing the symbol and grinned at me.

"What did you think?"

I shook my head, unable to form words.

"Good? Bad?" He prompted.

"You're incredible," I finally gasped.

He grinned, standing up so he could put the drumsticks in his pocket once more.

"You know," I started, "I only just realized that I don't even know your last name."

He chuckled and sat down beside me on the couch. "It's Wade."

"Mine's Burke," I responded.

His lips twisted into a smile and he held out his hand. "Nice to meet you, Emma Burke."

"Back at ya, Maddox Wade."

It grew quiet between us and the way he stared at me had me squirming.

"What's your middle name?" I asked, hating the silence between us. Besides, I itched to get to know him better.

"Carson," he replied with a chuckle, draping his arm over the back of the couch. His fingers hovered dangerously close to my upper arm and Goosebumps broke out across my skin at his nearness. "What's yours?" He asked. "Wait... let me guess..." He tapped a finger against his chin. "Tallulah."

I snorted. "Tallulah? How the hell did you come up with that?"

He grinned crookedly. "Your mom seems like the type to give you an off the wall middle name," he shrugged, "and that was the first one to pop into my head."

"It is kind of different," I admitted.

"It's not Moon, is it?" He asked.

"No!" I laughed. Sobering, I added, "Although it's close."

"Oh God," he tilted his head back, his Adam's apple bobbing with his laughter.

"It's Rayne," I finally told him. "But spelled R. A. Y. N. E. instead of rain."

"Well, thank God for that," he chuckled.

"My mom is a bit of a hippy," I shrugged. "I guess it could've been a lot worse."

"Yeah, you could've been Emma Moon... which sounds like a stripper name." His eyes sparkled with barely contained laughter.

I snorted, laughing so hard that tears streamed down my cheeks.

He started to laugh too and I smiled at how easy it was being in his presence. I didn't feel the need to try to be someone else. I was just... Emma.

"Well, I'm definitely not a stripper," I continued to laugh.

"I don't know," he eyed my chest, "with those curves I think you could pull it off."

"Maddox!" I shrieked, playfully swatting at his arm.

He pretended to wince. "That hurt."

"Oh, I'm sure the injury is life threatening." I turned towards him, studying his face carefully.

"Why are you looking at me like that?" He asked with wonder.

I shrugged. "You've lived here for a while, right?" I asked.

"Yeah, my whole life." He answered with a tone that suggested he was curious as to what I was getting at.

"How have we lived in the same place for all these years and only just met?"

"Because," his voice lowered and he leaned towards me so that there was little space between us, "we weren't meant to meet then. This is our now."

My eyes fluttered closed and his words felt like a tender caress against my skin.

He sat back once more and the spell was broken.

I opened my eyes and scooted away from him a bit, hoping to dispel the energy buzzing around us.

He stared at me intensely and I found myself squirming. "Are we friends, Emma?" His question startled me since I hadn't been expecting it.

"Yeah... I believe so?" It came out sounding like a question.

"Do you like me?" He continued.

"Yeah," I said again, "Why? What are you getting at?" I was extremely confused by this sudden turn in the conversation.

He shrugged. "What is it specifically that you like about me?"

"Maddox," I started, my brows furrowing together, "I'm confused."

"Just answer the question, please," he growled desperately.

I stared at him for a moment, extremely puzzled. His question wasn't harsh, just curious, but I still found it an odd thing to ask. "I like that you make me laugh," I shrugged. "I like that we have things in common—like music. I like that when I'm with you I'm *me*."

He bowed his head and he seemed almost relieved.

His eyes rose to meet mine, and his playfulness returned. "I thought you were going to tell me that you only liked me because I'm hot."

I rolled my eyes. "Maddox," I groaned.

"Sorry," he apologized, but his smile told me he wasn't sorry at all. He reached out, startling me, and grabbed a strand of my blonde hair. He began to wrap it around his finger.

"Maddox?" I questioned. "What are you doing?"

He jumped, looking at his hand and released my hair. He smiled sheepishly, like he'd only just realized what he was doing. "I couldn't resist. Something about you," his voice lowered to a whisper and he looked away, almost as if he wished I wouldn't hear his next words, "draws me in and I'm powerless to what I feel."

I sat silently, unsure of what to say, but luckily Maddox saved me from having to reply.

"Would you mind playing the piano again?" He asked, his eyes glimmering with hope.

"I'd love to," I smiled, my hands already itching at the thought of running my fingers along the smooth keys of the shiny black upright. My piano at home was old, out of tune, and falling apart. This one was perfect. In fact, it was so pristine that I had a feeling it was practically brand new. "Is there anything you'd like me to play?"

He shook his head. "Just whatever you want."

I stood up and walked over to the piano.

I sat down and ran the tips of my fingers along the keys. My body instantly began to hum with happiness.

I heard shuffling behind me and I turned to find Maddox lying down on the couch with his arms crossed behind his head. He smiled crookedly when he saw me watching him.

"Go on. Play."

I turned around, pretending I didn't feel his eyes perusing my body. Goosebumps broke out across my skin and I shivered.

I closed my eyes and began to play the first song that came to mind.

The music flowed from my fingertips, through the piano, and out into the room. My body swayed with it—feeling it, living it.

I played song after song, never wanting to stop.

The music made me feel alive, much in the same way Maddox did when I was around him.

Not just alive, but *free*—like nothing that happened to me mattered anymore. Something told me that finding someone that made me feel the way music did was a rare thing.

The music ceased as my hands fell to my lap. I turned around on the bench and giggled when I found Maddox fast asleep on the couch, snoring lightly.

I was sure after his late night travels he was exhausted.

The angular curves of his face were softened in his sleep, somehow making him even more handsome. There was a blanket sitting on the arm of the couch and I picked it up. Shaking it out I draped it over his body.

He blinked his eyes open halfway and yawned. "Lay down with me?" He asked in a sleepy voice that made my insides hum and dance.

"Uh-I-uh," I floundered.

He grasped my arm, opening his eyes a little wider so I saw a sliver of gray peeking through. "Please?"

How could I resist him?

"Okay, but only for a little while," I agreed.

He scooted over, trying to make room for me, but the couch was small.

He wrapped one arm around my body and pulled me against his chest. I was pretty sure this was called spooning—I was also pretty sure that my heart had stopped.

"Is this okay?" He whispered, brushing my hair away from my neck.

"Yes," I squeaked.

"Good," he murmured, and I swore he pressed his lips to the skin just below my ear in a kiss, but the touch was so quick and light that I couldn't be positive.

He grew quiet and a few minutes later his breath grew heavy

when it tickled my neck, so I knew he'd fallen asleep.

I felt like an intruder curled up against him—like I was playing a role in someone else's life, but selfishly I did want this life to be mine.

I wanted to have the starring role in Maddox's life, and that scared me more than anything else ever could.

CHAPTER ELEVEN

"WELL, THIS IS interesting," someone laughed.

I blinked my eyes open and rubbed the sleep from them. Maddox groaned, tightening his arms around me and squeezing...

"Did you just squeeze my boob?" I shrieked, sitting up.

"Sorry," he grinned, "it was a reflex."

"Uh-huh, I'm sure," I mumbled, standing up from the couch. I avoided eye contact with a smiling Ezra and brooding Mathias. My shirt had ridden up and I hastened to pull it down. I wrapped my arms around my chest, like that could protect me from the penetrating stare of Mathias. There was something about him that set me on edge. I wasn't afraid of him, but something about him told me to keep a safe distance. I wondered what could've happened in his life to make him so unhappy.

Ezra smiled at me, pushing dark colored curls from his eyes. Looking from me to Maddox he said, "Hayes wants to hang out."

"Who's Hayes?" I asked.

Maddox spoke before either of the other guys could say anything. "He's a friend." He eyed the other two, like he was daring them to dispute him.

I couldn't understand what was going on. "Oookay," I drew out the word. "I'll head home then," I mumbled, then realized I didn't have a car.

"Nonsense," Ezra grinned, glancing over at Maddox with a victorious smile, "you'll come with us."

"Come with you?" I repeated. "To do what?"

"Bowling," Matthias answered in a lazy drawl. "Fucking bowling, because there's nothing else to do in this stupid little town."

"Hey," Maddox pointed towards the door, "we currently have a ball pit in our yard. I'd say there's plenty to do."

Mathias rolled his eyes. "Whatever. I'm going to smoke." He stormed outside, pulling a pack of cigarettes from his back pocket.

"He's such a joy," Ezra deadpanned. "Sometimes I can't believe you guys are twins. Hell, if you weren't identical I wouldn't know."

Maddox chuckled. "I'm pretty sure he came out of the womb with a chimp on his shoulder."

"Chimp?" I laughed. "I'm pretty sure it's, 'chip on your shoulder.'"

"In Mathias' case it's a chimp," he chuckled, "a very large, very hairy, very smelly, chimp."

Ezra and I both laughed. I couldn't help picturing the tall, brooding, Mathias with a chimp on his shoulder. Yeah, it was a pretty funny sight.

Maddox stood up from the couch and stretched his arms above his head. "Alright, let's go, but we're taking your car. No way am I going to listen to Mathias bitch about sitting in the back of mine."

Ezra chuckled. "Mathias bitches about everything."

"It's true," he shrugged. "I'll be right back." He ran up the steps and I looked questioningly at Ezra, who simply shrugged in reply to my questioning gaze.

Maddox wasn't gone long, and when he returned he wore a black beanie. Strands of his brown hair stuck up in the front. "Alright, let's go."

We headed towards the door, with me lagging behind. I smiled at the sight of the drumsticks in Maddox's back pocket. He almost always had a pair with him—like it was an important extension of himself.

I followed the three guys into the garage and stared at the row of vehicles. Normal people didn't have this many nice cars. Their parents must have made a lot of money.

I tried not to gawk too much when Maddox held open the door to a shiny black SUV. The thing was huge—more like a tank than a vehicle.

The leather was cool against my bare legs and buttery smooth.

Maddox closed the door and jogged around to climb in on the other side. Ezra was driving, obviously, and Mathias joined him in the front.

"What kind of car is this?" I asked—once again showing my lack of knowledge when it came to cars.

"A GMC Yukon," Ezra answered, glancing at me in the rearview mirror as the garage door rolled up.

Ezra reached over and turned on the radio. The volume was blasting and he hastily turned it down to a decibel that wasn't deafening.

I didn't recognize the song, but I did recognize the name of the band flashing on the fancy touch screen display.

"Hey, this is Willow Creek," I commented. "They're from here. I've never heard any of their music before."

Maddox coughed beside me, and when I turned to look at him he was glaring at Ezra.

Mathias huffed and reached for the dial. "No one wants to listen to this garbage."

Ezra didn't reply, he was still looking at Maddox—with the car idling in the garage. I didn't understand the silent battle that seemed to be taking place between the two. I wished now I hadn't said anything.

The drive to the bowling alley was distressingly silent.

The silence made me nervous, because I felt like I'd done something wrong.

I was glad when Ezra parked the car and I could leave the tension behind—hopefully.

I walked ahead of the guys and straight into the building.

They came in and I looked over my shoulder, gaping at them. Ezra now wore a baseball cap that pushed down his curls and Mathias was wearing a beanie similar to Maddox's but his was gray. What was up with the hats?

We grabbed our shoes from the lady working at the front and Ezra pointed to one side of the alley. "Hayes is supposed to be over here."

We followed him into to the darkened room. The chairs and tables glowed purple and green so you could see where you were going and some kind of country song blared from the speakers.

A tall guy waved to us from the last alley.

"Someone remind me, why the fuck are we bowling again?" Mathias grumbled, but Hayes heard him.

"Because bowling is great and I really wanted a hotdog," Hayes smiled.

I reared my head back, taking in his monstrous height. The guy was a giant—probably six foot five. Sandy blond hair fell into his blue eyes and a light dusting of stubble dotted his jaw. He was handsome in an all-American sort of way.

"Hi," he smiled at me, and Maddox's hand fell possessively

on my waist. "I'm Hayes, and you are?"

"Emma," I smiled.

"Nice to meet you, Emma." My name rolled off his tongue like it was an exotic wine. Maddox growled at my side and Hayes chuckled. "I'm not hitting on your girl, so calm down."

Maddox's hand fell away and he grumbled, "I knew that."

I didn't bother correcting Hayes on the fact that I wasn't Maddox's girl, because it kinda felt like I was.

Mathias sat at one of the chairs with his legs kicked up on the table while Ezra entered our names into the computer. "Are we going to play or have a pissing contest, boys?"

Hayes smiled, shaking his head. "Welcome to the family," he shrugged in a *what-are-you-going-to-do* kind of way.

It took us a few minutes to get everything set up.

The guys went first, all of them getting a strike except for Mathias who ended up getting a spare. He kept bitching about it too and I was really tempted to tell him to shut up. His negativity was giving me heartburn.

It was my turn and I was terrified that I was about to make a fool of myself in front of the four guys.

I grabbed my bowling ball—a swirly purple one that Maddox picked for me—and walked up to the lane.

I squared my shoulders and breathed out, acting like I knew what I was doing.

I swung my arm back and let the ball go... only it didn't go the way it was supposed to.

It flung off my fingers and rolled back towards the guys.

My cheeks flamed and I wanted to crawl into the nearest hole and die.

Mathias was the first to start laughing, which shocked me, but the others were quick to join in.

The other people near us started to stare, and my mortification grew.

Maddox grabbed the ball and stalked towards me. I gulped.

Something told me I was in trouble—of the sexy and dangerous kind, because Maddox knew how to play with me.

He handed me the ball.

"Like this." His voice was a gruff whisper in my ear. With a hand on my waist he positioned me, and then used the other to move my arm. I felt like a puppet on a marionettes strings, willing to let him do whatever he wanted to me.

When had I become so pathetic? It was like my backbone had snapped.

"And then," his lips brushed my cheek and I swore he had to be doing this on purpose, trying to break my resolve, "you let it go."

He'd said something before this spiel but I had missed it.

I hoped it wasn't important.

He released me and my body felt icy without his touch to warm me.

I took a deep breath, staring at the pins and trying not to think about the way his eyes felt perusing my body.

I swung my arm back and let the ball go.

It went into the gutter.

"Dammit," I cursed, pissed at myself.

Maddox chuckled. "Don't worry, I'll help you again."

I hated to inform him, but I was pretty sure it was his 'help' that messed me up this time.

We waited for the slow progression of the ball and Mathias made obnoxious snoring sounds. One of these days I was going to go off on him for his rude ways.

"How about I help this time?" I startled at the sound of the new voice and turned to find Hayes standing behind me with the ball clasped in his hands. I hadn't even realized the ball had come back.

"I was helping her," Maddox growled.

"That looked like flirting, not helping," Hayes grinned at me and not Maddox. "Why don't you let an unbiased third party help Emma out?" This time he did look at Maddox.

Maddox's eyes shifted to me and he grunted, "Okay." I guess he realized that he really had no claim to me and was being ridiculous anyway.

Hayes gave me some basic instructions and helped position me. There was nothing flirty in the way he touched me and his touch didn't set my body aflame like Maddox's had. Hayes was truly just trying to help me.

This time when I let the ball go it roared down the lane, knocking over all but two pins.

"Yes!" I screamed, jumping up and down. "I did it!" I jumped into Hayes' arms, giving him a hug. "Thank you."

"You're welcome," he chuckled warmly.

At the sound of a crash Hayes set me down and we turned to see a fallen chair and Maddox stalking off. I frowned, looking from Hayes to the other two guys. "I-I didn't mean to—"

"We know," Ezra interrupted, "Maddox is just being..."

"Possessive," Mathias supplied with a sly smile.

"I should go apologize," I mumbled.

I turned to leave but Hayes' hand wrapped around my arm, urging me to stay. I looked up into his eyes and he said, "Give him a few minutes to cool off and realize what an ass he was."

"Are you sure?" I frowned, picking at the hem of my shirt. "I feel bad."

"Positive." He nodded his head towards the table. "Sit tight for a bit."

The three guys took their turns, but when Maddox's name popped up he still hadn't returned. I felt horrible knowing that this was my fault.

Ignoring Hayes' pleas to stay I went in search of Maddox.

It didn't take me long to find him near the front entrance playing with one of those claw machines.

I stepped up behind him and the way his body stiffened told me he knew it was me.

"Maddox," I whispered hesitantly.

"What?" He grumbled, his eyes briefly connecting with the reflection of mine in the glass case.

"I'm sorry," I said. "It was just a hug. I didn't mean to make you mad."

"I know," his head lowered with shame, "and that's why I'm upset. I *shouldn't* be mad, but I am. You're not mine, but it feels that way, and seeing his arms around you... I didn't like it."

"I'm sorry," I said again, "I should've thought of your feelings."

"No," he shook his head, glaring at my reflection, "you shouldn't have. I was being stupid."

"Maddox," I started, at a loss for words.

He whipped around, the stuffed teddy bear he'd won falling into the chamber. "I get it, okay. You don't like me the way I like you and I need to get over it. I have to... I have to stop *wanting* you." He let out a weighty sigh and his eyes shifted to look at the wall.

"I do like you!" I screamed, for once not caring how much attention I attracted. His head whipped back so he could look at me. "It scares me how much I like you as *way* more than a friend. I don't want to have these feelings, but I do. I'm just scared." My eyes lowered to the ground, and I kicked the toe of my converse against a ripped patch in the carpeted floor. "I'm scared of what I feel for you. I only just met you," I raised my arms, meeting his eyes once more. "I'm not ready for more. Give me time."

Silence stretched between us like an endless sea and my chest heaved with each breath I took.

"I can do that," he finally said.

My breath rushed out of my lungs like the air from a deflating balloon.

He smiled slowly and I smiled in return.

"We're good?" I asked.

"Yeah," he chuckled, ducking his head in embarrassment. "Sorry for being an asshole."

"You're forgiven, but only if you get me a drink," I jested.

He laughed, reaching down to grab his prize. "I can do that, and here."

He handed me the teddy bear. It was small and wore a blue shirt with the name of the bowling alley on it. "Now every time you look at it you can think of me."

"I most definitely will," I assured him, clutching the bear to my chest. "But he needs a name."

Maddox tilted his head, looking closely at the bear. "Harold."

"Harold?" I laughed.

He shrugged. "It's a very distinguished name."

"Okay then, Harold it is," I giggled, inhaling the buttery smell of the teddy bear. I guessed the smells of the bowling alley had seeped into it.

"Shall we get some drinks and food then?" He nodded his head towards the small café.

My stomach rumbled at the mention of food.

"Yes," I agreed, following him to the line.

The line moved slowly so we waited a good ten minutes before we could place our order. Maddox ordered enough food for him and the guys and I ordered what I wanted... plus a Coke.

Maddox gasped. "Emma, you can't get a Coke."

"Why?" I asked.

"Because I love Diet Pepsi, and Pepsi and Coke are not friends."

I raised my brows at him. "I'm getting Coke."

He mumbled something and the lady manning the register looked at us like we were crazy. She rattled off the total and he pulled his wallet out of his back pocket—the one without the drumsticks.

She swiped his credit card and handed him the slip to sign. She did all of this with a scowl on her face, like we were pesky teenagers ruining her day. We might've been teenagers, but I didn't think we were pesky. Maybe I was wrong.

After signing the slip we stood off to the side to wait for our drinks and food—which took another fifteen minutes. I was shocked the other guys hadn't come looking for us. Maybe they didn't miss us yet... or maybe they thought we were otherwise occupied.

Oh God.

Now I was going to be scared to look them in the eyes and I hadn't even done anything wrong!

Before I could really start freaking out they called our number and Maddox grabbed the two trays of food and I grabbed the one with our drinks on it. We stopped off at a condiment station, grabbing everything we'd need.

When we finally returned to the guys they'd grown tired of waiting for us and had finished the game. They were already halfway through a second one.

"Food," Hayes grinned, rubbing his flat stomach, "y'all are saviors."

"So," Ezra looked between the two of us, "all is forgiven?"

"There was nothing to forgive," Maddox shrugged, ripping open a packet of ketchup with his teeth. "I overreacted."

The other three guys exchanged looks and then their gazes rose to me. They all looked at me curiously, like

I was some exotic animal.

Mathias spoke first. "I think you've bewitched my brother."

Maddox chuckled. "Maybe she has. Look at her, she's enchanting."

I shook my head, ignoring their conversation.

I grabbed a hot dog and fries. "Maddox, can you hand me my Coke?" I asked, since that tray was closer to him and too far for me too reach.

He gasped dramatically. "That's right, guys, Emma has gone to the dark side and ordered Coke."

"What is wrong with Coke?" I laughed, taking the cup when he handed it to me.

"Pepsi is so much better," he shrugged, eating a fry.

I opened a pack of ketchup and squirted it on my hotdog. "In my defense, I don't drink a lot of soda, but if I have the choice I prefer Coke. I mean, it's not that Pepsi is bad," I rambled, "it's just not my favorite."

Maddox pretended to wince. "You wound me. I thought you were the most perfect girl ever when you chose Diet Pepsi on our date, and now I feel like I've been betrayed."

I laughed, unable to hide my smile.

When I looked up Ezra was watching me closely. He hastily lowered his gaze, like he was embarrassed at getting caught.

"Was there something on my face?" I reached for a napkin.

Ezra looked up and shook his head, his black curls bouncing from beneath the baseball cap. "No..."

"Oh," I replied. "Why were you looking at me like that then?"

His smile grew shy, almost embarrassed. He looked between Maddox and me, and replied, "You make him happy."

I choked on a piece of hotdog—like full on coughing until I cried, struggling for air.

Maddox reached over, beating my back.

I finally managed to get the hotdog down and took a large sip of Coke.

"Sorry," I said breathlessly, "that caught me off guard."

Luckily, neither of the four guys said anything. Maddox's hand didn't fall from my back, though, and now he rubbed soothing circles in an effort to calm me.

We finished eating and played a new game—Hayes won.

When we left the bowling alley, Maddox and I hung back from the other guys.

"Did you have fun?" He asked me.

I nodded enthusiastically. Besides the choking fit today had been great, one of the best ever. "I did. I like your friends... and Mathias."

"Don't lie, no one likes Mathias," he chuckled, rubbing his jaw.

"Okay, so maybe I'm not his number one fan," I admitted sheepishly, "but I do like him... somewhat."

"Well, that's more than most people," he shrugged.

"The way I figure, every single person has a reason for acting a certain way."

"True," he agreed, "but Mathias and I have shared many of the same hardships and I don't act like an asshole."

I stopped walking and tilted my head to look at him. "Yes, but Mathias is also a different person from you. He would process things differently. I guess you can cope better." And then I reached up and stroked the side of his face in a gesture that was all too loving for the kind of relationship we had. "I'm sorry," I stuttered awkwardly, my hand falling, and my eyes darting to the ground, "I shouldn't have done that."

What was wrong with me?

"It's okay," he replied, his gray eyes searing me.

I nodded, reading so much in his eyes that I didn't— *couldn't*—want to see.

"Hurry the fuck up!" Mathias called with this hands cupped around his mouth.

Maddox gave me a small smile. "Come on, I'll have Ezra drop you off at home."

We started forward again, my arms hanging limply at my sides.

I itched to reach out and hold his hand.

What the hell had he done to me?

CHAPTER TWELVE

THE NEXT DAY passed slowly.

Oh, so, slowly.

In fact, it wasn't even over yet.

Darkness was only just now beginning to settle in the sky.

Maddox hadn't called or texted me at all today, which was unusual. I figured he was busy, and that was fine. I wasn't his girlfriend. He didn't owe me an explanation, but I hated how lost I felt without him. It wasn't normal. You shouldn't have such intense feelings for someone you just met, but I did, and I couldn't stop them. I was beginning to think I didn't *want* to stop them.

I pressed the heels of my hands into my eyes, blocking out the sight of my bedroom ceiling above me. I wished this simple act alone could erase the foreign feelings invading my body, but I knew nothing could do that.

I rolled over, clutching my pillow to my chest.

Sadie had been busy today—she went into the city with her mom—and unable to distract me from my thoughts that were consumed by Maddox.

"Emmie?"

I startled and looked over to find my mom standing in the doorway—two cups of hot tea clutched in her hands.

"Are you okay?" She asked, stepping inside and sitting down on my bed. "You look like you don't feel good. Do you think you're sick?"

Yes, I was sick if Love-Sick-Fool counted.

"I'm fine, mom," I forced a smile, "I'm just really tired."

Her lips thinned as she looked at me, almost like she didn't believe me.

"Well, drink this and if you are coming down with something it will help."

She held the cup out to me and I took it. Once the cup was in my hand hers flitted out to touch my forehead.

"You don't feel warm," she mused.

"See?" I quirked a brow. "Just tired."

She sighed and looked up at a poster taped to my wall—one of a Broadway show, no boy bands for me.

"Is this about Maddox?" She asked, her gaze falling to me. "Did something happen between you two? He didn't hurt you, did he? I swear to God, if he hurt you—"

"No, mom," I laughed, smiling for the first time that day. "I'm just being a typical surly teenager. Don't worry about me, please," I begged, reaching out to grasp her hand.

She sighed heavily, like the weight of the world was on her shoulders. "I'm your mother, Emma. I worry. I will *always* worry about you."

I set my cup of tea on the table beside my bed. I reached forward and wrapped my arms around her. "I know that, mom, but I promise there's nothing to worry about right now."

"Okay," she sighed, running her fingers through my tangled hair. "How about we order something to eat and have a movie night? Sound good?" She asked, pulling away.

"It sounds great," I smiled.

"Good." She stood up and headed for the door. "Oh, and Emma?"

"Yeah?" I asked.

"Brush your hair."

I rolled my eyes. "Okay, mom."

She smiled and disappeared down the hall. I brushed my hair like she asked, but didn't bother to change out of my sweats and tank top. After all, she hadn't said anything about that and I wanted to be a bum today.

"I ordered steak and cheese subs," she said when I walked into the kitchen. With a smile, she added, "I'm sorry I'm not one of those moms that cooks you a fancy meal all the time and makes brownies for school functions."

I laughed, sitting down at the table with my cup of tea. "Don't worry, I think you're a great mom even if you don't cook. Plus, you do make me tea." I played with the string on the tea bag.

She finished her tea and pointed towards the living room. "Should we pick a movie?"

"Oh, yeah," I shook my head, following her.

We ended up settling on *Bride Wars* and it had just started when our food arrived.

Besides the subs she'd also ordered cheese fries and mozzarella sticks. It was heaven.

We laughed and talked through the movie, and I reveled in how nice it was to spend some time with my mom. Since she worked all the time it was rare that we did anything.

The movie ended and by the time we cleaned up it was after nine—which was really still early, but I figured I could go to bed and read for a while.

I said goodnight to my mom and headed to my room.

The twinkling lights I'd hung up on the wall lit the now darkened room.

I grabbed my book and Maddox's iPod. I put the buds in my ears and pressed play, listening while I read.

I hadn't read more than two chapters when my phone began to vibrate. I pulled the ear buds out and set my book aside as I searched for my phone, which was currently lost beneath the sea of blankets.

I finally located it and answered, "Hello," sounding breathless.

"Come outside."

"Maddox?"

"Yeah," he answered slowly. "Didn't my name come up on the caller ID?"

"I didn't look," I mumbled. "So, you're here?" I asked, sneaking over to my bedroom window and peeking through the blinds.

"Yeah, I can see you Emma."

I squeaked and jumped away from the window, dropping the phone in the process. While I scrambled to retrieve it his boisterous laughter echoed over the line.

"You're mean," I hissed when the phone was back in my possession.

My declaration didn't faze him. He kept laughing.

"I'm hanging up now," I swore.

"Wait!" He sobered. "Come outside, please?" He begged. "Let's go get ice cream?"

Did he say ice cream?

"I'll be out there in a minute."

"OH MY GOD, this is so good," I moaned. "I love ice cream."

Maddox watched me with a wide-eyed expression. "I can

tell." His eyes zeroed in on my tongue on the spoon and my cheeks began to heat.

"But I'm curious, why the ice cream?" I asked, taking another bite of its raspberry chocolate swirl goodness.

"I wanted to apologize for today," he shrugged, taking a bite of his own vanilla ice cream.

I might've been upset earlier about not hearing from him, but I didn't want him to know that. The last thing I wanted was for him to start thinking I was dependent on him.

"Why?" I asked, sounding indifferent.

"I felt bad for not calling you."

"You don't need to call me," I told him. And it was true. Even if I had been upset, I didn't have a claim to him. He didn't have to share every part of his life with me.

He tilted his head. "Anyway," he continued, "I wanted to see you and I wanted ice cream so this seemed like a win-win. I also wanted to tell you that I've cleared my schedule for tomorrow and we're going to do something fun."

The way he said it made 'fun' sound super scary.

"Cleared your schedule?" I asked, my lips turning up into a smile. "You're nineteen and unemployed, what kind of schedule could you possibly have to clear?"

He chuckled, wiping ice cream from his lip. "A very busy one full of awesomely amazing things that would blow your mind."

"Let me guess," I held up a finger, "cleaning Sonic's cage?"

"That's on Thursday's," he replied with a chuckle.

"So, are you going to tell me what this fun thing is that we're doing tomorrow?"

"No," He looked at me like he was crazy. "The surprise is part of the adventure." And then he flicked his ice cream at me, some of it landing in my hair. "See? Suuurprise!"

"Oh, you asshole!" I laughed, flicking my own ice cream at

him. It landed in a blob on his forehead.

And then a full on ice cream war broke out between us. I guessed it was a good thing that the ice cream place was one of those little stands and we were sitting outside.

"Mommy!" A kid called. "I want to do that!" The kid pointed at the two of us flicking ice cream at each other.

"No, don't even think about it," she groaned, probably cursing our existence for giving her kid ideas.

Our laughter filled the air in a raucous roar.

I couldn't remember the last time I had this much fun.

We didn't stop our fight until all the ice cream was gone and we were both covered in its stickiness. Random giggles kept escaping my mouth as Maddox took my hand and we ran back to his car. People looked at us strangely, but I didn't care. I was happy and when you're happy you don't care what other people think. Their thoughts and opinions cease to matter.

"Where are we going?" I asked, when Maddox drove in the opposite direction of my house.

"The park," he answered.

"The same park we got arrested in?" I questioned, my voice sounding stern.

He laughed heartily. "Yes, the very same one, but I promise that no one will get arrested tonight."

"Mhmm," I mumbled, fighting a smile, "that sounds like a promise you might not be able to keep."

He shrugged. "I guess there's always the small possibility... but I doubt stargazing can lead to an arrest."

"Stargazing?" I asked, tilting my head.

He chuckled, pulling into the parking lot.

"Yes, stargazing. You know, where you lay on the ground and look up at the sky."

I wanted to tell him that sounded romantic, but then I worried he'd interpret my words in the wrong way, so I kept quiet.

He grabbed a sweatshirt from the back of his car and handed it to me. "Here, you might need this. It's getting cold out."

"I have ice cream on me," I told him. "I don't want to get your sweatshirt dirty."

He shrugged. "I'll wash it. It's no big deal."

Since the temperature was dropping I took the sweatshirt he offered me and fitted my arms through the large sleeves. The thing nearly swallowed me whole.

Maddox's hand reached for mine, but he let it fall before our hands connected. He cleared his throat and looked away, like he was hoping I had missed the gesture.

Maddox strolled through the park, looking for a spot where we could look up at the sky and not have our sight shielded by the tops of the trees. After five minutes of walking he finally picked a spot he believed to be good enough.

He lay down on the ground and I followed his lead, stretching my body out.

My hand itched to reach for his, much the way he had for mine.

I finally clasped my hands together on top of my chest in the hopes that the urge would disappear.

It didn't.

"There's the North Star," Maddox pointed.

I squinted my eyes, trying to see what he saw. "Uh-huh," I nodded, pretending I saw.

He rattled off a few more and I was shocked by his knowledge of astronomy. I'd never been interested in the skies or the stars. I'd always been more focused on fictional worlds and music, and maybe that was my problem. Life had been passing me by until I met Maddox. Now I actually felt like I was living it—an active participant in my destiny and future.

"It's pretty," I whispered. My words felt like such an inadequate description of the beauty above me, but I was at a loss for words.

"It's extraordinary," he supplied.

"Yeah," I agreed.

"Emma?" He whispered into the darkness.

I sat up a bit and looked at him. "What?"

He stared at me for a moment, his silvery gaze making me shiver with the intensity. He swallowed thickly and his Adam's apple bobbed. "Never mind." He looked away.

"Say it," I pleaded, my voice no more than a whisper.

His face contorted like he was in pain. "No."

"Maddox," I urged. "Now you have me worried thinking it's something bad."

"I just... I wanted to know if I could hold your hand." He looked away. Mumbling, he added, "It's stupid."

I bowed my head, trying to hide my pleased smile.

I lay down and said, "You can hold my hand. I wouldn't mind."

"Are you sure?" He asked, sounding young.

And at nineteen he *was* young. Maddox seemed to know so much more than me—to have so much life experience—that I kept forgetting that he was nearly as young as me. In some people's eyes we were still very much children, and not the adults we pretended to be.

"Positive." I smiled up at the twinkling stars and laid my hand within his reach.

His fingers intertwined with mine and my body zinged with an electricity only Maddox could produce.

I scooted closer to him until our legs touched. He cradled our joined hands on his chest and I wondered if his smile matched mine.

Suddenly, the starry sky above us didn't hold my attention

anymore.

I turned my head to look at him, studying the elegant arch of his nose and his pouty lips. He sensed my eyes on him and turned too.

Our eyes connected and he reached out with his free hand to caress my face with the backs of his fingers.

There was nowhere else I'd rather be than right here with him.

It was scary and exhilarating all at the same time.

I knew I was falling, and falling hard. I only hoped Maddox would be there to catch me.

CHAPTER THIRTEEN

MADDOX'S SLEEK SPORTS car wound around the windy road. Rocks jutted out to our right and on the left side of the road was a straight drop down to the river.

I wasn't scared. Not at all.

That was a lie. I was totally freaking out—especially since he was driving like we were in a race, then he pulled off on the side of the road where several other cars were parked. Dust floated up around the car when it came to a stop.

"What are you doing?" I asked, holding onto the seatbelt strap like it was my last hold on humanity.

"Parking the car," he said like I was stupid.

"I can see that, but *why?*"

"Because we're going zip lining." He stated with a proud smile.

My body suddenly buzzed with excitement and I forgot all about the scary road I'd been bothered by.

It was kind of funny that I'd been terrified of this stupid road and Maddox's crazy driving, but not the thought of zip lining. Clearly, I was weird.

I hurried out of the car and together we crossed the road. I followed him down a narrow path, wondering how he ever found this place.

The gravel path soon turned to dirt and I spotted people up ahead.

"We're really doing this?" I asked.

He glanced down at me and a small chuckle escaped his lips. "Yes, Em."

Maddox introduced himself to one of the men and I figured this must be the guy in charge.

I rubbed my hands together and Goosebumps broke out across my skin and my whole body bubbled with an excited energy.

It was mostly guys standing around—some clearly working the zip lining rig and others getting strapped into harnesses. There was a lone woman and she seemed to be working here.

"I'm Brad," the guy reached out a hand to me.

"Oh, I'm Emma." I hoped he hadn't been waiting long for me to respond. Oftentimes I got too lost in my thoughts to notice what was going on in the real world.

"Nice to meet you," he said, smiling pleasantly. If I'd had any fears about doing this his smile would've put me at ease. "Let's head over here and fill out some paperwork."

It took us about ten minutes to fill out the paperwork and sign a waiver. Once that was complete and Brad was satisfied, he and another guy that introduced himself as Jim helped to harness us.

My heart thundered in my chest.

Fear was beginning to settle in my body, but I wasn't going to back out. The thrill would be worth it.

The harness cut into my hips and thighs, but at least I didn't have to worry about it falling off of me. The people working this clearly knew what they were doing.

"Who's going first?" Stan asked the two of us.

Maddox raised his hand to volunteer. "No chickening

out," he warned me.

"I won't," I assured him, grinning. My legs began to shake with adrenaline. We were going to fly—at least that's the way I looked at it.

They fixed a helmet onto both of our heads and then lined up Maddox to strap him on.

"See you on the other side." He grinned at me and gave me a thumb's up before taking off. He let out a cry of joy as he flew down the line, over the river, and onto the other side.

I watched in awe.

Maddox reached the end and the people working that side unhooked him from the line and helped him out of the harness.

"Your turn," Stan told me. He went over some instructions and I listened carefully even though I already knew this information from when he told Maddox.

My heart skipped a beat when they strapped me onto the line.

"One, two, three," Stan counted.

And then I was falling, only I wasn't falling, I was *flying* just like I thought I would.

I spread my arms out like I was a bird, and let out a scream of delight. This was amazing. The world zipped by me in a swirl of green, blue, and gray. Within seconds I reached the other end and it was over all too soon.

I felt high, or maybe drunk was a better term for it.

Yes, drunk on life.

On the possibilities.

A man unhooked me from the rig and helped me out of the harness.

Maddox stood off to the side, watching me closely while grinning like a fool.

Once I was free I ran into his arms, crashing into him. He

stumbled back a step and tightened his arms around my upper body.

"That was amazing," I breathed into his neck.

"I'm glad you liked it."

I tilted my head back to look at him. His eyes were a stormy gray filled with longing.

"Kiss me."

The words were no more than a whisper on my tongue, barely audible.

He startled, looking at me like he couldn't believe he heard me right.

"Kiss me," I said again, my voice stronger this time. "Please kiss me, and don't stop."

"Never," he vowed, taking my face in his large hands and angling my head back to kiss me.

Oh, boy.

This kiss was nothing like the first.

He'd been right—he did make me forget who I was. Heck, he made me forget where we were or that an entire world existed outside of our lips.

Not even the hoots and hollers from the zip-lining guys could break through the fortress.

His tongue swiped against my lips and my mouth parted on a breath.

Maddox was devouring me. There was no other word for it.

My fingers tangled in the soft, short strands of his dark hair. I felt lost in him, in *us*.

My hands moved down to his shoulders, holding onto him. I needed the support, because his kiss was leaving me dizzy.

"I told you," he whispered, smoothing my hair back off my forehead.

"Told me what?" I asked, confused. He'd left me breathless and with my world spinning.

"That you'd ask me to kiss you."

And then he kissed me again.

I was pretty sure I'd be content to let him kiss me for the rest of my life.

A few minutes ago I thought the most exhilarating thing I had ever done was go zip lining.

But I'd been wrong.

This, right here, was it.

Admitting my feelings—asking for what I wanted—*that* was the most exhilarating thing I had ever done.

MADDOX AND I sat in a little diner, on the same side of the booth holding hands.

I laid my head on his solid shoulder, unable to wipe the smile from my face.

I felt giddy—on top of the world.

Nothing could touch me or ruin this day.

Who knew something like this could make me so immeasurably happy?

I looked up at Maddox and he grinned down at me with a crooked smile.

I could've missed out on something great if I'd been stupid.

I guess all it took was me zip lining into the unknown to finally gain some clarity.

"What are you thinking about?" He asked, his eyes scanning my face.

"You. Us." I admitted.

He twisted a piece of my dirty-blonde hair around his finger. "Good things I hope." He lowered his head to brush his lips lightly against mine.

I got the impression that now that I'd asked him to kiss me he was never going to stop, and I was perfectly okay with that.

"Mhmm," I hummed, "of course." I stiffened a bit and looked up into his gray eyes. "Does this mean I'm your girlfriend?"

"Well," he slung an arm around my shoulders and played with the saltshaker with his free hand, "I want you to be, but that's really up to you." He wouldn't look at me and I knew it was because he didn't want me to feel pressured into anything.

"I want to be." I probably said the words too quickly, but let's face it, I had no experience when it came to this sort of thing.

"Then you are." He grinned and kissed me again, just a light quick peck.

"Here you go," the waitress said, setting down our plates of food. We'd both ordered burgers—and of course Maddox got a Diet Pepsi.

"God, I'm starving." Maddox's arm fell from my body as he basically dove for the burger.

I couldn't blame him, though. I was hungry too.

As if zip lining hadn't been enough of an adventure today, we were also headed to the aquarium. Since the location of the zip-line was well on the way to the aquarium he figured this was easiest.

But we'd both grown hungry and somehow ended up stopping at this diner.

I reached for my own burger. All I'd had for breakfast was a protein bar, so to say I was hungry was an understatement.

Since we were both so hungry it didn't take us long to finish and leave—Maddox left with a to-go cup of Diet Pepsi and I left with a boyfriend.

Holy shit.

Maddox was my boyfriend.

I had a boyfriend.

I was pretty sure this was the craziest thing to ever happen in my life—even crazier than meeting Maddox in the first place.

It took another hour drive to get to Baltimore, but I didn't mind. We chatted easily about random things. I learned that when he was five he fell out of a tree and broke his ankle. And that he had a scar on his shoulder from crashing his BMX bike at seventeen.

They were little things, but it made me happy to find out more personal bits and pieces about his life.

I knew we both still had a lot more to open up about. Me with my dad, and him with his real parents, but that stuff was harder and would come with time.

Maddox found a parking garage that claimed to have some available spaces and pulled inside. We wound around and around, looking for one of those so-called empty spaces.

We finally found one. On the roof. And there wasn't an elevator.

"Dammit," he cursed. "Figures."

"It's okay," I assured him. "There's nothing wrong with walking."

He slipped out of the car and I followed. It took us forever to go down the six flights of steps. But Maddox made it fun by singing a song. I would've sang with him, but I didn't know the words to the song.

We burst outside and the summer heat burned down on us. It was nearly scalding.

Maddox pulled his dark sunglasses from the V-neck of his shirt and slipped them on along with a beanie. "It's this way." He nodded to our right, reaching for my hand.

I fit mine inside his larger one, my body humming pleasantly.

The harbor, shops, and nearby restaurants was all crowded

to the point that we had to elbow our way through. People roamed the water in some kind of dragon looking paddleboat. "We should do that," I pointed.

Maddox looked in the direction I pointed and laughed. "Whatever you want, Em."

We walked up to the line for the aquarium. It wasn't as busy as I anticipated and soon we were headed inside with tickets clasped in our hands.

I was awed by the bright colors of the fish and coral. I'd never seen anything so stunning before. We often forgot to stop and appreciate the simple things in life—the bits of beauty nature afforded us on a daily basis.

"This is incredible." I looked around in awe. I gasped when a blacktip shark swam overhead. "Wow."

Maddox chuckled. "You look like a kid in a candy store."

"I feel like one." My head was on a swivel, trying to see everything at once.

"Come on, let's go to Shark Alley." He took my hand, dragging me away. I guess he'd decided I had gawked long enough.

"There are more sharks?" I asked, my voice spiking with excitement.

"Yes," he chuckled, leading me through the building.

"This is the best day of my life!" I exclaimed, like an over-excited little kid jacked up on sugar.

Maddox's laugh grew louder, echoing around us and causing more than a few people to turn and look at us.

Shark Alley turned out to be relatively boring. We sat in the middle of a ring-shaped aquarium and the sharks, and other creatures, swam around us. I wanted some action.

From there we headed to the jellyfish exhibit. I became enamored with the strange orb like creatures.

"I want one as a pet," I declared to Maddox.

He laughed. "Really? A jellyfish as a pet? That sounds dangerous."

"Says hedgehog boy."

He snorted at my new nickname for him. "Hedgehogs aren't dangerous, though."

"But they are an uncommon pet," I countered.

"And a jellyfish is a non-existent pet." He laughed, rubbing his stubbled jaw.

He had me there so I didn't bother arguing with him.

"Wanna go see the dolphins now?" He asked, leaning against one of the jellyfish tanks and appearing bored.

"Dolphins!" I squeaked. "They have dolphins?! Why didn't you tell me sooner?!"

Maddox's eyes widened in surprise at my exuberance. "I didn't know I should tell you."

"Dolphins are my favorite animal!" I resisted the urge to clap my hands and dance around. I was going to see a dolphin! A real, live, dolphin. I was pulsating with excitement.

Maddox began to laugh. "I'm never bringing you to the aquarium ever again. You turn into a crazy person."

It was true.

I tried to tone down my excitement as we headed to the dolphin cove.

When I finally saw the dolphins I let out a shriek that had Maddox covering his ears. "You have got to stop doing that," he winced. "I think you busted my eardrum."

"Sorry," I shrugged sheepishly, "I couldn't control it."

"Uh-huh," he muttered like he didn't believe me.

An employee stood by the tank explaining different facts about dolphins. I joined in with the group that was already there, listening carefully.

"Any questions?" The staff member asked.

My hand shot up and she pointed at me. "Can I pet one?" I

asked, dancing on the balls of my feet.

She laughed. "Of course. They're very playful."

I walked over to the tank and listened to her instructions. When one swam up I extended my arm slowly and let my finger glide over its thick blubber.

"It's so soft," I whispered in awe. It was nothing like I had expected.

Another dolphin swam up and I petted that one too.

Maddox was going to have to drag me out of here. I never wanted to leave.

Maddox came to stand beside me and petted one of the dolphins as well. "Whoa," he gasped. He laughed when the dolphin then rolled over to get his belly rubbed. "He likes me."

"Actually that one is a female," the staff member said.

"She *likes* you," I bumped his shoulder playfully. "The dolphin is totally flirting with you."

He laughed, glancing at me and smiling adorably. "Everyone flirts with me. Have you seen my face? I'm irresistible."

"Uh-huh, sure you are," I nodded.

"You *are* my girlfriend, so that means you couldn't resist me," he winked.

I smiled, ducking my head.

The dolphin nearest me splashed some water at me like she was mad I'd stopped petting her. "Sorry," I told her. "He's distracting me."

Maddox laughed beside me and I joined in with him.

We played with the dolphins for a little while longer before heading out. I hated to leave them, but I knew we couldn't monopolize their time since other people wanted to play with them too.

"Still want to do the paddle boat?" Maddox pointed.

"Of course..." I paused, looking at the prices. "Are they for real? That's way too expensive. Forget it, we're not doing this."

I started to walk off towards the shopping area.

Maddox grabbed my arm and pulled me back against his solid chest. "You want to, so we will."

"Maddox—" I pleaded, but he wasn't listening.

He shook his head and basically carried me over to the guy who manned the boats. He paid and we walked down the steps to the little dock.

"You pick." He pointed to the different colored dragon boats.

"Yellow," I said.

"Thank God you didn't pick the pink one," he laughed.

"Now you just make me want to pick that one." I warned him, with my hands on my hips.

"Too late, I'm already in this one." He said, slipping into the yellow boat and onto the far side. He reached a hand up to help me down.

The boat wobbled with our combined weight, but we both managed to hold our balance and sit down. I reached over and untied it from the dock and we began to paddle.

"This is fun," I smiled, letting my fingers skim the water and the sun warm my face.

"I'm glad you think so."

"Thank you for today," I smiled, reaching over to touch my fingers to his cheek. "It's seriously been one of the best."

Still peddling, he leaned over and kissed me. "I think we can both agree on that."

I smiled at his words—the kind of smile that hurt your cheeks—and I knew that with Maddox I would never stop smiling like this.

He was different.

CHAPTER FOURTEEN

Two WEEKS PASSED and the stifling July heat rolled in. Even in Maddox's air-conditioned guesthouse my tank top still stuck to my body with a fine sheen of sweat.

"It's too hot," I whined, crooking my arm over my eyes where I laid on the cool floor.

Either he ignored me or he couldn't hear me over the drums.

I had no idea what he was playing, it didn't sound like any song I knew but I quite liked it.

A moment later the banging of the drums ceased.

"We could always go swimming. You know, that's what the pool is for when it isn't filled with balls."

"You did hear me," I mumbled, turning my head towards the area where the drum kit sat. I still couldn't really see him, just his sneaker-covered feet, since I was lying on the floor.

He chuckled. "Yes, I did. But I wanted to finish the song. Now, do you want to go swimming or not?"

"I don't have a bathing suit," I argued.

I heard him stand up from the stool and his boots clomped across the floor before stopping in front of me. He lowered to a squat and stared down at me. "Unless you're naked under there," he eyed my clothes, "then I think you'll be just fine."

I wrinkled my nose. The idea of stripping down to my unflattering grandmaish underwear in front of Maddox was not appealing.

"I was lying, I'm not that hot."

He threw his hands in the air, exasperated. "Women," he muttered. His eyes softening, he said, "I'll take you to Target for a swimsuit then."

"No, it's okay." I stretched my arms out on the cool hardwood floor. "This floor has accepted me as one of it's own. We're family now."

He stared at me for a moment, his lips twitching with the threat of a smile.

Instead of saying anything he reached down and grabbed me up into his arms.

"Maddox," I groaned, "this is silly."

"You're the one that's claiming my floor is now your family, so who's the silly one again?"

I groaned. "Just put me down."

"Nope," he said, and I knew he had to be grinning, "we're going to Target and getting you a bikini... a really slutty one." I swatted at his behind and he chuckled in response. "And then we're getting Slurpee's."

"Slurpee's?" I confirmed as he carried me outside and to his car.

"Yep. On hot days like this it's absolutely necessary to have a Slurpee."

He set me down then and opened the car door.

The heat rolled out from the vehicle and I nearly fell down. "I think I'm going back to the floor."

"Don't even think about it." He blocked my way.

I grumbled and slid into the car, the hot leather nearly burning my bare legs.

"Let's go somewhere cold," I told Maddox when we got in, "like Antarctica."

"Sorry, but we're not cuddling penguins today," he chuckled, cranking up the AC. "Target will have to do."

"LOOK, EMMA!" MADDOX called. "I found the perfect one!"

I glanced over to find him grinning and holding up the skimpiest bikini I had ever seen. I looked down at my ample chest and then at him. "That wouldn't even cover my nipples," I blurted.

He laughed heartily and returned the skimpy garment to where it belonged.

I grabbed a simple navy top and bottom with sunflowers on it. I liked it and it wouldn't be overly revealing. I also wouldn't look like a nun either.

Since we were already in Target Maddox wanted to go look at the pool things. He ended up adding five of those noodle things to the cart, along with squirt guns, floaties, and a few other items.

"Do you think you got enough stuff?" I joked, pushing the car towards the checkout area.

"I think so," he said, completely serious.

After checking out he stopped at 7-Eleven for Slurpee's just like he said he was going to.

When we got back to his house Ezra was lounging by the pool. "Did you get me one?" He asked, pointing at the Slurpee in Maddox's hand.

"No," he shook his head, "sorry. But I did get pool stuff."

Ezra lowered his sunglasses and his eyes lit up at the sight of all the bags.

I left the guys alone and headed inside the guesthouse to change into my bikini. I swung the plastic bag around and around, nearly whacking Mathias with it when I walked inside and ran into him.

"Sorry," I apologized, putting a hand to my racing heart. I was glad that I'd managed not to spill my red Slurpee on his crisp white shirt. "I didn't know you were here."

He grunted in response and moved around me to head outside.

He was so weird.

I shook my head and locked myself in the small bathroom to change.

I hadn't been in there long when I heard the door to the guesthouse open and close.

"I'm going to change," Maddox called, and I heard the sound of his feet on the steps.

Once I was in my bikini I slipped my shorts on. I knew it was silly since I'd be taking them off to get in the pool, but I hated the idea of walking outside and facing Mathias and Ezra without them. I headed out of the bathroom and threw away the plastic bag.

My hand was on the knob to head outside when I heard Maddox coming down the steps.

I turned to look at him and all coherent thought went out the window. His body was a work of art. I mean, I had no idea abs could be like that—so defined, sculpted, and perfect.

He chuckled, his lips turning up in a crooked smile.

I floundered and hurried to turn back around, but the door opened at the same time and slammed into my face.

My hand shot up to my nose and I felt the sticky warmth of blood on my fingers.

"Oh God." My voice was muffled sounding.

Maddox rushed forward and grabbed me by the shoulders,

turning me around.

Ezra stood there apologizing profusely.

"Let me see it," Maddox pleaded, trying to pry my hands from my face.

I shook my head.

"Emma," he warned, his eyes flashing silver. Growing exasperated with me he grabbed me by the arm and towed me towards the small kitchen area. Ezra hovered behind us, still mumbling that he was so sorry.

Maddox lifted me by my hips up onto the counter.

"No, no." I pleaded when he tried to pry my hands from my face again.

"Silly girl," he muttered, smoothing my hair behind my ears, "let me see."

With tears pooling in my eyes I let my hands drop. My face hurt—like I'd walked face first into a concrete wall... which I guessed was kind of what happened. Only it was a door... not a wall.

Maddox winced when he saw my face.

"Is it that bad?" I asked. "Do you think my nose is broken?"

"Oh, God! Did I break her nose?" Ezra exclaimed, echoing my question.

Maddox shook his head. "I don't think so. There doesn't seem to be enough blood for that and it doesn't look crooked. Go get me a cloth," he told Ezra.

Ezra disappeared, clearly happy to be assigned with a task.

"Be honest," I pleaded, resisting the urge to cover my face again, "how bad is it?"

"I think it might bruise," he shrugged, inspecting my face. He took my chin between his fingers and tilted my head in different directions. "You're definitely going to be sore for a little while."

"Great," I huffed. I was going to have a bruise and puffy

nose all because I'd been drooling over Maddox. It was like the universe was trying to punish me for being happy.

Universe: *Oh, look! Emma is ogling her smoking hot boyfriend! Let's ram a door in her face!*

Ezra returned with a dampened washcloth and handed it to Maddox, who then gently dabbed at the blood on my face.

"I'm so sorry, Emma." Ezra started in again.

"It was an accident," I told him. "You didn't know I was standing there. I'm not mad," I promised.

The door to the guesthouse opened again and I looked to see Mathias stroll in.

"What happened to your face?" He asked, looking between the three of us. "Did you try to kill her or something? Should I get the shovel?"

Maddox shook his head at his twin brother. "No, she had a very unfortunate encounter with a door."

Mathias winced. "Looks like it hurts."

"It does," I muttered.

Mathias came over to stand beside his brother in front of me where I sat on the counter. He inspected my face much the way Maddox had.

"Get her some ice you idiot." He finally told Maddox.

Maddox balked like he couldn't believe his brother was bossing him around. He handed the cloth to Mathias and said, "Finish cleaning her face off, please. I'll have to go into the main house, I know we don't have anything in the freezer here."

I was surprised when Mathias didn't argue about tending to me. I'd gotten the impression that Mathias didn't like me—or anyone for that matter. It shocked me even more when he tenderly wiped away the last of the blood from my face.

Ezra hopped up on the counter beside me, but seemed to have stopped apologizing—at least for the moment.

"Can you breathe through your nose?" Mathias asked.

I tried. "Yeah," I answered.

"Good." He gave me a small smile and I figured that was a lot coming from him. Up this close I noticed his eyes were a bit different than Maddox's. While Maddox's gray eyes usually looked silver, Mathias' were darker like the stormy gray clouds you saw before a storm. With a nod of his head, like he was agreeing to a thought he'd had, he walked off and out the door.

Maddox came busting in only a few seconds later with an icepack wrapped in a cloth. I tried to take it from him, but he insisted on holding it to my face.

"I don't need you to be my nurse," I mumbled.

"Well, I'm going to be," he stood his ground.

Ezra sighed. "I'm so sorry, Emma."

"It's okay," I assured him, for what felt like the thousandth time. "Go swim or something. You don't need to stay here."

He nodded and jumped off the counter. "Holler if you need me."

Once he was gone Maddox lowered the icepack and frowned.

"What's wrong?" I asked. "Is it getting worse?"

He shook his head. "No, it's not that... I just... I feel weird inside."

"Huh?" I looked at him like he'd lost his mind.

"What I mean is, I've never felt so terrified in my entire life. I don't like seeing you hurt." He reached up and tenderly stroked the side of my face. I relaxed into his touch, closing my eyes. I never thought being with a guy could be like this—so easy and happy. My dad had always been a jerk, even when the alcohol hadn't been a problem. I'd never had a good male figure in my life, and I guess along the way I'd come to believe all guys would be like my dad.

I wrapped my arms around his neck. "I'm not as breakable as I look. Don't worry about me, please."

He chuckled, giving me a small smile. "I don't think I could stop worrying about you if I tried." The look he gave me was so intense that I felt it all the way down to my toes. He pressed the icepack to my nose once more. "I think if you keep icing it the swelling will go down quickly."

"Well," I grinned, putting my hand overtop his, "at least I'm not hot anymore."

His laugh boomed around us. "Yes, at least there's that," he agreed.

"THE SWELLING HAS gone down a lot," Maddox commented. "It doesn't even look that bad anymore."

I peered up at him where I was lying with my head in his lap. "You're such a liar."

The movie continued to play on the large TV in the basement of the main house, but neither of us was currently paying any attention to it.

"I would never lie to you, Em. I promise it's better. I should probably get you another icepack though." I sat up from his lap and he stood. "I'll be right back," he promised.

I gave him a small smile. It was all I could muster. The day's events had really knocked me down.

While he was gone I went to use the bathroom. I'd only seen part of the main house when he brought me down here but everything looked so pretty and shiny. But you could tell it was lived in. It wasn't one of those places that looked so pristine that you were scared to sit down on a couch for fear of leaving behind a miniscule stain. I was also quite taken with the cape cod style of the home. Most homes in this area didn't look like this, and I liked it. It made me feel like I was vacationing by a beach up north.

I washed my hands and inspected my appearance. Maddox hadn't been lying. The swelling had gone down some—but in its place a bruise was forming.

I had just sat back down on the large sectional couch when Maddox returned with the fresh icepack and popcorn.

The buttery smell invaded my senses and my mouth watered.

He handed me the icepack and sat down, draping a blanket over our bodies.

I curled against him, soaking in his warmth. I still couldn't believe that I was with Maddox—that he was my boyfriend. I hadn't been planning on him, but I was discovering that it's the unexpected things in life that make it so great.

He placed the popcorn bowl in his lap and I reached for a handful.

I popped a piece in my mouth and moaned. "This is so good." It tasted like the kind of popcorn you got from the movie theater, not from the grocery store in a box.

"If you think I make fantastic popcorn, wait until you see my cooking skills," he boasted with a proud smile.

I narrowed my eyes. "I thought you said your freezer was empty?"

He chuckled. "That's only because mom likes to make dinner for us," he shrugged. "She likes to make sure she sees all of us at least once a day."

"I think it's nice that you call Karen mom," I commented, laying my head on his shoulder.

I felt, rather than saw, him smile. "She is my mom. Just because we don't share blood doesn't make her any less of a mom to me, and I always want her to know that."

I tried to resist the urge to sigh dreamily. "You're a good guy, Maddox."

"No, I'm not," he answered quickly, glancing down at me. "I'm selfish."

"Why do you say that?" I questioned, my brows furrowing together with curiosity.

He looked away with his jaw clenched tightly. I noticed his hands start to shake where he held the bowl in his lap.

"Maddox?" I prompted. "What's wrong?"

The shaking stopped and he schooled his features. "Nothing. Never mind."

I stared at him, puzzled. I couldn't figure out what was going on, but I felt like it was important.

"You can tell me anything, Maddox. I hope you know that."

"I do, Em," he winced.

"Then what's the problem?"

He took a deep breath and looked down at me. "There's no problem, I swear."

I stared at him for a moment, contemplating his words. I finally nodded, and said, "Okay." If I was going to make this relationship work I had to learn to trust him. If he was keeping a secret from me, which it felt like he was, then I had to believe he had a good reason for keeping it.

He's not like your dad. I repeated the mantra over and over again in my head. But somehow I didn't feel any better, because another voice kept piping in with, *What if he is?*

CHAPTER FIFTEEN

"I THOUGHT WE'D take it easy today, but still do something... fun." Maddox smiled, standing on my front porch.

I rubbed the sleep from my eyes. "I just woke up. Fun is not on my agenda for a few more hours." It was already after noon, but I'd been up late reading.

"You're going to have to put it on your schedule then, because we need to be there in thirty minutes."

"Where is there?" I whined, blocking the sun from my eyes with my hand.

He snorted. "Did you really think I'd tell you?" Pushing his way inside he waved a hand at me. "Go get ready. You have ten minutes before I come after you and dress you myself."

"You wouldn't." I glared at him as I shut the door.

"I would," he replied with a grin.

"Ugh." I shoved my fingers through my messy hair and stomped back to my room. Thank God I'd showered last night and didn't have to worry about that. I grabbed a pair of shorts, a tank top, and a cardigan with an Aztec design. I tried my best to tame my hair, but it was sort of a lost cause. At least the swelling in my nose was practically gone, and a little bit of concealer and foundation hid the bruise.

Grabbing my bag I darted out into the living room and ran smack into Maddox's hard chest. His hands clasped around my arms to steady me.

"Oh you're ready," he frowned. "How disappointing for me. I was quite looking forward to dressing you myself." He winked, causing my cheeks to heat with color. He held me at arms length, appraising my nose. "Looks good today. Ezra's still torn up about it."

I laughed. "He's not even the one hurt and I feel like I need to get him a Get Well balloon."

"We should," Maddox agreed. "It would only make him feel even sorrier."

I winced. "It was an accident. I really hate that he feels so bad."

Maddox let go of me and started towards the door. "He should feel bad," he mumbled.

I let the subject drop, because I didn't want to deal with the teasing I'd get if I told him the only reason it happened in the first place was because I was gawking at him.

I followed Maddox to the car, which was still running, and busted out laughing when I saw Sonic sitting on the dashboard.

"The hedgehog is coming with us?"

"Of course," Maddox gasped. "He's like our team mascot."

I snorted. "But you don't bring him everywhere with you."

"Well, zip lining was not hedgehog appropriate. Today's activities are."

"Good to know," I nodded, sliding into the car.

Maddox got behind the wheel and placed Sonic in his lap.

He drove through the neighborhood where his house was, so I assumed we were going there.

I was shocked when he pulled into the driveway of a different home. Several other cars were parked in the driveway and on the street.

"Why are we here?" I asked, unbuckling my seatbelt.

"You'll see," he sing-songed.

I followed him to the front door where he rang the bell. I heard the sounds of several voices on the other side and the door opened to reveal a little old lady standing there. Her gray hair was bushed around her head, and she was hunched over. Her blue eyes were kind and sweet and her smile was blindingly happy.

"Are you here for the knitting party? Karen said one of her sons was coming with his girlfriend."

I smiled, pleased that Karen had called me his girlfriend. I immediately scolded myself for being a lovesick fool, though.

"That would be us," Maddox grinned, and I looked up noticing for the first time that he had Sonic perched on his shoulder. "I'm Maddox, this is Sonic, and—"

"I'm Emma," I interrupted him, holding my hand out to the woman.

She ignored my hand and reached her thin arms out to hug me. She smelled like peppermint.

"I'm Maise," she replied. "I'll introduce you to the rest of the ladies."

She led us through her beautiful home and to a back porch, where five more ladies sat, plus Karen. I smiled at Karen, giving her a small wave.

"You both already know Karen, obviously," Maise spoke, "this is Alice, Margaret, Beth, Jane, and Mary."

Hellos echoed around us, and Maddox and I responded.

"This is Maddox, Karen's son, and his girlfriend Emma." She introduced us to the group.

Maddox and I took a seat on one of the couches and Maise handed each of us a ball of yarn and knitting needles.

"I can't believe I'm doing this," Maddox muttered, grabbing Sonic and putting him back on his shoulder—the hedgehog had been trying to climb on his head.

I pointed to the knitting needles. "Just pretend they're drumsticks."

He wrinkled his nose and tapped them against his knees. "Yeah, that isn't working for me."

I laughed. "It was worth a try."

Maise cleared her throat, and we both looked up.

She guided us through instructions on how to fix the yarn around the needle and make our first stitches. It seemed easy enough.

A little while later Maddox cursed, "Fuck."

The room had been filled with the quiet chatter of the ladies voices but everyone shut up at Maddox's exclamation. He looked up, his eyes wide like a deer caught in headlights.

"Oops." He mumbled. "It fell off." He pointed to the crumpled pile of yarn in his lap.

Masie sighed. "Then start again and try to keep the cursing to a minimum."

"Sorry," he bowed his head, looking truly ashamed of himself. It was cute.

He started again, going slower this time.

I smiled proudly at my neat rows of stitches. I might actually manage to make a scarf.

"It's too quiet in here," Maddox mumbled, from beside me. His face brightened. "I know…" He set his scarf—or whatever the lopsided thing was that he was attempting to make—aside. He steadied Sonic with one hand and grabbed his phone and some earbuds from his pocket. He handed me one and put the other in his ear, turning on the music.

"Ah!" I cried, when it blasted.

"Sorry," he mumbled, quickly lowering the volume.

He picked the knitting needles back up and went to work once more.

I knew it sounded crazy, but Maddox made knitting look hot.

A few minutes later he poked my shoulder and I turned to look. He had Sonic in his lap with the small piece of fabric he'd knit lying across the hedgehog's back. "Look, Emma, I made him a cape! He's Super Sonic!"

I snorted, slapping a hand over my mouth to stifle my laughter. It was no use, though. Pretty soon the both of us had dissolved into laughter and tears ran down my cheeks.

"Super Sonic? You couldn't come up with something better?" I wiped the tears from beneath my eyes.

He shrugged, his grin huge. "It was the first thing that popped into my head."

I shook my head at him, fighting a smile. "Maybe you can start a trend of hedgehog capes."

Maddox picked up Sonic, cradling him to his chest. "What do you think Sonic? Do you want to be my model?"

The hedgehog wiggled his nose. I wasn't sure if that was meant to be a yes or no.

"Sonic says he'll be my model." He returned the hedgehog to his shoulder once more.

I looked up to find all the old ladies watching us and staring at Sonic like he was some kind of rodent.

"What is that creature?" One of the ladies asked. I was pretty sure it was Alice.

"He's a hedgehog," Maddox replied.

"Huh," she muttered, and returned to knitting.

I looked up at Maddox and smiled.

Only Maddox Wade would sit in a room with a bunch of old ladies and knit a scarf with a hedgehog on his shoulder for me.

He went out of his way to make me happy—to make me feel special.

He was remarkable, and I might've been young, but I knew enough to know that most guys weren't like him.

I swallowed past the lump in my throat and looked down at the colorful yarn in my lap.

What was he doing to me?

I breathed deeply, fighting the panic that threatened to choke me.

I knew what I felt for him was too much, too soon. I was turning into one of those girls I made fun of for claiming they loved a guy after one date.

"Emma," Maddox's voice sounded concerned. "Are you okay?"

"Yeah, I'm fine. Just a little thirsty." My voice came out sounding breathless.

"I'll go get you some water, dear." Maise smiled, tapping my knee kindly as she left the room.

"Are you sure that's it?" Maddox asked, his silvery eyes radiating with concern.

"Positive," I assured him.

He still looked at me doubtfully, but let it drop.

My panic was beginning to ebb when Maise returned with a bottle of water. I took it from her and drank it greedily.

"Better?" Maddox asked.

"Yes," I replied, sitting the bottle on the floor.

He stared at me a moment longer before turning his attention to Maise. "What do I do if I want to end this here?" He asked, holding up the small piece of fabric.

"Why would you want to do that?" She asked. "That's nowhere near being a scarf, sweetheart."

"I know, but I want it to be a hedgehog cape."

Maise turned her gaze towards Karen, as if to say she couldn't believe Maddox would dare ask such a thing. Karen shrugged with a small smile.

"Alright," Maise sighed, coming over to show him how to finish it off.

Once it was done Maddox stuck it to Sonic's quills and smiled proudly.

While I finished my scarf Maddox stayed beside me with Sonic sleeping in his lap, humming along to the song he was listening to. I'd long ago tuned the music out.

Maise helped me finish my scarf, like she had Maddox. I knew my scarf was hardly the prettiest thing anyone had ever made, but I was quite proud of it. I knew I'd always cherish it, and this day. And it was all thanks to Maddox.

As we walked outside to his car, I stood on my tiptoes and quickly kissed his stubbled cheek.

"What was that for?" He asked.

"For being you."

He grinned at my words and started to say something, but was interrupted by Karen coming outside and calling for us. We paused, waiting for her.

She came hurrying towards us. "I'm glad I caught you. I was afraid you were already gone."

"What do you need, mom?" Maddox asked. He didn't say the words rudely, he sounded genuinely concerned.

"I was wondering if Emma would like to come to dinner?" She looked at me, smiling kindly as she waited for my reply.

"I'd love to," I answered honestly.

"Great," she clapped her hands together. "I'll see you for dinner then."

She waved goodbye and headed to her own car.

"You okay to hang out at the guesthouse?" Maddox asked.

"Yeah, of course," I replied.

It didn't take us long to get to his house.

He placed Sonic in his cage—and the hedgehog immediately burrowed his way under his igloo to sleep.

"I have something I want you to take a look at," Maddox said, bowing his head. He seemed unusually shy.

"Okay," I replied, following him over to the desk that was always covered in paper. I'd never inspected them before, but now that I was up close I could see that they were covered in song lyrics and music.

He grabbed a few papers up and nodded for me to follow him to the piano.

He lined up the papers and looked at me rather bashfully. "Will you play it while I sing?"

I started. "Of course... you wrote this, didn't you?" I asked.

He nodded. "I've been working on a few different songs for a while, but I got the idea for this one a few weeks ago and I haven't been able to get it out of my head since. I think I finally have it right, though. If you hate it, tell me. I trust your opinion."

"I'm not going to hate it." I looked at him like he was crazy.

He shrugged. "It's possible."

He then waved his hand for me to start playing. It didn't take me long to recognize the song—he'd been playing the same one on the drums yesterday.

He sang softly at first and I could taste his fear in the air. He truly thought I was going to hate the song. But it was beautiful, absolutely amazing, and in my (un)biased opinion the greatest thing I had ever heard.

His voice, just like the song, grew with more strength.

Unable to help myself I started to sing with him—a song about love, hope, and forgiveness.

My voice was quiet and high compared to his low gravel, but somehow our voices blended beautifully together.

I wanted so desperately to look at him, but I kept my eyes on the sheets of music in front of me. I could feel his eyes on my face though, and it was nerve-wracking.

The song ended, the last note still lingering in the air.

I turned to look at him and found passion burning in his eyes. I wasn't prepared when he grasped my face and tugged me impossibly closer.

He slanted his mouth over mine, kissing me deeply—with his heart and soul.

I kissed him back, grasping the collar of his white t-shirt.

Our lips moved together to a song of our own making.

One of his hands lowered to the nape of my neck and he hummed happily in the back of his throat. I pressed my chest against him and let out a small sound when his other hand grabbed me by the hip, pulling me onto his lap. I rocked against him—kissing him with all the passion I possessed.

He pushed against me and my elbow hit several of the keys on the piano. Neither of us was bothered by the clamor.

He pulled back, just a breath, and whispered, "What are you doing to me?"

He didn't give me a chance to respond. His kiss was electrifying. It burned me straight down to the core—branding me forever.

I grasped his stubbled cheeks in my hands and from this position I hovered above him.

The piano stool teetered and I squealed when we lost our balance. We fell, and Maddox wrapped his arms around me. He tucked me against his chest so he took the brunt of the short fall.

We looked at each other for a brief second before bursting out in laughter.

"That was some kiss," he chuckled, reaching up to tuck my hair behind my ear. I was still lying on his chest and had no intention of moving.

"Who said it was over?" I said boldly, closing the short distance between us.

Our lips connected once more and my body flooded with electricity. One spark could set me on fire.

He rolled us over so he was now on top with my back against the floor. His strong arms caged me in and my legs wound around his waist. I tugged his hips down to mine and we both let out soft moan.

I'd never experienced these types of feelings before, and it was scary how intense they were with Maddox.

"Emma," he murmured against our lips.

I panted, unable to respond.

His tongue ghosted against mine and I tugged at the short strands of dark hair near his neck, urging him on.

"What the fuck?" The door slammed. "Thank God your fucking clothes are on. I live here you know and I don't need to see this stuff."

Maddox's lips left mine and he rolled off me. His chest rose and fell in soft pants. He reached a hand down to me and pulled me up.

"Good to see you too, Mathias." Maddox groaned, clearly irritated by his brother interrupting us.

"Whatever," Mathias mumbled, walking to the refrigerator and grabbing a bottle of orange juice. He poured himself a glass and stared at us. "Neither of you are even sorry, are you?"

We both shook our heads.

"Don't act like you weren't the same way with Remy," Maddox challenged.

Mathias' face morphed from mildly irritated to full on livid. His face turned red and a vein threatened to burst on his forehead. He threw the glass of orange juice and it shattered on the floor near our feet. I let out a small scream and grasped tightly onto Maddox's arm.

"Do not fucking say her name ever again!" Mathias roared, pointing an accusing finger at Maddox. "She is none of your fucking business!"

He grasped the countertop so tightly that his knuckles turned white.

With another roar he stormed up the steps and I jumped when the door to his bedroom slammed.

Maddox and I both stood silently, neither of us knowing what to make of the what went down.

When a minute passed I finally had to do something. "I'll get a rag to clean this up," I mumbled, skirting around the broken glass.

My words seemed to get Maddox moving. "I'll get the dustpan," he muttered.

Together we managed to clean up the mess. Both of us were quiet, lost in our thoughts.

When the last of the orange juice was wiped away I looked at Maddox. "What was that about?"

He sighed, dumping some of the glass he'd brushed up into a trashcan. "That's Mathias."

"He's quite explosive, isn't he?" I asked hesitantly.

Maddox nodded. "He doesn't handle much well." His jaw clenched and he looked away. I wanted so desperately to ask him to elaborate, but I kept my mouth shut. When he was ready to tell me he would.

"What do you want me to do with this?" I asked, holding up the soiled rag.

He took it from my hand, holding the small trashcan in his other. "I'll take it inside and put it in the washer. What time is it?" He asked me.

I pulled out my phone and looked at the time. "Four."

He nodded. "Mom will have dinner ready soon. She likes for us to eat early."

He started towards the door and I said, "Is Mathias coming?"

He looked towards the stairs. "Not likely."

"Oh," I frowned.

"Don't worry about him," Maddox mumbled. "Trust me, he doesn't deserve your sympathy."

"But he's your brother," I said, confused.

"And he's also an asshole," he replied. "I might love the guy, but even I know better than to go near him when he's like this."

I sighed, following him out of the guesthouse.

We entered the main house through a set of French doors that opened into a cozy living room. Maddox turned down a hall and I followed him. He opened the door to a laundry room that was larger than the bathrooms in my house. I couldn't believe that people lived in homes this large—and I knew this home wasn't even as large as some.

He tossed the soiled rag in the washer and headed to the kitchen, getting rid of the trash bag full of glass and fixing a new one in place.

Karen was cooking away, but didn't question anything. To her it just looked like he was changing the trash. She had no idea why, and I wondered what she'd think of Mathias' outburst if she'd been there. I got the impression that she wouldn't put up with that kind of behavior.

"Is there anything I can do to help?" I asked her. I hated standing around feeling useless.

She smiled at me over her shoulder. "It would be wonderful if the two of you could set the table."

"No problem, mom," Maddox chimed.

He showed me the silverware drawer while he gathered the plates.

Despite the fact that he said Mathias wouldn't bother joining us I noticed he still set a place for him.

Ezra came sauntering into the kitchen just as we finished with the table.

"Hey," he greeted me, slinging his arm around my shoulders, "I didn't know you were joining us for dinner."

"Your mom invited me," I told him.

"Mom's thrilled to have a girl hanging around the house," Ezra joked.

"Stop it." She scolded her son.

He chuckled and took a seat. "Dad called and said he'd be a little late."

Her brows furrowed together. "He didn't call me."

Ezra propped his elbow on the table and his head in his hand. "He said he did. You know how you get absorbed in cooking. You probably just didn't hear it."

She reached into the front pocket on her apron and pulled out a sleek phone that looked identical to the one Maddox had gotten me. "Oh, you're right," she laughed.

Ezra shook his head. To me he said, "I don't know why she doubts me."

"Maybe because when you were ten you lied about *everything*," Maddox chuckled, pulling out a chair for me. I sat down and he took the spot beside me.

"That was nine years ago," Ezra defended. "She should have restored her faith in me."

"*She* is standing right here," his mom scolded, placing a dish filled with some sort of casserole on the table.

"Sorry." Ezra bowed his head. Even though he was nineteen, he clearly respected his mom and still acted very much like a little boy in her presence.

She finished placing the various dishes on the table and by the time she sat down a man's booming voice called through the house, "I'm sorry I'm late!"

I looked over to see a tall, handsome man enter the room. He wore a nice suit—and when I said nice, I meant *nice*. His dark hair was trimmed short, sprinkled with a few gray hairs, and his face was clean-shaven.

The man startled when he saw me, placing his briefcase on the floor by the archway. Loosening his tie he smiled. "I didn't know we had company. I'm Paul," he held a hand out for me to shake.

"Emma," I replied, taking his offered hand.

He smiled kindly and his eyes turned to Maddox.

Maddox squirmed in his chair, but didn't say anything.

"I'm assuming she didn't just wander in off the streets..." Paul paused, waiting for Maddox to elaborate.

I swore there was a slight tinge of pink to his cheeks, but as quickly as I saw it, it was gone. "She's my girlfriend."

"And here I thought you told us everything." Paul tapped Maddox on the shoulder as he strolled towards his wife who sat at one of the heads of the table. He lowered and kissed her cheek, whispering something in her ear. Heading to the empty seat across from her, he said to Maddox, "I always knew you'd be the first to go down."

Ezra snorted.

And Maddox tried to fight a smile.

I felt like I was missing something.

"Excuse me?" I asked, looking between Paul, Ezra, and Maddox.

"I always knew Maddox would be the first to fall in love," Paul answered simply.

If there had been water in my mouth I would've spit it out. "What?" I gasped.

Paul shrugged. "Just callin' it like I see it."

I'm pretty sure I turned as pale as Casper the Friendly Ghost.

Love?

Maddox didn't *love* me.

It wasn't possible.

We'd only known each other a month. That was not enough time to fall in love.

I sat there, shaking my head. My appetite was suddenly gone.

Maddox groaned beside me and growled, "Thanks dad, now you've gone and scared her to death." To me he said, "Breathe, Emma."

Breathe? What was breathing?

Oh, right, that thing where you inhaled oxygen.

"She's not going to pass out, is she?" Ezra voiced. "Should we splash water on her? I think that's what they always do in the movies with these sorts of situations."

"Shut up," Maddox snapped. "Emma," he took me by the shoulders and turned me towards him. "Please, stop freaking out."

"Freaking out?" I panted. "I'm not freaking out."

He raised an eyebrow in disbelief.

"Okay, fine," I relented. "I'm freaking out."

"Here," he grabbed my water glass, "drink some of this. It'll help."

I really didn't see how it would, but I was willing to try anything to calm my racing heart. I took slow sips of the cold liquid and it did somehow manage to help alleviate my nerves.

Once I was calmed down, Karen cleared her throat and asked, "Where's Mathias? Is he not joining us?" She eyed the empty place setting beside Ezra.

Maddox grumbled, "He's in one of his moods sulking in his room."

"Oh." Karen mumbled. "I'll save him a plate then." Changing the subject once more, she asked me, "So, Emma, will you be attending college in the fall?"

"No," I shook my head, "I'll be a senior in high school."

She smiled. "That's wonderful. Senior year was the only year of school I actually liked. It was also the year I met Paul." She pointed her fork at her husband.

"Really?" I asked, suppressing the urge to laugh as Maddox piled food on both of our plates. "So, you're high school sweethearts?"

"Yes," she smiled wistfully.

I looked between the two. You could see how in love they were, even this many years later. It gave me hope that some loves could last.

Shaking her head, Karen addressed me once more, "What do your parent's do?"

"Oh, uh, my mom's an artist," I stuttered. "She mostly does pottery and things like that. And my dad is gone."

"Oh, I'm so sorry to hear that," she frowned. "Dealing with the death of a parent at such a young age is a difficult thing. My mom died of breast cancer when I was a sophomore in college and it was devastating."

I winced. "He didn't die," I frowned, huffing out a breath, "he left us. He *chose* to leave us." I looked down at the table when I felt the familiar burn of tears prick my eyes.

Karen let out a startled gasp, floundering for something to say.

"Would you mind if I used your bathroom?" I asked, not meeting anyone's eyes. I might've told Maddox about my dad leaving, but it was something I *hated* talking about.

"Not at all," Paul replied, clearing his throat. "It's just down the hall. Second door on your right."

I pushed away from the table and scurried into the bathroom.

I closed and locked the door behind me, leaning my back against its surface.

I breathed in and out deeply for a moment.

Sometimes the fact that my dad was gone hit me hard. I

liked to pretend I didn't care, but deep down I *did*. What girl didn't need her father in her life? And mine was just gone. Not because he was dead and had no choice in leaving, but because he couldn't stand my mother or me. I *knew* we were better off without him. He wasn't a good man, but he was still my dad. Fuck, my feelings were so messed up. One minute I hated him, and the next I missed him. It was all so stupid.

I moved over to the sink, running some cool water. I splashed some on my face to refresh me. It helped, but I was still upset.

I took a deep breath, focusing on the silvery damask design of the wallpaper.

"Emma," a fist rapped against the door, "can I come in, please?"

"I'm fine," I muttered, hoping he'd go away.

"Emma," he pleaded again. "Let me in."

For some reason I felt his words of *let me in* were referring to much more than just letting him into the bathroom.

"Fine," I sighed, turning the lock and opening the door.

He slipped inside and the door closed.

The bathroom was one of those small powder rooms and much too tiny to contain the two of us. His chest pressed against mine and his hands came up to cup my cheeks.

He swiped his thumbs underneath my eyes, his normally silver eyes nearly black. "I hate seeing you cry."

"I didn't know I was." But he was right, silent tears fell down my cheeks.

He swallowed thickly. "Your dad is an asshole for leaving you. You're wonderful and so is your mom. Some people don't know how to cherish what they have, so instead they destroy it." His tongue flicked out to wet his lips and he looked at me with a serious expression. Normally Maddox was all carefree smiles, so this was a new side of him. "Sometimes I'm thankful that I had such a rough start to life, because it makes me appreciate every good thing I have in my life. Like getting to have dinner with my family, and you, I didn't have that growing up. *Please*," he begged, "don't let that man make you bitter. Don't let him win, Em. You deserve to be happy and you can't do that if you don't let him go."

My face crumpled and I began to sob. "I hate him so much, Maddox. I hate how mean he was to my mom and me. But I think I hate him even more because I love him and that makes me angry. It's this vicious cycle that never stops."

"Shh," he hushed, wrapping his arms around me. "Let it out, Em. Let it all out."

"He chose to leave me," I cried against his chest, soaking his shirt with my tears. "I wasn't good enough for him."

"That's not true." He shook his head, his chin brushing against the top of my head as I clung to him. "He wasn't good enough for *you*."

He smoothed his fingers through my hair as I clung to him like he was a life preserver and the only thing keeping me afloat.

I felt his lips press lightly against the top of my head.

"You know," I choked, "it's like that day at the fair you knew I needed you to save me." I whispered the last part, like I was scared to breathe life into the words.

"No, Emma, it was me that needed you. Never forget that."

And then he just held me, and I knew that everything was going to be okay.

CHAPTER SIXTEEN

MADDOX: I HAVE TO GO OUT OF TOWN FOR A FEW DAYS.

The text message flashed on the screen of my phone. I currently sat on my bed with a book in my lap, the afternoon sunlight streaming in through the open blinds.

EMMA: DID SOMETHING BAD HAPPEN? I couldn't stop myself from asking.

MADDOX: NO. NOTHING LIKE THAT. I'LL BE BACK IN TWO DAYS... TOMORROW EVENING IF I'M LUCKY.

EMMA: I'LL SEE YOU SOON THEN.

MADDOX: I'LL MISS YOU.

I'd be lying if I said I wasn't going to miss him too, but he wasn't my whole life. Besides, this was a good thing. Sadie had been bitching at me the last few days for not hanging out with her. I couldn't blame her for being irritated with me, and I felt bad for blowing her off. Things had been so new and exciting with Maddox that I'd started neglecting my best friend.

After telling Maddox I'd miss him too I sent a text to Sadie, asking if that girl's day she'd talked about was still open. She was quick to reply.

SADIE: HOW ABOUT YOU COME OVER TONIGHT? SLEEPOVER? PIZZA? AND THEN WE CAN GO SHOPPING TOMORROW.

EMMA: SOUNDS GOOD.

"HE IS SO hot," Sadie sighed dreamily, drooling over the half-naked guy on her TV. I think he was supposed to be a werewolf or something. I wasn't sure, since I didn't watch much TV. Shows made me bored for some reason, which was why I stuck to music and books. "Don't you think he's hot?" She asked me.

"Sure," I agreed. I was currently too busy devouring a slice of pizza to check out the guy.

"Ugh, you're no fun," she groaned, pushing my shoulder in jest.

I smiled. "Hey, look at it this way, at least we don't have to fight over who gets him."

"Bitch, he's mine," she narrowed her eyes, fighting a smile. "You know how those dark-haired, dark-eyed boys make me."

I giggled. "Yeah, they make you throw your underwear across the room."

She rolled onto her back laughing. "It's true." Sobering, she said, "I'm putting myself on a strict no dating policy for senior year."

I snorted.

"What?" Her eyes widened. "You don't think I can do it?"

"Nope."

"I'm going to prove you wrong." She jutted out her chin defiantly.

"You'll last a day," I grinned, taking another bite of pizza.

"You have such little faith in me," she shook her head. "You're my best friend, you should be cheering me on."

"I think you have some pom poms in your closet if you need me to cheer," I joked. Sobering, I added, "Seriously, I think it's good for you to focus on something other than boys for a change."

She reached for a slice of pizza. "I don't want to be that girl anymore. You know," she shrugged, "the slut."

I rolled my eyes. "You're not a slut, Sadie." I knew for a fact that she'd only had sex with one guy. She might've been provocative, but she didn't jump into bed with every guy she batted her eyes at.

"That's not what the people at school think," she sighed. "I want to show people, and myself, that I can stand on my own two feet and do something for me. No, not just that," she frowned. "I want to prove that I can *be* someone."

"What do you mean?" I asked.

She shrugged and dropped pizza crust into the box. Rolling onto her back she stared up at the fan as it went around and around. "This is senior year, Emma. Then it's the real world. It's scary. I have to figure out what the hell I'm going to do with my life."

"I'm in the same boat, you know," I told her.

"I know."

"So," I ventured to ask, "what do you think you're going to do after we graduate?" Wasn't that the million-dollar question?

"I don't know," tears pricked her eyes, "and that scares the shit out of me. I need a plan, and I don't have one beyond buckling down."

"Well," I smiled, hoping the gesture offered her a small amount of reassurance, "at least that's a start."

"Enough serious talk," she dabbed at the moisture pooling beneath her eyes, "I'm missing my show."

I laughed gathering up our trash into a small smile.

One of the things I loved most about Sadie was that one-minute we could discuss something serious, and the next she could make me laugh.

I tried to pay attention to the show, but I honestly had no idea what was going on. All I knew was there were a lot of half-naked guys on it—and that was clearly why it appealed to Sadie.

"I hope you're ready for a long day of shopping," Sadie warned, as I fixed to go to sleep in the pull out trundle. Her parents had insisted on having one, since Sadie and I had many sleepovers over the years.

"Ugh," I groaned. "Shopping."

"Hey," she pouted, "brighten up that attitude and maybe I'll suck it up and let you browse through the flea market for a little while."

"You have yourself a deal."

"I'M PRETTY SURE my sweat is sweating," Sadie complained, pulling her long brown hair off her neck and fanning herself.

"Don't be dramatic," I warned her, focusing on the jewelry stand I was browsing.

"I think I'm going to die," she panted.

I pulled a bottle of water out of my purse and handed it to her. "Here, drink this."

She took it and chugged it down greedily. "Why does it have

to be so hot?" She whined.

I turned and glared at her. "I spent five hours at the mall with you, and we've only been here thirty minutes. Stop bitching."

She frowned. "How are you not hot?"

"I am hot," I told her, "but I'm not complaining."

"Fine," she relented, "I'll keep my mouth shut."

Something told me I'd be lucky if she was quiet for five minutes.

I browsed through a few more of the stands, picking up a few necklaces, a cardigan, a pair of worn chestnut colored cowboy boots, and a handmade metal drummer and drum set made out of nuts, bolts, and other odds and ends. I just couldn't resist getting it for Maddox. I was lucky that when I found it Sadie had abandoned me to go sit underneath a shaded tree.

"I'm done," I called as I approached her.

"Thank God," she wiped sweat from her brow. "Can we get some dinner now? I need a cool place to lay down and a table sounds like it would be pretty perfect."

I snickered. "Whatever you want."

I waited a moment for her to get up, but she didn't move. "I think I've lost the function of my legs." Pouting her glossed pink lips, she poked one of her legs. "Move," she demanded. Looking up at me, she said, "They're not moving."

"Such a baby," I laughed, reaching out a hand to haul her up.

"I hate this heat," she whined. "And my hair keeps frizzing." She reached up to bat it away.

I shook my head, walking back to the parking lot.

I put my bag in the trunk—trying not to laugh at the other fifty bags that belonged to Sadie.

"Where do you want to eat?" She asked, cranking up the AC.

"Wherever you want. I honestly don't care."

"TGI Friday's it is, then," she chirped. "I want some of those green bean things so I can trick myself into thinking I'm eating healthy."

I snorted. "Sounds like a plan."

By the time we got there the restaurant was packed and we ended up having to wait thirty minutes to be seated.

When we were finally seated at a booth in the back I was ready to go to bed. Shopping was exhausting.

Sadie seemed to agree since she immediately flopped her head on the table and groaned. "My feet hurt."

"You shouldn't have worn those shoes." I wiggled my own toes, encased in a pair of comfy converse.

"Uh, you're right." She sat up, propping her head in her hand. "I would take these off right now if I didn't think I might kill everyone in a five foot radius with the smell of my feet."

I laughed as I pictured the people around us falling to the floor from the fumes. "Yeah, you better leave them on."

The waitress came by for our drink order and before she left Sadie demanded her green bean appetizer thing. It didn't sound that good to me, but she swore it was the greatest thing ever.

"We haven't talked about lover boy in a while," she mused, looking down at her nails, trying to pretend that she wasn't curious.

"There's nothing to talk about," I shrugged. Since I hadn't been able to bring Maddox to the barbeque I'd decided it was fate intervening and saying that I needed to keep him to myself for a little while longer. It wasn't that I thought Sadie would try to steal him from me—she certainly wasn't like that—or that I thought Maddox would choose her over me. It came from a place of, for once in my life, wanting something that was just for me. I felt like I had a whole separate life—no, world—with

Maddox and I'd grown to love it. I wasn't ready to share yet, but if things got more serious I would introduce her to him. But for right now, I liked things the way they were.

The waitress set our drinks on the table and Sadie began to peel the paper away from the straw. "I'm starting to think he isn't even real."

"He's real," I assured her. Being honest, I added, "I just don't know where this is going between us, and I'd like to keep things low-key for now."

"So, basically you're saying that you won't introduce him to your best friend?" She raised an elegant brow.

"Basically," I confirmed.

"This hardly seems fair," she pouted. "As your best friend I should know all the details of your life. Keeping secrets is wrong, Emma." She smiled so I'd know she was only joking. "It's okay, though. I won't bring him up anymore. I'm just glad you've finally gotten yourself a boy. But," she leaned towards me, "if you turn in your V-card to him, I better be the first one to know."

"Sadie," I groaned, rolling my eyes.

She laughed, sitting back in the booth, and turned the conversation away from Maddox.

I was glad I'd gotten to spend the day with her, and yesterday evening too. I hadn't realized how much I was missing girl time.

Despite that, by the time she dropped me off at home I was ready for bed. I was completely exhausted and my feet hurt from so much walking. Clearly, I was out of shape.

I tossed my purse on the couch, placed my bag on the floor, and was kicking off my shoes when the doorbell rang. I sighed. Had I left something in Sadie's car?

I opened the door and took a prompt step back. "Maddox," I gasped, "what are you doing here?"

"Surprise," he grinned, holding out a bouquet of pale pink tulips. "For you," he handed them to me.

"I-I thought you weren't getting in until tomorrow." I stepped back, waving him inside.

"I told you I might get back early," he shrugged, smiling down at me, "so I wanted to stop by and see you."

"You're incredible," I whispered.

His lips pulled into a grin. "I try."

"Let me put these in a vase." I nodded my head towards the kitchen and he followed. I grabbed a clear vase and filled it with water. "I'm just going to tell my mom you stopped by." I pointed to the door that led to the garage that served as her workshop.

He nodded, preoccupied by looking at the framed family photos on the wall beside the kitchen table.

I stepped into her studio and she looked up from the pot she was painting. "Did you have fun with Sadie?"

"Mhmm," I nodded, "it was nice to hang out with her."

"Good." She stared intensely at the pot, working on some sort of intricate circular design.

"I just wanted to tell you Maddox stopped by." I tossed a thumb over my shoulder. Normally, I wouldn't bother my mom while she was working, but I didn't want her to think I was hiding things by not telling her Maddox was here.

"Oh, okay," she smiled. "Don't do anything stupid." She gave me a stern look.

I laughed. "You have nothing to worry about mom."

"He's a teenage boy, therefore he's the one I'm worried about. I might like him, but I know what he's thinking about right now and it's not seeing your seashell collection. Don't show him your clam, Emma."

I stood there open mouthed.

"Oh, God. Ew. Mom!" I slapped a hand over my eyes, like

my hand alone could block the visual in my head. "I cannot believe you said that!" I gagged. Like, seriously?! Who said that?!

She chuckled. "Okay, let me rephrase then… don't show him your vagina."

I'm pretty sure my mom just wanted to see me turn ten shades of red and stand there sputtering like an idiot.

"Please, mom! Stop!" Now I covered my ears. "Where's the bleach?" I asked. "I need to remove this nastiness from my mind."

She just kept laughing at me.

I finally walked out, leaving her to her hysterics.

Maddox tilted his head when I stepped inside the kitchen. "Interesting conversation?"

Oh, dear God! Please let him not have heard that exchange!

"No," my voice went high.

He raised a single brow, clearly not believing me.

I grabbed the vase of tulips and carried them back to my room, setting them on the dresser. They brightened up the space, and I found myself smiling at them. They were such a sweet gesture.

Maddox flopped on my bed and wiggled around. "Comfy," he grinned, crossing his hands behind his head.

I blushed. Even though Maddox had already seen my room I still felt uncomfortable having him in it. It suddenly felt so… girly.

The walls were painted yellow—not mustard yellow, but a light buttercup shade. I'd strung twinkling Christmas lights on the wall where my bed was, and they cast a golden glow on the room. A blue and teal quilt covered my bed and all the furniture was mismatched. I loved it, but I wondered what Maddox thought when he looked at it.

"Come lay down." He patted the empty space beside him.

I started forward, but then stopped.

"Hang on," I held up a finger, "I got you something."

Leaving Maddox lying on my bed I scurried to the living room and grabbed the bag from the flea market.

I sat down on the bed, pulling out the bubble wrapped metal drummer.

"Here," I handed it to him, "I hope you like it."

I suddenly felt very unsure if I should have gotten it or not.

He smiled at me, peeling away the tape and bubble wrap. He held the drummer and drums up, twisting it around. A slow, crooked smile lifted his lips. Turning to me, he said, "Em, this is the greatest gift anyone has ever given me. Seriously, this is amazing. I love it. Wow," he murmured, examining it from every angle.

"Really?" I asked, "you're not just saying that?"

"I love it," he repeated. "It's such a thoughtful gift." He continued to stare at it with a smile. "You didn't need to get me anything, you know?"

"I know," I replied, "but I wanted to."

He stared at me for a moment. His eyes were such an intense silvery gray color that I found myself squirming from his gaze.

"I-it reminded me of you and I had to get it," I stammered, needing to fill the silence.

His look never wavered and butterflies took up residence in my stomach.

He set the object aside and before I could blink he had me pinned to the bed. His muscular arms formed a barricade around me.

My breath rushed out of my lungs as he stared down at me. My heart thumped so loudly that I knew he had to hear it.

"Thank you."

"Thank you?" I repeated his words.

He nodded, a strand of brown hair falling over his forehead. "Yes, thank you for the extremely thoughtful gift."

"Oh, right," I stammered, "you're welcome."

His eyes darkened to the color of storm clouds. "I'm thinking I should kiss you. You know, as a proper thank you."

"You think so?" I gasped breathlessly.

He lowered, so his body was pressed against mine and his lips were only a breath away. "I know so."

He closed that last miniscule of distance, kissing me like a man that had been deprived of oxygen and I was his air—the only thing keeping him alive. His fingers tangled in my hair, pulling me impossibly closer and guiding me against him.

I wrapped my arms around his neck and moaned into his mouth.

It didn't seem possible that one person could create a hurricane of emotions inside you, but Maddox did that to me. He'd stirred up the calm waters my life had been and now everything was a chaotic storm. And I loved every minute of it.

He kissed me until my lips were red and chapped—branding me for the world to see that I was his.

He rolled over and curled my body against his chest.

"Goodnight, Emma." He whispered, kissing the skin where my neck met my shoulder.

I thought it would be impossible for me to go sleep after that kind of kiss, but I was exhausted. With Maddox's body heat wrapped around me like the coziest blanket in the world, I drifted off to sleep, having the sweetest dreams I'd ever had.

CHAPTER SEVENTEEN

THE ROUGH CLEARING of a throat had me blinking my eyes open sleepily.

"Hi, mom," I yawned.

"Morning, Emmie... Maddox."

"Maddox?" I questioned.

She raised her brows and nodded her head.

I startled. I was still half asleep or I would've noticed sooner that a body was wrapped around me. He had me cocooned to his chest and his head was buried into the crook of my neck. His warm breath blew softly against my skin. He was sound asleep. At least we were both fully clothed so my mom couldn't accuse of us anything.

"Sorry," I mouthed. "We fell asleep."

"Obviously," she grumbled, putting on a motherly face. "I like him, I do," she said in a hushed whisper, "but I'm not okay with this."

I winced. I hated displeasing my mom. "I'm really sorry."

She nodded her head, as if my words somehow made it better. "I'll make breakfast. Wake him up."

I nodded, assuring her that I would.

With one last glance at us she left my room.

I tried to roll over, but Maddox's arm had me pinned to the bed. I tried to shove his arm off, but that didn't work. I finally pinched him and that got him moving.

"What the hell, Emma?" He cried, rolling onto his back and rubbing his eyes.

"My mom." It was only two words but his eyes widened in horror.

"Is she pissed?" He asked, scrubbing his hands through his already sleep mused hair.

I nodded.

"Fuck," he groaned, sitting up. "I'm really sorry. I was planning to leave once you fell asleep, but then I went to sleep too, and—"

"It's okay," I interrupted him. "We just can't let this happen again or she might kill me... and I'd really like to graduate high school."

He snickered. "Okay. No more sleepovers."

Something in his tone told me that there would, indeed, be more sleepovers.

Before I could give that much more thought I let out a squeak and rolled out of bed onto the floor.

"You okay?" Maddox asked.

"Yep," I cried, wanting to hide behind my hands. I'd suddenly realized that I'd just woken up in bed with Maddox and my hair was bound to be a mess and oh my God what if my breath smelled awful? I cupped my hands over my mouth and breathed, inhaling the scent a bit. "Ugh," I groaned. "That's nasty."

"What's nasty?" Maddox asked, striding around the bed and over to me.

"Nothing!" I cried, jumping to my feet. He probably thought I'd lost my mind. Maybe I had. I reached up, trying to tame my wild hair.

"I'm going to go brush my feet."

"Your feet?" Maddox repeated, biting his lip to stifle his laughter.

"I meant my teeth!" I ran past him and out of the room, straight into the bathroom. I slammed the door closed and leaned against it. I let out a pent up breath. Oh my God, that was mortifying. My feet? Seriously? Sometimes my brain and mouth did not communicate.

Even behind the closed door I could still hear him laughing. At least I amused him.

I shook my head and went to brush my teeth and hair, trying to make myself look halfway decent and not like the spawn of Satan... which was what I usually looked like when I just woke up.

When I padded back into my room I found it empty. I changed into a pair of shorts and loose tank top that showed off a bit of my stomach. It wasn't something I'd normally wear, but I was hoping to make Maddox forget about that embarrassing bit about my feet.

I found him sitting at the kitchen table, laughing with my mom. A plate sat waiting for me, along with a cup of tea.

"You look nice," Maddox grinned, surveying my body as I took a seat. "I can't say the same for myself." He winked, plucking at his wrinkled t-shirt.

I wanted to tell him that he always looked good, but I figured his ego didn't need any more inflation.

I took a bite of bacon and said, "Mmm, this is good, mom."

She smiled. "I figure the least I can do is make you a nice breakfast since I'm rarely around for dinner in the evenings... and now your time is... preoccupied." She nodded her head at Maddox and he ducked his head to hide his smile.

When Maddox looked up he grinned at me.

"What?" I asked, lifting the cup of tea to my lips.

He nodded at it. "Tea Rex?"

I let out a soft laugh. "I had to have it."

"I can see why," he chuckled. "It suits you. It's quirky."

My brows rose. "Quirky? I'm not sure most girls would appreciate being called quirky."

He smiled crookedly, his silver eyes flashing. "But you're not like most girls. That's one of the things I like most about you."

"You like that I'm weird?" I suppressed a laugh. "That hardly seems like a winning attribute."

He shrugged, stabbing at his scrambled eggs. "I didn't say you were weird, Emma. I was just trying to say that you're different and I think that's a very good thing. You're not like other people."

We stared at each other, completely oblivious to the fact that my mom was still in the kitchen.

I swore the air began to crackle with electricity between us.

I'd only ever read about this kind of thing in the many books that lined my bedroom walls. Never, in a million years, had I believed it was real.

I broke eye contact first, unable to handle the intensity a moment longer.

We finished eating breakfast in relative silence.

I grabbed up our plates and proceeded to wash them in the kitchen sink. I heard the door to the garage close and knew my mom had gone into her studio. It had never bothered me how much she worked, I knew that for her it didn't feel like work. It was where her passion lay, just like me with music. Although, I doubted I'd ever pursue music as a career.

A moment later I felt Maddox step up behind me and my rambling thoughts cut off.

"Let me help." He grabbed a clean, but wet, plate from my hands and a towel to dry it with. He wiped it dry and set it aside, bracing his hands on the counter. He tilted his head towards me and I stopped what I was doing. "I want to show you something."

"Uh," I paused. "Okay?"

I didn't know why it came out sounding like a question.

He cracked a smile, his silvery eyes oddly serious.

I thought he was going to say more, but he took another clean plate from my hands and went about like nothing had happened.

Boys.

They were so damn confusing.

I really wondered what he could possibly want to show me. I thought it could be another 'adventure' but the serious look in his eyes had me doubting that. I felt like something important was about to happen, but then again I could've been reading too much into the situation.

We finished with the dishes and Maddox wanted to stop by his house to change before we went wherever it was that we were going.

I waited in the car, because frankly I didn't want to run into Mathias. I still hadn't recovered from his outburst over the girl named Remy.

In under ten minutes I saw Maddox emerge from the guesthouse. He'd changed into a different pair of jeans, a white shirt, with a button down jean shirt on top with the sleeves rolled up. When he turned around to shut the door I laughed at the fact that he had his drumsticks in his back pocket.

He hopped into the car, tossing the drumsticks in the cup holder, and backed out of the driveway, not uttering a word about our destination.

I decided to sit back and enjoy the ride. There was no point in stressing myself.

Twenty minutes later he pulled off the main road and onto a dirt road. I knew this road led to a pretty shitty neighborhood with run down houses—well, they were actually trailers—and scary people... mostly drug addicts.

"Why are we going here?" I asked, whipping my head back and forth.

Maddox winced, scratching at his stubbled jaw. He tapped his fingers against the steering wheel as he thought. "I've been thinking... since you had the breakdown in the bathroom." I winced, remembering how I'd cried on his shoulder like a complete baby while babbling about my asshat of a father. He glanced at me briefly before continuing, "And I realized I haven't been very forth coming about my life before Karen and Paul took us in as foster kids. I want to change that... so, I thought it best to start at the beginning."

I swallowed thickly. I didn't know what to say. This certainly wasn't what I had expected when he told me he wanted to show me something today.

"Maddox—" I started, but he held a hand up to quiet me.

"You don't need to say anything."

He pulled off the road onto a path that definitely wasn't a road and drove a short ways before stopping. Trees closed in around the vehicle, obscuring it and us from the sight of others.

He cut the engine and held the key in his hand. He didn't look at me, and I felt that he was probably giving himself a pep talk.

He took a few deep breaths and undid his seatbelt. He glanced at me with an indeterminable look on his face. "Are you ready?"

"Are you?" I countered. It seemed like the more important question.

He nodded his head, looking out the windshield. "Yeah, I am."

He climbed from the vehicle and I followed.

He slipped a pair of dark sunglasses on and looked over his

shoulder where I stood by the car.

"Come on," he nodded.

"This way?" I pointed ahead. "I thought we were going that way?" I then pointed behind us to where the trailer park sat. "I thought you were just trying to hide your car. I'm no expert, but this looks like too nice of a car to have around here," I rambled.

He chuckled and came to my side. "No, we're not going *there*. Once I left I vowed never to go back."

"But we're here?" I was so confused. I wished he'd just get to the point.

"Even when things were really bad, I had one place to go— one place that didn't hold bad memories, only good ones. That's what I want to share with you today. My sanctuary." He reached for my hand and entwined our fingers together. "I'll tell you the ugly parts of my life too, the parts that are broken and ruined, but I want to show you the beauty first."

Without another word he guided me forward, pushing through the overgrown brush and errant tree limbs.

"It's not far," he told me.

He was right, within a minute we pushed through the last of the brush and a small creek appeared. I stopped and closed my eyes, listening to the sounds of the water flowing.

Opening my eyes, I smiled at him. "So, this is your happy place."

He sat on the ground, resting his arms on his drawn knees. "Yeah." He stared out ahead, his eyes shielded by the sunglasses.

To our left sat a large willow tree. A tire swing was tied to one of the limbs.

Maddox saw where my gaze had landed. "Ezra, Mathias, and I hung that up one year. I think we were ten." With a laugh, he added, "I thought I was such a dare devil climbing up there and tying it on." He shook his head and scrubbed his hands over his face, skewing his sunglasses. "We were so young," he said softly under his breath.

My brows furrowed. "You're still young."

His eyes narrowed as he righted the sunglasses. "Sometimes I feel so fucking old." He ran his fingers through his hair and it stuck up wildly. "Life was cruel to me early on, and while we lucked out—and things are great now—the past still haunts me."

I sat down beside him and wrapped my arms around his strong bicep. I then rested my head on his shoulder. He stared straight ahead at the creek. I knew he'd continue when he was ready.

"Sometimes I wonder if things were always so fucked up," he started, "if maybe there were some good times with my parents and I was too young to remember, but I tend to think not." His head drooped for a moment before he returned his gaze to the creek. "When we were really little, they used to yell and scream at us. Then once we got to be about five, both my mom and dad started hitting us."

I winced. *Five* was *'really little,'* but the way he said it made it sound as if he was so much older.

"My dad was an alcoholic like yours," he turned to glance down at me. "He was a mean drunk. He'd shove us into walls and scream in our faces. But I'd take that shit any day over my mom..." He trailed off, lost once more in memories of the past.

"My mom was just... *cruel*," he sneered, glaring at the ground. "She hit us more than my dad did. But... hitting wasn't her first weapon of choice. She liked words and," he looked to me once more, almost as if he was measuring whether or not I could handle what he was about to reveal, "she liked to choke us."

"Choke you?" I gasped. "*Why?*"

He shrugged. "I don't know... I think maybe she liked the

thrill of it, of seeing the light fade in our eyes."

I wanted to throw up. What kind of mother could do that to her children?

"My dad died when we were seven. He crashed his car into a tree, because he was so drunk. She got worse after that. *A lot* worse," he added. "Paul and Karen lived in the trailer beside us—that's how we became friends with Ezra. They never knew how bad things were for us, or they would've intervened. Sometimes I wish I'd been strong enough to tell them what was happening, but I was terrified of my own mom—of what she might do to me." He swallowed thickly. "Mathias had it worse with her than I did. He was slow in school and had trouble reading, so that made her mad—even though she's to blame, it's not like she ever read to us or helped with homework. Anyway," he shook his head, "Mathias' teacher sent home a note from school one day when we were in sixth grade—something about how he was failing reading and she thought my mom should have him checked out for dyslexia. She was pissed when she read the note..." His teeth ground together and he removed his sunglasses to rub his eyes. "Even though I wasn't the one in trouble I ran away from her—scared she'd hurt me too. I hid underneath my bed and I heard Mathias fighting against her, trying to get away—we were both still really scrawny then," he laughed, but there was no humor in the sound, "I heard her drag him into the bathroom and the door slammed." His eyes pinched shut and his body trembled.

Even before he continued I was certain I knew where this was going.

"She tried to drown him in the bathtub like... like he was fucking animal or something." I expected him to be crying, but he wasn't. Instead anger simmered beneath the surface of his skin. His fists tightened like he wanted to swing out and punch something. "The most ironic part of it all is the fact that *she* was the animal. She was a drug addict and a whore—that's eventually what got her arrested and led to us being put in the foster care system. She was trying to trade sex for drugs from a cop that was working undercover. We were thirteen then, and even though we were rid of her," he stared straight ahead, his jaw set, "the damage had been done and it was irreversible."

He ripped at the grass, caking dirt beneath his fingernails. "Maybe it's because I didn't get it as bad as Mathias, or maybe I just coped differently, but for whatever reason I haven't stayed angry like him." He turned to glance at me. "My brother isn't an asshole for no reason, it's because she made him that way."

I winced, my heart breaking for Mathias and Maddox. No child should ever go through what they did.

"While we lived here," he waved a hand, "*this* became our solace. When things got rough we got out of the house and ran here. After all, the Collins' couldn't always let us into their home—and that was the first place my mom looked for us anyway. She never learned about this place. It was all ours."

A look stole over his face, one of peace and maybe even happiness.

"Nothing bad ever happened in this spot, and that made it special—no bad memories could haunt us here. We don't come here very often anymore, at least I don't, but it will always be special."

He trailed off, his eyes growing distant.

"You know, normally," he continued, "we would've ended up in a hellhole when we entered the system, but the Collins' stepped up to the plate. We basically lived at their place anyway—they'd moved out of the trailer park but were still close enough that we all rode the same bus, so we'd go there in the evenings. They saved us," he said with surety, "without them Mathias would be even more fucked up than he is, and me? I know I wouldn't be sitting here with you right now," he cracked a smile, "and I wouldn't feel so happy. I owe them everything. They loved us when no one else did—for years I struggled to find a way to repay them for their kindness, but I finally realized I already had, just by loving them back." He looked out at the creek, watching the way the sun shimmered on the surface. "They're the reason we got into music. They thought music might be a healthy outlet for our anger."

"Mathias plays too?" I had no idea that his twin had any kind of musical talent.

"Well," he chuckled, "he sings. He can play the piano too, and a little guitar, but he prefers singing."

"I would've never guessed," I said honestly.

"Mathias keeps to himself, don't take it personally."

"Why'd you choose the drums?" I asked curiously.

"I don't know," his lips turned down, "it just felt right."

We grew quiet—the only sounds around us were the creek, the rustling of leaves, and the caw of birds.

I let go of his arm and he stretched his legs out, coaxing me to lie down and put my head on his leg. He looked down at me, his face oddly serious. "You know," he started, reaching down to brush an errant blonde curl off my cheek, "I thought it would more difficult to tell you, but it was surprisingly easy." His fingers moved from my cheeks to outline my lips.

"Thank you for trusting me enough to tell me," I whispered.

His eyes zeroed in on my lips, following the path his fingers burned as he traced their contour. "You're too good for me."

"That isn't true," I grabbed his hand, wrapping my fingers around his and laying our joined hands on my chest. "I'm not too good for you. I'm average, Maddox. I'm just a girl and you're just a boy. But together," I reached up with my free hand, clasping his jaw so he was forced to look down at me, "we're more. Maybe not perfect, but we're something pretty extraordinary."

He grinned at that. "You could be a poet, Emma." He'd removed his sunglasses and they sat on the collar of his shirt, so I didn't miss his wink.

I laughed. "Maybe if you're nice to me I'll let you use it in a song."

"Or maybe you could write one with me?" He was still smiling, but his eyes shimmered with seriousness. "You told me you write."

"Me? Write a song with you?" I laughed. "Yeah, right. I can barely write a paper for English class." I *did* write songs though—at home, where no one would ever see them. I began to pale, recalling a long ago conversation where I'd told him I wrote songs. Jesus. Why couldn't I keep my mouth shut around him?

He bit down on his delectable bottom lip to stifle his laughter. "Writing a song is nothing like writing an essay. An essay comes from here," he tapped my forehead, "and a song," his voice lowered to a husky whisper and his darkened, "comes from here." He laid his hand on my chest, right over my heart. It started beating wildly at his touch, and with the way he grinned I knew he noticed.

"What are you doing to me?" The words tumbled out of my mouth, reminding me of a set of Jenga blocks falling to a table.

"Falling in love with you," was his quick reply.

I didn't know who made the first move, I guessed it didn't really matter, but suddenly I was in his lap with my legs wrapped around his waist as he kissed me passionately.

It was the kind of kiss that scorched your soul.

He nipped at my bottom lip and I wrapped my arms around his neck.

My chest pressed against his and I had the sudden urge to

feel his bare skin against the palms of my hands. Almost as if he sensed what I wanted he stripped off both of the shirts he wore.

His bare skin scorched my palms.

"You're so beautiful," he whispered in between kisses. His hand found the nape of my neck, drawing me closer as his tongue brushed against the seam of my lips.

I opened for him, begging, wanting all he could give me.

My heart raced and my blood rushed through my veins.

I wanted him.

All of him.

Here.

Now.

I rocked my hips against him, needing to ease the ache I felt, and he grasped my thighs.

"Em," he whispered, "Emma, you have to stop."

He rolled over, pinning me to the ground and my hands above my head.

"Stop," he panted, his eyes so dark that there was only a thin ring of silver left. My lips ached from the loss of his. His tongue flicked out to wet his lips. "I want you, Em, God I want you so fucking bad. But not here, not like this."

I closed my eyes, realizing what I'd done.

"I'm sorry," I whispered.

"Don't be sorry," he shook his head. "Not for that, please."

My lower lip trembled and I was seconds away from tears—I felt like I'd basically thrown myself at him and been shot down. I knew realistically that wasn't what happened, and I'd gotten caught up in the moment, but it still hurt.

"Emma," he frowned, "don't cry. I'm trying to do the noble thing here, and your sad face is making it very difficult."

I managed a small laugh.

He smiled. "And can you honestly say you'd want our first

time to be here?" He smoothed his fingers across my cheekbone.

"No," I replied. "I'm sorry," I repeated. "I don't know what's wrong with me."

He chuckled and ducked his head against my neck before rising to his feet. "There's nothing wrong with you, Em," he reached out a hand to help me up, "it's called hormones."

I still felt embarrassed and flustered as he grabbed his shirts, putting them back on.

He wrapped an arm around my shoulders and drew me against his body, kissing the top of my head. "Stop thinking about it, Em."

I let out a soft laugh. He could read me so well—*too* well sometimes.

Before he could guide me away, I asked, "What is this place, exactly?"

He looked out towards the water, his face darkening with... was that regret? "It's Willow Creek."

CHAPTER EIGHTEEN

I FOLLOWED MADDOX back to his car—trying my best to forget about basically throwing myself at him. My cheeks were already heating just thinking about it, and I willed the redness to disappear. I needed something—anything—to talk about.

"So, you said Karen and Paul lived here too?" It was the first question that popped into my head.

He nodded, unlocking the car and we both climbed inside.

"How'd they get away?" I winced at my choice of words. It sounded so harsh and callous. "I'm sorry, I didn't mean it like that... I just meant that..." I rambled, unable to form a coherent sentence.

He reached over and squeezed my knee, leaving his hand there in the process. "It's okay. I know what you meant." He paused, appraising his next words. "Paul was able to get a promotion at work and they had to move to be closer—but they didn't move into the house they live in now, if that's what you're thinking." His hands tightened around the steering wheel.

He was obviously tense, and I worried that it came from telling me about his mom and dad—that maybe he'd told me before he was ready.

Maddox interrupted my thoughts with a statement of his own. "Your mom said your birthday is in a few weeks."

I winced. "What else did she tell you?"

He grinned at that—and even though his eyes were concealed behind the dark sunglasses I knew they were lit with laughter.

"She said you used to dress up and sing these little songs you made up."

My face reddened and I struggled to breathe. I could remember being five years old and dressing up in my sparkly red dress, black shoes, and getting into my mother's makeup—which wasn't much since she barely wore any—and singing a song about... cheese. Yes, cheese. Pretty much all the songs I made up related to my love of same random thing. Usually food. What could I say? I was always hungry.

"Hey, my songs were not *little*," I disagreed, "they were brilliant." The songs I wrote now were only for myself, though, and no one—not even Maddox—was ever going to see them.

"Do you still remember them?" He asked, an eyebrow rose in interest.

I squeaked. I felt like a cornered rabbit, and if we hadn't been in a moving vehicle I would've run away. "Maybe."

He laughed, trying to hide his smile behind his hand as he drove. "That's cute."

I wrinkled my nose with distaste. I wasn't sure I liked my boyfriend calling me cute. It seemed like a putdown, somehow—like something you'd call your little sister. Then again, I was probably being overly defensive due to my non-existent boyfriend experience. In the past I spent more time trying to push guys away than trying to figure them out.

"Mathias wants me to pick up some lunch to bring back with us, and then I was hoping I'd get to see you put those song writing skills to the test."

I blanched, shaking my head back and forth. "I'm hardly a skilled song writer," I defended. "Not like you," I added softly, remembering the day I played the song he wrote on the piano while he sang. The song had been beautiful—something I imagined someone much older than Maddox would've written. The songs I wrote paled in comparison.

"How would you know if you haven't let anyone hear them?" He countered.

Damn him. He had me there.

"What if I'm not good at it?" I asked in a small voice. I hated the thought of failing at something I loved so much.

He pulled into the parking lot of a local restaurant and turned off the car. He took his sunglasses off and leveled me with an indignant look. "How can any of us know if we're good at anything if we never at least try?"

I tried so hard not to smile, but I failed. "Okay, Yoda."

He chuckled. "I'm shocked you know who Yoda is if you didn't know Sonic the Hedgehog."

He was never going to let the hedgehog thing go.

I shrugged. "I watched them with my dad once." I didn't want Maddox to think I was going to burst into tears by talking about my dad again, so I was quick to add, "This is where Mathias wants us to get his lunch?" I pointed at the building.

Wait, lunch? Didn't we just eat breakfast?

My eyes widened when I looked at the time on my phone. It was after twelve—nearing one. Had we really killed that much time at the creek? Apparently so.

"Yep," Maddox nodded, hopping out of the car. He leaned his head through the open door. "Come on."

"Aren't you picking it up?" I asked, perfectly happy to stay behind in the car. You know, to avoid people and all that jazz.

He shook his head. "*We're* eating here, while Mathias will eat alone and suffer in his self-imposed solitude."

My lips quirked at that, and I exited the car, following him into the building.

Before we entered the building he tugged on a beanie. Seriously, what was it with him and hats?

I followed him into the darkened building. It was relatively empty of a lunchtime crowd, although the bar did hold a few occupants. Maddox led me to a booth in the back and a waiter appeared quickly with menus.

"Have you ever been here before?" Maddox asked, twisting his bottom lip with his fingers as he perused the menu.

"No," I answered shortly.

He set the menu down, looking like I had offended him. "This place only has the best food ever. 'Tis a shame."

"I guess it's another first I'll experience with you," I said, and then immediately hid behind the menu because I started thinking about the naked kind of firsts. Seriously, my brain was all kinds of fucked up lately.

Maddox laughed at me, like a full belly laugh, which only served to leave me even more embarrassed.

He finally managed to compose himself and picked up the menu once more.

The waiter returned and we both ordered iced tea. I got a sandwich and Maddox ordered half the menu. I wished I was joking and I hoped that *some* of that food was going to be boxed up for Mathias.

Since my thoughts had already headed in that direction I thought now might be a good time to ask about the mysterious Remy.

"I've been wondering…"

"Yeah?" He prompted, his eyes skimming the restaurant like he was searching for something or someone.

"What's up with Remy?" I finally asked. "Who is she to Mathias? I mean, I assumed it was his girlfriend, or ex-girlfriend more likely, but then that night at dinner your dad said he knew you'd be the first to have a girlfriend." I knew I was rambling so I quickly shut my mouth. I hated to pry, but after Mathias went all Godzilla and threw a glass at us I thought I deserved to know—especially if I was about to willingly subject myself to his obnoxious presence.

The waiter sat down our drinks and Maddox nodded in thanks, waiting for him to walk off before he continued.

"Remy and Mathias..." He winced. "They dated briefly when they were sixteen."

"And that's it?" I asked. There had to be more to the story than he was letting on.

"Mathias is private—there are lots of things he doesn't even share with me—so I honestly don't know that much. She never really came over to our house, but we'd all hang out. They were always all over each other, and they argued a lot. They've both got a temper and Remy didn't back down from his shit. She moved before our senior year of high school and they broke up. Mathias has been an even bigger asshole then usual since then, but I honestly don't know what transpired there. I have a feeling we may never know." He sat back and draped his arm across the top of the booth.

I frowned, suddenly gaining even more sympathy towards his moody and arrogant twin.

"Did he love her?" I didn't know why, but the question felt important to me.

He shrugged, taking a sip of his iced tea. "I guess in the only way Mathias Wade knows how to love—and that's to destroy." Maddox didn't seem bothered by his own harsh words about his brother. I think it bothered him that Mathias was so... broken... but he'd come to accept his twin as he was. Maddox straightened and I heard his boots stomp against the concrete floor. "Forget about my brother, let's talk about what we're going to do for your eighteenth birthday."

I squeezed my eyes shut. "No."

"No?" He chuckled. "I thought most girls loved talking about their birthdays and all the expensive shit they wanted."

"Not me," I shook my head. I used to love my birthday, until one year my father destroyed it in a drunken rage. It never felt the same after that—like it was tarnished somehow.

Maddox seemed to pick up on my feelings. He leaned forward, his hands crossing with interest. "Why?"

It was only one word, but it still made me squirm.

"Why do you think?" I countered with a question of my own, buying more time.

He quirked a single dark brow. "I'm going to go out on a limb here and guess your dad."

"Ding, ding, ding we have a winner."

His face wrinkled with disgust. "What did he do to ruin your birthday?"

I couldn't believe I was actually about to recount this story. I was eight years old and my mom had made me invite the entire third grade class, and not just Sadie. I'd been so embarrassed when my dad stumbled into the backyard drunk, muttering random nonsense under his breath. I was used to seeing him like this, but the other kids had no idea what was going on and had begun whispering amongst themselves.

"He showed up to my birthday party drunk," I mumbled. Closing my eyes I remembered the way the breeze had blown against my face—the orange balloons swaying. "Then proceeded to smash my cake and throw up in my lap."

Maddox snorted.

"It's not funny!" I cried.

"Sorry," he sobered, hiding his mouth behind his hand.

"I was traumatized," I defended. "Now whenever my birthday rolls around that's all I remember."

His eyes flashed with a silvery fire. "We're going to change that this year."

I shivered at the promising tone in his voice.

"What do you have in mind?" I asked, trying to pretend I wasn't all that interested in what he might come up with.

"I don't know yet," he rubbed his stubbled jaw in thought, "but I'll think of something."

I didn't doubt him.

"HERE'S YOUR FOOD asshole." Maddox tossed the bag of food at Mathias' chest.

Mathias fumbled to catch it. He'd been sitting on one of the barstools in the guesthouse's kitchen and hadn't been expecting us.

"Fuck, Maddox." Mathias managed to grab the bag before it fell to the floor. "I'm going to stick my cigarettes on your stupid hedgehog's fucking quills."

Maddox laughed, completely unaffected by his twin's words. "We both know you'd never waste your precious cigarettes to do that."

Maddox headed to the refrigerator, grabbing a bottle of blue Gatorade. While he spoke to his brother I headed to the side of the guesthouse that housed the instruments and simple couch.

Papers still sat scattered across the desk, and I wondered just how many songs he was working on. Skimming the papers, I guessed a lot.

I had a journal at home filled with songs—all written neatly and kept in some sort of order. *This* was a mess. Although, as I peered closer, I had to admit that he had ridiculously good handwriting. Couldn't he suck at something?

Another pair of drumsticks sat on the desk. I couldn't resist picking them up and tapping them against the top.

"Don't do that." A hand shot out, grabbing the sticks from my hands.

I pouted. "That wasn't nice." I wrestled them away from him and laughed in triumph, waving them in the air. "They're. Mine. Now." I accentuated each word by tapping the drumsticks against his chest.

He leveled me with a glare. "Don't do that."

"Do what, play with your sticks?" I grinned evilly.

"That sounded dirty." He fought a smile.

"You have a very dirty mind then," I told him, putting the drumsticks back on the desk.

I looked around, surprised Mathias hadn't interrupted us with a smartass comment, but he was gone.

Noticing my puzzled look Maddox said, "Mathias went to the main house to eat."

"Oh."

He grinned. "What? Are you suddenly afraid to be alone with me?"

"No," I scoffed.

"You should be."

His lips descended on mine, his hands on my hips. He lifted me onto the table, stepping between my legs.

He nipped lightly at my bottom lip and I'm pretty sure a moan escaped my throat. I really hoped he didn't hear it.

His fingers delved into my hair, musing it even more.

When I lost all ability to breathe he stepped back. He breathed heavily, looking down at me with a searing gaze.

"Afraid now?"

"Hardly," I panted.

He grinned at that. "Then I'll have to try harder." His eyes dipped to the swell of my breasts. Normally I would've covered my chest in mortification, but his kiss had killed a few of my brain cells and I couldn't move if I tried.

He dipped his head once more and I closed my eyes in anticipation, but his lips didn't touch mine. Instead he kissed my cheek, leaving me desperate for more. Jerkface.

"Think you can get off the table so we can write a song?" His hands landed on the table beside my thighs so he was now eyelevel with me.

He knew that there was no way I was peeling my body off this table. "You put me here."

He chuckled. "Oh, Emma." He helped me off the table and I stumbled against his side. "Go sit over there." He pointed and I saw that there were pillows, blankets, and beanbags sitting on the floor. They weren't normally there and I couldn't help wondering if he'd had this planned.

He carried over the papers where he'd already started songs, as well as blank sheets, and pencils. He sat them on the floor in front of me and went back, opening Sonic's cage.

I didn't even blink when he sat down with the hedgehog on his shoulder. At this point it was commonplace. I wouldn't have even been surprised if Sonic was wearing his knitted cape—he wasn't, though.

I stared at the spread out papers, grabbing a random one and starting to read.

Finished with that one I skimmed another.

I peeked at him, trying not to laugh at how adorable he looked with his hair ruffled and Sonic on his shoulder.

"These are really good, amazing actually," I waved the papers in my hands, "remind me again why you need my help?"

"Because I want it," he whispered.

I swallowed thickly, the look in his eyes was indescribable.

"I guess we better get started then," I smiled. I grabbed a piece of paper and one of the pencils. "Do you have anything specific in mind for this song?"

His eyes flashed a stormy gray. "Yeah, I want it to start with the piano and slowly build to the crescendo. As for lyrics... I hadn't gotten that far."

"It looks like we have our work cut out for us then," I laughed. My brows furrowing, I asked, "Do you mind me asking what you do with these songs?"

"I record them," he responded.

"Are you trying to get a record deal?" It was an honest question. Maddox never talked about his lack of a job or spoke of what he wanted to do in the future.

He looked away from me and mumbled, "Something like that."

I ignored him and tapped the pencil against the paper as I thought.

The words came to me easily and I scribbled them across the paper.

Maddox watched with rapt attention as I worked. I purposely sat with my shoulders angled in a way that he wouldn't be able to see the words on the paper.

Minutes passed before he couldn't take it anymore. "Can I see it?"

"No," I scolded, "not yet."

True, he'd asked for my help so we were supposed to be writing it together, but I wanted to get all my thoughts out on paper before he saw it.

By the time I finished an hour had gone by.

I looked over, laughing when I saw Maddox had dozed off. He lay in one of the beanbags with Sonic sleeping on his chest. They were quite the pair.

I almost hated to wake him—almost being the key word there.

I found a drumstick lying on the floor—seriously, he had

them everywhere—and reached over to give his knee a tap. Okay, so I basically hit him with it, but whatever.

He sputtered awake, grabbing his knee. Sonic was knocked off his chest and into his lap with the motion.

"What was that for?" He groaned, rubbing the spot. "I think you gave me a bruise."

"Aw, poor baby." I pouted. "Here." I shoved the papers at him and scooted as far away as I could manage. No one—and I mean *no one*—had ever read one of my songs. I'd stopped singing them around the house about the time I stopped writing about cheese.

I honestly couldn't believe I'd let him talk me into this. He was such a charmer.

His mouth fell open the further he read and I resisted the urge to cringe. My songs were always so personal—like a diary entry—and it felt very much like I was baring my soul by letting him read one.

He picked up the pencil, crossing a few things out and adding his own lyrics.

Oh my God! He hated it! He totally hated it and he was trying to fix it.

I hid my face behind my fingers.

I couldn't stand the silence so I blurted, "It's okay if you hate it."

He was still quiet.

And then his hands were on mine, prying them away from my face.

His soft gray eyes met my blue ones. "Emma," he said my name slowly, "the song is amazing, truly. It... it blew my mind."

"But... but you were scribbling on it," I stuttered.

He grinned. "I'll admit to tweaking it a bit, but not much. Do you want to see what I changed?"

I nodded and he handed me the papers. He was right, he

didn't change much, and what he did was for the better. It made it a stronger song.

"Normally I go through at least ten drafts before I get the lyrics right, and you just... did that in no time." He shook his head, running his fingers through his dark hair. "You're really kind of amazing."

I grinned. "Are you just now figuring that out?"

"No," he laughed, "I knew it the moment I saw you. It's why I talked to you in the first place."

His words warmed my body with a pleased flush.

"Now, the *really* hard part," he held out a hand to help me up. "Piano time."

Once again I found myself seated on the bench in front of the piano with him. The bench was so small that it left no room between us.

"I was thinking something like this..." He started to play, and I closed my eyes.

The notes drifted off and I opened my eyes in time to see him shrug. "Something like that. You're better at this than I am."

"Hardly," I snorted.

I'd heard enough to pick up on the sound he wanted, so I played while he wrote everything down.

Music was second nature to me—as easy as breathing.

I loved that it was the same way for Maddox. It allowed us to connect in a way many other people couldn't. It was a special bond we could share.

"I want you to start from the beginning," he said, standing up. "Just give me a minute."

He headed over to his drum set and pulled the drumsticks out of his back pocket. "Now you can start."

I laughed, shaking my head at his bossiness, but did as he asked.

I'd played a quarter of the way through the song when he started in on the drums. Just a rumble at first before it built— just like he said he wanted it to do.

We finished the song and he jumped up with the drumsticks clutched in his hands. He pointed the drumsticks at me, biting his lip excitedly. "*That*, Em, is what you call a hit song."

"You think so?" I asked, still doubtful about my lyrics.

"I know so," he chimed. He moved from behind his drum set and over to me. He bent down and pressed his forehead against mine. "You remember how you told me you didn't know what you wanted to do after high school?"

I nodded.

"I think you just figured it out."

"What?" I asked, confused.

"You're a song writer, Em. Plain and simple."

I gaped at him and then started laughing. "No, I'm definitely not."

"You are and I'm going to make you believe me when that song is a hit."

I snorted. "In case you're forgetting, we're two teenagers writing songs in your guesthouse. It's not going to be a hit."

"You'll see," he grinned.

And something told me I would.

CHAPTER NINETEEN

SEVERAL DAYS LATER I found myself hurrying to keep up with Maddox's long-legged stride in downtown Winchester. The sun was just beginning to set, bathing us in a red-hued glow.

"Where are we going?" I asked.

Maddox grabbed my hand and drug me down the street. Apparently I wasn't walking fast enough for him. As per usual he was dressed in jeans—with his drumsticks in the back pocket—a black t-shirt, and a beanie.

"If I told you that it would spoil the surprise." He glanced at me over his shoulder, his lips rising in a smile.

Damn these surprises.

I narrowed my eyes before he looked away. "Will this surprise also send me running down the street screaming?"

He chuckled. "I don't know... depends on what you're afraid of. You did tell me you'd jump out of a plane with me, and I don't think this is nearly as scary as that."

"I really don't like not knowing what *this* is," I growled. Something told me I wasn't going to like what he had planned.

"My lips are sealed."

"I'm going to unseal them," I grumbled.

He merely laughed at me.

He finally stopped and opened the door to a local coffee shop. I knew this place.

"Oh, hell to the no," I pried my hand from his. "I know what you're trying to do and it's not happening." I shook my head.

"Emma," he groaned—he rarely ever used my whole name so I knew he was serious—"People deserve to hear our song. I want to see their reactions."

I sputtered, "Absolutely not." I didn't consider myself a shy person, I just wasn't social, but putting myself on a stage singing in front of people seemed too much for even me.

"Em," he reached up to tenderly cup my cheek, the sweet look in his eyes nearly melting. "Please do this for me."

Oh God, he was giving me the puppy dog eyes. I almost expected his bottom lip to turn down.

He leaned in closer, brushing his nose along the line of my jaw. "Please," he begged again.

My eyes fluttered closed and I let out a small moan. "You're not playing fair."

"I never said I would."

"Fine, I'll do it." I gave in easily. I had to trust Maddox when he said the song was good—and really that's what scared me more than singing, the fact that this song came from my heart.

Maddox grinned triumphantly. "Thank you." He kissed me quickly, pulling away before things could get heated.

He stepped away from me to open the door to Griffin's—the local coffee shop/restaurant... it was kind of a weird place where mostly teenagers and college students hung out—and I instantly missed the heat of his body.

Upon stepping inside I was met with the heavenly sent of coffee and cake.

"Hey, Griffin," Maddox called to the burly owner, who manned the register.

He lifted his hand in a small wave. "You guys playing

today?" He asked.

"No, just us." Maddox slung an arm around my shoulders.

Griffin chuckled. "I'm kinda relieved your brother isn't here. I had to break up a fight the last time he was."

Maddox sighed beside me. "Sorry about that."

Griffin shrugged. "It's in the past. Can I get you guys anything?"

Maddox looked to me.

"I'll have an iced coffee." I reached into my bag for my wallet.

"I'll have the same," Maddox told him, reaching for his own wallet in his back pocket.

I was determined to beat him. He was always treating me, now it was my turn. I bumped him with my hip, hard enough that he stumbled and dropped his wallet.

"Here," I handed Griffin a ten dollar bill.

The older man chuckled. "I like you."

"Jesus, Em," Maddox grumbled, wiping dust off his wallet, "I think you gave me another bruise."

I laughed. "Sorry, I had to."

Griffin handed me my change and went to make our drinks.

"I would've bought it," he grumbled, sliding his wallet back in his pocket.

"I know you would've," I assured him. "But I wanted to get this."

He mumbled something under his breath about me being so damn bossy sometimes. My lips lifted in a smile.

Griffin handed over our drinks and I followed Maddox to a table in the back corner that was partially hidden by a wall.

The coffee shop was fairly busy, but not as crowded as it was on open mic night. I'd come with Sadie once and the place had been *packed* with little room between bodies.

I began to fidget with nerves—first tugging on the ends of

my hair, and then playing with the straw wrapper. I knew it was only a matter of time before Maddox dragged me onto the small stage and all the people here heard our song.

Maddox seemed equally as restless. He sat drumming his fingers against the top of the table. Then again, Maddox was always drumming or tapping on something.

"Can we get this over with?" I finally hissed.

He chuckled, his eyes crinkling at the corners. "We're singing a song, not going to the dentist. You don't just get it over with. You have to wait until it feels right."

"In that case, this doesn't feel right. I think we should leave."

I started to stand, but he grabbed my arm to keep me from running away. "Not so fast."

I sat back down. "What if people hate it?" I asked him, letting him see just how much that thought worried me.

He leaned forward with a contemplative look. "The way I see it, there are always going to be the ones that love you and the ones that hate you—let's face it, people love to tear others down, but as long as you're confident within yourself then nothing else matters."

"I was talking about the song, not myself," I countered.

He grinned, stifling a chuckle. "The same principle applies. If you're confident with the song, what others think shouldn't matter to you."

Why did he always have to be right? It was annoyingly unfair.

I squared my shoulders and jutted my chin out. "I believe in our song."

"I believe in *you*." He stood up and kissed my cheek before nodding towards the stage.

He didn't need to say anything. I knew this was it.

I followed him to the stage. There weren't any drums, but

there was a guitar and a keyboard. Maddox picked up the guitar and sat on a stool, pointing at the keyboard for me.

Once I was on the stage, seated behind the keyboard, all my nerves disappeared.

I loved this song and I was proud of it. More than just the two of us deserved to hear it.

Maddox introduced us to the people hanging around the coffee shop.

"This is a little something we wrote together and I hope you guys will love it as much as we do."

He nodded at me and I knew that was my cue to start playing.

I took a deep breath, bracing my fingers above the keys.

And then I started to play.

You could tell the people were worried at first—since it started out so slow—but once we started singing and the song built towards the middle they got more into it.

It was an indescribable feeling watching people fall in love with our song.

When it ended I couldn't stop the goofy smile that lit my face.

I don't think I'd ever been happier in my entire life than I was right now.

I stood up from behind the keyboard, but before I could leave the stage Maddox had me in his arms, sealing my lips in a kiss that stole my breath. I clung to his shoulders, my cheeks heating with a blush as people gathered around the stage started to whistle and call at us.

When Maddox felt that he'd kissed me thoroughly he pulled away enough to put his forehead against mine.

I could see that he wanted to say something, it was there on the tip of his tongue, but he stopped himself.

He took my hand and we headed back to the table to grab

our drinks before leaving.

I heard someone call after us as the door closed behind us, but Maddox didn't slow. In fact, he quickened his strides.

I basically had to jog to keep up with him as we headed to his car. Once safe inside he glanced over at me.

"After that adrenaline rush, I'm thinking we should do something else crazy. We're on a roll here."

I raised a brow. "Like what?" I had a feeling I already knew what he was going to say—and it was going to happen eventually anyway.

"I think it's time to go skydiving."

I buckled my seatbelt and smiled at him. "You know I'm in."

He grinned, his laughter filling the car. "You might be the only girl on the planet more scared to sing a song she wrote, than to jump out of a plane."

I shrugged. "There's no judgment with jumping out of a plane. You just do it. Singing a song you wrote... that's personal. Like someone reading your diary."

His eyes sparkled with that information. "You have a diary."

"*No*," I drew out the word.

Before pulling away from the curb he grabbed his phone. "Would you mind if the guys tagged along? I mentioned it to them awhile ago and they were pissed I was going without them."

"I don't mind at all," I assured him. Sometimes I spent so much time alone that it was all too easy to forget that he had friends, and I had Sadie. I'd been completely neglecting her this summer. If the situation was reversed and she'd ditched me the entire summer for a guy I'd be pretty mad. We'd hung out a few times, but not like we normally did. I was going to have to learn how to prioritize. I didn't need to spend all my time with Maddox.

"Great," Maddox grinned, either not noticing that I was lost in my thoughts or choosing not to comment on it.

I sat quietly while Maddox called Ezra to round up the guys. I heard him giving directions to the skydiving place.

I didn't feel nervous at all. Maybe there was something wrong with me. But I actually felt exhilarated at the thought of jumping out of a plane. It felt like I was literally going to spread my wings and fly.

I just hoped I didn't go splat.

MADDOX, MATHIAS, EZRA, Hayes, and I all stood being instructed on what we could and could not do.

It was quite a lengthy explanation they went through.

Basically the gist was: Don't be a fucking idiot.

Easy enough.

We got strapped into the harnesses and my body buzzed with an excited energy.

This was hands down the most insane thing I'd ever done.

I knew a sensible person would be afraid—but all common sense had left me the moment I met Maddox. He had me throwing my rulebook out the window and living life to the fullest.

Once we were suited up they herded us onto the plane, going over a few more rules again. Since we were newbies we all ended up being strapped to an instructor.

I ended up paired with Tyler—an instructor that was only a few years older than us, and insanely good-looking in a California surfer type of way.

"Hi," he smiled, his blue eyes shining.

"Hi," I replied, glancing towards Maddox. He had his teeth barred and I swore he was growling.

"Down boy," Ezra told him, like he was a dog.

I couldn't help laughing and Maddox seemed to relax some when he realized he had my attention.

"What made you guys want to go skydiving?" Tyler asked. His question seemed to address all of us, but he stared at me. I squirmed, feeling uncomfortable. I mean, his question was innocent enough, but the way he was looking at me wasn't. His eyes perused my body lazily with a cocky smile curving his full lips. I imagined they didn't get very many girls willing to throw their body out of a plane, so he was probably intrigued by that.

"We just fucking wanted to," Mathias sneered, piping in before Maddox could say anything. "And while you're at it, maybe you could stop looking at my brother's girlfriend like you want to fucking lick her. M'kay?"

Maddox's lips quirked into a smile at his brother defending him. Ezra just laughed while Hayes shook his head. I stood shocked. I didn't think I'd ever heard Mathias use so many words at one time.

Tyler's head dropped and he took an uneasy step away from me.

The man that was supposed to be diving with Mathias switched places with Tyler. I guessed they wanted to avoid any unnecessary drama—and they might've been afraid of Mathias. His glare was icy and probably made small children cry.

Once the switch was made my new partner set about attaching us.

Maddox reached for my hand, giving mine a reassuring squeeze. I smiled at him, trying to show that I wasn't scared and he didn't need to worry.

Within minutes we reached the altitude we needed to jump.

This was it.

No turning back.

"Who wants to go first?" Tyler asked.

My hand shot in the air. No way was I letting the guys go first.

Maddox chuckled at my enthusiasm, ducking his head to hide his smile.

"Alright then," the guy strapped to me said. I didn't know his name.

The door slid open and I took a startled step back as the air swept into the plane. The guys laughed at me, but I ignored them.

"Ready when you are." The man told me.

I closed my eyes.

One, two, three.

And then I jumped.

CHAPTER TWENTY

"THAT WAS AMAZING! Fantastical! Absolutely magical!" I exclaimed, twirling around in the grass.

"Someone make her shut up," Mathias groaned, puking his guts up.

"You're just jealous, because she didn't get sick and you did," Maddox countered. He came to stand by my side, his fingers grazing my hip. I stood on my tiptoes placing a light, chaste kiss on his check.

Mathias wiped his mouth with the back of his hand. "I can't fucking believe people do that for fun."

Maddox rolled his eyes. "Do you think you could try speaking without using a variation of the word 'fuck' in every sentence?"

Mathias laughed. "I don't fucking think so."

Maddox grumbled and turned to me. "He's ridiculous."

"He's your brother," I countered.

"And if we weren't identical I'd never know we were related," he retorted. Mathias overheard and gave him the finger.

"I fucking love you too, princess," Mathias sneered.

Maddox narrowed his eyes. "Now you're just saying

it to spite me."

"Yes I fucking am," Mathias replied, trudging through the grass towards the building.

Maddox turned to me, his expression unreadable. "Be glad you're an only child," he grumbled. "Siblings suck."

I laughed, taking his hand in mine. "You love him."

He sighed, pinching the bridge of his nose with his free hand. "Yeah, I know. That makes it worse."

"Are you guys coming?!" Mathias called over his shoulder. Hayes and Ezra were specks in the distance.

"Yeah, yeah," Maddox waved him on.

"You know," I piped in, my voice low enough that Mathias wouldn't hear, "I'm really surprised he said what he did on the plane."

"Me too," Maddox agreed. "But Mathias is really protective of his family," he glanced down at me briefly, "and he considers you a part of our family."

My throat caught at that. "W-what?"

He grinned, drawing me close so he could press his lips to my forehead in a tender kiss. "You're not going anywhere, Emma."

I closed my eyes, reveling in his words. They were nice to hear. I was falling hard for Maddox and now I was starting to think maybe I wasn't the only one that felt that way.

Once in the parking lot we split up from the guys. The other three headed to Ezra's massive Yukon while Maddox and I made our way to his sports car. My poor little Volkswagen had barely been driven any this summer. I'd probably be lucky if it ran by the time school started.

"You know," Maddox started, buckling his seatbelt, "I've realized something."

"What?" I asked.

"We didn't need these adventures... yeah, they were fun, but we don't need them to have a good time. Being with you is enough."

My heart stuttered, skipping a beat in my chest. Since I was the least romantic person on the planet, I said, "Does this mean we don't have to go on that hike now?" If I recalled correctly the hike was the only thing we hadn't done.

He laughed heartily. "We don't have to do the hike."

"Thank God," I breathed a sigh of relief. "I was already dreading the blisters I was going to get from that."

He smiled at me—and that smile alone made my whole body flood with happiness. I'd never known that my feelings could be so in tune with someone else's, but with Maddox we were in sync.

I knew then that I was in love with him.

This wasn't the kind of love that was fleeting.

It was real and true.

It was a forever kind of love.

This realization didn't scare me—not the way it might have a few months ago. Instead, it made me smile. I'd managed to find the one person on the planet that was absolutely perfect for me.

"Where are we going now?" I asked, laying my head on his shoulder watching the world whip by us through the windshield.

"Does it matter?" He asked.

"No," I replied.

As long as I was with him I knew only good things could be headed my way.

"I'VE ALWAYS WANTED to come here," Maddox told me, parking the car along the side of the road.

We were high up on the edge of the mountain and I knew that straight down below us was the river.

Maddox slipped from the car, walking to the edge.

I did the same, sitting down so my legs dangled over the side.

Below us I could see people at the water's edge. It was flowing too fast for swimming or kayaking. It was beautiful though—the way the water lapped against the rocks and the greenery of the trees blanketing the area.

Maddox sat down beside me, looking up towards the sky before speaking. "Sometimes I forget just how beautiful it is here." He closed his eyes, letting out a deep breath. "For so long all I wanted to do was get away, and now I can't imagine living anywhere else."

I wrapped my hands around his arm and laid my head on his shoulder. "I know what you mean."

"Do you ever think you'll see him again?" He asked suddenly.

"Who?" I replied, confused.

"Your dad," he whispered.

I shrugged. "I doubt it. Yeah, it sucked that he left, but I'm better off with him gone. If he showed up tomorrow and apologized for everything he's done, then *maybe* I could forgive him and move on... but without an apology, he isn't worth my time. People should own up to their mistakes instead of brushing it under the rug. I *can't* forget about what he did, but I could forgive him if he asked me to—if he proved to me that he deserved it. But I don't think I'll hear from him ever again. I used to not be okay with that..." I trailed off. Refocusing, I added, "But now I am." I lifted my head to look at him. "Why do you ask?"

He shrugged.

"Maddox," I urged.

He glanced out at the water, a muscle in his jaw twitching. "I've been thinking about my mom lately... and wondering if I could ever stomach seeing her again... and I don't think I can. I know the past is the past, but I can't forgive her for everything she did to us. Especially to Mathias. Does that make me a shitty person?" When he looked at me I could see the worry swimming in his silvery gaze. "Does that make me just like her?"

"No, not at all," I said quickly. "You went through a lot and someone like your mom—I'm sorry, but I don't think they change. Some people are just mean."

"You're right." He cupped my cheek, kissing the top of my head. He swallowed thickly, looking down at the water and kicking his feet against the ledge. "I never want to end up like her."

"You won't."

"How can you be so sure?" He asked, his eyes full of pain. I didn't like seeing him hurt like this.

"Because you're already nothing like her. You're a good, kind person."

He winced, like my words had stabbed him. "I'm a liar."

"No, you're not," I shook my head.

"I am." His jaw tightened and when he looked at me I swore there were tears in his eyes, but the moisture disappeared quickly. "But I can't regret my decisions. I won't."

"Maddox, what are you talking about?" I was completely lost. Where was this coming from?

He shook his head rapidly back and forth. He stood up, extending his hand for me. "Now's not the time."

"When will be the time?" I pestered. Something was really bothering him and I wanted to get to the bottom of it.

He looked away from my eyes and once again stared beyond at the breathtaking view.

"Never."

CHAPTER TWENTY-ONE

"HAPPY BIRTHDAY TO you," my mom sang, barging into my room before the sun was up, "Happy Birthday to you! Happy Birthday dear Emma! Happy Birthday to you!"

August twelfth. My birthday. I was shaking with excitement—*not*.

I threw a pillow over my face and groaned, "Thanks, mom."

My bed dipped when she sat on the end. She pried the pillow from my face. "I was thinking we could go to Marigold's for breakfast. Get some egg sandwiches."

"That sounds good, mom," I yawned. I'd come home late last night from Maddox's. We'd ended up having an all day Lord of the Rings movie marathon in the basement. Even Ezra, Mathias, and Hayes had joined us. I knew from some hints he dropped last night that he had something planned for my birthday, but I didn't know what. I only prayed it wasn't a party. I didn't do parties. Ever.

"Should we invite Sadie?" She asked.

I brightened at that. "Yeah, I'd like that."

"Alright, get out of bed, shower, and get ready." She tapped my foot before standing.

"Is that your way of telling me I stink?" I frowned.

"No," she laughed, "that's my way of telling you your hair looks like a rat's nest."

"Thanks, mom," I groaned, rolling out of bed. "Mornings suck," I grumbled, heading to the bathroom.

"Oh, Emma, don't be dramatic," she sighed, going to the kitchen—probably to make tea.

I showered, making sure to use half a bottle of conditioner on my hair to work out the knots and tangles.

I blow-dried my hair, trying to make it look halfway decent. Most days I just didn't care. But for my mom to comment on it, it had to be looking pretty bad.

I perused my closet for something to wear and ended up settling on my go to of shorts and a tank, but I opted to wear a loose one-shoulder sweater on top. It was cream colored and made my blue eyes appear even bluer.

I grabbed my phone off the night table and sent Sadie a quick text about breakfast. She was quick to reply that she'd go.

"Are you ready?" My mom asked, sitting at the table with her cup of tea.

"Yep," I nodded.

"Your hair looks better," she smiled. "You didn't happen to pull any furry creatures out of there, did you? Or maybe a hedgehog?"

I blushed, remembering the day I thought I'd lost Sonic. "No furry creatures here." I bent over, shaking my hair around.

She laughed at me, grabbing her keys off the kitchen counter. "Oh, Emmie," she sighed. "Are we supposed to pick Sadie up?" She asked, setting her mug in the sink.

I straightened. "Yeah."

She put her keys back down and said, "Oh, I want to give this to you first."

Before I could ask what it was she headed back to her room and returned with a carefully wrapped package.

I sat down on the floor—chairs were for the weak—and started ripping the paper off.

I lifted the lid of the box off and gasped. A pretty floral dress sat on the bottom, but it was the gold watch on top that had my mouth falling open.

"Mom," I choked. I knew, without even picking it up, that it was expensive. "It's so pretty. You didn't need to spend so much."

"I know," she smiled down at me, "but it's your eighteenth birthday and I wanted to do something special. I even had the back engraved."

I picked it up and flipped it over so I could read the tiny letters inscribed on the back.

Emmie,
I believe in you. Always.
Love, Mom.

I stood up, the watch clasped in my hand as the box fell to the side, and hugged my mom. "Thank you so much. I love it and I love you."

She hugged me back fiercely, like she never wanted to let go.

I'd never thought about it before, but it was probably scary for my mom knowing that this was my last year of high school.

It was scary for me too, in the sense that I had no idea what I wanted to do, and I wasn't sure if I was ready to leave my mom. It was terrifying thinking about going out on my own, but it would have to happen one day.

She let me go and I stepped back to snap the watch on my wrist. I was already thinking about wearing my new dress later for Maddox's mysterious plans. I carried the box with my dress back to my room and set it on the bed.

"I'll be in the car!" My mom called, and I scurried out of my room.

When we got to Sadie's house she already sat outside on the front porch steps, her eyes glued to her phone's screen. She looked up at the sound of the car and smiled. She stood, grabbing up a gift bag.

I already sat in the back and I reached over to push the door open so she could join me.

"Happy Birthday, bitch," she said, laughter twinkling in her voice as she handed me the bag and closed the door. I started to grab the tissue paper, but she stopped me. "You might want to wait." Her eyes flickered to my mom.

I paled. "What did you do?"

"Nothing bad," she assured me, reaching for the seatbelt.

"I don't believe you," I hissed, holding the bag out like it was grenade.

"Why do you have such little faith in me?" She sighed. "It's an awesome gift. I just want you to wait to open it."

"Okay," I said slowly, sitting the bag on the floor.

"How are things with lover boy?" Sadie asked.

"Great," I smiled.

She grinned evilly. "Then I got the perfect gift."

Screw waiting. I grabbed the bag, ripping away the tissue paper.

"What the hell?" I held the tiny lacy black bra and panty set in my hands. "No way." I shook my head, shoving it back into the bag. "You are the worst best friend in the history of best friends."

"Hey, just trying to help you out here." She raised her hands in defense. "That bra is a miracle worker. It makes your boobs look twice as big."

I crossed my arms over my chest. "I don't think I need any help in that department, thank you very much," I grumbled.

243

She laughed, grabbing her breasts. "Well I do."

"Then you can have it." I handed her the bag.

"Don't be absurd," she shoved it back in my hands. "You need some sexy lingerie. There you go."

I glared at the offending bag.

"There's also a gift card in there so you can go back and get more." She waggled her brows. "Because I know you'll want more."

"Stop it," I hissed, my whole face flaming. This would've been mortifying at any time, but having my mom driving the car made it a hundred times worse.

"And," she whispered, "condoms too."

"I need air!" I gasped, reaching to push the automatic button but apparently my mom had the child's lock on. "Air, please," I begged, trying to roll down the window with my bare hands. I wasn't opposed to jumping out of the moving vehicle to escape this conversation.

My mom obliged and as soon as the window was down I stuck my head out of it like I was a dog.

Sadie giggled. "Stop acting like you're five."

I wished I could, but I wasn't like her. I couldn't talk about sex as easily. It made me uncomfortable and squeamish.

"I was only kidding, Emma," she groaned, tugging on my shoulder to pull me back inside the vehicle. "You don't need to freak out. It was a joke."

When I managed to compose myself I slipped my head back into the vehicle and my mom rolled up the window. "I'm sorry," I mumbled, glancing at Sadie sheepishly.

"It's okay," she laughed it off, "but you've got to get over it eventually. You're not going to be a virgin forever."

I squirmed restlessly in my seat and whispered under my breath so my mom couldn't hear. "It's not the idea of sex that scares me, it's just talking about it. I feel like it should be a private thing."

"Oh. My. God." Sadie's mouth popped open. "You've already slept with him, haven't you? And you didn't tell me!"

My mom's eyes flicked up to look at me in the rearview mirror.

"No," I sputtered, "of course not." I scoffed at the idea that she'd suggest such a thing. Had I thought about it? Yes. I knew I was ready. I knew he was it for me.

She smiled slowly—like the cat that ate the canary. "But you want to, don't you? That's why you got so embarrassed."

"Shut up," I mumbled, looking away.

"Aw, my best friend is officially all grown up."

I whipped my head in her direction. "And your best friend is really beginning to question this friendship."

"Okay, shutting up now." She mimed zipping her lips and throwing away the key—but the effect was kind of lost when she smiled through the whole process.

"We're here," my mom announced.

I had never been so excited to get out of the car before.

I basically tumbled outside, catching myself before I could scrape my knees on the sidewalk. I straightened, pretending that hadn't happened—but Sadie's snicker let me know she saw.

"Don't say a thing," I growled.

"I wasn't going to." She hid a giggle behind her hand.

I hurried into Marigold's before I could make an even bigger fool of myself.

Two of the three tables were already taken, so Sadie and I snagged the last one, leaving my mom to place our order with Betty.

My mom joined us a few minutes later and crossed her fingers together, leveling me with *the look*. I was a second away from asking her what I did when she spoke. "Since you haven't let me throw a birthday party for you since you were in elementary school, I'm telling you right now that I *will* be throwing you a graduation party next summer. We have to at least celebrate that."

"Sure, mom," I agreed. I didn't need, nor want, a party but it was clear to me that she wanted one, so I'd suffer through.

"We should do a joint one," Sadie chimed in. "We could do something bigger and nicer than two separate parties."

"That's an excellent idea," my mom smiled. They launched into a conversation about all party related things, while I wanted to hide beneath the table to avoid a party that wouldn't be taking place for nearly a year. Actually, the thought of a graduation party didn't give me hives the way a birthday party would. What *really* scared me was the fact that I was going to be graduating and thrust into the real world. I wasn't ready. Not. At. All. Couldn't I stay a kid forever? That would be great.

In no time Betty was bringing drinks and our breakfast sandwiches to the table. "Happy Birthday, sweetie," she told me with a bright smile.

"Thanks." I smiled back.

My stomach rumbled at the sight of the food. I hadn't realized how hungry I was, but now I was starving.

I devoured my sandwich like I was never going to see food again, but I didn't really care.

"I'm stuffed," I declared, shoving my empty plate away from me.

As if conjured by my words Betty breezed over to our table again, this time with an elegant cake on a platter.

"Your favorite," she declared, "lavender cake with lemon icing."

Tears pricked my eyes at the kind gesture. "Thank you so much," I told her honestly. "And thank you." I turned to address my mom and Sadie. "I don't know what I'd do without the two of you."

"Don't make me cry!" Sadie pointed a finger at me, waving her free hand at her face as if the motion alone would dry the tears in her eyes.

I ignored her dramatics and turned to my mom. "Seriously, thank you for putting up with me for the last eighteen years. I know things haven't always been easy, but no matter what you've always been there for me, and I can't thank you enough for that."

My mom clambered out of her seat and wrapped her arms around me. "I love you so much, Emmie. You're the greatest thing to ever happen to me. Never forget that."

I hugged her back just as fiercely. I knew I was lucky to have a mom as amazing as mine.

When we broke apart I saw that Betty had returned with candles. "Shall we light them now?" She asked with a kind smile.

"Absolutely," I nodded.

She stuck eighteen candles into the top of the cake and lit them. The three of them began to sing and then it was time for me to make a wish and blow out the candles.

Only I didn't make a wish, because I had everything I could possibly ever want.

MY PHONE RANG and I hurried to answer it when I saw Maddox's name flashing on the screen. He still avoided texting me if he didn't have to. It was one of his quirks I'd grown to love.

"Hey," I answered the phone, sounding rather breathless.

"I'll pick you up at seven. Wear something nice."

I wrinkled my nose. "Are we going out?"

He chuckled. "I'm not answering *any* of your questions, but dress nice, and I'll be there at seven," he repeated.

"I have a car, you know." I put a hand on my hip, getting into a defensive stance even though he wasn't here.

"Yeah, and I'm pretty sure that thing needs to be driven to the nearest junkyard. It has rust all over it."

I gasped. "How dare you mock my car? Daisy has been a faithful companion."

He grew quiet and then his warm laugh sounded over the line. "You named your car Daisy?"

"Well you named your hedgehog Sonic," I countered, then wanted to smack myself in the forehead for such a silly comeback.

"And it's a damn good name—Mathias stop that! You're going to eat it all before we're done!"

"Uh... what's going on?" I asked.

"Nothing," he mumbled. "I've gotta go."

Before I could respond the line clicked dead. I stared down at the screen, shaking my head. What the hell just happened?

Since I still had a few hours before I needed to get ready I played the piano for a while and then read for a bit.

I decided to put a little bit more effort into my appearance than I normally did. My hair was already curly, but I did my best to tame the tendrils so I didn't look like Medusa. I even took the time to put on more makeup. When I finished I swore a different person stared back at me in the mirror.

I checked the time and saw that I had thirty minutes until Maddox was supposed to arrive—which meant he'd probably be here in fifteen.

I put on the new flower print dress my mom bought me. It was navy with large pink and orange flowers. The straps were thicker and thankfully it didn't dip low in the front. A thin brown belt cinched it in at the waist. I twirled in front of the mirror. The smile on my face was one I hadn't seen in a long time—and I knew I owed my newfound happiness to Maddox.

Turning away from my reflection I grabbed a cream colored cardigan, just in case I needed the extra warmth, and slipped on a pair of flats.

My phone rang and before I could say hello, Maddox said, "I'll be there in five."

I shook my head, and hung up, before heading outside to wait on the front porch.

I heard the low rumble of the car's engine before it appeared on the street.

I started towards the car, but he jumped out and held up a hand, "No."

Well then.

He ducked back inside the car and reappeared with a vase full of flowers.

"Those are beautiful," I gasped as he neared me. I grabbed my key and unlocked the door so he could set them inside. "Orchids, right?"

He nodded, grinning. "One for each day we've known each other."

My eyes widened in surprise and my mouth fell open slightly. "Maddox." His name was no more than a gasp on my lips. I was touched beyond words.

He headed straight back into my room with the flowers, sitting them on the nightstand. He appraised them for a moment and nodded in approval.

He whipped back around and his smile nearly blinded me. "Happy Birthday, Em." He said softly, taking my face in his large hands. Before I could respond he angled my head back, lowering his lips to mine in a soft kiss that still managed to flood my insides with butterflies. When he pulled away he placed a tender kiss on the end of my nose. A breathy sigh escaped my lips at the sweet gesture.

He reached down and clasped my hand in his. "I really hope I can make this birthday special for you." With his free hand he glided his fingers along my cheek. "I want you to love your birthday again, instead of dreading it."

"You're one of a kind," I whispered. Most people wouldn't care the way Maddox did. His heart was so kind and pure, that at times I felt undeserving of his affections.

He shook his head, a small smile playing on his lips. "No, that's you, Em." He kissed my forehead and guided me out of my room and outside. He opened the passenger door for me and before I lowered into the car, he caught me by the arm and pulled me against his chest. "You look beautiful." His breath caressed the skin of my cheek and my body shook from the intensity of my feelings. I felt weak in the knees—and that was something I thought only existed in books and movies.

I swallowed thickly—trying to dam back the flood of emotions I felt—and looked him up and down the way he had me. I don't know how I'd missed it earlier, but he was dressed nicely in a pair of dark gray dress pants, with a crisp white button down shirt tucked into them, topped off with a black belt. He looked absolutely lickable. Yes, lickable.

When I didn't say anything, but continued to peruse his body with my eyes, he grinned wickedly. "Like what you see?" He leaned in, sweeping my hair over my shoulder so his lips could touch my ear. "Because I promise you'll love it even more when all my clothes are off."

I gasped and my arm whipped out to smack him in the shoulder. "Maddox," I scolded, but he simply laughed at me as I slipped inside the car.

I was pretty sure he only liked to say things like that to see what kind of reaction he could get out of me. Next time I was going to call his bluff and tell him to strip.

Oh God.

What if he wasn't bluffing and he actually started to take off his clothes?

I might die.

Of either embarrassment or the sight of his too perfect body.

My cheeks heated at the visual that began to play out in my head.

Stop it! I scolded myself, hoping the flush left my cheeks by the time Maddox jogged around the car and slipped in the driver's side. I did not need him asking questions, because when he did I usually ended up spilling the truth.

I buckled my seatbelt and didn't bother asking him where we were headed. It would've been a waste of my breath, because there was no way Maddox would tell me anything.

Since he told me to dress up I figured he was taking me to a fancy restaurant. Not really my scene, but it was the thought that counted.

However, I was surprised when he ended up driving to his house.

"Did you forget something?" I asked, my brows furrowing.

"Nope. This is our destination." He grinned, slipping out of the vehicle.

I scurried out and to his side—terrified that he'd thrown me a surprise party. I prayed to whichever god would listen that there was no party.

He wrapped an arm around my waist and guided my shaking body forward.

Please, no party. Please. I'm begging you.

My eyes had squished shut and when he swung the door open and I heard no shrieks of 'surprise!' I figured it was safe to open my eyes.

The guesthouse was surprisingly empty.

I stepped inside, half expecting someone to jump out at me.

Finally I turned to Maddox, my hands clasped together. "I'm so confused."

He smiled, crossed his arms over his broad chest and leaned against the wall. "Did you really think I'd throw you a party after you told me you didn't like that sort of thing?"

I shrugged. "Maybe."

He shook his head, his lips upturned slightly. He stepped forward slowly, like a lion stalking its prey. He took my cheeks between his hands and stared into my eyes. "That would not be the way to get you to love your birthday again. We're keeping things simple."

"Simple?" I repeated.

"Yes," he whispered, brushing his lips lightly against mine. It wasn't even a kiss, just a simple caress, but I still felt it all the way down to my toes.

He stepped back and I looked around, noting that the lights were dimmed and candles were scattered all over the place— already lit. It created a warm glow throughout the space.

"I gave the guys a heads up that we were almost here and they lit them. I don't want you to think I almost burned the house down," he chuckled.

"It's beautiful," I whispered in awe.

"This isn't even the best part." His voice lowered and his hand found my waist, pulling me against his body.

"I-It's not?" I stuttered.

He grinned, nuzzling my neck. "It's only beginning."

With those words he guided me into the small kitchen and motioned for me to sit on one of the stools.

"Birthday surprise number one... you get to watch me make you dinner." He smiled boyishly, backing towards the sink.

"And what will you be making Chef Wade?"

He washed his hands and swiveled to face me. "Your favorite."

252

"And what's my favorite?" I asked, raising a brow.

"Pizza." He answered with confidence.

I grinned. "I guess I've made no secret of that."

He grabbed a canister of dough from the refrigerator and before he could pop it, I asked, "Can I do it?"

"It's your birthday," he frowned, "you're supposed to sit there and watch me work."

I laughed. "But I want to help."

He grinned, his silver eyes flashing with my words. "Okay," he agreed, "only because it will be more fun."

I hopped up from the barstool and took the canister from his hands. "This is my favorite part," I told him, defending my actions.

He chuckled in response, opening a cabinet and grabbing a pizza stone. "Have at it, Em."

I smacked the canister against the counter and it popped open. I took out the dough, smoothing it onto the stone in a perfect circle.

Maddox grabbed the sauce and toppings from the refrigerator while I worked.

"This was a great idea." I smiled up at him, unable to hide my joy.

He dumped some sauce in the middle of the pizza and grabbed a spoon from a drawer to spread it around. Unable to control myself I stood on my tiptoes, kissing his stubbled jaw.

He smiled down at me. "What was that for?"

I shrugged. "It was because I wanted to."

He chuckled, lowering his head. "And maybe I want to do this." He pressed a light kiss to my lips. Even though it was only a quick touch of our lips it left my whole body tingling... and thinking about the fact that I'd put Sadie's gift to use. Yep. I was wearing the lingerie. But I was never telling her that. She'd be too satisfied with being right.

To distract myself from any possible naughty thoughts I grabbed the bag of cheese and began sprinkling it on the pizza.

I usually only ate cheese pizza, but we ended up adding green peppers, onion, pepperoni, and sausage, before sticking it in the oven.

Maddox set the timer and turned towards me. "How's your birthday so far?"

"Pretty perfect," I confessed.

His grin was infectious. "Good." He reached for his phone and pressed a button. Music began to play from a speaker and he grabbed me around the waist. "Dance with me," he whispered in my ear.

I nodded, lacing my fingers with his as we slow danced through the kitchen.

He lifted my arm spinning me around and into his chest. I let out a giggle, clinging to his neck. I was so full of happiness that I was ready to burst.

He began to sing the lyrics of the song softly under his breath.

He twirled me again, this time dipping me down and kissing my neck. I couldn't wipe the smile off my face, and I didn't want to.

When he stood up straight I tightened my arms around his neck, my fingers delving into the short strands of his hair.

"I love you." I stared into his eyes as I said the words, refusing to back down. Even if it was nerve-wracking laying my feelings out for him, I wasn't going to be ashamed.

His smile was blindingly bright. One hand stayed on the curve of my hip while his other found the nape of my neck. "Say it again." He pleaded with a look of awe on his face.

I leaned closer. "I love you." I swept my lips lightly over his as I said the words. "I love you." I brushed my lips against his jaw. "I love you." This time I stood on my tiptoes so my lips met his ear.

He lowered his head to the crook of my neck and my eyes fluttered closed. "I love you too," he breathed, then placed his lips lightly against the spot where my pulse raced. I shivered at the words. I hadn't expected them to sound that good rolling off his tongue.

For a moment we simply clung to each other, our words lingering in the air.

I loved him.

And he loved me.

I felt complete with that knowledge.

He brushed my hair away from my face, staring into my eyes. He opened his mouth, as if to speak, but silenced himself. With a low growl he dove for my lips. We crashed together, clinging to one another like we were the only thing holding each other up. He fisted the fabric of my dress in his hand, raising it dangerously high. One of my legs wrapped around his waist and before I could move any further he grasped my hips and lifted me onto the counter—all without breaking our kiss. With me sitting on the counter we were now at the same height. He stepped between my legs, grasping my thighs.

"I love you," he murmured against my lips.

I smiled at his words, loving the sound of them.

He placed light kisses along my jaw and down my neck. His lips headed even lower, towards my breasts, but then the timer went off and he jumped away from me like he'd been burned. He smiled sheepishly, running his fingers through his brown hair. He turned away from me to grab the pizza and while he wasn't looking I fanned my hands around my face. Holy Hell that had been hot—in both senses of the word.

He turned the oven off and grabbed the pizza, setting it on a rack above the counter.

After that kiss I'd lost my appetite.

All I wanted was Maddox.

And that was saying something, because I really did love pizza.

He left the pizza to cool and closed the space between us. His palms rested on the counter beside my hips. So close, but not close enough.

He leaned in, peering into my eyes. He tilted his head slightly to the side, his tongue flicking out to wet his lips.

"So, you love me?" He smiled happily.

I wrapped my arms around his neck. "Yes... do you need to hear me say it again?"

His eyes darkened with warmth. "I'll always want to hear you say it."

"Forever?" I asked hesitantly.

He cupped my cheek, smoothing his thumb over my skin. His eyes flicked from my lips to my eyes and he let out a small sigh. "For as long as you'll have me."

"Forever then," I reaffirmed, kissing him.

He broke the kiss before it could get too heated. "I want to give you your present... well one of them," he shrugged. "Wait here," he held up one finger.

He jogged up the stairs and returned a minute later with a package. It wasn't the best-wrapped package, but I wasn't going to diss his wrapping skills, because frankly it was better than anything I could do.

I ripped the paper off—I wasn't one of those people who removed it neatly. I always tore it off like I was an animal.

Beneath the paper was a plain brown box with colored duct tape holding the ends together. "Do you have a knife?" I asked him.

"Oh, yeah." He opened a drawer and handed me one.

I cut into the tape and opened the flaps.

Whatever was inside was wrapped in a thick brown paper. "You really don't want me to see this present do you?" I laughed.

He chuckled, ducking his head to hide his smile. "It came like that."

I lifted the item out and pulled away the paper, smiling at the object.

"I know it's silly," he started, "but it reminded me of us, and you like to drink tea, so..." He trailed off, looking slightly embarrassed. "If you hate it, just tell me, it won't hurt my feelings."

I clutched the mug to my chest. "Are you kidding me? This is my new favorite mug, it has officially beat out Tea-Rex."

He grinned. "Good."

I held the mug out, smiling at the design.

It had two hedgehogs on it, one stuck to the other, with the apt quote of: *I'm stuck on you.*

"It's perfect," I whispered. To some it might've seemed like a stupid gift, but for me he couldn't have gotten anything better.

"Do you want to see your second gift?" He asked, taking the box and paper so he could throw it in the trashcan.

I nodded eagerly.

He took my hand and I hopped off the counter. He led me over to the side of the guesthouse with all the instruments and Sonic's cage... only there were two cages now.

"What did you do?" I gasped.

"Your mom said it was okay..." He scratched the back of his head nervously.

"Did you seriously get me a hedgehog?" I asked, peering into the cage.

He shrugged. "I know I joked about it, but then your mom said you liked taking care of Sonic so I thought you might want one of your own."

"Where is it?" I asked, peering into the cage. I clapped my hands together excitedly. I might not have been able to keep a fish alive, but babysitting Sonic had proved that I could take care of a hedgehog—you know, except for losing him on my bed.

"Sleeping," he replied. He opened the cage and lifted up the little igloo thing, his body blocked the hedgehog from my sight. He gently nudged it awake and scooped it into his hand, slowly turning so I could finally see it.

"It's so tiny!" I squeaked, reaching out for the baby hedgehog.

He set it into my hand and it peered at me for a moment before falling back asleep.

"Is it a boy or a girl?" I asked.

"Boy, that way if you ever want to bring him over he can play with Sonic and we don't have to worry about any babies surprising us."

I laughed at that, gently stroking my finger along the small quills. It was the cutest thing I'd ever seen. "I'm taking your throwaway name and naming him Aquilla the Hun," I declared.

Maddox laughed. "Sonic and Aquilla... that ought to be interesting."

Since Aquilla clearly wanted to sleep I put him back in his cage and fixed the igloo in place. I wrapped my arms around Maddox in a tight hug. "Thank you so much. You've definitely made this the best birthday ever."

He grinned. "It's not over yet."

"It's not?" I gasped.

He shook his head. "Nope. There's more."

"You're spoiling me," I declared.

"Only because I want to. But before I show you the rest, I think we should eat."

I'd completely forgotten about the pizza, but now that he

mentioned it I was starving.

He grabbed a pizza cutter and sliced it, placing pieces on two plates.

We sat side by side at the bar and he waited for me to take the first bite.

I let out a small moan. "Oh my God, this is delicious. We should make pizza every day."

He threw his head back, letting out a throaty laugh. "That good, huh?"

"Phenomenal."

He took his first bite and nodded his head in agreement. "You're right. This is delicious. Mom would be proud."

"We should take Karen a piece."

"Tomorrow," he agreed, "tonight is about you."

My body warmed at his words. We finished eating and set about cleaning up the kitchen together. While we cleaned we both sang along to the music he was playing—a few months ago I wouldn't have been able to sing along, but since he had given me his iPod I knew a lot of the songs now. At one point we started dancing again, so it took us longer to clean up than it normally would have, but I didn't care.

Once the kitchen was clean Maddox turned to me and wrapped his arms around my waist, pulling me against his chest. "Do you want your cake now?"

"You got me a cake too?" I asked, surprised.

He shook his head, grinning proudly. "No, I made you a cake." He paused, "Well, we all did. Mathias, Ezra, and Hayes helped too. So I can't promise it's the most delicious thing ever, but we tried."

Tears pricked my eyes. "That's the sweetest thing ever."

He chuckled, "You might not be saying that once you see it."

"Why?" My brows furrowed together with confusion.

"Well..." He started. "I'll show you."

He'd hidden the cake in a cabinet and brought it out to sit it on the counter. "It's yellow cake with chocolate icing—your mom said that was one of your favorites. We tried to make a layer cake, but it fell apart, and now it's kind of a blob."

"It's beautiful," I said.

"Beautiful?" He laughed. "Hardly. I also wrote Happy Birthday Emma on it, but you can't really tell now," he frowned.

"Maddox," I grasped his arm, "this is seriously so sweet. I don't care if the cake is a giant blob. It's the thought that counts."

"Are you sure?"

"I love it," I assured him. "Now stop frowning and let's eat some cake."

"Okay, okay," he chuckled. He stared at the mess of cake and mumbled, "I think we're going to need bowls, not plates."

"You're probably right," I agreed, lifting the glass top off.

He spooned some of the cake into a bowl and handed it to me, doing the same for himself.

"I can't believe the four of you made me a cake." I was still in a state of disbelief.

"It was fun," he shrugged. "Except Mathias kept eating the icing, so Hayes had to go buy more."

"Is that why you were yelling at him on the phone earlier when you called me?"

He chuckled. "Yeah. He wouldn't stay out of it. And then he kept telling us what to do... and laughed when the cake fell apart because we wouldn't listen to him."

"Does that mean Mathias was right?" I giggled, picturing the four guys arguing over the proper way to make a cake.

Maddox shrugged. "Probably. But I'm not telling him that."

Instead of sitting on one of the chairs I ended up cross-legged on the floor. Maddox joined me, stretching his legs out and resting his back against the cabinets.

"This is really good." I licked chocolate icing off my lip.

"Even if it's a lump and not a cake?" He asked with a raised eyebrow.

"That makes it better," I grinned.

We finished the cake and then he took my hand, guiding me to the stairs. "Your last present is up here... it's not really a present, it's..." He shrugged, looking sheepish. "You'll see."

I was very curious now.

At the top of the stairs there were two doors, one on the left and one on the right. He turned to the right one. He swung it open and motioned me into his bedroom.

I'd never seen his room before and my eyes flitted around curiously. The walls were painted a dark gray color. All his furniture was black with chrome accents. His bed was covered with a light gray comforter that was so fluffy I was pretty sure I could get lost in it.

But what took my breath away was in the corner.

He'd made a makeshift tent with twinkling lights strung around it. Blankets and pillows littered the floor and books lined the perimeter.

"You like to read so... I wanted you to have your own spot."

I threw my arms around his neck, kissing his cheek. "This is the best thing ever."

I released my chokehold on him and scurried over to the fort—I was calling it a fort anyway—and dropped to my knees on the pillows. One in particular caught my eye and I laughed. "Anatomy of a Hedgehog," I read on the pillow. Beneath the words was a picture of a hedgehog with lines jutting out. The line pointing to the hedgehog's bottom said, *'curlable posterior.'*

I lifted up the pillow, quirking a brow. "Really, Maddox?"

"There had to be a hedgehog," he declared. "Hedgehogs everywhere."

I put the pillow back and patted the empty space beside me for him to join. When he did I stretched out on my back, staring up at the top of the fort. Now that I was closer I could see that the each of the twinkling lights had a paper star attached to it.

I swallowed down the lump in my throat. "Thank you for the best birthday I could've ever asked for."

His eyes grew serious and he reached out to tuck a piece of hair behind my ear. "Does this mean you like your birthday now?"

"It means I love it," I whispered.

"More than you love me?" He joked, rolling onto his side and sitting up slightly so he looked down at me.

"Never."

He stared at me with an intensity that left me breathless. I'd never had anyone look at me like that before. Like I was everything.

He lowered his head, closing the space between us in tiny increments that drove me wild. When he was almost to my lips he stopped. I let out a small sound of protest. "I'm going to kiss you now," he growled low in his throat, "and I'm not going to stop until you forget your name."

I quirked my lips. "Promises, promises."

He chuckled and brushed his lips against my neck before gently nipping the spot with his teeth. "I always make good on my promises, Emma."

His lips sealed over mine and my back arched off the pillows. My hands sought his shoulders, needing something to hold onto, because I was pretty sure his kiss was about to make me fly away.

He pulled away enough to speak. "What's your name?"

"Emma," I rasped.

He grinned wickedly and kissed me again. Or maybe *devoured* was a more apt description. He nibbled lightly on my bottom lip and then his tongue smoothed over the spot, making me gasp. His hands delved into my hair, pulling slightly—enough that I felt a small sting, but not hard enough to hurt.

I was pretty confident in saying that every time we kissed it got better.

He pulled away again. "What's your name?"

My brows pulled together. "E-Emma?"

"Almost there," he growled.

This time his kiss set my whole body on fire. I felt heated all over and I clawed at him like a wild animal, trying to undo the buttons on his shirt. He broke away enough to rip the buttons off the shirt. Yeah, he *ripped* them. It was actually kind of hot.

He tossed the shirt over his shoulder, not caring that he'd just ruined what appeared to be a very expensive dress shirt.

When our lips collided together I stopped caring about the shirt too.

I ran my fingers along the dips of his abs, wondering how they'd feel pressed up against me with my dress gone.

He grasped my neck, tilting my head back. His hips pressed against mine. I let out a small gasp at the sensation, wrapping my legs around his waist.

His lips moved against mine slowly, leisurely, but with no less passion than he had exuded moments before. There was something infinitely better about this kiss—like we had all the time in the world.

He tore away from my lips, his chest rising and falling with every breath.

"What's your name?"

"I don't know," I panted, "and I don't care."

He grinned triumphantly, having won.

"Don't rub it in," I warned.

"Let me revel in my victory," he chuckled, all too pleased with himself.

I shook my head, my body aching to close the space between us. "Just shut up and kiss me."

Luckily he didn't argue with me.

After all, it was my birthday and he had to listen to everything I said. Right?

His fingers glided down my side, lighting me on fire. He wrapped his hand around my thigh, holding me more tightly against him. I gasped against his lips when he pressed into me.

He placed tender kisses to my neck and my body bowed off the pillows. "Maddox," I panted.

"What?" His voice was equally as breathless. "Tell me what you want," he murmured, tugging my bottom lip between his teeth and letting go.

I closed my eyes, swallowing thickly.

"Look at me," he growled, taking my chin between his fingers. "Tell me what you want."

The look of intense longing in his eyes made me shiver. I was sure the same look was reflected in my own eyes.

"You," I gasped, "I want you."

He lowered his head my chest, his ear over the spot where my heart beat madly.

"Are you sure?" He asked.

My heart sped up and he grinned.

"Positive." I assured him.

He lifted up slightly, staring down at me. I stared right back, refusing to look away.

Whatever he saw in my eyes must've been enough, because he nodded once and then he was kissing me again.

He lifted the dress from my body ever so slowly, like he was unwrapping a gift and wanted to savor every moment.

His eyes perused my body all over once it was gone—taking in the lacy bra and panty set I wore. Right now I was thanking God for Sadie.

"You're beautiful," he whispered, his eyes rising to meet mine, "and I love you."

I wrapped my arms around his neck and pulled him down so I could whisper in his ear, "Show me."

Our lips collided yet again and the rest of our clothes began to disappear.

Right there beneath the cover of the blanket fort and the glow of the starry lights he made love to me.

And it couldn't have been more perfect.

CHAPTER TWENTY-TWO

MY FIRST THOUGHT upon waking was: *Man, Maddox's chest actually makes a really good pillow.*

I smiled, slowly blinking my eyes open. He was already awake, smoothing his fingers through my tangled hair.

"Morning," he grinned, kissing the end of my nose.

"Mmm," I hummed, reveling in the feel of his fingers skimming my bare back, "morning."

I cuddled closer to him, burrowing against his side. I never wanted to move from this spot or his arms. Seriously, I would've been content to stay right here forever as long as someone brought us food. Maybe we could sweet talk Mathias into being our butler—although he'd probably try to kill us in our sleep.

"How do you feel?" Maddox asked, taking my chin between his fingers and tilting my head up so I met his eyes.

I stretched my stiff muscles, taking inventory of how I felt. I didn't feel profoundly different like I'd had some sort of awakening. I still felt like me, just a little sore, and happy and in love.

"Amazing." It was the honest to God truth.

"Good," he rubbed his forehead against mine, his hair

tickling me. "I was afraid I might've hurt you."

I shook my head rapidly. "No, no. Everything was perfect." *Because of you*, was what I left unsaid.

Maddox had been kind and gentle with me, his patience endless. Last night had been far more than I'd ever expected for my first time. It wasn't something I pictured often, but when I did it was usually dark and awkward and the worst thing ever. But with Maddox it had been so much more and I knew it was because we truly loved each other. That fact alone changed everything.

I splayed my hand on his chest, then began drawing random designs.

I knew that no matter how much I didn't want to leave our fort I was going to have to go home. If my mom was aware I hadn't come home last night I was surprised she hadn't already shown up here knocking down doors. I mean, she was more lenient than a lot of moms, but she was still a mom, so I knew she wouldn't be thrilled about me sleeping over at Maddox's. And she'd probably have a heart attack if she knew what we did. Yeah, parents were probably—okay, definitely—aware of what most teenagers were up to, but it didn't mean they wanted that information thrown in their face.

"I should probably go home," I whispered, almost afraid to voice the words out loud.

Maddox grasped my hand—the one I'd been using to doodle on his stomach—and entwined our fingers together.

"You're right—" I deflated at his words even though it should've been better that he was agreeing with me. "—But I'm making you breakfast before you go."

"Can we make it together?" I asked.

He chuckled, the sound rumbling through his chest, which my ear was currently pressed against. The steady *thump, thump, thump* of his heart was quickly becoming my favorite sound in the whole world. It was like a drum that beat only for me.

"We can do whatever you want." He sat up, the blanket pooling at his waist. His eyes flicked over my body unabashedly taking me in. A blush threatened to blanket my skin but I willed it away. His lips quirked into a half smile, and he leaned down. "I love you, Em." He pressed his lips ever so softly against mine. I was beginning to think I liked these kisses more than the soul scorching ones. There was something about the tender kisses that made me feel even more loved and cherished.

I grasped his hair between my fingers, holding him against me for a moment longer. "I love you too," I whispered against his lips.

His face split into a grin.

I wondered when, or if, we'd ever get tired of the impact of those words.

He stood, grabbing a pair of boxers and jeans from a drawer. He left the belt undone and chose to forgo a shirt—which left my eyes to feast upon his perfectly sculpted chest and arms... I really hoped I didn't get hit in the face with a door this time for looking. Although there were no doors near me so it would be more likely that the fort would collapse on top of my head.

That thought alone propelled me from beneath it and into the middle of his bedroom. I kept the blanket clutched to my body as I crawled around on my hands and knees in search of my clothes.

Maddox stood watching me with his arms crossed over his chest and an amused smile tugging up his lips. "What are you doing?"

"Looking for my clothes." Seriously, where were they? He'd basically ripped them off of me like a mad man so I knew they had to be on the floor somewhere. Jesus, did he throw them so far that they ended up in another dimension?

"Uh... Em," he crouched down beside me and I ceased my frantic search, "they're right there." He pointed to his bed where they lay folded neatly.

"How'd they get there?" I asked.

"House elves," he replied with a chuckle. Sobering, he said, "I picked them up earlier."

"You were up?" I asked.

"I wanted to lock the door in case Mathias showed up," he shrugged. "He doesn't normally barge into my room but there's a first time for everything and I didn't want him to see you." His eyes darkened with possessiveness. "So I picked up your clothes while I was up." He shrugged.

"Well... thank you," I smiled. I reached for my clothes and saw that he was still watching. "Look away," I growled.

He grinned crookedly, tilting his head. "I've already seen everything there is to see, Em, so don't get embarrassed on me now. Besides, you watched me get dressed," he winked.

Damn him.

I grumbled under my breath and let the blanket drop. I knew I was being silly, but it felt different to be standing in front of him naked now than it did last night. Then we'd been in the heat of the moment, now we were just... us.

My heart thumped so hard that I was sure he could see it pulsing through my skin.

I dressed as quickly as I could, but never looked away from him.

When I was clothed he grabbed me by the waist and kissed me passionately, making my head spin. I forgot to breathe for a moment, so when he let me go I ended up gasping for breath like I'd just run a marathon.

He smirked, clearly pleased with his kissing abilities. He turned and unlocked the door. I followed him downstairs still in a daze. I'm pretty sure that kiss killed a few of my brain cells.

He turned on the lights and I blinked a few times from the sudden brightness.

"What would you like?" He asked, opening the refrigerator. "We have... eggs... and cereal... that's pretty much it breakfast wise."

"Let's make scrambled eggs." I reached around him to grab the carton. "Do you have any bread? We can make toast too."

"Uh... no," he frowned. "I'll go grab some. I'll be right back." He kissed my cheek quickly as he passed, almost as if the gesture was automatic.

While he did that I went to work on making the eggs.

"What the fuck are you doing?" A voice boomed.

I jumped, letting out a small scream. The bowl of eggs I was whisking nearly flew out of my hands but I managed to keep it from making a mess. I turned around to face Mathias.

"Making breakfast, obviously."

"Oh, fuck, Emma. I'm sorry." He squished his eyes shut, and appeared truly apologetic. "I thought you were someone else."

My brows wrinkled. "And who did you think I was?"

"I thought maybe I brought a girl home last night and she hadn't taken the hint to get the fuck out." He yawned, pulling out one of the barstools.

I stared at him, processing his words. "You *thought* you might've brought a girl home last night. Meaning, you don't even *remember?*"

"God, stop fucking yelling at me." He groaned, shoving the heel of his hands against his eyes.

"I'm not yelling," I glared. The unmistakable stench of alcohol wafted off of his breath, flooding me with memories of my dad.

He groaned, laying his head against the cool countertop. "I think I drank too much."

"You *think?*"

"Can you hand me a bottle of water?" He asked. "Please," he added, his eyes softening and his voice less gruff.

"Only because you asked without cussing," I sighed, opening the refrigerator door. I slid one of the bottles over the counter to him.

"Thanks." He gave me a grateful smile.

Maddox returned with the bread and Mathias winced when the door slammed closed.

"I'm surprised to see you up," Maddox said to his brother as he passed, "I thought you'd forgotten what it was like to wake up in the morning like a normal human being."

Mathias' gray eyes flashed with anger. "If I'm not a normal human being what the fuck am I?"

"An asshole," Maddox replied easily.

"Fuck you," Mathias sneered. "And here I thought if you finally got laid you might start being a joy to be around." He nodded his head in my direction.

Maddox's jaw tightened with anger and his fists clenched at his sides.

My cheeks began to redden and the bowl of whisked eggs did drop out of my hands from surprise this time. The gooey eggs splattered all over my legs and I cringed.

Maddox shook his head roughly back and forth. "Don't talk about her like she's nobody."

"Whatever," Mathias shrugged, standing up and grabbing his bottle of water. He started towards the stare. "It was a fucking joke. Maybe you should lighten up some."

"Nobody is laughing." Maddox glowered, but Mathias never seemed fazed by his brother's anger.

"See you later," Mathias called, disappearing up the stairs and acting like he hadn't just majorly pissed off Maddox.

Maddox turned around to face me and I hastily bent down

to grab the bowl. "I'm sorry. I didn't mean to drop it—"

He grabbed the bowl from my hands and tossed it in the sink. "I don't care about the bowl, I care about *you*. Are you okay?"

"Yeah," I shrugged, looking away from his eyes and to the floor.

"Talk to me, Em." He grabbed my chin forcing my eyes to his. "Tell me what's going on in that pretty little head of yours."

I didn't want to voice my fears, because I didn't want to even entertain the possibility that it could be true, but Mathias had already put doubts in my mind.

I squirmed uncomfortably, staring at the ceiling. I mumbled, "Did you just use me for sex?"

He let go of my chin like I'd burned him. "God, no. Em, I can't believe you'd even think that." He shoved his fingers through his hair, looking hurt.

I shrugged. "I didn't think that, not until—"

"My asshole of a brother opened his mouth." He let out a heavy breath. "I love him more than I can even possibly describe, but he always likes to cross the line. He's just bitter, because he doesn't have what we do." He wrapped his arms around me, hugging me to his chest.

I wrapped my arms around him, returning the gesture.

"I hope he finds it one day," I whispered, meaning it.

"Me too." He agreed. "But I'm afraid that day might never come."

MADDOX TOOK ME home and stayed long enough to help me clear a spot for Aquilla's cage and get him set up in his new home—aka my bedroom. The hedgehog was so tiny and cute—

even cuter than Sonic, but I might've been biased.

I lay across my bed now, staring at the ceiling with a giddy smile on my face. Last night felt like a dream, but my sore muscles argued that it was real.

It seemed so unbelievable.

This whole summer did.

I remembered zip lining with Maddox and asking him to kiss me afterwards—cementing our relationship.

I'd started the summer with no plans—and with two weeks until school started it was safe to say I'd had the best summer of my life.

Maddox and our adventures had been completely unexpected, but the greatest thing to ever happen to me.

Still unable to wipe the silly smile off my face I headed into the bathroom to shower. Since I planned on hanging around the house most of the day I dressed in a pair of gray cotton shorts and white t-shirt with a faded design of a butterfly on the front.

I padded into the kitchen to make some tea—planning to use my new cup from Maddox—and heard something clatter in the garage.

I opened the door and poked my head inside. "Mom?" I called. "Is everything okay?"

"Yeah," she responded, "just cut myself. Can you grab me a Band-Aid?"

"Of course."

I headed down the hall to the bathroom and grabbed a Hello Kitty Band-Aid—they were the only kind we had.

The doorbell rang and my mom called, "I'll get it," as I closed the medicine cabinet.

I walked into the kitchen to find Sadie standing beside my mom. "Hi," I smiled at my best friend. I opened the Band-Aid and my mom held her palm out for me to affix it to her cut.

"That's probably not going to stay on long," I warned her.

"It'll be fine." She grumbled, heading back into her studio.

I'd have to keep an eye on the cut, though. Once, she'd needed five stitches, and had insisted she was fine. She ended up with an infection.

"We need to talk, *now*," Sadie hissed, grabbing my hand. She dragged me to my bedroom and slammed the door closed. I hadn't noticed it before, but she was livid. I couldn't understand where her sudden anger was coming from. What had I done? "Sit." She pointed to my bed and I suddenly felt like I was in for an intense interrogation.

She then shoved an *US Weekly* magazine into my hands.

With her hands on her hips she glared. "I'm so pissed right now that I can't even think straight. I can't believe you would keep something like this a secret from me. I thought we were best friends! And now I feel like you don't even care about me!" She started to yell, shaking with anger. "We're supposed to tell each other everything and you kept something this big a secret from me! That hurts, Emma. It really does." She frowned, tears clinging to her lashes. She was truly upset, but I had no idea what she was accusing me of and what the magazine had to do with this.

"I'm lost," I told her honestly.

She snorted, looking away. "Emma, you're dating *Maddox Wade*."

I narrowed my eyes. "How do you know his name?" I knew I'd never actually told her—having always evaded the topic. Yeah, that was shitty of me, and I'd willingly own up to it, but I still felt like she was making a bigger deal out of this than necessary. I didn't tell her his name? So what. She knew I was seeing someone and she'd been okay that I didn't want to talk about it. What was with her sudden change of heart?

She looked at me like I was stupid. "He's Maddox. Fucking. Wade."

"Yes," I replied. "That's his name. But I don't know what's so important about his name. I'm so confused right now." I was beginning to panic. What the hell was she getting at?

"Oh my God," she gasped, her hand flying her mouth. A single tear snaked down her cheek. "You don't know, do you?"

"Know what?" I hissed through my teeth, urging her to get to the point. "And why the hell did you shove this at me?" I waved the magazine through the air.

"Turn to page fourteen." She sat down and took it from my hands before I could even flip it open. Once she had it on the right page she handed it to me. "There," she pointed. "See."

I squinted at the grainy picture. "What the hell?" I gasped, my stomach rolling. The picture was grainy, like it was taken on a cellphone from quite a distance, but it was obviously me—if you knew me that is—and Maddox. My head was turned towards him and he looked down at me, both of us smiling. Drumsticks rested in his back pocket and I recognized our clothes from when we sang at Griffin's.

"Read it." Sadie pointed to the caption.

My eyes dropped away from the picture to read:

Maddox Wade of the band Willow Creek has been spotted with an unidentified female companion that is believed to be his girlfriend. The two were seen together at a local coffee shop in Maddox's hometown. According to our source the duo even sang a brand new original song. Looks like love is in the air, which Willow Creek boy will be next?

I threw the magazine down, clutching my stomach.

"I'm going to be sick." I slapped a hand over my mouth,

running to the bathroom.

Panic snaked through my veins, suffocating me. This couldn't be real.

Please don't let it be real.

But it had to be.

The proof was in a freaking magazine.

"Emma!" Sadie cried, running after me. She grasped my hair as I heaved over the toilet. She rubbed her other hand soothingly against my back. "I thought you knew," she sobbed, "I'm so sorry. I thought you knew," she repeated.

I flushed the toilet and stood to brush my teeth. Tears coursed down my cheeks and I could do nothing to stop them. I was so full of rage that I was ready to explode.

I walked stiffly back into my bedroom and sat on the bed. I wrapped my arms around my chest, like I was trying to hold myself together. I couldn't even begin to process this.

"He didn't tell you?" She asked, even though it was unnecessary.

"No," I whispered. "I didn't know." I ripped at my hair and screamed, "God, I was so stupid! It was all right there in front of me and I couldn't see it!"

She handed me a tissue and I used it to dry my face.

"I feel so naïve," I sobbed.

"You can't blame yourself, Emma," she said softly, sitting down beside me. Her thin arms wrapped around my shoulders. "You don't listen to that kind of music, or read magazines. Hell, you barely watch TV and you don't even have a Facebook. You're kind of a mutant freak."

That got a small laugh out of me, but I quickly sobered.

"Seriously, I was so stupid. He plays the drums, has all that music equipment... Sadie," I shrieked, pulling out of her grasp as new tears poured down my cheeks, "he even took me to his special place and guess what it was called?"

"I don't know," she frowned.

"Willow Creek."

"Well, shit. You are kinda stupid," she joked.

"This is insane." I pushed my hair off my forehead and then began to flap my arms. "Jesus Christ, I'm hot."

"You are turning a bit red," she agreed.

Whenever I got angry it was like my temperature heated to two-hundred degrees.

"I can't believe it was right in front of me all this time and I didn't see it. Sadie, I was in the damn car with him and his friends when a song of theirs came on the radio. I made a comment about Willow Creek being from here and none of them even thought to tell me." My voice grew higher in pitch the madder I became. "I feel so used." My shoulders sagged in defeat. "What was I? His fucking plaything?"

Sadie winced. I hardly ever cussed or got this worked up over anything.

I mean, holy shit, my boyfriend was famous. This was insane. This kind of thing just didn't happen in real life. It was like I'd been transported to an alternate universe.

"I don't know," she whispered.

"He told me he loved *me*," my voice cracked. "Now it all feels like a lie."

Every look.

Every touch.

Every kiss.

All of it felt tainted now.

"We had sex," I hissed, "and now he's probably bragging about how he finally fucked me and screwed me over, because I'm the dumb naïve little girl that didn't know he was fucking famous," I shrieked, my hands fisted. My fingernails dug into the palms of my hands, leaving scratches.

"Emma," Sadie looked at me sadly, truly remorseful for

dumping this kind of news on me, "what are you going to do?"

I took a deep, calming breath, and squared my shoulders. "What any sane person would do... I'm going to cut off his balls and feed them to his hedgehog."

She sat up, grinning evilly. "I'll help."

I grabbed my car keys off my dresser. "Then let's go."

CHAPTER TWENTY-THREE

"COME ON, START," I begged my car, turning the key. This time—the fifth try—the engine caught.

"Maybe we should take my car." Sadie pointed to the street as I backed out of the driveway.

"I'm not opposed to running him over and I don't think you'd approve of blood on your tires."

"You're right," she stared straight ahead. "I'm really sorry, Emma."

"You have nothing to apologize for. You're the only one to tell me the truth while he hid it from me, and so did Mathias, Ezra, and Hayes. I swear to God if they're there too I might punch them all." I flicked my gaze towards her. "Remind me to thank your brother for teaching me the proper way to punch someone."

She ignored that statement. "Hold up," she clutched the seatbelt, "you mean to tell me you've met *all* of them?"

"Yes," I growled, "those lying, worthless, pieces of shit."

"Is Ezra as hot as he looks in pictures?" She asked dreamily. "He has that gorgeous black wavy hair. God, I just want to run my fingers through it."

"Whoa, whoa, whoa," I shrilled, "whose side are you on?"

"Yours, of course. It was an innocent question," she frowned.

I shook my head, focusing my eyes on the road.

My anger was building by the second, but beneath that I was *hurt*. I loved Maddox and I trusted him too, and that's what pained me the most—the fact that I'd been so blinded by those two feelings that I hadn't been able to see the truth staring me right in the face. People were right when they said love made you a fool.

It felt like an hour had passed by the time we made it to his house, although I knew it had only been minutes.

"Stay here," I growled at Sadie.

"But what if you need backup?" She asked. "I have pepper spray."

I stopped with my hand on the door. "You have pepper spray?"

"My mom bought it. It's in a cheetah print canister." She held her keys up proudly, shaking them so that I saw the can.

I shook my head. "Just stay here for now." I grabbed the offending copy of *US Weekly*, ready to beat him over the head with it.

"Okay," she sat back.

I slammed my car door closed—instantly feeling bad for taking my anger out on an inanimate object.

I marched up to the guesthouse door and reached for the knob. It opened and music blasted me. All four guys were oblivious to me for the moment.

A scream tore out of my throat as I stormed forward. I saw a pair of drumsticks lying on the desk and grabbed one with my free hand, throwing it at Maddox with more force than I thought I had. It connected with his forehead, bouncing off and onto the floor.

The music stopped then as all the guys turned to look at

Maddox who'd ceased drumming. He pressed a hand to his forehead, wincing in pain. He glanced up and spotted me, all the color draining from his face. "Emma, I can explain—"

"Explain, what?" I spread my arms wide. "That you lied to me? That you used me? Did you laugh at me behind my back? Did you even care about me at all?"

"Emma," he stood hastily, his stool clattering to the ground, "I love you. Stop this."

"Stop what? Stop telling the truth? You lied to me, Maddox!" I pointed at my chest, inhaling a heavy breath. Tears stung my eyes once more. "I have never felt so betrayed in all my life, not even the day my dad walked out on us and didn't even say goodbye."

He winced at my words, pain coating his features. "I never meant to hurt you."

"But you did hurt me!" I screamed. "Even if this was some stupid game to you, you still owed me the truth!" My chest heaved and I clutched the magazine so tightly that it started to crinkle. He stalked towards me and I shoved the magazine into his chest. He grasped it, not even looking at it. "*This* is not how I deserved to find out." My voice began to soften as the fight left me. "I'm a human being, I have feelings, and seeing the truth laid out to me in a magazine isn't fair." I choked on a breath.

"Guys, can you give us a minute?" Maddox asked.

The three guys shrugged and mumbled a few things, heading upstairs.

Once they were gone Maddox and I stood across from each other, neither of us saying a word.

"I never tried to play you," he finally said, his voice barely above a whisper.

"Then what do you call this?" I spread my arms wide. "This whole thing between us is a lie."

He winced like my words had stabbed him.

"God, Emma," he growled, hurt contorting his features, "it wasn't like that."

"Then tell me what it was like!" I poked a finger against my chest, leaning towards him.

His teeth clenched together, a muscle in his jaw ticking. "I wanted something for myself, okay? Because I'm a selfish fucking prick. The last year has been insane as our band has grown in popularity. *Everyone* wants something from us. And I was sick and tired of feeling used," he spat, tears shimmering in his eyes. "And then I met you and you didn't know who I was and... I felt like me again. I wasn't Maddox Wade the drummer from Willow Creek—I was just Maddox. I *craved* that."

"So, what? You only liked me because I didn't know who you were?" My own words began to slice me open.

"No!" He tore at his hair. "You're making this sound so much worse than it is!"

I flinched. "*I'm* making this worse than what it is?" I sputtered. "*You're* the one that hid your identity from me. I don't even know you!"

"Yes, you do," he took two steps forward, closing the distance between us. He reached up to clasp my cheeks in his hands. I flinched from his touch and he let his hands drop, his eyes haunted. "You know me better than anyone, Em." His voice was soft, pleading with me to believe him. "I've shared things with you that most people don't know about me. I know you don't believe it right now, but you are special to me, and I love you. That isn't a lie."

"Then why couldn't you tell me the truth? Did you think it would matter that much to me? Did you think I'd try to use you?"

"No!" He yelled, his hands flying through the air. "Jesus Christ, that's not what I thought at all! I tried to tell you so many times, I really did, I swear. But I never could. I just... the words would never come out right and..." He took a deep breath. "I was scared," he admitted. I started to reply but he cut me off. "I was scared to death that if you knew who I really was that my fame might push you away, and the last thing I want to do is live a life without you in it."

Tears coursed down my cheeks and I wiped them away as fast as they fell.

"Congratulations, Maddox," I sneered, wanting to hurt him as much as he had hurt me, "now you'll get to find out what your life is like without me."

With that I turned and started towards the door.

"Emma!" He yelled after me. "Please, stop!"

I did. My brain told me to move, but my heart said to stay.

I turned slowly and looked at him over my shoulder. He stood there, hurt shimmering in his eyes, and his fists clenched at his sides. His dark shirt molded to his tense muscles and he looked torn between staying where he was and coming after me.

Finally, he spoke. His voice was soft and cracking. "Loving you is my greatest adventure. Nothing else means anything without you."

"Then I guess you can live a life full of emptiness."

"Emma!" He roared again, starting towards me.

"Don't follow me!" I snapped, yelling at him. "You have no right to follow me! Just leave me alone! You've done enough damage! ... If you follow me I'll kidnap your hedgehog!" Yeah, that sounded like a good threat.

"*Emma*," his voice cracked. "Don't do this."

He fell to his knees and I closed my eyes as my heart ripped in two. I'd never experienced pain like this before and in that moment I swore it would never happen again.

"Too late."

I walked out the door and just before it closed I heard him cry my name again as the guys ran down the stairs.

I hurried to my car and raced away—just in case he did decide to follow.

Sadie stayed quiet, letting me cry.

Halfway home I couldn't see to drive through my tears. I pulled over and wrapped my arms around the steering wheel. My whole face was damp with tears. You would've thought I would have run out of them by now.

"Why does this hurt so bad?" I sobbed, my shoulders racking.

"Because you love him," Sadie whispered.

Her words made me cry harder.

I did love him. So much. And this wasn't fair. I'd deserved to know the truth and he hadn't given it to me. Maybe he was right, and it would've pushed me away, but he hadn't given me a chance. And now he'd betrayed my trust and that's what hurt the most. I gave it all to him and he only gave me half of who he was.

"Do you want me to drive?" Sadie asked softly.

I nodded. "And can we go to your house, just in case…"

She didn't need me to finish. "Of course."

"Thank you," I hugged her, my tears wetting her shirt, "you really are the greatest best friend in the whole world."

She laughed. "Are you just now figuring that out? I should be offended."

"No, I've always known." I assured her.

She let me go, giving me a serious look. "I know it doesn't feel like it right now, but you're going to be okay. Not today. And probably not tomorrow or even next week. But one day you're going to be okay."

"Thanks." I forced a smile but it quickly turned into a frown as more tears assaulted me.

I forced my stiff body from the car and switched places with her.

I laid my head against the window and closed my eyes, but darkness didn't greet me. Instead I saw Maddox falling to his knees calling my name, and my heart split even further.

I knew Sadie was wrong.

There was no getting over this.

Maddox had ruined me.

CHAPTER TWENTY-FOUR

"HERE," SADIE HANDED me a bowl of soup, "you have to eat something."

I shook my head, burrowing further under the covers of her bed. "I'm not hungry."

"You haven't eaten in two days. Please," she lifted the spoon, "you're worrying me." Her brow wrinkled and her lips turned down in a frown.

"I'll try," I conceded, only because I felt bad for worrying her. I sat up, the blankets pooling at my waist. She tried to feed me, but I glared. "I can do it myself."

"Okay." She handed me the bowl and spoon. "It's homemade chicken noodle soup."

I knew Sadie didn't make it, so that meant—"Did you tell your mom?"

She smiled sheepishly. "I kind of had too. She wanted to know why you were shut up in my room crying all the time."

"Have I really been that bad?" I asked, blowing on the hot soup.

She gave me a look like *are you kidding me?* "Yeah, it's been bad."

I winced. "I'm sorry."

The past two days had been hell. I missed Maddox more than I could describe. My heart ached for him. I'd never experienced a pain like this before—one that seemed to rip apart your insides leaving them raw.

My feelings were all over the place.

I loved him.

I hated him.

I missed him.

It was all so stupid and I was beyond angry.

I couldn't believe that he'd kept something like this a secret from me. If he really loved me like he said he did, he would've told me, right?

Sadie frowned, looking away. Her posture told me she was about to say something I wasn't going to like. She glanced back at me, her forehead wrinkled. "Can't you forgive him?"

I leveled her with a glare.

"He seems really hurt and sorry for keeping it a secret," she looked at me sadly. "Your mom said he's been stopping by several times a day to see you."

"And that's further proof as to why I should stay here," I frowned. "He *lied* to me, Sadie. About something big too. This wasn't like he told me he took the trash out and he didn't. This is... I mean, he's *famous*."

"So?" she shrugged. "He loves you."

I was tempted to throw the hot soup at her. "What happened to you? You were as mad as me," I hissed. "Besides, love doesn't fix everything."

"Well," she smiled sheepishly, "I talked to him. And Ezra too. They were at your house when I went to pick up your clothes. Not that you've changed." She wrinkled her nose and pointed at the dirty pajamas I was wearing.

"I'm *wallowing* and I'll wear what I want," I huffed. "This room is a no judgment zone."

"I think you're forgetting that this is my room, and therefore I can boss you around. Finish eating," she patted my leg, "then shower and change, please. I'm sick of seeing you so sad and maybe a shower will liven you up a bit."

I hated to tell her, but nothing was ever going to make me feel better.

"Yeah, sure." I agreed.

"I'll be back in fifteen minutes," she warned, eyeing me as she headed towards the door, "and if you're not in the shower I'll drag you there."

"I hear you," I grumbled. I paused, tilting my head. "I think maybe I should just go home."

She halted in the doorway. "Are you ready for that?"

I frowned. "He might show up, but it's not like I have to see him. I can't stay holed up in your room forever. I have to face this." My words sounded stronger than I felt.

She grasped the wooden doorframe, looking at me sadly. "I really think you should talk to him again."

"No," I hissed. The amount of venom in my tone surprised her.

She sighed, shaking her head. "Can you really blame him, though? For keeping it a secret? The guys deserves to have someone love him for who he is, not what he does. That's all he wanted, Emma."

"Stop it," I hissed. "I don't want to hear this." I needed my best friend to be on my side and she clearly wasn't.

"You don't want to hear it because you know I'm right."

I grabbed a pillow and threw it, but she was already gone and it thumped pathetically to the floor after colliding with the closed door.

I started to cry again—that's all I seemed to do the last few days—and tried to eat the soup. But it was useless. I didn't want to eat anything. I was miserable, and I knew the only way to move past this was to forgive him, but this betrayal cut deep and I wasn't sure I could look past it.

"I WAS BEGINNING to think I didn't have a daughter anymore." My mom stepped into my room with a cup of tea for me—thankfully not in the cup Maddox bought for me.

"Ha, ha, ha," I droned. I took the tea from her and set it on the table and opened the cage to check on Aquilla. My mom had been tasked with taking care of him for the last few days. I felt bad about that, but I'd needed the time away.

"What exactly happened?" She sat on the end of my bed. "Maddox told me his side of the story and now I want to hear yours."

I sat down too once I was sure Aquilla was still alive, and she began to braid my hair like she used to do when I was little.

I hated that she'd spoken with Maddox. I wished he'd just stay away. When he lied to me he forfeited the right to care.

Even though this was the last thing I wanted to talk about, I started from the beginning, telling her everything—okay, not *everything*, but enough.

She listened, nodding her head and making a comment now and then.

When I was done she stood up and headed for the door.

"You're not going to tell me I should forgive him?" I asked, surprise coloring my tone.

"Emmie," she paused in the doorway, "do I think you should forgive him? Yes, I do, but that isn't my decision to make. You," she pointed at me, "have to make it. Whether you forgive him or not is entirely up to you," she shrugged, "and I'll support you either way."

"This sucks," I mumbled, grabbing a pillow and hugging it to my chest.

She let out a small laugh. "Love is never easy, Emmie. In fact, it can be impossible. But love is always worth fighting for—if it's the right kind of love."

I let out a shaky breath. "This feels like one impossibility I can't overcome."

"That's your choice," she shrugged. "You either love him enough to fight through your pain, or you let him go."

"I *trusted* him mom, and he *broke* that trust like it was nothing." My lower lip began to tremble.

She came further into my room and sat down again. She wrapped her arms around my shoulders and hugged me. "Sweetie, I think you forget that Maddox is just a boy. He's young and impulsive. He thought he was doing the right thing, for him and you. There was nothing malicious in his deception. Can you blame him?"

Sadie had asked me the exact same question.

"I don't *know*." My voice cracked. I was too upset to think clearly and all I wanted to do was hate him, but no one seemed to want to let me do that.

She nodded her head and let out a small sigh. "Just think about things."

I groaned and flopped back on my bed.

I wanted to kick and scream and cry, but I'd already done all those things and knew they did no good.

I loved him so much, and a huge part of me wanted to find him and run into his arms—to beg him to never let go. But I *couldn't*. Not now, and maybe not ever.

I honestly couldn't imagine my life without Maddox, but I was mature enough to know that life did go on, and it wasn't like this was the *end*.

And yet, it still felt that way.

I covered my face with my hands and groaned.

Why did everything have to be so messed up?

Why did my emotions have to be all over the place?

Why couldn't there be some clear answer in my mind?

Forgive him or move on?

It just wasn't that simple though.

Life rarely ever had a clear path set out for you, and this was one of those instances where the path seemed to have completely disappeared and I wasn't sure I would be able to find it.

CHAPTER TWENTY-FIVE

FIVE DAYS LATER and I still hadn't forgiven Maddox.

He'd shown up plenty of times trying to talk to me. The first few times I refused to even see him.

Another time I opened the door and yelled at him before slamming it in his face—sure that after that explosion he'd leave me alone.

He didn't.

Why?

Because he said he loved me—and that tore me apart more than anything else he could have said, because I loved him too, but I was hurting.

"Please, Emma," he begged, his eyes pleading. "You have to believe me, I love you and I never meant to hurt you. This whole thing has spiraled out of control. Please, just listen to me."

"I don't want to listen," I growled.

He braced his hands against the front door, barring me from closing it. "I never intended to hurt you. I fell in love with you and it became impossible for me to tell you."

"Impossible?" I gasped. "Are you serious?"

He winced. "I didn't mean it like that. I just... I never wanted to hurt you."

"Stop saying that!" I screamed. "You did hurt me!"

He lowered his head and looked back up at me with pain filled eyes. "I'm so sorry, Em. I know you don't believe me, but I am. I'm so, so sorry I didn't tell you. I never meant to keep it a secret, but when I saw you didn't know who I was it just became so easy to pretend that other part of my life didn't exist."

Tears pooled in my eyes. I wanted him to shut up. I didn't want to hear this.

"Maddox," my voice cracked, "I need you to go away. Please. I can't think straight when you're around. Just give me a chance to breathe."

He took a step back and I closed the door.

"Please, Em," I heard him say through the door, "please forgive me."

I needed *time* and he couldn't seem to understand that.

I needed a chance to think things through and let go of this anger. I kept reminding myself that Maddox wasn't my dad. Maddox didn't leave me. He lied. And lying was bad, but he hadn't abandoned me, and I knew in my heart he hadn't played me like I originally believed.

But I wasn't ready to run into his arms and act like nothing had ever happened.

This was *huge*.

Since finding out the truth I'd spent more time watching TV and on my computer than I ever had.

And what I'd learned was Willow Creek was blowing up.

Their EP had dropped at the start of the summer, three of the songs soaring into the Billboard Top 100 and one even going to number one. The level of excitement for their full-length album was insane.

The bottom line was: the Willow Creek boys were famous.

Which meant if I stayed with Maddox, I was going to be thrust into the spotlight.

Hell, I already had. I mean they had a photo of me in *US Weekly*. And eOnline had posted an article about Maddox and me—and my name had been included. How they found that out was beyond me, but I was thanking my lucky stars that no one had shown up outside my house to try and snap a picture.

The whole thing was a lot to process.

The doorbell rang—for the third time today—and I was tempted to chuck the mug in my hand at the door.

I ignored the doorbell, heading back to my room and closing the door. After speaking to him yesterday I had no desire to see him today. If he couldn't respect my wishes for space then I would tell him to leave me alone and that I didn't want anything to do with him anymore—that I couldn't forgive him.

My heart clenched at that thought.

The stupid organ still yearned for him.

It was annoying.

All I wanted was to be able to think clearly and rationally, but I couldn't do that when my heart wanted other things.

And maybe that was the problem, love wasn't rational, it just *was*.

"Emma!" My mom called.

Dammit, she got the door.

"I'm busy cleaning my room!" I called back. It was a pathetic lie, but all I could think of off the top of my head.

"Emma!" She called again. "*Come here!*"

Oh no. She used her stern voice. I was in trouble.

I grabbed Aquilla from his cage and cradled him in my hands. I figured if I was holding the baby hedgehog I'd be less likely to chuck something at Maddox's head.

I padded down the hall, my eyes on the hedgehog in my hands as I cooed at him.

When I stepped into the living room and looked up I promptly took two steps back, shocked to see Ezra, Mathias, and Hayes standing there.

"What are you guys doing here?" I asked, putting a hand on my hip and holding the hedgehog in the other. I felt like they were ganging up on me and I was probably about to endure an intense lecture. *Great.* It was really beginning to feel like no one was on my side. It was unfair. I wasn't the one that lied about who I was. I didn't betray anyone's trust. Maddox did. But everyone seemed to think I should let this go like nothing happened.

Couldn't they see that I was hurt? I felt like I'd had my insides ripped out. The boy I'd fallen in love with had been keeping a *huge* secret from me. He was no longer *Just Maddox.* He was also *Willow Creek Maddox.*

My boyfriend was freaking famous.

Or ex-boyfriend.

Ugh, whatever we were. I didn't even know anymore. It was all so confusing, not to mention exhausting.

"We wanted to talk," Mathias spoke. "Can we sit down?" He pointed at the couch. "Or will you pelt us with a fucking drumstick?"

"Language!" My mom warned as she left the room.

I sighed. "It was in the heat of the moment," I defended. I hadn't apologized to Maddox about that when I spoke with him. I'd wanted to, especially when I saw the bruise on his forehead, but I'd once again been too mad to be sensible.

Today, I didn't feel quite as angry. More sad. Defeated.

And frankly, I was really starting to miss him.

I just felt so conflicted.

It was like my emotions were one big ball of tangled yarn,

and I couldn't unravel them. When I tried they just got more twisted.

"It was kind of funny," Hayes chucked, taking a seat. Even sitting the guy was a giant.

Mathias speared Hayes with a withering glare. "She could've given my brother a concussion. I don't find that funny."

Hayes' lips quirked into a smile, and even I had to smile. Mathias' fierce protectiveness for his twin was really quite adorable—even if I felt like throttling said twin.

Ezra sat down between the other two guys. He pushed his wavy black hair out of his eyes. "Why don't we just get to the point of why we're here? Okay?" He asked them.

"Sure, sure." Hayes agreed.

"He started it." Mathias pouted like he was five.

Ezra shook his head, sighing heavily.

Mathias turned to me, glaring. "We're here to talk about the fact that you broke my brother's fucking heart."

"Hey!" I cried, going on the defensive. "I'm not the one that lied!"

Aquilla curled into a ball in my hands, not pleased with my sudden outburst.

"Whoa, whoa, whoa." Ezra held his hands up in a placating manner. "We didn't come here to yell at you or try to make you feel bad," he glared at Mathias. "We just wanted you to hear our side."

"Yeah," Hayes agreed.

"Whatever," Mathias grumbled, crossing his arms over his chest and sitting back. He stared at the wall, his jaw clenched.

Ezra shook his head, his too long dark hair falling into his eyes once more. "We just wanted you to know that all of us wanted him to tell you."

"What?" I straightened. I hadn't been expecting that.

"We like you," Hayes piped in, "you're a nice girl and we

296

didn't think it was fair for him to keep the truth from you."

"But," Ezra cut in, "we also understood where he was coming from."

"I think all of us can agree, that it would be nice to know that someone loves us for who we are. Not that we're rock stars or have a hefty bank account." Hayes shrugged. "So, we did see where he was coming from to an extent. But we also thought that he should've told you early on. You're not like other girls, that was obvious to all of us," Hayes waved his hand to encompass all three of them, "and we thought you might not be okay with this life. And if that was the case, he should've let you go."

Oh God. I was going to cry again. Imagining my summer without Maddox and all our adventures was heartbreaking. Even if I was hurt I would never take back any of those moments for anything.

"Honestly," Mathias sighed, his features softening, "I did get into it a few times with him after this. You shouldn't have found out the way you did. It would've been bad enough if he told you himself now, but seeing it in a magazine," Mathias winced, "I'd feel betrayed too." His eyes darkened and he growled, "But he's my brother and I know how upset he is and he misses you. I might not believe in love, but he does, and he loves *you*. Maddox doesn't let many people in. Remember that." He stood up, looking around the room momentarily. "I'll be in the car if you need me."

The front door closed behind him.

And then there were two.

I eyed the remaining guys across from me. "I don't know what I'm supposed to *do*." My voice cracked. It was doing that a lot lately thanks to all the waterworks.

Ezra shrugged. "All I have to say is, if you do take him back I think you can count on the fact that he'll never fuck this up again. He truly is devastated—he hates himself for not telling you himself sooner. He knows he was wrong, Emma. He's not trying to dismiss that fact."

Ezra stood up and I did too, clasping Aquilla to my chest. I was surprised when he opened his arms to hug me. He was a little shorter than Maddox and leaner.

"I'm really sorry," he whispered. He headed for the door.

And then there was one.

Hayes stood, grinning boyishly. He towered above me, his blond hair shorter on the sides and longer on top. "Come here," he opened his arms and I hugged him too.

When he pulled away he didn't head straight for the door. He paused looking at me carefully.

"We leave for L.A. in three days and I don't know when we'll get back. They didn't want to tell you, because they didn't want you to feel pressured, but I think you deserve to know."

I nodded, swallowing past the lump in my throat. "T-thanks for telling me."

"Always," he nodded. He stepped onto the front porch and caught the storm door before it could close. I stared at him, damming the tears back. "We're a family, Emma, and no matter what, you're always going to be a part of that. Okay?"

I nodded. "Bye," I whispered.

"I'll see you later, Emma."

He seemed sure of that, but I wasn't. I wasn't sure of anything anymore.

CHAPTER TWENTY-SIX

I SAT ON the step of my front porch watching a plane fly overhead. I wondered, yet again, if Maddox was on that plane. Flying to L.A. to live his dreams, while I stayed behind and tormented myself with the decisions I had made.

After the guys showed up I expected Maddox to come by again.

He didn't.

Nor did he come the next day.

Or the next.

And today I knew he was leaving for L.A.

I didn't go to him. That thought broke my already splintered heart.

I didn't go to him, because I'm a selfish grudge holder.

I just let him leave.

I wanted to believe our love for each other was strong enough to weather any storm, but this was one of our own making. He'd lied. And I couldn't seem to forgive. But oh my God, I missed him more than I ever thought it was possible to miss someone. I felt like I was suffocating in his absence, like the air was slowly being sucked from my body.

I hadn't had this kind of reaction when my dad left.

The answer seemed obvious enough.

Go to him.

But he was gone now.

It was too late.

I'd let things go too far and now it was out of my control.

True, I could pick up my phone and call him, but after a whole week of *this* that didn't seem like enough.

Besides, there was a small voice in my head telling me he deserved more than me. A model. Or an actress. Not a girl who immersed herself in books and classical music. I was *nobody* and he deserved a *somebody*.

But he wants you. Another voice spoke up. I wanted to believe that voice so badly, but it was hard. We were so young, and Maddox was famous—I choked on the word—and therefore the odds were stacked highly against us.

Some things are worth taking a chance.

Was Maddox worth it?

Yes.

He definitely was.

Oh God.

A cry tore out of my throat and I ran into the house before one of the neighbors thought an animal was dying—because that's exactly what I sounded like.

"Emmie?" My mom called from the kitchen as I ran back to my bedroom. I heard her feet thumping against the floor as she hurried after me.

I collapsed onto my bed facedown, sobbing hysterically. "What have I done?" I mumbled, but it probably came out sounding like whathabidub because my mom responded with, "What was that?"

I rolled over and looked at her with my tear-streaked face. "What have I done?" I choked. "I threw away one of the best things to ever happen to me all because I was angry," I cried,

300

my lower lip shaking, "I feel like dad."

"Oh honey," she took me into her arms, "you're nothing like your dad."

"I abandoned Maddox," I muttered.

She kissed the top of my head. "You didn't *abandon* him. You were upset and hurt, so you did the only thing you knew you cold do to protect yourself and that was to walk away. There's nothing wrong with that."

"I miss him so much, mom," I cried. "I've ruined everything and now he's gone."

"Shh," she hushed me, "that's not true."

I shook my head, wiping away my tears. "They left for L.A. today, and Hayes doesn't know when they're coming back. It's over."

My mom took me by the shoulders, forcing me to look at her. "Nothing is over until you give up. Are you giving up?"

"I don't want to," I answered honestly. "I want to fight for him."

My mom's whole face lit with a smile. "Now there's my Emmie. I've missed her."

"Mom," I groaned, looking away.

"Now we just have to figure out how to get you to L.A." She beamed. I was pretty sure she'd wanted to tell me I was an idiot for pushing him away, but she knew I had to come to this conclusion on my own. Yes, I was hurt that he'd lied to me. Yes, I knew it was going to be hard dating a rock star. But I also knew Maddox was worth it, and that was the only thing that kept me from freaking out.

"But flights are expensive," I mumbled.

She gave me a stern look. "Don't play dumb with me. We both know you want to do this in person and that boy deserves more than a phone call from you." She looked away, frowning. "I don't think I've ever seen someone look so heartbroken." I opened my mouth to tell her that I'd certainly been heartbroken, but she cut me off. "He looked even worse than you, so don't start with me."

"You like him," I laughed.

She smiled. "He's a nice boy and I can see he loves you. That's all I've ever wanted for you, Emma—to be happy and have someone love you the way you deserve to be loved. I never wanted to see you go down the same path as me." She patted my knee and stood up. "I'll see if I can book you a plane ticket."

"No, mom," I shook my head. I held up a hand when she started to retort. "No," I said in a firm tone, "I want to do this on my own. I can take care of it. This is my mess and I'm going to clean it up."

She smiled. "I'm so proud of you, Emma."

I snorted. "I don't think there's much to be proud of."

"That's because you don't see what I see."

She disappeared down the hall and I grabbed my phone. I'd never called this number before, but I knew he was my only hope.

"This is Mathias," he answered on the last ring.

"I need a favor," I whispered, like as if Maddox might here me over the phone.

I heard some shuffling and what sounded like a door closing. "I'm listening."

"I need a plane ticket to L.A. I'll pay you back, I swear."

Mathias didn't smile often, and even though I couldn't see him I was positive he was smiling then. "Text me all your information and I'll have the ticket sent within an hour. A driver will pick you up too."

"Thanks," I sighed in relief. I'd been terrified that I'd waited too long and Mathias wouldn't want to help me. "I'll need someone to pick me up when I get there too."

"I'll take care of it," he assured me. "Just make sure you get here."

"I can do that," I nodded.

"And Emma?"

"Yes?" I questioned hesitantly.

"If you break his heart again I won't be quite as nice."

"Understood."

"And since I'm not a one-sided bastard, if he hurts you again I'll punch him for you—no more projectiles on your part, m'kay?"

I laughed. "You've got a deal."

"See you soon." He hung up.

"See you soon." I whispered into the air, a grin transforming my face. I was going to get Maddox back.

But what if he doesn't want you now?

If he didn't, then I'd just have to live with my choices—even if it killed me.

"HOLY SHIT," SADIE exclaimed, staring at the limo. The driver opened the door for me to slip inside, but Sadie cut me off and dove into the interior. "Emma! There are twinkling lights that look like stars on the ceiling! This is the coolest thing ever!"

I poked my head inside the door. "I called you to come over so I could say goodbye. Not so you could fawn over the limo." Mathias, unfortunately, hadn't been able to get me a plane ticket for yesterday, but I had a morning flight today.

"Right, sorry," she frowned, sliding over the seats and climbing out. "Are you going to be back before school starts?" She asked.

It was Saturday morning and school started on Tuesday.

"Of course," I replied.

She nodded and wrapped her thin arms around me in a tight hug. "Go get your man back." She slapped my ass as she walked away.

"Sadie!" I shrieked.

She simply laughed, backing away from the limo while giving me two thumbs up.

My mom stepped forward and I hugged her for as long as I could. I didn't want to let go—because this moment seemed symbolic. It was the first time I was ever really leaving my mom to go out on my own, and in a matter of months I would be graduating from high school and moving on with my life.

"Don't get into any trouble," she warned me. "I'm not bailing you out of jail."

I laughed under my breath. If only she knew.

"I'll see you in a few days," I told her.

"I'll miss you." Tears shimmered in her eyes and I wondered if she was thinking the same thing as me—that one day soon I'd be leaving home for good.

"I love you, mom," I smiled, slipping into the limo. "Don't miss me too much!" I yelled after Sadie who was hanging beside her car.

"Pssh, miss you? Never!" She cackled.

I nodded at the driver and he closed the door.

I sat back and closed my eyes.

I was about to get on a plane—and I'd never even flown before—to go across the country for a *guy*.

If someone told me that three months ago I never would've believed them.

Fate, it really was something else, wasn't it?

304

I STEPPED OUT of the airport doors, searching for Mathias'.

A hand rose in the air, and I glanced over, smiling when I recognized him. I moved through the crowd, my suitcase bumping behind me.

He leaned against a sleek black Cadillac Escalade, a navy blue baseball cap turned around backwards on his head. He was dressed casually in a pair of workout pants and shirt.

"Here let me take that." He reached out for my suitcase and put it in the trunk.

We climbed into the back of the Escalade. It was being driven by—

"Is he a body guard?"

"No, that's my boyfriend Hank," Mathias deadpanned.

The burly black man chuckled. "You wish, kid."

"I'm shocked he let you out of the car," I mumbled, looking out the window, taking in the palm trees and sunny skies.

"Hank and I have an understanding—he lets me do whatever the fuck I want—"

"Within reason," Hank piped in.

"And I pay his bills. He also keeps the grabby people away which is nice," Mathias shrugged. "Ezra had some girl try to cut off a piece of his hair. There are some psychos out there."

"Uh... that's... scary."

"Are you sure you can handle it?" His eyes glimmered with challenge.

I squared my shoulders, leveling him with a glare. "Of course I can." I knew it was going to be a huge adjustment—especially still being in high school—but there wasn't a doubt in my mind that didn't think Maddox was worth it.

Being without him had shown me just how powerful my love for him was. It wasn't going to go away, not ever, and I was going to fight for our happily ever after. I refused to think that I might live a life without him. I knew there would be ups and downs for us, and there was no telling what surprises the future may hold, but it would all be worth it.

"Where is he?" I asked, my eyes widening at the sight of the Pacific ocean.

"Photo shoot," Mathias replied. "That's where I'm supposed to be."

"Dressed like that?" I eyed his workout clothes.

"Hey, I showered," he pointed a finger at me, "besides, they'll have wardrobe for us."

My hands began to shake with nerves and I chewed on my bottom lip.

"Hey," Mathias said, placing his hand on mine. I turned to look at him and was surprised to see the compassion in his steady gaze. "It's going to be okay, trust me."

It might've seemed like an odd thing to trust brooding, anger-filled, snarky Mathias, but I did.

I nodded. "Okay."

While I believed him, that didn't take away my nerves. The last few times I saw Maddox I'd been less than friendly. I'd avoided him and snapped at him. And been a downright bitch.

If I were him I wouldn't forgive me so easily.

But I guess we were both in the wrong. Him for lying, and me for not listening to him.

I believed we could move past it, though.

He'd tried to reach out to me and I'd iced him out.

Now it was my turn to make this right.

"WE'RE HERE," HANK said, the Escalade coming to stop.

I looked at the plain square gray building. It hardly seemed like the place for a photo shoot, but what did I know.

Mathias and I climbed out of the vehicle. He pulled a lanyard out of his pocket with some kind of ID badge on the end.

"Come on," he put a hand on my back, guiding me forward. Hank trailed behind us, the silent protector.

He led me through a winding hallway and down some steps.

He stopped outside another door. "You ready?"

"Absolutely." I rubbed my hands together.

He swung the door open and nodded his head for me to go in. I could hear the clicking of a camera and saw lights blinking. I really hoped I didn't get in trouble for this.

"Go," Mathias urged, waving me on.

I nodded and took two steps inside. He followed me and veered to the left. I started to follow, but he held up a hand to halt me. He pointed over his shoulder to where Ezra and Hayes sat on a couch. When they saw me they both perked up grinning from ear to ear. Ezra gave me a thumbs up and Hayes flashed an encouraging smile.

"That way," Mathias hissed, waving me in the other direction that was blocked off by a white sheet of some sort.

I turned my back on the guys and took one step forward and then two.

And then there he was.

He didn't see me at first, since he was listening to the photographer's instructions. I watched him for a moment at how effortless it all seemed for him as he posed with his drumsticks over his shoulder. He was looking away from me at the moment, but then he lifted his head and his mouth parted in shock.

"Emma?"

He said my name hesitantly, like he was afraid I was a ghost his mind had conjured and with the one word I might disappear forever.

"Hi." I waved weakly. I was frozen in my spot, my feet refusing to move forward.

The photographer looked over his shoulder and spotted me, his brows wrinkling in confusion.

"Can you give us a moment?" Maddox asked the man.

He mumbled something unintelligible, the tone coming across as harsh, and grabbed his camera bag as he headed out of the room.

"What are you doing here?" He asked, tucking his drumsticks in his back pocket.

"I-I came to see you," I whispered, terrified to close the space between us, because I feared his rejection.

"To see me?" He pointed at his chest. "Why? Because I got the impression that you never wanted to see me again." He looked away momentarily, trying to hide the sadness in his eyes from me.

I shook my head rapidly back and forth. "I was confused and hurt. I shouldn't have been the last to know, Maddox. *You* should've told me. Instead you made me feel like I was an insignificant part of your life and didn't deserve to know the truth."

"It was never like that," he winced in pain. "It wasn't my intention to keep the truth from you, it just happened. I liked spending time with someone that only wanted to be with me for me. The more time that went by the harder it became to find the words to tell you. I'm so sorry for that. But I don't, for one minute, regret it. I wouldn't take back every moment I got to spend with you for anything." He took a step forward. "And you're right, you shouldn't have been the last to know about me—not when the whole world already knows who I am," he grinned.

"Don't get cocky," I narrowed my eyes.

He chuckled, taking another step closer to me.

"But you know what, Emma?" Another step.

"What?" I asked, my eyes zeroing in on his hips.

Another step.

And another.

And then his sneakers were pressed right up against my boots. He reached up, smoothing his hand down my cheek. He leaned forward, his lips pressing against my ear. "You really aren't the *last to know*, because you're the only girl that knows the *real* me, and you're the only one I'll ever *love*." He pulled away, grasping one of my curls between his fingers. "Forgive me?" He pleaded, his eyes sincere.

Tears shimmered in my eyes. "You already were."

He grinned at my words. "Does that mean I get to kiss you now?"

"Since when do you ask?" I laughed.

He took my face between his hands. "Good point."

He closed his mouth over mine and wrapped me in his arms.

I heard the guys let out whoops and cheers, making me smile into Maddox's kiss.

"Welcome home, Em," he whispered, his fingers curling into my hair.

I grinned at his words, my whole body humming with happiness.

He was right.

I was home.

Right here in his arms.

EPILOGUE
—EIGHT MONTHS LATER

"THIS IS STUPID," I groaned, "I don't even want to go." I complained, wincing when Sadie brushed through a knot in my hair.

"Shut up. It's prom. You're going. Even Maddox insisted upon it." She braided some strands of hair, pulling them back into a bun.

"I don't see why Maddox's opinion matters here, he's in L.A., so he shouldn't get to vote on whether or not I go. This isn't my thing," I insisted, eyeing the dress hanging on the back of my door. At least it wasn't that bad.

I'd picked it out on a shopping trip with Sadie and our moms. It had thin spaghetti straps, and dipped down into a V shape in the front—but luckily stopped before it became too revealing. The top was a light peach color fading into blue and purple in an ombre effect. It cinched in at the waist before flowing down. It wasn't a big ballroom dress or anything too flashy. It was simple and pretty.

"This is our senior prom, and I have forgone a date as a favor to *your* boyfriend, so that we can go as friends. So suck it up, princess." She stuck a flowered headband on my head.

"But everyone will stare at me," I mumbled, looking down at my lap.

This school year had been *awkward* to say the least. Everyone knew I was dating Maddox, so I'd gone from a nobody to the most popular girl in school in a matter of seconds. Everyone wanted to be my best friend in the hopes of getting close to the Willow Creek boys. It was annoying the lengths some people would go to, to try to get close to me. Luckily, I had Sadie, and she kept the crazies away with her cheetah print pepper spray. She made a good sidekick. Actually, she was probably the superhero while *I* was the sidekick, but I was okay with that.

She finished fiddling with my hair and stepped back. "Hair and makeup done." She clapped her hands together. "Now go put on your dress so I can see what the final product looks like."

"Yes, ma'am," I saluted her. I grabbed my dress off the back of my door.

She'd already changed into her dress—a pretty pale pink dress with silver detailing. With her tan skin and brown hair it was stunning.

I changed into my dress and turned to eye my reflection in the mirror.

"What do you think?" I turned to Sadie so she could see it from the front.

"If I were a lesbian I'd totally date you."

"Thank you," I rolled my eyes.

"Hey, that's a high compliment. There aren't many girls I'd switch teams for."

"Just stop talking," I told her, suppressing a laugh.

Sadie checked her phone. "We better get out of here."

"I thought we were supposed to be fashionably late?" I repeated her words from earlier.

"Emma," she eyed me, "we're already fashionably late. Prom

started over an hour ago."

"Ohhh," I frowned. "I didn't know."

"Obviously," she laughed.

I followed her out into the living room where my mom and her parents waited. After snapping more than enough photos it was time for us to leave. We'd planned on just driving Sadie's car, but when we opened the door a limo sat parked on the street.

"Maddox," I smiled, sighing dreamily.

Sadie groaned. "I hate it when you get that dopey look on your face."

"You're just jealous that you're not in love."

"It's true," she shrugged. "One day. I hope."

"It'll happen," I assured her.

"Miss Burke," the driver called, opening the door.

Sadie and I hurried forward—well, as fast as we could go in heels.

A small part of me hoped that Maddox would be waiting for me in the limo, but of course it was empty. We'd facetimed earlier and it had been good to see him. I hated that he was so far away in L.A. I'd flown out at Christmas—my mom had been okay with it since Karen and Paul were there—and while I was in L.A. Maddox had dragged me to the recording studio so that we could record our duet. It was one of my fondest memories. And thanks to Maddox I no longer was scared of what the future held after graduation. I knew what I wanted to do, and that was to write songs. I didn't feel this impending fear when I tried to see my future. Instead, I felt peace.

The drive to the hotel where prom was being held was short, and my nerves started up once more. I *hated* being stared at, but I knew that's what I should expect. I already experienced it every school day in the halls.

"Show time." Sadie called, bounding up the steps of the

hotel while I trudged along like a fifty-pound weight clung to my ankle.

We stepped into the ballroom, a really loud techno song playing in the background. Blue lights pulsed, giving the ballroom a club vibe.

I watched the way some of our classmates danced and wrinkled my nose in disgust. Um, ew.

"Come on, let's dance," Sadie dragged me onto the dance floor with our classmates. A few eyed me, but surprisingly most people seemed oblivious to my presence. I guessed their minds were otherwise occupied for the night. Thank God.

Between the dancing and the heat of the packed bodies it didn't take long for a fine sheen of sweat to coat my skin.

"I'm going to go get water," Sadie said, backing away from me. "You want some?" She asked, but was looking over my shoulder. I turned to see what she was looking at, but didn't see anything besides our classmates.

"Yeah, get me water," I told her, but when I looked back she was already gone, having abandoned me.

Great.

I started to dart off the dance floor, but was halted in my tracks when a familiar song began to play on the speakers.

A song that—as far as I knew—hadn't been released to the public yet.

I whirled around, trying to find the DJ—to demand to know how he got his hands on *my* song—and instead collided with a very solid chest.

"Whoa, Em. You're going to give yourself whiplash."

My heart skipped a beat and I closed my eyes, scared to believe it was really him.

"I'm here," he whispered, his fingers skimming along my neck and down my arm. "You can open your eyes now."

I did and was met with a silvery gaze. "H-how?" I stuttered.

"I thought you were in L.A. this morning?"

"Did you really think I was going to let you go to prom without me as your date?" He asked, raising a dark brow. I noticed that instead of a tux he wore a crisp button down white shirt, a black bow tie, and black pants. I was sure that if I looked he'd even have his drumsticks in his back pocket.

"Well, yeah," I finally replied.

"Oh, Em." He grinned, shaking his head. "Why do you ever doubt me?"

I eyed him.

"Right," he chuckled.

"The song?" I asked, lifting a hand in the air as if I could touch the notes and our words.

He grinned. "The record label agreed to put it on our album as a bonus track."

"Are you serious?" I asked, my eyes threatening to bug out of my head.

"I wouldn't joke about that, Em."

I squealed and threw my arms around his shoulders, squeezing him tight.

"Careful." He wiggled away, reaching into his pocket. "You might squish Sonic."

My mouth fell open. "You brought your hedgehog to my prom?"

"Of course. Sonic deserves to go to prom too," he grinned, lifting the hedgehog onto his shoulder. "Look, I even knitted him a bow tie." He pointed to the item dangling around the hedgehog's body.

I dissolved into a fit of laughter.

Maddox simply grinned at my amusement. I think it was his goal to make me laugh as many times as he could in a day.

"Can I have this dance?" He asked, holding out his hand.

I looked from the hedgehog into his silvery eyes. "Yes, and each one after it."

His smile was blinding as he wrapped a hand around my waist and pulled me against his body. We swayed with the music—our music, and I smiled as I imagined all the adventures that were yet to come.

THE END

BONUS CONTENT

INTERVIEWER: IT'S SO nice to sit down with the both of you today. Your song *My Only* is climbing up the charts. Many people didn't know that you could sing Maddox. Is there anything else you're holding out on telling us? Any hidden skills?

Maddox: I'm a very skilled kisser. Like the best in the world.

Emma: Shut up.

Maddox: What? You don't agree? You've always seemed pretty impressed with my skills to me. I mean, it's not like I've ever made out with myself to know, but you always make these little noises—

Emma: I hate you.

Maddox: That's not what you told me last night. I'm pretty sure you told me you loved me and called me a God.

Emma: I'm leaving. You can finish the interview by yourself.

Maddox: Aw, don't go, Em.

Interviewer: <clears throat> Can you tell us how you got the idea for *My Only*?

Maddox: I think that's pretty obvious. She's the only one for me and I'm the only one for her. Case closed.

Interviewer: Are there any plans for a wedding in the future?

Emma: Uh... no. I'm only nineteen. There will not be a wedding anytime soon.

Maddox: Don't you want to marry me, Em?

Emma: Eventually.

Maddox: I can live with that.

Interviewer: Looks like we're out of time. Congratulations on the success of *My Only* and the whole debut album.

Maddox: Thanks man. <turns to Emma> I think I need to show you just how amazing my kisses are.

Emma: Oh God. You have that look that says I'm in trouble.

Maddox: <laughs> Oh you're definitely in trouble.

Emma: <screams and runs out of the room>

Maddox: You can run, Em! But I'm always going to catch you!

NEVER TOO LATE

Coming April 21, 2015

- A WILLOW CREEK NOVEL-

Remy. Is. Back.

I'd never met anyone quite like Mathias Wade.

He was brooding and arrogant, but I loved him anyway.

Together we were wild and uncontained—a hurricane raging.

Then I had to leave and words were
exchanged that could never be undone.

But I was back, and Mathias better watch out,
because this bitch wasn't finished with him.

Game. Set. Match.

All is fair in love and war, right?

(Recommended for readers 18+)

ACKNOWLEDGEMENTS

I always say writing the acknowledgements is the hardest part of any book. I'm always afraid I'm going to forget someone—or that I'm always saying the same exact thing in each one.

Last to Know is a story I've wanted to write for nearly two years, but it was never the right time. Well, Maddox and Emma made it known that *now* was the time for their book to see the light of day. I absolutely loved going on all their adventures with them—their ups and downs—and I hope you guys did too.

This book wouldn't have been possible without the help of my betas. Haley, Stefanie, Becca, and Kendall, I'm thankful to have you all on my side to tell me when things aren't working—or when something is just right. Thank you for loving this story as much as I did and shaping it into what it is.

Grammy! Thank you for always being there for me and dealing with my craziness. You're one of a kind. Now, seriously, stop reading my "dirty" books. Ha!

Mom and dad, I'm so thankful that you guys supported my dreams. I know I don't say it enough, but it means so much to me to have you guys on my side and to know I've made you proud.

Regina Bartley, without you and all the late night writing

sprints this book might still not be done. I love that the both of us always seem to be working on a book at the same time and can cheer each other on. Thank you for always being there to talk me down off the ledge, to run scenes by, or just for other randomness.

Regina Wamba—Cover Design Goddess, thank you for creating the perfect cover for this story. It's sweet and simple and has that magazine cover vibe I wanted. Plus, HEDGEHOG! Thanks for not thinking I was crazy when I asked for that... or maybe you did and just didn't say anything...

Eric and Lailah, thank you so, so, so much for bringing Maddox and Emma to life. I can't imagine this cover without either of you. It's exactly what I wanted and I think you both captured the carefree love and silliness of Maddox and Emma's relationship without even having to try, haha!

Enjoy excerpts from Authors Anne Carol and Jamie Canosa

Never
let Go

ANNE CAROL

Is it possible to find your soul mate
on the other side of the world?

Beth Johnson is an ambitious high school senior from
suburban California with a secret passion for writing. David
Somers is a charming young Englishman who wants nothing
more than to play guitar in his up-and-coming rock band.
Though worlds apart, when fate brings Beth and David together
in London in the summer of 1979, sparks fly. After Beth
receives upsetting news from home, she finds herself drawn to
David's warm character, and an all-consuming love develops.
Theirs is the kind of love one never forgets, and as Beth's stay
in London nears the end, the young devoted couple must face
the inevitable question: will their romance fade with the
passing of summer or will they realize their promise of never
letting go?

Excerpt

"FEELS LIKE I'M taking a ride into the center of the earth!" I said, eyeing the lengthy escalator. I clutched the handrail as it carried us down to the train platform. Mom and I had walked a few blocks up to the nearest Tube station, passing uniformed schoolchildren and businessmen along the way. The Tube was London's answer to the underground train, and the crowd of people moving through the turnstiles proved it was a popular way to travel.

We stood on the cement platform until we saw headlights and felt a *swoosh* as the train pulled in. Squeezing our way onto a train bound for Baker Street, I quickly grabbed the metal bar above me, accidentally elbowing a woman.

"Sorry!" we both said, swiftly avoiding eye contact. I thought it was weird that she apologized when it was clearly my faux pas. This was definitely not California.

● ● ●

LATER THAT EVENING, after Mom and I spent the day touring museums and checking out a library, our whole family walked up to the local pub for curry night. I found it liberating not being tied down to a car, like we were in Garden Valley. Walking to dinner in my hometown was practically unheard of.

Just before entering the neighborhood eatery, I smoothed

down my hair since the cool humidity fluffed it up more than I cared for. My appearance was soon forgotten, though, in favor of my rumbling stomach, which was called to attention by the exotic smell of Indian spices. We glanced over the menu behind the bar and put in our orders.

Situating our group at a large wooden table in back, we started going over the events of the day. Uncle Ned was in the middle of telling a story about a great-aunt when the meals were finally delivered.

"Oh, this smells good!" I said, picking up my fork.

I dove into my chicken curry, but stopped halfway when I felt someone watching me. Looking across the room, I noticed a pair of deep chestnut eyes fixated on me. A tiny gasp escaped, and I quickly looked away.

"What's wrong, Beth?" Jenny whispered.

"There's a guy over there staring at me," I said, feeling my mouth dry up. "Is there something on my face?"

She laughed quietly. "No, you're fine. I imagine he's staring at you because you're pretty."

Embarrassed now, I said, "Oh, stop."

I tried to ignore him, but then Jenny pointed her head in his direction. "Are you talking about that bloke with the brown hair?"

Peeking over at him, I nodded.

"I know him. He goes to my school. His name is David... mmm... Somers, I believe," she said, checking out the cutie dressed in a crisp collared shirt and black pants.

"Oh, David?" Aunt Ellie perked up and turned in her chair to spot him. "I had him as a pupil several years back. Nice boy, good family."

Jenny raised her eyebrows at me. "Would you like me to introduce you? He seems smitten."

"No!" I whispered, looking down at my rice.

"Too late, he's coming this way."

I nearly choked. I didn't know why I was such a mess. He was just a good-looking guy, but no, there was something about his stare that was so... hypnotic. Nobody had ever looked at me like that before. My heart fluttered as I watched him approach Aunt Ellie, who practically fell over herself greeting him.

"David! What a lovely surprise."

"Hello, Mrs. Johnson," he said in a smooth accented voice, which unexpectedly sent my pulse racing. "I won't keep you. I just thought I'd pop over and say hi." He swept a long section of his hair off his forehead and buried both hands in his front pockets.

"Oh, well I'm happy you did. Now you can meet my family." She proceeded to first introduce Uncle Ned and Jenny, and then moved on to my parents. I wondered if she purposely saved me for last.

"And this is Jenny's cousin, Beth."

"Hello, Beth," he said with a sheepish grin as his hands remained stuffed in his pockets.

Something possessed me to reach my hand out to him. "Hi, David. Nice to meet you."

Appearing caught off guard by my gesture, he withdrew his hand and gently shook mine, creating a surge of electricity which traveled up my arm and all through my body. As I pulled away, our eyes met briefly, but long enough for me to know there was something special about David. Suddenly I wanted to know more about him. And I knew he felt the attraction, too, because he could hardly take his eyes off me as he returned to his table.

There was an awkward silence after he left; my family clearly picked up on the spark in the air which now spanned the room. I wondered what my folks were thinking, but of course nobody said anything. After a minute or so, the conversation picked up again, much to my relief. Only Jenny chose to recognize the obvious.

"He likes you," she whispered.

I shook my head, facing downward as I felt my cheeks heat up.

"Feeling alright, dear? You look flushed," Mom observed.

"Perfectly fine, Mom," I said quickly, wanting the attention off me.

Yet I still had the full attention of one David Somers, who gazed at me on and off throughout the meal. It was difficult not to stare back, and a few times we even exchanged shy smiles. I tried to be discrete, so as to appear I was still a part of our family discussion. Jenny noticed my preoccupation, though, and I had a feeling we'd be talking about David later that night.

● ● ●

AS IT HAPPENED, I was the one who brought him up.

"So tell me about him," I asked as I sat on my bed, watching Jenny rifle through her dresser drawer.

She raised an eyebrow. "I assume you mean David?"

I nodded.

"Well, he's a year ahead of me, which means he officially finishes school next month, though Upper Sixth Form students no longer attend classes now that the exams are complete. I'm not sure what he studied or if he's going on to university. I don't know him that well." She looked away, appearing deep in thought. "He was dating someone a while back, but they've since broken up. As of a few weeks ago, I hadn't seen him with anyone else. I think he keeps busy with his music."

She shut her drawer and crawled into bed.

"Music?" I pictured him sitting, poised over a baby grand piano.

She perched herself up on one side, facing me. "Yeah, he's in a band."

"Really? What kind of music do they play?"

"Not sure. He must play guitar because I've seen him carrying a case around," she said, giving me a pensive look. "Why are you asking about him? What about your boyfriend?"

I braved a look at my bedside photo and grimaced. "I don't know."

"What is it, Beth?" she asked.

"You want to know the truth?"

She leaned forward and nodded.

I hadn't planned on talking about my turbulent relationship with Rick, especially when I was still getting to know my cousin all over again. But since the opportunity arose, I decided it wouldn't hurt to explain the reality of the situation.

When I was through rehashing the drama, she got eerily quiet. Then, to my surprise, she reached over to my framed photo and turned it face down.

"What'd you do that for?"

"Beth, you deserve better. Gorgeous or not, he's not a nice guy. Why are you still with him?"

"Geez, you sound like my friend Melissa." I slumped against my pillow. "And as I've told her... I don't know. Honestly, I almost dumped him last weekend, but I think the hopeless romantic in me wants to hang on and see how things turn out at the end of summer."

"I guess I can understand that. But from my perspective it doesn't look promising. Sorry to be blunt."

"It's not like I haven't heard it before."

I was ready for a change of subject, so I asked Jenny if she had a boyfriend.

The way her eyes brightened up told me she did, and she

began to tell me about Simon, whom she'd been dating for three months.

"And he is so funny. One day in class he—" she stopped, probably when she noticed that I was nearly comatose. "Beth, have you heard anything I've just said?"

"Of course," I said, my eyes remaining shut. "Can't wait to meet him."

"Alright, we'll talk more tomorrow. Clearly you need sleep."

"Good night, Jenny."

"Good night, Beth. Sweet dreams."

And I did have good dreams, filled with warm brown eyes and a breathtaking voice.

Available now!

FALLING TO *Pieces*

JAMIE CANOSA

Suffering the bitter tongues of her alcoholic mother and cruel boyfriend, Jade struggles just to look at herself in the mirror. She hates her life, her insecurities, her ineptitudes, but most of all... Jade hates herself. She wants nothing more than to disappear, and everyone seems happy to let her. Until Kiernan Parks moves back into town.

Jade's been crushing on him ever since kindergarten, when his family moved away. But now he's back, and looking better than ever.

Hiding is a way of life for Jade, but Kiernan insists on uncovering the real girl he's sees trapped inside her. On drawing her out of her shell, and showing her that she is someone worthy of love.

Together, they fight back the darkness she's living in. But when they finally step into the light, will the secret Kiernan's been trying to keep buried destroy Jade, once and for all?

For some people, happy endings are a fairytale.

EXCERPT

BEEP-BEEP-BEEP

I groaned into my pillow and swatted aimlessly at the offensive piece of technology blaring at me from the nightstand until I finally made contact and silenced the foul beast. The numbers glaring back at me with angry red eyes refused to compute in my sleep riddled brain. An hour starting with a five should only exist in the PM. The lazy sun hadn't even deemed it a reasonable enough time to rise and shine yet, and here I was dragging my sorry butt out from under the covers.

My body screamed for 'five more minutes' on a cellular level, but not today. Today was going to be different. Today was going to be better. Today *I* was going to be better. And that required time to prepare. It was the first day of senior year, and the day I'd been promising myself for months that I would finally get it right. *It* being life in general.

Rolling out of bed, I pushed my dark tangled hair out of my face to look, bleary eyed, into the cracked mirror positioned precariously against the wall above my dresser, and sighed. Maybe I should have gotten up earlier.

Conditioner burned my eyes as goose bumps sprouted across my bare skin being pelted by the icy spray. Even at this unreal hour, the water heater wasn't strong enough to keep up with the demands of the building's tenants for more than a few minutes. Rusted metal rings scraped along the curtain rod—a sound far too harsh for my pounding head—as I groped for a towel behind the faded orange plastic curtain.

I was no stylist, but an epic battle with a hairbrush, layer of clear lip gloss, and swipe of mascara later, things were looking up. I'd raided my closet and dresser the night before, digging through every last piece of clothing I owned, and found the selection to be . . . underwhelming. It had taken almost half the night to decide on the outfit currently laid out on my bed. Individually, the pieces didn't look like much—dark jeans, black cami, and a three-quarter length purple fuzzy sweater, which had been a birthday gift and was one of the few genuinely nice things I owned—but paired together, I thought I'd done a decent job.

Two-year-old scuffed and worn gray Converses didn't exactly match, but my shoe selection was even more lacking than my wardrobe. Faded floral wallpaper reminiscent of the nineteen-fifties—or possibly *from* the nineteen-fifties—peeled and curled away from the walls I ricocheted off of as I hop-stumbled my way down the hall toward the kitchen, trying to pull them on.

"You're making a racket out here, Jade," Mom grumbled, shuffling into the room, running a hand through her thinning hair, while I rooted through the cabinets for some bread. *Bread.* The almighty pantry essential. How could we not have a single slice of bread? "What are you doing up so early?"

"Sorry." To be honest, I was kind of surprised she'd noticed the time, though I wasn't surprised in the least that she'd forgotten what today was. "School starts today."

"Aren't you done with all that nonsense yet?"

Yeah, science, math, English, social studies, all *that* nonsense. "One more year."

She made a noncommittal grunt as I abandoned my exploration of the cabinets and turned my attention to the fridge, instead. There was food in this house somewhere. I just had to find it.

"Make yourself useful and hand me a drink." At seven in the morning, most normal people would probably reach for the milk, or orange juice, maybe a glass of water, but not us. Oh no, not here. Here we had our own way of doing things.

Vaguely noting that the aluminum mountains had, indeed, turned blue, I passed the can off to my mother without really looking her in the eye.

"What the hell is on your face? Jesus, Jade, if you're going to look like a whore, at least get paid like one."

There are those plastic phrases we all say that are drilled into us from the time we're old enough to speak. Things we say out of force of habit or to be politically correct. Things like 'it's nice to meet you', or 'nice try', or 'thank you', 'you're welcome', or even 'God bless you'. Things we don't always—or even usually—mean. Things that cover a deeper, more sinister truth. Usually, one has to look beneath the words, between the lines, to find their true meaning. With my mother, there was no need for translation. She was straightforward and honest. Said what she meant without regard for feelings or appearances. She didn't care what people thought, so she made no attempt to mask her contempt for the human race in general. Daughter included.

I scooped up the dented metal toaster, scowling at my reflection as she disappeared down the hallway to the hushed pop-fizz of her breakfast being cracked open. Dabbing at my lips with a paper towel, I considered removing all of it, but I didn't have time to mess with the mascara if I was going to make it to school on time without raccoon eyes.

●　●　●

SOME THINGS NEVER changed, like the rotation of the Earth around the Sun. School was undoubtedly one of those things. It was pretty much a given that high school had consisted of the same slamming lockers, clicky groups, and stench of week-old meatloaf since the dawn of time. Craterview High was no exception. It was a well-choreographed ensemble, where everyone had their place—the geeks, the Goths, the athletes, the brains, and the brawn—and there was a place for everyone. Except me.

I skated the outskirts, ducked and weaved between the clearly defined crowds, and did my best to hide in plain sight. But not this year. This year I was going to do the impossible. I was going to *change* things. Or, at least, find a place to fit in. Either way, things were going to be different.

"Hi, Jade. How was your summer?" Susie was busy decorating the interior of her locker with mirrors and photos of her friends. We'd been locker neighbors for going on four years, and she was always spouting off empty phrases like that, the minimal required interaction between two people forced to share such close quarters for so long.

"Fine. How was yours?" Part of me wished she wouldn't bother. I could rarely open my mouth without making a fool of myself, so I made it a point to open it as little as humanly possible. My own brand of damage control I'd perfected over the years.

"It was great. Kensie, Ella, and I took a senior trip to Spain for three weeks. We just got back a few days ago. I'm still exhausted from the jet lag."

She stood there, watching me, and I knew she was waiting for some regaling of my own amazing summer adventures. Thing is, I didn't have any. I couldn't even make up a story like that. And she knew it. Everyone knew it. She just wanted me to admit it.

"Sounds like fun." I stuffed my extra notebooks on the upper shelf of my locker.

"It really was. Hey, I like your outfit." That's what she said.

What I heard was: *You look like you tried really hard and failed anyway.*

I glanced down at myself and grimaced. She was right. At home it had seemed relatively great, but here in the halls of Fashion High, surrounded by name brands that probably cost more than my entire wardrobe put together, I looked pathetic. I looked like the Purple People Eater, for crying out loud.

"Um... thanks." It felt dumb to thank her for making fun of me, but she'd been perfectly nice about it. So I did what I always did, I ducked my head and ran for cover.

I found it in the girl's bathroom near the cafeteria. No one had lunch until after noon, so all morning it was the ideal place to hide when necessary. I knew this because I found it necessary more often than not.

Sulking at my reflection in the mirrors lining the wall above the sinks, I ran my hands over the stupid purple fuzz. I wanted to take it off and shove it in the trash bin, but the shirt underneath definitely wouldn't comply with the school dress code. I could just see it now, being pulled out of class for indecent exposure and forced to wear one of those baggy tees the nurse always had lying around that looked—and smelled— like something a grandmother would wear. No, thanks.

Different, my ass. This year was going to be exactly as bad as every other year had been and would be for the rest of my natural born life. Why I even bothered trying to convince myself otherwise, anymore, was a mystery even I couldn't solve.

The warning bell rang, and as good as hiding out there for the rest of the day sounded, I knew I needed to get to class. My schedule was going to be challenging enough this year without the added obstacle of detention. Casting one last scathing glare at the mirror, I threw open the door and no sooner stepped into the bustling hallway than the strap on my backpack snapped, sending all of its contents scattering across the floor. *Unbe-freaking-lieveable.* I was cursed.

Feeling very much like the butt of some cosmic joke, I chased my books, folders, and pens around the feet of my classmates, trying hard not to burst into tears as I publicly humiliated myself once again. All of which led to me stumbling into chemistry late. And there he was. Seated in the back row, short blonde hair artfully spiked in all the right ways, black button-up hanging open over a plain white tee and rolled to his elbows, revealing some seriously ripped forearms. Those were new, as was the silver stud in his left ear, but I'd recognize Kiernan Parks anywhere. I should, I'd been crushing on him for twelve years.

Suddenly, I was five-years-old again, standing at my cubby in that horrific pink dress with little white hearts all over it, which might have been cute if it hadn't been two sizes too small and bordering on indecent for a kindergartener, when Kiernan Parks—the cutest boy on the playground—walked right up to me in front of the whole class and handed me a pink heart Valentine with red doily lace around it. I'd fallen hard right that moment. But then he'd just up and left, moved away with his family to who-knows-where, and I never saw him again. Until right now. And he was staring at me.

Everyone was staring at me. Maybe that's because I was standing at the front of the classroom, gaping like a fish out of water. I could feel the flush spread across my face and down my neck, and I was fairly certain my entire body was fire engine red by the time I plopped into my seat.

Thank you, Jesus, Mr. Walkins picked back up wherever he'd left off when I made my impromptu appearance and everyone's attention was drawn back to the front of the room.

Well, almost everyone. Flipping through my text, I cast a peek toward the back of the room where Kiernan's gaze collided with mine. He stared back, completely unabashed at having been caught watching me. I tried to exude the same confidence and failed miserably. Dropping my eyes to the desk in front of me, I forced myself—with no small effort—to keep them glued to the book for the remainder of the period.

The moment the bell rang, signaling the end of class, I scrambled out of my seat like it had caught fire—possibly from the heat still radiating from my face—barely scooping all of my books up before getting caught in the human traffic jam at the door.

My small size was good for something, at least. I was able to slip through the masses without receiving any serious bodily harm. Using his much larger bulk to his advantage, Kiernan managed to do the exact same thing and somehow ended up right beside me as I stumbled haphazardly into the waiting arms of Doug. *Just great.*

"Hey, sexy." Doug slung an arm around my shoulders, dropping a rough kiss on top of my head. "How's the first day going?"

"Um... it's fine. I—"

"Yo, man, what's up?" Doug broke away from me just long enough to engage in some sort of 'bro-hug' with one of the guys from his team. "See ya after school, man. So what was I saying? Oh yeah, my day's been awesome. Charlie's in my calc class, so you know that won't be a problem, and coach said..."

He was always doing that, asking a question and then answering it himself. I really didn't need to be present for most of our conversations, so I usually tuned him out. Kiernan stood just outside the classroom door, parting traffic like a rock in a river, watching us. Something flickered across his face, but he didn't stick around long enough for me to figure out what it

340

was. Tossing his bag over his shoulder, Kiernan headed down the hall in the opposite direction. I watched him go, thinking about the last time I'd seen him, wondering if he remembered me, until an abrupt shake drew me back to the present.

"Are you even listening to me at all?"

"What? Oh... I'm sorry, Doug, I was just—"

"Not listening to me."

"I was thinking."

"Well, don't hurt yourself." His words stung and I withdrew further into myself as his arm wrapped tighter around my waist. "Let's go, we're gonna be late."

I allowed Doug to steer me upstairs all the way to the door of his next class, where he gave me a quick peck on the cheek before following some of his friends inside. Looking at my own schedule, I groaned. *Figured.* My next class would be on the exact opposite side of the building, wouldn't it?

With a huff, I hefted my books in my increasingly sore arms and hightailed it through the halls, desperate not to have a repeat of first period. Thankfully, I managed to make it there just as the bell rang and slipped into a desk without anyone noticing. So much for doing things 'right'. The best I could hope for was to slip by unnoticed. To that end, I was equally relieved to find Kiernan Parks and I did not share English composition.

Available now!

ABOUT THE AUTHOR

Micalea Smeltzer is a bestselling Young and New Adult author from Winchester, Virginia. She's always working on her next book, and when she has spare time she loves to read and spend time with her family.

Follow on Facebook:
https://www.facebook.com/MicaleaSmeltzerfanpage?ref=hl
Twitter: @msmeltzer9793
Instagram: micaleasmeltzer
Pinterest: http://www.pinterest.com/micaleasmeltzer/